Further acclaim for *The Turn-around* . . .

'This brilliant novel never stops being a highly entertaining book.' *Spectator*

'A novel that is superior by far to anything this season offers.' *Le Figaro* magazine

'A masterly technician of the novel.' *Le Nouvel Observateur*

'An indisputable novelist is born to us.' *Le Monde*

'Uncommonly intelligent, entertaining, civilised and humorous, in every way a delight to read . . . *The Turn-around* is truly a remarkable novel.' *Scotsman*

The Turn-around
Vladimir Volkoff

Translated from the French by Alan Sheridan

CORGI BOOKS
A DIVISION OF TRANSWORLD PUBLISHERS LTD

THE TURN-AROUND

A CORGI BOOK 0 552 11941 5

Originally published in Great Britain by the Bodley Head Ltd.

PRINTING HISTORY

Originally published in French as *Le Retournement*
Bodley Head edition published 1981
Corgi edition published 1982

This book is set in 10/10½ Plantin

Corgi Books are published by
Transworld Publishers Ltd.,
Century House, 61–63 Uxbridge Road,
Ealing, London, W5 5SA

Printed and bound in Great Britain by
Cox & Wyman Ltd, Reading

A tout seigneur, tout honneur.
The Turn-around
is respectfully dedicated to
Mr Graham Greene

V.V.

1

'A fizzling spook always turns into a hack!' Tolstoy would declare whenever one of my reports struck him as wordy or overwritten.

I never managed to find out whether he was related to the great writer of the same name. If anyone did ask him, he would turn his sea-dog's gaze upon him for a second, then reply with polite obtuseness: 'I don't know who you're talking about.'

When the questioner was a general or an Under-Secretary of State, it was worth watching.

Was Tolstoy right?

It is a fact that a number of officers who specialized in what is generally known as Intelligence have made names for themselves in what is no less generally called Literature. It is also a fact that Mr Philby, whose memoirs Mr Greene was kind enough to preface, had a low opinion of the writer's gifts as a spy. But there is no reason to accept the Master Spy's opinion, nor any reason to believe that Messrs Rémy, Nord, Fleming and Le Carré did not succeed in the cold before triumphing in the sun. After all, did not Mr Philby himself, the model mole, drop the mask for the pen? On balance, therefore, I tend to attribute Tolstoy's stock response to spite rather than insight. Nevertheless, my own case bore out what he said; ten years after hanging up my grey overcoat forever, I can't resist the itch to get my story into print.

There is also, I think, a deeper connection between the two professions than Tolstoy, with his exclusively pragmatic turn of mind, was capable of seeing. I'm not referring to some compensatory mechanism: yes, silence does weigh heavily on our sealed lips and when, at last, the wax begins to crack—either because we have been ordered to break it and to take up the trumpet of propaganda, as in Mr Philby's case, or because it has worn away with time, as with Mr Popov (not my Popov, the other one, Dusko), or because we wouldn't stop at treason to pull out the gag, like Mr Agee—the logorrhoea that comes pouring out takes quite naturally the form of a book. The deeper we sink into silence, the more tempted we are to get up on a soap-box and make ourselves heard. But this, I think, is a secondary manifestation of the essential symmetry between the man of words and the man of silence, between the ham and the thug, linked together as they are by the common use of the mask. Personally I would almost go so far as to reverse the Tolstoyan formula and declare that a successful master-spy is a failed novelist.

He was born to write novels—he thinks up schemes; to invent names—he concocts pseudonyms; to bring language to life—he communicates in code. Instead of creating characters, he subtly changes individuals by slipping into their lives pinches of yeast from time to time. Like the writer, he throws an impalpable, but no less effective, net over the world and pulls. They are both illusionists, though one sells himself for the limelight, while the other would damn himself to stay in the shade of the wings. You sit next to Mr Durrell in a café, or pass Mr Gehlen in the street; they both look like honest burghers; you have no sense of having been close to a giant spider, whose sole passion is to spin intrigues, only to unravel them later—and whose sole appetite is resolutely cannibalistic. Indiscretion and ingratitude characterize scribbler and spook alike; laws have little hold on them—they have their own rules and doctrines; both are masters of mystification, their art is so secret that they feel responsible to no one; however much they may pretend to 'serve' (the nation, the public, it's all one), 'art for art's sake' remains their *ars vitae*; the only virtue they admire is a certain professionalism; a well laid plot is about the only thing that can bring tears to their eyes. 'That third act was beautifully put together!' says the one. 'That was quite some trick he played on me!' exclaims the other. They belong to the same species and, in my opinion, since the one creates out of nothing and the other secretes only cultured pearls, the writer remains the fullest embodiment of their common principle. Captain Tolstoy is a novelist who has missed his vocation; I am a novelist learning his trade.

That is why, from the outset, I have fallen into a trap that, with more experience, I could have avoided. My master, M. Lebossé, the author of the handbook, would have said that I am trying to solve with a single equation a problem containing two unknowns: I would like at one and the same time to recount a memory that still torments me and to construct out of it a work of literature, which is tantamount to having one's cake and eating it. A memory is a perspective; a work of art is always a more or less cubist painting, in which one sees both sides of the guitar, the inside and the outside of the water jug. How are these two aims to be reconciled? My good friend Divo would have worked out some unorthodox, non-Euclidian solution, but I have yet to find one that allows me to bring together the external action I witnessed, and in which I played a small part, and the internal action, the motive force of the other, which took place in a single head—not mine. The simplest, but clumsiest solution would be to resort to the omniscient narrator (and why not, after all?), but I am self-indulgent enough to want to hear my own piping voice telling my own story. Anyway, it seems odd to speak of oneself in the third person: 'Volsky went out at 5 o'clock!' Who do you think you are? Julius Caesar? I thought of letting each of the three of us tell the story in turn: I first, then Popov, then Tolstoy. The trouble was Tolstoy: any talent he may have had as a 'novelist' has become so completely submerged in his job that if I tried to get him to describe what took place no one would believe it. It would have been fun, all the same, to present myself, as seen by him, with that mixture of scorn and affection that he felt, I think, for 'little Volsky'. It was a solution fraught with danger, so I abandoned it in favour of a patchwork of memory and imagination, filling up the gaps in my knowledge as best I could, juxtaposing the authentic and the fabricated.

I say the authentic, but who can guarantee the veracity of his memory? To begin with, who would dare to trick out a

supposedly true account with dialogue? I shall soon be presenting Lester and, in order to avoid indirect speech, I shall try to
reconstruct snatches of our conversation; but however faithful I
wish to be to the style and content of what we said, it is obvious
that I cannot recapture the exact words spoken by us. The pure
novelist, who attributes words to imaginary characters, is in a
happier position. Perhaps I should have transposed everything
into fiction, without concern for the historical truth. On the
other hand, is there such a thing as a pure novelist? Is not the
novel itself a hybrid species? Is not the novel *from the outset* a
restoration? The restoration, often unconscious, of an
experience?

So rise up, friend Lester, to your full six foot two, as you
would say (but you'll soon have to say almost two metres, for
metric prose is already colonizing your country), rise up to your
full height, which, when I was standing next to you, made me
look like one of those little fish that swim around sharks, feeding
on what is stuck between their teeth, rise up to your full red-
haired height and burst out into one of your gigantic fits of
laughter, slapping your thighs and my back, shoulders shaking,
mouth open to the tonsils, eyes almost closed, conveying,
beneath eyelids creased into a laboriously ribald expression, an
underlying seriousness. You thought you were being very
clever, friend Lester, when you used to play the little boy who
never grew up, which you thought I thought you were, and, to a
certain extent, you weren't wrong, for, when you looked around
for a convincing character for yourself, you chose the one you
had really been a few years before, before you were put, somewhat belatedly, through the Company mill. But the vigilance in
your eyes betrayed you. You came from a world where one does
not really believe in original sin; you had learned about evil
much too late in life and, once your eyes were open to it, they
never really closed again.

'Hi there, boyo. How's tricks?'

'My respects, Major.'

He talked to me in an odd, half-intended mixture of everyday
American English and slightly out-dated French slang; I replied
either in the strictest military French (which did not exclude the

occasional crudity), or in a British English that I liked to think was impeccable. I later realized that the hilarity I triggered off in Lester was not always to do with the character I was playing, but sometimes with the actor. One point to him. As for his rank, I addressed him by it so that he would realize that we knew more about our Allies than our Allies chose to tell us, and that it was no use trying to pass himself off as a captain out of some habit of self-effacement, the occupational disease of our profession. One point to me.

That day . . . I have the date in front of me in a brown diary, swollen with age, which is still my principal source. On that page—it was a Tuesday—I had written the word 'toothache'. It isn't simply a question of inventing a code that doesn't look like one: one also has to avoid any risk of verification. That is why this diary, which might have been seen by others, was filled with embittered allusions to my health—a health which, in reality, gave me no reason for complaint. Anything to do with teeth was a reference to Lester. There was no need to note the time and place: it was always 11.45 a.m. at the *Cuisse de Grenouille*.

This particular frog's leg was situated half-way between Lester's office near the Champs-Elysées and mine at the Invalides. The name of the restaurant struck my American counterpart as deliciously 'françay'. It was I who suggested that we meet over lunch: since the Americans are not in the habit of overloading their stomachs in the middle of the day, this gave me the advantage. The rather steep bill bothered neither of us. Usually it was his Company that was paying, sometimes my Shop. The walk was pleasant.

Lester—occasionally I stood some distance away to observe him—turned up on foot, swivelling his hips and throwing his legs outwards, like a cowboy. He wore a plaid shirt, tight trousers, a belt slung low over a portly belly, sometimes a small, narrow-rimmed hat, with a pheasant's feather stuck in the ribbon; in chillier weather, a tweed jacket with leather elbows. It was his liaison officer's outfit. On occasion I have surprised him exercising other functions: he might then be stuffed into a tight-fitting, three-piece navy-blue or brown suit, white shirt, matching tie and handkerchief, only the shoes and thick socks

11

betraying the longitude under which he was born.

I, too, arrived on foot. I left early, of course, had a few words with the guard commander and walked up the Boulevard de La Tour-Maubourg, congratulating myself that my colleagues would soon be wandering off to the evil-smelling canteen where I, too, usually ate, against the wishes of my protesting stomach. Pausing for a few tempting seconds in front of the caviar shop, I crossed the Seine. I love the inimitable presence of this river: it has been domesticated for so long that one thinks of it as a person rather than as a mass of water. I set foot on the right bank, which I pretended to look down on, but whose charms were not lost on me: those airy spaces and, in autumn, that infinitely delicate play of rusted metal, verdigris, dull violets and slate blue, filled me with sudden joy. I felt young and clever.

Sometimes we met on the sidewalk.

'Look at that dame's legs!' cried Lester, grabbing my arm and jerking his head at the elegant nylon-clad calves of some female passer-by gloved by Hermès and shod by Ferragamo.

'Major! Major!' I replied, 'How did you ever manage to leave your native Texas?'

This was a new way of showing him how well-informed we were, because in fact he did come from Texas. This in itself was unusual, since most of the officers of the Company seemed to come from New England.

We then walked side by side, two and a half of my steps to one of his. If there was a transport strike in France, Lester never failed to say:

'Look, buddy, tell me the truth. Did you come by bus or métro today?'

The day America made a fool of itself in the Caribbean I bought some braces, which I asked Lester to send to Uncle Sam to spare the blushes of the civilized world. If we had no pleasantries of this kind to exchange, we arrived in silence at the door of the *Cuisse de Grenouille*. There, I would stand back stiffly, though I was usually the guest.

'Age before beauty!' exclaimed Lester, who was ten years older than I.

He grabbed me by the scruff of the neck and shoved me into

the restaurant. We were early, and our table at the far end was free. We marched towards it. I suppose we must have looked rather like a pilot-boat towing an ocean liner. Is that why Lester laughed? He'd always found it funny that he found me funny. He often said that for him I was the embodiment of France, which, in view of my Tartar origins, certainly had its funny side, but I knew what he meant: I was small, frivolous, snobbish, behind the times, insignificant, and yet he was forced to take me seriously, just as his vast country and its enormous secret service was forced to take France and my Shop seriously, against his will no doubt, but not altogether because he had no alternative; there was also an inadmissible liking, an involuntary respect, an irrepressible weakness. Lester was a Texan; I am convinced that he believed it to be morally wrong to like anything that was of merely average size; to do so was unhealthy, unnatural even. He believed that if a thing wasn't viable, it should be destroyed as cheaply as possible, yet, curiously enough, he discovered in himself a perverse liking for tiny objects: *petits fours*, snails, cockles and, at another level, little Europe as represented by little Lieutenant Volsky.

And so, that Tuesday, we met on the even-numbered side of the Avenue Franklin-Roosevelt and Lester asked me pointblank: 'When are you going to wear a monocle?'

Unlike Lester, I never disguised myself as a liaison officer, and when I met him I wore what I always wore: suits cut by the best military tailor I could afford, plain ties, slightly pointed shoes when the fashion was for square toes, and the other way round. That day, I was wearing, I remember it quite distinctly, a new, double-breasted suit, with wide, pointed lapels, in style somewhat reminiscent of a frock-coat, in colour somewhere between a smoky-grey and mauve, cut from wool that was both soft and slightly rough to the touch, and which I loved to rub between my fingers (the trousers have long since gone, but the jacket still hangs in my cupboard; I don't think I could bear to part with it). Lester must have thought of me as a stray Blimp among the spooks, while in fact I was a novelist who found it convenient to assume the roles both of the spook and of the dumb, bigoted soldier.

13

'I don't need a monocle to see the hornets' nest you've stirred up with Freeman,' I replied. 'It's what in our tongue we call the great stingaroo, Major.'

I loved to make up French sayings, which he then slipped into his conversation with great glee. He put on his unpleasant smile, the corners of his mouth turned down in so many inverted commas, and looked at his watch.

'Not much time today, boyo. Got to get the jaws working and no eyeing the blondes.'

'Why, pray?'

It is always insolent to ask an Intelligence officer why.

He put on a different smile, his eyes lit up and widened, his tongue trembled on the edge of his parted lips. At first he gave himself the pleasure of not answering at all; then, after a while, he said:

'Well, fella, you're not going to know. That gives you the stingaroos, doesn't it?'

He put his big hand on my shoulder, in brotherly fashion, to soften the blow. He was, after all, an excellent chap, even if he had little talent as a 'novelist'.

'Good afternoon, gentlemen. Good to see you both. Your table is ready. We have duck *ballottine* today—need I say more? An aperitif as usual? Arturo, the same as usual for these gentlemen.'

The *patronne* was at her cash-desk, a corpulent, well-corsetted woman, expensively dressed in black. Her deep, carrying voice suited the style of the place: a seriousness in the gastronomy and service alleviated by a familiarity in the welcome.

For Lester, 'the same as usual' was a dry Martini, which, in his case, consisted of a frosted glass filled for the most part with gin, with an impaled olive floating on the surface; for me, it was a Scotch. At the time, I could hold my liquor well enough, but I was already suspicious of mixtures: the cocktail is the effective invention of a practical nation that usually drinks to get drunk.

'*A la bonne vôtre,*' said Lester, trying to get his legs under the table.

'Cheers!' I replied, in what I considered the best British way. The ritual had begun. Arturo—he and I had our secret

14

accounts—knew his orders: he refilled the glasses as we emptied them, in the ratio of three for the American and two for me, never at the same time. The bill listed three martinis and three Scotches. Lester paid without batting an eyelid, which led me to believe that he had not seen through my ploy.

Perhaps this is a good moment to say something about our jobs. I was in charge of relations with the British Secret Intelligence Service, the Central Intelligence Agency and the *Bundesnachrichtendienst*, the purpose being to exchange a few rotten tips for really valuable information. The principal qualification for the job was an ability to speak their respective languages, while drinking their respective national drinks. These I possessed to a greater or lesser degree, but there were, apparently, other qualifications, too, including the skills of a street vendor, which I conspicuously lacked. The British major, a young, fair-haired chap who could still miss a day's shave, and the old Teuton captain, a red-faced old tough nut who was never happier than when recounting his campaigns in France and Russia (the old boy imagined he was pleasing me twice over), began by jibbing at the bills and ended by making our meetings less frequent. If Lester did not imitate them, it was because he applied the doctrine of his Company: quantity first. It is easier to get a lot of dubious information than a single dependable item and, after a number of cross-checkings, they add up to a similar result. They need staff, organization, computers. This kind of operation is not, therefore, within the reach of European budgets, but America blithely stuffs any old rubbish into Langley's digestive tube, which assimilates and rejects, sometimes knowing perfectly well what it is doing. Such was the fate of the half-truths I passed on to Lester. In exchange, he gave me information that was generally accurate enough, but unusable. Nevertheless, my Shop was glad to get hold of such information, for it helped to maintain in specialist circles the myth of its own usefulness. Now, this myth had to be safeguarded for several reasons, some good and some bad, but for one reason above all, one, whose existence Lieut.-Colonel Rat himself, head of the *Groupe d'études scientifiques et techniques*, alias GEST, alias my Shop, did not so much as suspect.

However, it should not be thought that our exchanges were carried out with the rustic simplicity I am now using in the interests of clarity. Usually, the information we presented openly, as on a plate, was strictly devoid of interest. The kind of information we really swapped was quite different, the sort of thing we might let slip when taken off guard, or in some sudden access of emotion. Neither Lester nor I was taken in, of course, but what would become of horse-riding if one was allowed to mount on the right?

As we drank, we ordered the meal. I don't remember what we had that day. Lester always consulted me, but never gave me the satisfaction of following my advice at the time. When we next met, he 'chose' what I had recommended on the previous occasion. I soon noticed this trick and set about trying to get him to eat some of the more risky dishes: kidneys, brains, *brochettes*, tongue. 'Soul food,' he would grumble, but he would force himself to eat it out of a desire to educate himself in the mysteries of French cuisine. I would love to have got him to eat tripe or ox-tail, but unfortunately these delicacies were not on offer here.

Lester had just disappeared behind his menu when suddenly his great rudder of a nose emerged. There was some odd geometrical correspondence between the half unfolded piece of card and that nose, for which it seemed to act as a sheath.

'Greek Fire, now. What exactly is he firing?'

The nose disappeared again, but the triangular pavilions of the ears remained visible. Not that Lester expected an interesting answer, but chess-players take care with their opening moves, however harmless they may be.

Greek Fire was the pseudonym of one of the few informants handled by GEST. The information obtained from him by Captain Tolstoy, his contact, was so valuable that first the other French services, then the Allies, had suspected a real gold mine. False trails had to be laid to conceal Greek Fire's speciality, which was nuclear physics. Lieut.-Colonel Rat, who had the cunning of the 'storyteller', if not the intelligence of the 'novelist', found the solution: he divulged the informant's pseudonym and began to attribute to him a mass of information coming from other sources, some of it deliberately false. Greek

Fire had become a geyser producing the true, the false, the ordinary; on an industrial scale. This resulted in an immediate devaluation. In specialized circles he came to be known as the boloney factory. The stuff he produced was evaluated at C/6, sometimes lower. In order not to get lost in this mass of inferior, and often inaccurate information, Rat himself took to writing 'greek fire' with small letters, when it was the real stuff, and, like an old spinster, hugged his secret to himself.

However, the identity of the informant remained inviolate: even Rat himself did not know it; only Tolstoy knew by name the one mole that had infiltrated into the enemy's trenches.

'And how's Popeye?' I retorted.

'Popeye', which I pronounced in the French way, which never failed to make Lester laugh, was not the pseudonym, but the nickname of an informant whom the Americans had managed to plant in Soviet scientific circles. The Company idolized him and was extremely jealous of all the information received from him. Lester shrugged his shoulders.

'*Popeille*, as you call him,' he continued sententiously, 'is a gentleman. Your Greek Fire is the tart of intelligence.'

During the hors-d'oeuvre we talked of this and that, politics perhaps, the weather, some fashionable singer, '*pitites femmes*', as Lester would say, food, Jaguars, Corvettes. When the main course arrived, we moved, by association of ideas, to official matters, exchanging news concerning the health and moods of our respective bosses, drawing up a professional balance-sheet of the previous two weeks, hazarding a few predictions as to the next two, in short, acting out our roles as ordinary liaison officers. This part of the conversation could have been carried out by telephone; we attached no particular importance to it: it simply served as a justification for our meetings and allowed us to swap our choicer pieces without appearing to touch them.

The cheese arrived. For cheese Lester had the passion of those who, late in life, discover perfect sensual pleasure. I took the opportunity to order a half bottle of *Nuits Saint-Georges*: wine is drunk more quickly in half bottles (we had now reached the fifth) and, as usual, I was trying to knock out my host, in the hope of getting him to say more than he should. I was beginning to succeed, that was obvious; not that he showed the slightest sign of drunkenness, but precisely because he showed none (except that his triangular ears were getting redder and redder). However, it was obvious that he was exercising excessively strict control—a sure sign of a relatively advanced stage of intoxication. For my part, I fumbled for the stem of my glass and stumbled over English words: in short, I was emitting the most reassuring signs. Between the Roquefort and the Bleu d'Auvergne Lester lit a cigarette. He looked at his watch. He was waiting, I think, for me to chip in my contribution. But I wanted him to be more drunk than he was: I decided to take my time.

By the time the coffee arrived, my major was beginning to feel a bit drowsy. It was not so much the alcohol. On top of the bacon, eggs and porridge of his breakfast, his stomach had had to digest not the usual snack of roast beef on a slice of toasted whole-meal bread, but an entire lunch at the *Cuisse*. There was no doubt about it, Lester could drink. The only effect that alcohol had on him was to loosen his tongue, an unfortunate characteristic in a man of his profession. But he had found a cover for it. As soon as he felt that a flood of words was about to pour out of him, he turned his thoughts away from secrets and told dirty stories. At that time, thanks to him, I had a repertoire of dirty stories that would have been the envy of a sergeant in the Marines. I can hardly think of it now without some embarrassment. Lester could not have known that one day his system would play him up; I was not even aware myself that the day had arrived.

His ears already scarlet, Lester ordered an Armagnac. Sensing that he was about to be overcome by an irresistible desire to talk, but still the prudent intelligence officer who knew his own weaknesses, he launched into a long series of jokes. I didn't have to pretend to laugh. There was something diabolically titillating in the spectacle of this convinced Calvinist who, in order not to betray state secrets, opened the sluice-gates to a veritable flood of priapisms and scatology. My laughter, I admit, was not entirely genuine, and hardly charitable. But it enabled me to change attitude without arousing suspicion. I was unbuttoning,

18

opening up, I was no longer wearing the metaphorical monocle. I was becoming what Lester believed every man to be at bottom—a son of a bitch; he was delighted to see his simple pessimism confirmed by the abasement of so distinguished a specimen as I. Sometimes I have gooseflesh when I think of the pair of us sitting there. Suddenly Lester moved his outstretched legs and jolted the table; the coffee spilled on to the tablecloth. I loosened my tie, congratulating myself at finding a gesture so untypical of me. Lester stopped to gather breath and I lent over towards him:

'Major?'

'Yep?'

'You wanted news of Greek Fire.'

It was part of our game to pretend to pass bits of information to one another against the wishes of our bosses: it gave a seal of authenticity to our confidences.

'Yep?'

'Would you be interested to know who the new resident of Bureau T in Paris is?'

Slowly Lester's eyes became serious once more: it was odd to see them suddenly sober up in his still flushed face.

'Popov, Igor Maximovich, counsellor at the embassy, in charge of relations with the cryptos.'

My eyes sparkled with mischief. Lester was well aware, because he used the same subterfuge, that in fact I was acting on orders. But there was just a chance all the same that he might think that the information came from Greek Fire, whereas in fact it had been transmitted in the normal way by the SDECE. Popov had been in Paris for two weeks; the relative freshness of the information made up for its doubtful importance: sooner or later the Company could not fail to discover the counsellor's real job; meanwhile, I was giving my friend Lester the pleasure of being the first to tell his superiors.

Suddenly he broke into an enormous burst of laughter. It was no longer the dirty laugh of a few minutes ago, but an arrogant, insulting hilarity: the laugh of Goliath before the fight with David. Over the table he pointed a stiff forefinger at me; it sprouted a few hairs and the nail, I remember, was chipped. It

19

was as if he was pointing me out for everyone to make fun of. Heads turned towards us.

'Ah! Little Frenchie, little Frenchie!' he spat out, rather like a lion talking to a gnat.

Then he made a mistake. He made to look at his watch again, but held back. Had he not done so, I would never have linked the revelations to come and the fact that he was in a hurry. But this reticence aroused my suspicions. I pretended to look annoyed:

'I fail to see what is so funny . . .'

He hesitated for a moment. In principle, he could, indeed ought to, have kept quiet. But his need to talk was not satisfied; his flow of filth had been interrupted; anyway, how could he resist an opportunity of poking gentle fun at his puny ally? Lester was so convinced—and quite rightly—of the superiority of his own service to mine! Nothing he could tell me could have the slightest effect. He was quite right, of course: it would require an unforeseeable combination of circumstances for me to imagine that I could put his gossip to any real use.

He rested his elbows on the table, pushed his cup away, nearly knocking over the vase of anemonies, which I caught just in time.

'What do you know about Popov?' he asked severely.

I knew nothing. GEST did not dabble in counter-espionage. The Big House had told us about Popov simply as an act of charity, because Bureau T of the first department of the KGB dealt with scientific and technical information and we were the poor relation of that family.

'Nothing more than what Greek Fire . . .'

Lester nodded slowly.

'Very clever, you Frenchies, very clever! They were right to tell us to watch out for you. Know what? Your Popov, Igor Minimovich . . .'

His eyes grew so big, so round, I wouldn't have been surprised to see them drop out and roll across the tablecloth.

'Well, what?'

'He's been stationed three years here, five there, four somewhere else, and he's a . . .' He let the word fall as if it was an obscenity:

'Widower! Does that fill a gap?'

I had obviously made a fool of myself trying to tell Lester about something he knew far more about than I did. In the profession, one could hardly drop a bigger brick. The only course left open to me was to exploit my inferiority.

'It might fill two if I knew what you were talking about.'

'What? The little Frog doesn't know that the Commies never leave a diplomat in the same job for more than two years if he's a bachelor, a divorcee or . . . a widower?'

Again, he spat the word out like an obscenity, delighting in his power. It was too late to pull back:

'For him, they go further: they provide for all his needs.'

'How do you mean?'

Lester's eyes lit up. He believed he was purveying his dirty stories again.

'Popov is fixated on blondes like that.'

He outlined a pair of ample breasts with his hands.

'His wife . . . He took less than a year to kill her.'

'Kill her?'

'Wear her down, you know what I mean.'

He choked with laughter.

'He needs it to keep going. But it pays off! It certainly pays off! So the Commies, who can afford it, change his secretaries every six months. *Regularly* twice a year. It's the regularity the computer picked up. And it's been going on for seven years . . . always blondes like that.'

Again he crudely outlined a pair of breasts over his own chest.

'When it's over,' he concluded, 'they are given two weeks to recuperate at Sochi, all expenses paid. They need it. They look like this.'

He sucked in his cheeks and, with his two index fingers, formed bags under his eyes. Then he sat up and drained his glass of the last drops of Armagnac. I had introduced him to it and now he preferred it to any other brandy or liqueur.

His eyes suddenly took on the cunning look of people who have drunk too much.

'That's how it is, kid. I must be off.'

I don't know what came over me at that moment. Perhaps it

21

was simply that the autumn weather was too beautiful to face going back to the office. Anyway, when I say that a spy is a 'novelist', I don't just mean that he elaborates and organizes his plots, but also that he allows himself to follow up unexpected avenues, to take risks, to give a helping hand to coincidences.

'Very well,' I said. 'I'll go along and tear a strip off Greek Fire. He mustn't be allowed to get away with that sort of thing. It's the least I could do, Major.'

It was intended as an apology. He smiled with muted arrogance.

'That's all right. You don't do so badly, given what you've got. The bill!'

He got up without staggering. I knew he would make for the lavatory—he always did. I in turn looked at my watch:

'I'm in a bit of a hurry, too. My respects, Major.'

He replied with a wink. He evidently thought that after my discomfiture I had only one wish: to clear out as fast as possible. He threw a credit card on the table and walked heavily, but firmly, in the direction of the lavatory. Suddenly he paused, came back and shook me warmly by the hand. No doubt about it—he had more feeling than I had. He finally dragged himself off and disappeared.

On my way out I stopped Arturo: 'Take your time over the bill.'

We had an odd relationship, Arturo and I. When he was serving at table he behaved irreproachably, with a flow of 'certainly, sirs' and 'right away, sirs.' When we were conspiring together, he became a quite different man. He assumed the airs of a burlesque *mafioso*, and whispered in my left ear: 'O. K., boss.'

I could trust him: it would be another five minutes before the major got his card back.

Five minutes isn't long to find a taxi by honest means. I strode off in the direction of the Champs-Elysées. Suddenly I spotted one moving towards a somewhat spectacular old lady standing on the kerbside. The ruthless conditioning known as good breeding nearly ruined my scheme. Nevertheless, I dashed up and got to the taxi door first. The old lady looked me up and down: her cold eyes stared from a wrinkled face surmounted by grey curls, and a toque was set rakishly to one side. I grabbed the handle with a furtive gesture that I can still feel in my muscles.

'Mmmonssieur,' she exploded, 'this taxi is mine!'

It belonged to her by divine right. I turned my back on her and opened the door.

'Mmmonssieur, your behaviour is unspeakable!'

In thirty years, thanks to television and the democratization of education, no one will speak with such sublime arrogance. I threw myself into the seat, banging my left kneecap against some metal protrusion.

'Driver!' ordered the old lady. 'Ask this gentleman to get out. It was I who signalled to you.'

Cars were hooting behind us.

'Work it out between you,' said the driver. 'I haven't got all day.'

I was dying to kiss my victim's feet, or at least to ask her for her address so that I could send her a bouquet of tea roses. But I knew that if I began to apologize I would end up by giving her the taxi. I banged the door in the marquise's face.

The driver let out a sigh. He did not approve of my behaviour:

'Well? Where's it to be?'

He was a fat Italian, full of pasta and salami. Dead to all sense of shame, I then did what one does in films. I showed him my card, which clearly showed me to be a secret service officer. Technically, GEST belonged to the War Ministry, but we were issued with secret service cards. It was the first time I had ever used mine in the field. I remember I was rather worried about the taxi fare: we were not supposed to spy on the Allies without orders from above and I had no desire to finance my escapade out of my own pocket. I prayed that Lester would not go too far.

'Oh, I see! Another one!' said the driver philosophically. 'There's nothing but secret police in this country. Where to, then?'

At that time, the various secret police organizations were proliferating at such a rate that the Ministry of the Interior was forced, from time to time, to dynamite the surplus. I didn't work for the secret police, thank God, but their reputation could be

23

useful: I did not set the taxi-driver right. I explained to him what I wanted him to do. He heaved a great sigh, did a U-turn in the Impasse d'Antin, and double-parked, facing away from the Seine, fifty yards down from the *Cuisse*. Out of the rear window I saw the old lady in the toque fix us with an admirably disdainful look. If by any chance she reads these lines and recognizes herself, I would like her to know this: none of the men who have lost their lives through any fault of mine—there have been three or four—haunt me as she has done. This, I confess, says nothing either for my humanity or my sense of proportion, but no absolution offered by any Church will cure the petty, but everlasting shame I burdened myself with that day. Enough!

Arturo had kept his word so well that I began to wonder whether he had understood what I wanted and whether Lester hadn't in fact left just after I had done. A senator wearing a hat, a furtive couple in a hurry, two red-faced businessmen, busy trying to do each other down, came out of the *Cuisse* at longish intervals. My remorse mounted: I would have had plenty of time to get a taxi without stealing this one. At last the tall gangling figure appeared: his triangular head thrown back in a movement of annoyance, red ears erect like radars, plaid shirt and hipster trousers conveying the young image the major wished to project on Tuesdays.

'That's him.'

'The Yank?'

In all probability, the Americans have never done the slightest harm to this man, but we are all equipped with a little xenophobic organ, the constant, but moderate use of which I am sometimes tempted to regard as a sign of health. Anyhow, this taxi-driver, who had been hostile to me at first, took to the hunt with alacrity as soon as he saw it was foreign game I was after.

'Don't worry. I won't let him get away. I'm used to it, sir.'

The last word was forced out as a supreme concession. What one gained, at that time, by passing oneself off as one of the government's hired killers!

Lester looked to the left and to the right, out of habit rather than precaution. Would he go down towards the Seine or up the street towards us? He went down towards the Seine. I had lost my bet. But not my prey. With Mediterranean panache, and to the rightful annoyance of some twenty car owners, my taxi-driver performed another U-turn, this time in the middle of the avenue, and set off in pursuit. Lester turned into the Rue Jean-Goujon, walked about a hundred yards, snatched the parking tickets tucked under the windscreen wiper of an illegally parked Plymouth, crumpled them into a ball, tossed them over his shoulder, caught them a well-aimed kick, doubled up his long body, inserting it into the vehicle, and drove off.

My driver seemed to have spent his whole life tailing people and, since I had no experience of this side of my job, I was delighted to leave him to it. It was only the clicking of his clock, which seemed to get faster and faster as we left Paris, that spoilt my pleasure. In the end I was relieved when we pulled into Orly: I had visions of us ending up in Marseille.

'Why didn't you tell me he was an official? And he didn't even have a CD plate on his car!' my driver grumbled as he saw the Plymouth slink into the enclosure reserved for the diplomatic corps. 'Right. Get out here. You'll reach the arrival-hall before he does. I'll be waiting for you by that white shed. You'll recognize me, won't you?'

He obviously didn't have a high opinion of my professional abilities. Rightly so, perhaps. In any case, he was so taken up by the chase that he didn't even ask me to pay his fare so far: if the chase went on, he wanted to be part of it. I must confess, I wasn't really surprised: I may be a cold fish, but I'd always had the ability to take people into my confidence. Do they want to exploit me or help me? Whichever it is, I've never lacked willing assistants.

Lester had obviously not come dressed like that to catch a plane. He must be meeting someone. My memory may be play-ing me false, but it seems to me that it was from that moment that I had a fairly explicit intuition concerning if not the iden-tity, at least certain characteristics of the individual he was meet-ing. Following the driver's advice, I did not try to tail my man through the parking lot, but went directly into the arrival-hall and looked for an observation post. Again, my training had left me woefully inadequate. I thought of buying a newspaper and making a hole in it, 'to see without being seen', as in Arsène Lupin, but this did not seem a very efficient method. There was little I could do by way of disguise: I took off my tie and jacket. At a distance, I'd look different enough for Lester not to recognize me. I walked up and down, then posted myself in front of the stand of some obscure airline company, whose employees had obviously gone off for a drink. Standing with my back to the counter, in the most natural pose I could assume, I had a good view of the whole hall. If Lester got too near, I could always turn my back.

After a few seconds, the mass of passengers, all different, all alike, the medley of their clothes, their incoherent movements, began to dance before my eyes. It was like an op-art painting: where did it begin? In what direction was it moving? How could one distinguish a single cell from ten thousand other almost identical ones? It moved in waves, twisted in and out, formed wrinkles, shimmered. I was so hypnotized by the spectacle I would never recognize Lester. I would have to pay my taxi-driver and explain my absence to the colonel.

In fact, everything worked out perfectly. The Texan stood out from the crowd by a head: his reddish shirt provided a further point of reference. I followed him to the arrival gates of the international flights. He stood out among the mass of friends, grandmothers, guides and lovers, arms folded on his chest, legs apart, like a sea captain. All I could see of him was the back of his neck, but I knew that his eyes would be focused on the arriving passengers, who, in irregular spurts, emerged from the limbo of customs-officers and police like dazed chicks falling from an incubator. Once, he looked at his watch, but he made no other movement. Thirty yards away, I had slipped into a telephone booth, pretended to talk and hoped against hope that no old lady would come and tap on the window. I had my jacket slung over my shoulder, my index finger through the loop. I had distributed the contents of the pockets between my trouser pockets, which had become heavy.

Lester had calculated his time well: we didn't have to wait more than twenty minutes. Suddenly he raised one of his arms; his body swung to one side and he cut through the crowd, using his shoulders like an ice-breaker. Again, my heart stopped beating: Lester would disappear and I would have come for nothing. But no: there he was, coming back, with the expected booty: his booty, which was also mine.

I was drunk with success. Not that I intended to use my discovery at once—except, at most, to record the event and file it away—but I had had my revenge on an arrogant Ally, an Ally whom I had tried to teach about something he knew better than I did, and the fact that this revenge would have to remain secret satisfied my 'novelist's' instinct all the more. Besides, Rat would pay for my taxi.

Carrying in one hand a miniature white case with gilt corners, Lester used his other hand to propel before him the astonishing passenger he had come to meet. Judging by the confident, determined, self-satisfied look on his face, one could tell that he regarded the specimen beside him as one of outstanding beauty and, in effect, people did turn round and look, but more out of amazement, I think, than admiration. An enormous head, made still more enormous by a bouffant coiffure of platinum-blonde hair, fluttering false eyelashes, a black beauty spot on a cheek of Tyrian pink, a toothy smile gleaming with saliva, shoulders stretched like a bow, a belly as tight as a gong, hips worthy of a mother-goddess, legs with the right curves, but of a really excessive calibre beneath the short skirt, the whole structure held in an architectural thrust hardly sufficient to sustain the monumental corbelling that completed the façade—there could be no doubt that this particular combination of physical charms had been selected for sheer volume out of thousands of candidates drawn from a population numbering a hundred million females.

As usual, the Company had spared no expense.

2

'Lieutenant, lieutenant, the general has asked for you three times.'

Mme Krebs, the Shopkeeper's secretary, wore check blouses, beige or mauve or turquoise, with small, well-starched, white collars. Yet her large, beautiful, moist eyes, floating in her placid, uniformly apricot-coloured face, seemed to belie such signs of innocence, suggesting rather a permanent dream of sensual ecstasy. As she breathlessly informed you that the general had been asking for you, she appeared, at the same time, to be calculating your hidden potential.

'Had it been you, Mme Krebs, it would have been more tempting.'

It was amusing to say suggestive things to Mme Krebs: she so skilfully pretended not to understand them.

'Kiril Lavrovich, I have the honour to convey to you my profound sympathy,' declared M. Alexandre with comic gravity.

'I sought you in the typing pool, but in vain,' Divo teased me gently.

'Lieutenant, I'd go if I were you,' said Puzo, a finger raised. Puzo usually contrived to be funny in any situation, though no one ever knew whether he intended to be or not.

Everyone laughed; there was no question of refusing the general's invitations. I slowly lowered my crossed feet, which I had placed on the corner of Puzo's desk. Slowly because I was proud of my stomach exercises and not at all ashamed of my black silk socks, perfectly held up by garters of English manufacture.

'Mme Krebs, if I'm not back within an hour, you will know

that I have given up forever the happiness of earning your favours.'

Not everybody acted with such *sang-froid* when summoned by the general, but I had long since learnt that, in the army, if one was to propagate the idea of one's own importance, one should cultivate the most detached attitude possible to one's superiors—in the French army, at any rate.

Puzo peered at me anxiously through his rectangular bifocals, with their thick black frames. At the mere mention of a rank, he was overcome by voluptuous sensations of panic.

I can hardly think of Puzo without a kind of remorse: what influence his destiny has had on mine, and how little I really know of him! I will try at least to describe what he looked like. What one noticed first of all was a round head beneath a circle of pepper-and-salt hair, cut pudding-basin fashion, fairly long at the back and at the front. Under the fringe, the face of a rather manly woman, fleshy, with lumps, swellings, folds of fat, one or two excrescences, one or two cysts, scattered haphazardly over the surface, like scraps of meat added to make up the weight. Green eyes of great gentleness. No neck. A fat, sexless torso, breasts and stomach forming vague protuberances, each merging into the other and further disguised by a black sweater, forming horizontal folds. In fact it was the trousers which ultimately determined the sex (as they do for small children)—this being the time when women still wore skirts in the office. With his head stuck into his shoulders, his round body like a ginger jar (his head forming the lid), his small, graceless voice, Puzo, in fact, suggested neither male nor female, but rather a neutered cat.

Puzo was not his real name. Let us say that he was called Pudelevich. But he was a creature of many nicknames. He had been called Poodle, Pudo, Poopoo, Uncle Pud, Pudoli-Pudola, Pastorelle (because M. Alexandre thought he looked like a woman pastor), but in the end we settled for Puzo, which means 'belly'. Although M. Pudelevich deserved this nickname on account of his corpulence, he also owed it to rather more esoteric reasons, difficult to convey in the French language (that beautiful, two-hundred-year-old corpse that the French persist in prostituting in everyday life, when Frenglish is obviously better suited to their present needs). To begin with, the word *puzo* is usually stressed on the first syllable, and we found it wildly amusing to stress the second. Furthermore, the section already had Divo, which is pronounced as a trochee in Russian, but which we pronounced in the French way as an iambus. Between Divo and Puzo, 'marvel' and 'pot belly', both wrongly pronounced in such a way as to rhyme to some extent, a parallelism was set up that was all the more comic given that no two people could have been more different than little Divo with his hard, crisp, dry manner, his crewcut, his icy smile, his suits with their excessively wide lapels, his starched pocket handkerchiefs, and fat, moist, sweating Puzo, whom those with a keen sense of smell did not care to approach too closely, for he only felt at ease with you if he was tapping you on the arm, patting you on the back, breathing under your nose or down your neck.

Nevertheless, Puzo was the best Russian interpreter in the French service, after, perhaps, Prince A . . ., who was on the private staff of the Head of State. He was at home in all the scientific disciplines, specializing particularly in the vocabulary of nuclear physics. He was often consulted by the National Centre of Scientific Research, travelled frequently to the Soviet Union and to the United States, and spoke on the radio, expressing opinions which, owing to the constraints of moderation, were of sibylline obscurity. His work as chief translator to GEST was little more than a home port: it provided him with a regular income, which could be supplemented from time to time by his work as an interpreter.

But there was more to him than this. Under the pseudonym Quatre-Etoiles ('four stars like the restaurants', he explained humbly, in his falsetto voice, 'not like the generals'), he was regarded as the greatest living writer of French erotic literature. I tried to read his books. The novellas, great dazzling creations, were not without charm. I found the novels quite unreadable on account of their incredibly elaborate style: they were all about Tibetan princesses, wearing two chrysoprases and a smarragd, riding round the rings of private circuses on motorbikes, under the whip of slave-drivers wearing solid-gold chastity belts, while behind the grills of private boxes, lying on leopard skins, sexually obsessed, but impotent oil magnates indulged in pastimes that I refuse to describe. I could not say whether Puzo saw himself in the role of the magnate or of the slave-driver; M. Alexandre suggested that he identified himself with the princess; Divo opted for the motorbike.

In fact, we had no reason to ascribe to him the preposterous perversions that we were pleased to invent for him. There was one passion, however, which we knew to be his, a passion, it is true, that went beyond all decent limits. Its object was quite simply the Head of State. A dozen times a day, Puzo would interrupt his work, and ours, to recount some moving incident, to share with us some wonderful remark the great man had made, to show us some little-known photograph, or to rail indignantly against some disrespectful comment made in the press or by a colleague. 'But this is treason!' he would exclaim, raising a finger. Tears would come to his eyes when he remembered the single occasion when his idol, then a mere cavalry colonel, heaped on him a long stream of abuse, which Puzo had piously committed to memory and would trot out at the slightest provocation. He preserved in a leather desk-pad decorated with poker-work the report the still shaky French spelling of which had earned him this summons from his then commanding officer. He subscribed to *L'Argus* and received *all* the articles in which the Head of State was mentioned, and stuck the favourable ones into scrap-books, which he took the greatest pleasure in showing to anybody who was willing to be shown them. On his desk was a bottle of glue specially intended for this use: woe betide any of us who borrowed it.

It should be remembered that it was a time when a certain newly fledged foreign government was busy pickling the friends of France in brine, and a time when the Head of State, whom some regarded as responsible for these excesses, had become the great stumbling block of the army, while remaining its absolute head. I particularly remember that a sumptuous edition of the *Memoirs* had just appeared; for days representatives of the publishing house had been displaying copies of the new book in the canteen, and General Silbert marked his new appointment by sending a memo round the whole of his Division, recommending 'the acquisition of this exceptional work by all personnel, military and civilian, established or non-established, loyal to France and to the Republic.' We would have had a good laugh at the general's expense if we'd dared to, but the memo was couched in an almost comminatory style, and we had to be content with averting our eyes before the tables laden with the superb, shiny, tri-coloured volumes. Puzo, of course, had ordered the whole set on the first day and, that Tuesday, he had just received Volume I, which he stroked with loving, if not entirely clean fingers, well licked to turn the heavy pages on which the prose of the beloved was laid out.

I got up slowly and, to show my lack of concern, I looked around for something to say to someone.

'M. de Pudelevich,' I said to him in French (Puzo, who had been born somewhere on the edges of the semi-imaginary countries of Central Europe, knew Russian perfectly, but he preferred to speak to us in French, in order to stress his loyalty, and I outdid his own wishes by endowing him with an aristocratic, but quite imaginary, 'de'). 'M. de Pudelevich, you really ought to put Mme Krebs into your next novel, you know. I'd love to see her riding around on a motorbike, wearing nothing but three chrysoprases.'

'Oh, no!' said Mme Krebs. 'I'd be too frightened on a motorbike.' Her light little tongue moved over her dark lips.

'Now then, Kiril Lavrovich,' M. Alexandre declared, 'you mustn't keep the top brass on brass tacks!'

He laughed with his deep, fine voice. Despite a rather childish sense of humour, he had carefully manicured hands, kindly, courteous manners, the benignity of an *ancien régime* grandee.

There was no one in the corridor—we used to say that the paving dated from the seventeenth century, the woodwork from the eighteenth, the pink marbled linoleum from the nineteenth and the neon lighting from the twentieth. But a pool of light outside Captain Tolstoy's office showed that his door was, as usual, open. He was the only officer in GEST to sit at his desk in full view of all who passed by. I never discovered whether it was because of claustrophobia, to disguise his mysterious activities,

32

or to supervise the comings and goings of the staff. I purposely did not look in his direction as I passed, but he caught sight of me and called out:

'Volsky!'

I stopped in spite of myself.

'Sir?'

'The general has been looking for you.'

'Yes, I know. I'm on my way.'

He made a great show of looking at his watch. I didn't have to account for my activities to Captain Tolstoy, who was Rat's adjutant only for the sake of appearances; in fact, he commanded an ultra-secret section, specializing in the manipulation of informants, called, heaven knows why, 144.

'It's very kind of you, sir. Don't worry on my account.'

He smiled with all his gleaming teeth; his sea captain's eyes, incongruous in an infantryman, twinkled with amusement. I had asked him to mind his own business; he had made a note of it, but would go on doing as he pleased. After a time, which he dragged out on purpose, he said: 'Well, run along. I'm not detaining you.'

This meant: 'Don't pretend you don't care. You're in a hurry, but, if I wanted you to, you'd have to stay where you are, in my doorway.'

It was an admission that gave me no pleasure, but I had to admit that in every hierarchy that mattered to me at that time, Tolstoy was placed above me. Professionally, he was a 'career' officer, I was only 'on the active list'. In rank: he had a stripe more than I on his epaulette. In age and experience: he had really seen fighting, whereas I had merely fished in troubled waters. He had a title, a rather recent one, it is true, but a title nevertheless. In terms of responsibility: he was Greek Fire's case officer, while I ran errands. In imagination: he conceived and elaborated his own networks, I simply laid connections between Rat's networks. In self-possession and insolence: I had only competence and a measure of impertinence. In a certain undeniable form of purity, of an almost chemical kind: I was always in two minds, Tolstoy was always incorrigibly himself. It was not simply a matter of innate quality, of course; there was

33

also a measure of skill involved. He managed to present all his characteristics as advantages. Even the fact that he was married, which was already ridiculous enough, and burdened with half-a-dozen children, whom he took off camping in a caravan in summer, to save money, a somewhat domestic activity for a warrior, he managed to turn to his own advantage. He had married a French girl of good family, and that justified everything. It was true that I wrote, and he didn't, but I had not yet published anything and, even if I had done so, he would have regarded it as yet another weakness. He would probably have asked me, as the Chevalier Descartes asked his son, if I was bound in calf. On reflection, there is one thing I pride myself on, and that is that, while recognizing all Tolstoy's superiorities, even suffering from them, I never became embittered by them: I admired him too much to bear him any grudge.

On that occasion, as usual, I could think of nothing to say and swallowed his insinuations.

A labyrinth of corridors and staircases blocked by various obstacles (doors, some padded, others not, orderlies, registers, signatures, checks) brought me to a corridor lit by concealed lighting, with oak-panelled walls and a crimson carpet. The doors bore no names, only numbers. Were one to open one at random, one might equally well find oneself in the general's office or in a broom cupboard; the numbers were moved from time to time 'to confuse the enemy.' It was one of Silbert's inventions. I was looking for room 121, I think. It took me some time to find it. A warrant officer in civilian clothes, with reddish hair and a mischievous face, addressed me from behind a colonel's desk:

'Wait here.'

'Sir,' I added firmly.

He looked at me as if he couldn't believe his ears. The headquarter staff NCOs behaved just as they liked. Strategically, there was only one chair in the room. His. I sat down on a table taking care to push a file off on to the floor as I did so. He looked at the file. I looked out of the window. I had the feeling I was about to be given a good-dressing-down by the master: I wasn't going to begin by abasing myself before the servant.

For the time being, it was the servant who was keeping me waiting: five minutes on principle, five more minutes for my behaviour. I saw him look at his watch: a methodical man. After precisely ten minutes, he got up, cast another sad look at the file, crossed the room and disappeared without knocking through a door surmounted by a green light. Through the window I could see a handsome rectangular courtyard: the walls needed cleaning, but the proportions were sublime. Examples of artillery from different periods were arranged in ranks: slim culverins, gaping howitzers, Gribeauval cannons bearing the French coat-of-arms, an elegant 75 that looked as if it could go off at any moment. Tall, small-paned windows, surmounted by scrolls, opened on to offices bathed in white-violet neon light, a piece of shoulder here, a bit of foot there, half a typewriter, a table covered in yellow papers whose contents it would not have been too difficult to make out with a good pair of binoculars.

I could hear the general shouting. I was supposed to be trembling with fright. The warrant officer came back, looking as sinister as an undertaker. He glanced down at the file, hoping that I would have picked it up by now. He sat down again behind his desk. It was now the master's turn to keep me waiting. I knew the ritual—I'd practised it myself—yet, for all that, it worked on me. I wondered how much time the general thought I needed before I was fit to appear before three stars. The artillery had destroyed true nobility. Gunpowder had produced, as if by magic, that fireworks display known as the Renaissance. The Jacobins and Napoleon had won all their battles with Louis XVI cannons. The Russian artillerymen were deeply attached to their guns, gave them nicknames and patronymics, and wept if they were captured by the enemy. Nicholas I, who despised over-decorated officers, once turned to an old captain, bedecked with ribbons and medals, and asked: 'Whose aide-de-camp were you?' The old boy replied, 'This one's, your Majesty!', affectionately tapping his favourite gun . . . Despite the help of the artillery the palms of my hand were sufficiently moist and my throat acceptably dry when, at last, the general's metallic voice boomed down the intercom:

'Send Volsky in.'

The warrant officer looked up and nodded his head in the direction of the door: what was about to happen was my own doing, he washed his hands of the whole business.

I went in.

General Silbert was not highly regarded by us, not only because of his circular concerning the literary works of the Head of State, but also because of the demagogic manner in which he had assumed his command. After the customary introductions, he began by summoning the personnel individually, beginning not at the top but at the bottom. All the secretaries had already been interviewed; my turn had hardly come; Lieut.-Colonel Rat, the head of the service, would not be summoned for another three weeks.

The office was enormous, half in light and half in shade, because the blind of the first window had been raised and that of the second left down. In the middle of the dark part sat the general, his eyes hidden behind blue-tinted spectacles. He was still young, short, but of fine bearing, with closely cropped, thick, bristly hair, black at the roots, iron-grey at the ends, full cheeks, flecked with a recalcitrant beard despite an obviously demanding razor, a small, greedy mouth, tinged with purple. I knew all the tricks, the waiting, the blinds, the dark glasses. Their familiarity was reassuring. After all, the poor fellow had already had time to earn the disapproving nickname of 'Steel Wool'.

'Lieutenant Volsky reporting, sir.'

We were both wearing civilian clothes. I refused to indulge in the gymnastics of courtesy he was expecting.

'Where've you been?'

The voice was sonorous, the consonants aggressive, the lightning about to strike. One would have been forgiven for thinking that Silbert had learnt how to command from a textbook.

I was tempted to reply, 'In the outer office, sir. For the last three-quarters-of-an-hour,' but I said nothing of the kind.

I crossed the room. Two upright, leather-upholstered brass-studded chairs stood opposite the desk. I put my hand on the back of one of them and almost sat down. I always behaved informally with Rat, and had lost the habit of performing the

36

external marks of discipline. At the last moment, I realized the enormity of what I was about to do. I dropped my hand.

'I was lunching with my CIA major.'

Perhaps I stammered a bit.

Silbert looked at the travelling clock on his polished wooden desk, on which various expensive accessories—leather-handled scissors and paper-knife, IN and OUT trays with lids made of the same leather, a large pad, a small pad in a nickel stand, coloured crayons, sharpened like stilettos—were arranged in perfect order. It was after five o'clock.

'Good lunch?' he asked, with heavy sarcasm.

With a touch of low humour, of a kind Rat would have appreciated, I answered: 'At our Ally's expense, sir.'

I was sure that Silbert was about to attack me about expenses. He changed tactics with disconcerting rapidity: 'Had you nothing to do in the office?'

I replied virtuously: 'I don't think so, sir.'

That was it! I had fallen into the trap. And I didn't yet know it.

He sat back in his chair. It took me some seconds to realize that he was not reproaching me with my extended absence. He asked me point-blank:

'What do you *do* here?'

The emphasis gave his question a menacing quality, but I still did not know what Steel Wool was getting at.

'Here, sir?'

He impatiently tapped his blotting-paper with his paper-knife; he wouldn't hold out much longer; the storm was about to break.

'In my Division. In GEST. You understand French?'

Was he referring to my foreign origins? I replied dryly: 'I am technical assistant to the head of the service.'

'What does that involve?'

'I'm at the colonel's elbow. If he doesn't need me, I lend a hand to the translators. I liaise with the Allied special services for scientific and technical information.'

Silbert paused for some time; I was probably supposed to fill the gap by listing my other responsibilities. He was being fair;

he was giving me my chance. But I could hardly tell him that I was writing a long novel, that I worked as a reader for a publishing firm, and that much of my time was taken up by a pretty Italian mistress. I refused to invent fictional duties and said nothing. The minute he had allocated to me expired and, as if I had just concluded a long list of activities, Silbert said:

'Is that all?'

He looked at me, his head thrown back, with all the superiority lent him by his sitting position and dark glasses.

I wondered what new job he was going to find for me. I was already beginning to worry for my novel, when he went on:

'Translations—translators are paid for that. The errands you run for Lieut.-Colonel Rat could just as well be done by a courier. Liaison with the Allies—don't make me laugh!' (He showed no desire to do so.) 'You pass on dubious information to them and bring back stuff that isn't even dubious.'

Scrupulously, he gave me time to reply. Until now I had been proud of the fact that my leisure activities were being paid for by the taxpayer. I had always disdained to appear to be working. I slightly rectified this position and awaited what was to come next.

'I intend to send you back to your regiment,' said Silbert. He had the good grace to add a few words by way of explanation. 'You draw your salary. Your record is appalling. I'm carrying no passengers in this Division.'

I stood there petrified, but he was a fair man, so 'What have you got to say for yourself?' he added irritably.

Sending me back to my regiment would mean a posting abroad: Tahiti or Ouagadougou. I had nothing against foreign travel, in general, but I did not relish the prospect of going off to the ends of the earth to supervise the polishing of boot soles (between the studs). In Paris, I was half-way to success; I was well in with certain literary circles; I was in demand, socially; I had sentimental ties. So I had no intention of policing the colonies. Should I resign? To do what? Work eight hours a day, with three weeks' holiday a year? Anyway, once one has had a taste of the secret service, it's difficult to give it up. I had no desire to sell insurance after playing at putting the finishing

38

touches to some international crisis. On the other hand, Silbert was right: I wasn't earning my keep—well, that's me to a T!

I can no longer recall the exact moment when the idea came to me, but I remember that I argued more or less like this: since I was about to be sacked in any case, why not risk everything on one last daring throw? I walked over to the window. The general looked at me with surprise. I came back. All fear had disappeared.

'Hasn't the colonel told you about Operation . . .'

I glanced out of the window.

'Operation Culverin, which I'm in charge of?'

It was late afternoon. It was hardly likely that Silbert would demand an explanation from Rat before the following morning.

'Culverin? Culverin? No. What's it all about?'

'The operation is classified as *very secret*, sir'.

The Shop came under Silbert's overall supervision, but he wasn't part of it.

'Tell me about it. That's an order.'

He still thought he was in the field. I could have demanded orders in writing. But supposing he gave me written orders? I wanted to lay a bait for him. I also wanted to prevent Rat from altering any of the details of the plan, which was already working out well for me, if only because it would be easy to spin it out.

'Culverin is an operation directed at Major Igor Popov, head of scientific and technical espionage in France. The idea is to turn him, sir.'

Silbert took a quick, sharp intake of breath, producing a hissing sound as he did so, then bit his lower lip.

Such an operation would not normally come within the activities of the Division. It was just possible, however, given exceptional circumstances, that it might do so. I could see a number of questions were running through Steel Wool's head: personal and professional advantages, possible risks, relations with the parallel services . . .

'Who ordered Culverin?' he asked severely.

It gave me great pleasure to hear him repeat the name that I had just made up. It was like an adoption. Once the name was registered, everything would grow. But I had to answer. Who could have given such an order? It could have been Poirier, Silbert's predecessor, with approval from higher quarters. Or the Chief of General Staff. Or the Minister. Or even . . . the secret services short circuit with alacrity. There need not necessarily be any written trace. Secrecy has its advantages . . . The general placed the red crayon in place of the green, then a steel ruler in place of a compass, with calculated brutality. It was as if he were reducing them to the ranks in front of the troops. In the end, I said, almost inaudibly: 'Orders came from "*Up There*".'

Brilliant! At the time, '*Up There*' cautioned anyone to prudence who valued his career. Silbert again fell silent. For the head of the Intelligence Division of the General Staff of the French Army a Soviet major was a big prize.

'Good,' he said at last. 'Rat will brief me on it. You may go.'

He could no longer speak to me with his customary sharpness. He was beginning to respect me: and he found that embarrassing. To put him at his ease, by way of compensation, so to speak, I clicked my heels and did a rather poor imitation of the correct about-turn.

The warrant officer didn't look up as I walked by. I looked around for the file I had knocked off the table; it was nowhere to be seen.

3

In the corridor leading to Lieut.-Colonel Rat's office—the floor
of this part of the termitarium was covered with red linoleum—I
saw Puzo's backside disappear round a corner with astonishing
nimbleness for such a volume. It was 5.35 pm and, despite his
intense loyalty, Puzo was always the first to leave the office. In
the secretary's office, Mme Krebs had put all her papers away,
slipped the cover over her typewriter, locked the filing-cabinets,
the cupboard and the safe, but she was still at her post, busy
putting cerise varnish on her nails and waiting until 5.45.

'Is the Shopkeeper there?'

Her eyes opened wide.

'Lieutenant! He might hear you.'

Lieut.-Colonel Rat did not in the least mind being called the
Shopkeeper. He took it as a compliment. In another service,
apparently, he had been nicknamed the Pimp. He liked Pimp
even better.

His desk was placed not majestically in the middle of the
floor, like Silbert's, but in a corner, next to the window, its side
against the wall. This little grey metal desk—it was identical
with those given to the translators and subalterns, was too low
for Rat, who bent over it like a mother over a cradle. The ink-
stained blotting-paper was practically invisible beneath a
heterogeneous mass of papers, chewed pencils, cigarette ash,
sometimes even the greasy wrapping-paper from a sandwich,
the whole suggesting a sordid humanity which, at that time,
turned my stomach. Rat himself, with his long, fleshless figure,
his lantern-shaped head, the bones visible beneath the old skin,
which hung in pockets under his eyes, under his cheek-bones

41

and on his neck, was alarmingly human. His yellow-white hair betrayed not only his age, but, by that very fact, his situation: he was quite obviously a career officer who, having been struck off the active list, had been promoted and, as a farewell present, re-enlisted under contract. How did this man of such limited intellect manage to get himself appointed head of such a specialized service as GEST? We often asked ourselves the same question, always concluding that personal connections must have had something to do with it. Perhaps. But we never guessed what must have been the main reason, namely, that GEST had to be commanded by a nonentity. In fact, Rat was not entirely devoid of professional talent; on the contrary, deception was as necessary to him as eating; for him, hypocrisy provided an almost sensuous pleasure.

I took a chair and told him the truth.

Not all the truth: Rat would have despised me if I had. I kept quiet about Silbert's initial intentions concerning me: he would learn of them soon enough, deduce my motives, realize that I had tried to manoeuvre him and would be grateful for having his opinion of human nature confirmed once again. For the time being, I admitted that by inventing Culverin I had wanted to gain time: we had an opportunity of making our mark that we would certainly lose if we had to get permission through the normal bureaucratic channels.

Rat's first reaction was the one I expected: he had cold feet.

'You've got yourself into quite a fix, haven't you?' he said.

His lower lip, which always seemed about to come away from the gum, trembled against the false teeth. He stuck a cigarette into the opening, as if to block up the hole, but to no avail. The cigarette just hung there, pulling the lip away still more.

'I thought I was doing the right thing, sir. In the interests of the service . . .'

He gave me a sidelong look through his tinted glasses: he, too, wore them, but his were yellow and more a protection for his eyes, I think, than an affectation.

'The service? The service has a broad back.'

'The general talked about cost-effectiveness, sir.'

In the army the word 'cost-effectiveness' strikes terror in all hearts : it can produce nightmares, ulcers, even suicides. I didn't know at the time that GEST was sacrosanct. Rat himself did not know. I saw a commission of enquiry marching through his terrified imagination. I saw him seeing himself boarding the suburban train of retirement . . . A little house at Athis-Mons, a garden with a fuchsia bed and another for leeks; a cantankerous wife who put on the radio at full blast; a wardrobe taking up half the bedroom; an Henri II sideboard dominating the dining-room; not even assegais or tom-toms on the walls, because he'd fought all his wars at an office desk.

'The general led me to believe . . . that heads will be rolling,' I added.

Rat's hands were covered with age spots, his fingers tobacco-stained, but, for some reason, his nails were those of a mandarin, not rounded but streaked. His fingers clenched; I noticed that his nails had left marks on the blotting-pad.

'Heads! That's going a bit far, my boy. One or two jobs will go, of course. The best course might be to suggest to the general myself a redistribution of responsibilities. For all the use Huchet makes of his secretary, for example . . .'

Age was taking its toll: reduce the personnel instead of increasing cost-effectiveness. Anyway, cost-effectiveness . . . In theory, GEST was responsible for all external-scientific-and-technical-non-operational-information-of-military-interest.   In reality, or rather to all appearances, it was a hodge-podge of Intelligence, constituted by a dozen teams of semi-amateurs whose work consisted for the most part in combing through specialized foreign journals for worthwhile, or filchable, ideas. In addition to this, Tolstoy handled a few agents of whom the only productive one was Greek Fire; we lent Puzo out to whoever wanted him; we were supposed to handle scientific and technical liaison with the special services of the various members of the North Atlantic Treaty Organization; Rat, with the title of consultant, pottered around between the National Centre of Scientific Research, the Service of External Documentation and Counter-espionage and the headquarters of the security police: that was about it. It did not amount to enough to justify the upkeep of a hundred soldiers and civilians, some of them very highly paid indeed.

'But if we reduce personnel, sir, we won't count for much in the Division.'

He knew that better than I did. I saw him seeing himself at a weekly meeting of service chiefs, pushed down to the end of the table. His wrists skimmed the surface of the desk, his fingers making the familiar gesture of gathering pinches of this and that.

'You realize that your excess of imagination may cost you your job?'

He meant that I had put his own in danger.

'The pleasure of playing a trick on the Allies is worth the risk, isn't it?' I was speaking for him. Personally, I liked the Americans, in spite of their protective airs. But Rat hated them. I suspected him of having been a Pétainist.

'You know very well we have no responsibility for counter-espionage.'

If he began by making objections to my scheme, my cause was not lost.

'As far as scientific and technical information is concerned, sir, you have a fairly free hand.'

'In any case, it would have been the responsibility of 144.'

I allowed myself a crafty smile.

'You would not necessarily have put all your eggs into the same basket.'

He looked up through his yellow lenses. I think he hated Tolstoy even more than the Americans.

'You're a good lad, Volsky,' he said. That meant: you're almost as good a pimp as I am. 'All the same, a high-ranking officer of the KGB, with diplomatic immunity . . . If it had been a chauffeur or a typist . . .'

'You know better than I do, sir . . .'—I could talk to him in this way, providing I was right—'. . . that the only Soviet personnel we have the slightest chance of turning are precisely the officers of the KGB. They are the only ones who have enough freedom to make contacts. Indeed, it would be much easier to turn Semichasny himself than the least of his orderlies. Popov is in charge of relations with the women's movement, the peace

44

movement, youth groups. He must move about alone, and not only to meet his informants.'

'You say he's a big shot.'

'And all the more vulnerable, because they trust him and he trusts himself. The Goliath complex, like the Americans. Anyway, even if we didn't pull it off . . .'

I didn't have to spell it out. If we failed, we would nevertheless have gained time and, who knows, with time, further promotion for the lieutenant-colonel. Sometimes the headquarters of Army Personnel promote you simply out of lassitude.

'No one would give the order to turn a major of the KGB without first finding something to pin on him,' said Rat. 'It's all right for the Yanks to try everyone in the hope of a satisfactory return of, say, .001%. We simply can't afford it. Anyway, turning . . . There's no reason to suppose that he'll go along with it. Still, if we can get him fired because of a little scandal, it would be worth it, wouldn't it? He's been there two weeks? Yes, but Silbert arrived two months ago!'

'General Poirier might have known that Popov had been transferred to Paris, mightn't he?'

General Poirier had, as they say, been allowed to exercise his right to retirement. Invulnerable, he now spent his days tickling the trout somewhere in Normandy. Rat and he had been close friends. Among other things, they shared an unshakeable dislike of our dear trans-Atlantic Allies.

'Poirier was a good fellow,' said Rat, raising a thumb.

Operation Umbrella was under consideration: always a good sign.

'I've nothing in particular to do tomorrow morning, have I?' Rat murmured dreamily.

I saw him seeing himself boarding a train at Saint-Lazare, and getting off again at some village station surrounded by green fields. Poirier would have come to collect him in an old Citroën, a Poirier with sharp little eyes set in a fat, red face, his chin prickly with white stubble, wearing an old pullover, perhaps, and corduroy trousers. 'My dear general . . . My dear old friend . . . What are you up to, eh? Some terrific scheme to get the

Yanks to . . . How about a drop of something rather special?' It could be arranged.

Rat asked me point-blank: 'Have you anyone in mind?'

GEST was more plentifully endowed with Professor Nimbuses than with Mata-Haris. I hadn't expected the Shopkeeper to move so fast. He was probably thinking that a few embarrassing photographs, even if they didn't lead, in the end, to a turning, might transform his two silver stripes into two gold ones. Fortunately, he didn't give me time to answer.

'In any case, it would have to be checked first. This woman, do you know who she is?'

'Penelope Barker, American. Just arrived from London.'

I had got my information from the air traffic police before leaving Orly.

'We might be able to ask our chaps in Washington what they think. But it will have to go through the Big Shop. Or through one of our own diplomats who has been stationed with Popov. Do you think that's his real name?'

'The chances are that it is. He's not a secret agent.'

'Do you believe in this obsession of his for well-endowed blondes? It seems a bit Freudian, naive and systematic. American . . . You know what I mean.'

'Maybe it's just what he likes. Personally I like refined, slightly plump brunettes.'

After all, I was doing all this for Frisquette.

'And this rather puritanical government provides him with his six-monthly ration of human flesh.'

'They're becoming civilized, sir. Still realistic and already civilized. That's their strength. They know the relative value of rules and exceptions.'

'He must deliver the goods, then, this Popov! And to think I gave him to you to sell cheap to the Allies! You don't think SDECE gave us the gen to make us think it wasn't important? Maybe they know what they're doing too? No, they wouldn't have said anything. They've done us a favour, a nice little favour!'

The idea of having a laugh at the expense not only of the Americans, but also of the Big House, our eternal enemy,

46

excited Rat beyond all my expectations. Behind the tinted spectacles, his eyes, usually dull with age, lit up with feline brightness.

'The register is no problem,' he murmured. 'Ours is full of erasures and Estienne has the Division's register kept by two fellows who get things wrong as often as not: I've already had occasion to check it.'

Then his lower lip, which still hung limp, trembled: 'Of course, there's the day-book.'

In our services it was the practice to record all mail, incoming and outgoing, in a special register (this apparently presented no difficulty), but it was also the practice to make two copies of all outgoing mail and to file one, analytically, in the archives, and the other, in numerical order, in the day-book. Now, modern armies being what they are, Operation Culverin could in no way be launched without a minimum of paperwork, if only to take care of certain secondary matters. There was no problem in antedating a few papers and slipping them into the appropriate files, at least as far as GEST was concerned, but it was impossible to give them a number that had not already been used. What might pass unnoticed in the file would immediately show up in the day-book, where the entry numbers had to be consecutive. I'm not of a very bureaucratic turn of mind and this down-to-earth objection seemed insuperable. I repeated stupidly: 'The day-book . . .'

Meanwhile, the prospects of Paris and Ouagadougou, polished soles and insurance, alternated in my mind.

Rat searched around his yellow, irregular teeth with the tip of his tongue, producing sucking sounds that inspired confidence.

'Would you bring it to me? Mme Krebs must have gone by now.'

Hopes rising, I got up and went into the secretary's office. Mme Krebs had indeed gone, but I knew (I like to know these things) where she hid the key of the steel cupboard (in her desk drawer, under the Kleenex). I found the large blue-grey file marked 'July-August' easily enough. (Silbert had taken up his command on the feast of the Assumption: some holiday!)

The file bore the following notice: 'All non-COSMIC

personnel acquiring knowledge of the enclosed documents come under the current legislation concerning espionage in peacetime.' This hardly concerned me; I was 'COSMIC'. Who thinks up these labels?

The colonel opened the day-book and, licking a finger with his long brown tongue, began to turn the pages. Almost all our outgoing mail was there: the ordinary, the *confidential* and the *secret*; only part of the *top secret* was included, another part, classified as 144 and numbered separately, was with Tolstoy. In principal, an operation like Culverin ought to have been his responsibility, but if, for one reason or another, it had been decided to keep him out of it, the corresponding mail would be found in the general day-book, probably in the form of a numbered reference to some special file. The trouble was, all the numbers had been taken. Unless Mme Krebs had missed one by mistake? We went on looking.

Minutes, circulars, reports, requests for explanations, information sheets, intelligence summaries, testimonials, orders. The same phrases recurred again and again: 'for onward transmission' and 'for information', 'I have the honour to' and 'I am astonished that', 'bring to your notice' and 'ask you to have the kindness to', 'your very great kindness' and 'regrettable negligence', 'special leave' and 'seven days' open arrest', occasionally illustrated with typographical illuminations due to the talent of Mme Krebs, and variously stamped from *Urgent Flash* to *Limited Distribution*, with perhaps some predilection for *Not to be communicated to the Allies*. The entire mass of material was in perfect order. Even the memos reminding personnel that it was forbidden to use the GEST telephone line for private calls were to be found in their periodic places: there was one every three weeks.

Rat closed the file and gave me a cunning look. At that moment, I still trusted him: he would surely find some way around it. He then delivered a blow that I was not at all expecting.

'And that's not all, Volsky. There's the other one.'

'The other one?'

Of course, you greenhorn! There was the Division day-book,

48

over which the red-haired orderly reigned, and which ought to contain at least one reference to Culverin, authorizing the appropriation of expenditure under this or that heading. Rat raised the skin of his forehead in successive folds, like the metal blind of a shop. I went to put the day-book back and hid the key under the Kleenex. The drawer reeked of *Sortilège*. Insurance? Or polished soles?

The Shopkeeper and I left together and walked down the stone steps, which had been made almost spongy by three centuries of boots. The deserted corridors sounded hollow. The odd light-bulb projected on to the seventeenth-century arcades, the Don Quixote-like shadow of the colonel, impaled by his umbrella, and mine, short and straight, like an I: an old king, leaning on his page, perhaps, out of a painting by Rouault or a play by Ghelderode.

The officer of the guard gave us a suspicious salute. It was not normal for staff to leave the building late. We walked in silence along the Boulevard de La Tour-Maubourg to the métro station. I continued on foot; the colonel, for reasons best known to himself, sometimes chose not to avail himself of his official car and went to sweat it out with the common people. He had already descended three steps and I was waiting politely for him to disappear in the crowd, when he turned towards me and, slapping the rail with his aged hand said:

'Tomorrow morning, at half-past ten, you will pop over to the Quai d'Orsay and, keeping a straight face, you will ask for M. Edme de Malmaison, and you'll worm a few secrets out of him.'

4

That night I had the preposterous idea of proposing to
Frisquette: after the wedding we would set out for Timbuctoo. I
mention this aberration simply to show how low my morale had
fallen. In any case, had I made my proposal, Frisquette would
have laughed in my face. The fact that Rat was sending me to
the Quai d'Orsay should have raised my hopes, but I didn't
entirely trust him. The Shopkeeper was quite capable of using
me to clear the ground, and then taking over the operation
himself. But supposing he did not intend to betray me, how,
even with the rather dubious complicity of Poirier, was he to
insert into the past an event that had not taken place? Do the
supernatural powers of 'novelists' extend so far? Is there a way
of getting round the day-book of history?

The next day, just as I was arriving at M. de Norpois' old
haunt, I got a stitch in my side. So as far as my diary was
concerned, 'stitch' now became the code word for the Quai
d'Orsay.

To my surprise, M. Edme de Malmaison turned out to be a
pleasant young man with a sidelong smile, and not at all the
subtle, solemn pontiff I had imagined. He was sitting at a desk
in the middle of an office panelled with elaborately carved,
unstained wood. He had taken off his jacket and his yellow
waistcoat combined very smartly with his grey silk tie. The
windows looked out on to the Seine, whose lead-coloured
surface could be glimpsed between the leafy trees. I explained
my mission: Colonel Rat would like confidential information
about Igor Maximovich Popov, counsellor at the Soviet
Embassy.

'I am entirely at Colonel Rat's disposal,' he said, forming his left eyebrow into a circumflex accent. 'It seems to me that SDECE . . .'

'We'd better not arouse their suspicions,' I interjected.

'Would they fumigate the lot of us?' He burst out laughing, resumed his sober mien, and gave me a sly, but courteous look. He had all the refinement of a man who had never wanted for anything.

'Monsieur,' he said, leaning his head to one side, 'I must let you into a little secret. Your respected chief and I have one thing in common.'

He paused to allow me to make the most of the surprise. One thing in common, Lieut.-Colonel Rat and M. Edme de Malmaison?

'And that is,' he went on, 'a strong and healthy antipathy to SDECE. Those idiots get us into the most unpleasant situations with foreign ministers and, when we complain, do you know what reply we get back from the Presidency? "That's their job!" Well, it's a stupid job, Monsieur, done by stupid men. Look at the mess they made of the kidnapping of M. Argoud in the German Federal Republic! The ambassador was in such a state! . . .'

This puerile outburst of anger suddenly subsided into a winning slanted smile: 'So you see, if I can do anything to play a prank on those people . . .'

The old-fashioned turn of phrase fell charmingly from that spoilt child's petulant lips. We were on the same side; together we were going to play pranks on those idiots at SDECE. It occurred to me that M. de Malmaison was not perhaps as young as he was paid to seem. Why had this diplomat so undiplomatically mentioned the taboo name of Argoud? To demonstrate to me that here walls do not have ears? To seal our complicity still further (which, he no doubt thought, could not fail to flatter me, and he was not wrong), he walked around his inlaid desk and came and sat down next to me in one of the two cane armchairs provided for visitors. He gave my knee a friendly tap: 'Let me know your desiderata. Or, as your respected chief would probably say, spit it out.'

There we were, accomplices, men on the same side and almost of the same world. M. de Malmaison knew his job.

'We want as much information as possible about Counsellor Popov. Date and place of birth. Family background. Education. Health. Political history. Official career. Actual career. Awards. Working habits. Private habits. Vices. Gossip. In short, everything. All available photographs. Do you think that's too much?' (Malmaison was observing me seriously, but impenetrably.) 'That's not all. Photographs of his dead wife. Photographs of his secretaries, with the dates when they began working for him and when they left.'

'By when?'

'Suit yourself.'

He formed a little Gothic cathedral with the fingers of both hands.

'I have three categories of deliveries. A, which I can give you now. B, which I shall manage to gather in the office. C, which you will have to resign yourself to not seeing if you don't want to rock the boat. Now, let me see what I can do about A. Pray excuse me a moment.'

He left me alone with the magazines. Instead of turning their pages, I began to reflect on the destiny of this man. While I had always been hard up, he had always been surrounded by comfort and good taste; while I tended naturally to contempt, to sarcasm, he seemed like a well-behaved child who succeeded in everything without effort. In actual fact, the reverse was possibly true: lacking ambition, I let things happen to me, while he directed his fate with a mastery that he was polite enough to conceal. He came back after about an hour and a half, carrying a thick, chalky sheet of paper, without letter heading, impeccably typed. The heading read: 'Confidential note on M. Igor Popov, counsellor at the Soviet Embassy (information provided by the embassy of the Soviet Union and collected from archives).' The parenthesis effectively contradicted the word 'confidential', which had no doubt been put there as a matter of routine.

Igor Maximovich Popov was born in 1928, I think. I can't recall the exact date, but I think it must have been March or April, for I remember noticing his sign of the zodiac: Puzo had taught me the basic notions of erotic astrology. His father had been a fitter, his mother a winding-machine operator; both were now dead. His secondary education had been at a high school, in Vladimir. Despite the fact that he spoke French perfectly, he did not follow the usual practice of his country and specialize in the area for which he was best suited. Instead, he took a general degree in physics at Moscow University. This suggested, though the dates neither confirmed nor disproved this hypothesis, that he had undergone a training period in a special school, disguised (necessarily) as months of voluntary work on the building sites of Novosibirsk. After graduating, Igor Popov published some articles—when? On what? In which journals? He then suddenly turned up as attaché at the Soviet embassy of some French-speaking central African state.

This appointment, if I am not mistaken, occurred in 1953. From then on, Popov's career followed a normal diplomatic course, except that promotion came, for no apparent reason, with increasing rapidity. Two or three African states, followed by the Lebanon, and, before long, Paris; from attaché to counsellor in a few years, in a system in which colonels are often passed off as chauffeurs: some secret and deserved rise must lie behind this inexplicably brilliant career. His speciality was contact with the paracommunist movements (an activity in which a degree in physics would not seem to be indispensable). The information confirmed that Popov was a widower.

'We shall continue our researches. Late this afternoon or tomorrow morning we'll have photographs and some bits of gossip. Then, as our contacts continue, I shall send you B and what I can gather of C. Will that do you?'

'Could I have copies of his articles?'

'We shall ask for them at the Rue de Grenelle. Or would you prefer us to get Moscow onto the job?'

The Rue de Grenelle was the Soviet embassy in France; Moscow the French embassy in the USSR. Malmaison gave me a sidelong glance, and smiled mischievously. Of course, as far as Rat and I were concerned, there was less danger in arousing the suspicions of the enemy than in alerting one's friends. The Rue de Grenelle it would be, then.

I returned to the Invalides, fearing that Rat may have decided that after all the obstacle presented by the day-books was insuperable and that the whole thing should be called off. Mme Krebs gave me some hope when she informed me that the colonel would not be in the office until the end of the afternoon. I spent the rest of the day with the translators, my attention divided between an electronics article and the feud being fought out between M. Alexandre and Puzo, under the sardonic eye of young Divo.

'You've been sweating over that adenosyntriphosphate for ten days now,' the chief translator grumbled. 'Dr Colineau wanted it for the day before yesterday.'

'Speed and quality do not go together, Monsieur le Pudestat de Pudelevich,' M. Alexandre replied, with benign dignity. 'You must understand that a stylish translation cannot be knocked together in a jiffy. Anyway, I can only enjoy my work if I'm given the time to do it properly.'

'You are not paid by France to enjoy your work,' Puzo retorted, under his breath, and he turned back to gaze with the rapture of a Spanish mystic at the coloured photograph that he had stuck inside the door of his locker.

As soon as Puzo's back was turned, M. Alexandre would sigh deeply, look at Divo and myself in turn, as if soliciting our attention as witnesses, raise his eyes to heaven as if in reproach, slowly nod his head and exclaim, in deep tragic tones: 'Why, oh why, could he not have died in the prime of life!'

Mme Krebs came in to tell me that the colonel would see me at 5.45. I managed to conceal my pleasure: obviously, he wanted to see me without risk of being interrupted. Then I had a sudden fear: was he going to tell me that a request to return to my regiment would be regarded favourably? The hours dragged on. Puzo knocked off first, then Divo, then M. Alexandre himself rose majestically, put on his tweed jacket (he worked like a young man, in the American style, displaying perfectly laundered pale shirts) and wished me fair winds and prosperous voyage.

GEST had disgorged all its personnel when, at last, at 5.44, I gave myself permission to cross the threshold of the corridor.

Only Tolstoy was still at his desk, behind his open door, and his icy eye caught me as I passed. I looked straight ahead of me, pretending to be unaware of his presence, but from the far corner of my right eye I saw clearly that he saw that I saw that he had seen me; my trick seemed to amuse him; his pink, pretty, almost feminine lower lip formed into a sadistic pout. For once, however, I had a kind of advantage: my late visit to the colonel must disturb him; intrigue him at least; a little.

In his half-lit office, by the light of a lamp with tilted shade, Rat was working at his little table, a forgotten cigarette hanging from the corner of his mouth. I placed the confidential note on some over-ripe banana skins and sat down. After a short while, the Shopkeeper pushed the papers he had been studying into a drawer; corners stuck out, pages were dog-eared, but he seemed quite unconcerned. He picked up my note and began to read without his glasses, which he had raised on to his forehead, which made him look like a skeleton in a diving-suit.

'Yes, I see,' he said at last. 'And what do you make of all that?'

The text, I recall, was full of double negatives, euphemisms, litotes and metalepses. The expression 'not without' occurred three times.

'The essence is conspicuous by its absence, sir. And there's nothing confidential about the note, in spite of its heading.'

'Volsky,' he said almost affectionately, 'you're an oaf. It's neither dated, nor signed; we could have got it when and from whom we liked. Confidential, you see? Good. And what do you read between the lines?'

'That Popov is in fact a KGB officer, as SDECE thinks.'

'Possibly. But what kind of a guy do you think he is?'

'With so little to go on . . .'

'Little or not, we must have a psychological profile if the high command is going to swallow Culverin.'

'Well, success, I suppose. Beginning life with very little, a hereditary proletarian as they say, with no diplomatic training, counsellor in Paris at thirty-five, major in the KGB . . . A brilliant career, no? Or perhaps the hard-working, but not particularly brilliant student who makes the best of his opportunities. Or perhaps he possesses some secret, some Party Open Sesame . . .'

'That would be too likely: they would never believe it. A brilliant civil servant in the Soviet Union? No, that's not very credible either. The good plodder, that's more typical. Anything else?'

'He was too young for the war.'

'Yes, there's more work to be done on that aspect. Hero's son?'

'I don't know whether his father . . .'

'It doesn't matter. A survivor's mentality. Loyalty, yes, gratitude, perhaps, but above all an ability to grab whatever he can, while playing the part of the pure revolutionary.'

'A cynical careerist?'

'Steady on! A good convinced Communist, but one who has supped full of horrors. Son of a conqueror. There'd be no point in biting off half of Europe if you have to go on eating nothing but cabbage and gruel.'

'Rome and Greece, sir?'

He did not even pretend to understand what I was talking about.

'Yes, mmm, you might make a note of that. Now, let's see. Malmaison has also sent me . . .'

He tore open an envelope. Two photographs slid out. I was impatient to see the face of the adversary that chance had sent me.

The first was a glossy photograph, of passport size, showing against a dark background a very light, bony face, with, it seemed, even lighter, but quite inexpressive eyes. The high forehead, with its slack skin, furrowed with curved folds, further emphasized premature baldness; at the front, the only hair remaining was above the ears, which stuck up like large, thick cactus leaves; on the top of the head what remained of the fair, almost white hair was carefully combed into straight parallel lines. Hollow, clean-shaven cheeks framed a mouth which, in repose, must have formed a thin straight line, but which was now embellished with a conceited half-smile, of the kind one sees on singers of the *Belle Epoque*. This antiquated trick of the trade had probably been forced on an unwilling subject by some poor hack of a photographer. A bow-tie suggested a certain superficial theatricality in an otherwise monk-like face.

The other photograph had been cut out of a newspaper. It showed the same individual taken on his left, from a low angle, flanked by two rather more blurred figures. Sitting on a platform, he was taking part in some discussion or, more likely, making some impassioned speech. The half-tone conveyed well the chalky tones of his skin and hair; his eyes seemed almost white. A sharp shadow underlined an over-developed jaw. Looking back to the other photograph, one noticed that in fact the nutcracker chin and jaws were unusually large, but ovoid in form and merging into one another without projection or hollow. In the foreground of the second photograph, a large aggressive hand, wrist bent, fingers half closed as if around a large ball, hammered out the words.

Certain primitive peoples are unable to recognize a familiar person or object in a photograph. I am not much more percipient myself where photographs are concerned. I still recall my perplexity when confronted by the psychological deductions that our history textbook derived from portraits of kings and ministers. I would stare at those faces laid out on the page, but I could find none of that overweening ambition, that self-satisfied vanity, that dazzling intelligence, that unbridled sensuality, which Messrs Mallet and Isaac identified at a glance. I had not changed. I racked my brains as best I could:

'He's losing his hair,' I declared limply.

Rat gave me a pitiful look. His extinguished cigarette was still hanging from his lower lip.

'Come on, Volsky! I seem to remember reading in your file that you had a "remarkable ability to put yourself in the place of others, an essential quality in an Intelligence officer".'

'Not in the place of a photograph.'

'But I'm not talking about this fellow. I'm talking about the high command. Enormous jaw expressing will-power. Forceful gesticulation. Wild eyes. Tartar cheekbones. An ambitious, dynamic individual, but one not incapable of spectacular transformation. There's something going on inside that head. Don't you feel it? The thin lips: he looks like an actor—or a cop.'

'And the sensuality, sir? You're not forgetting the blondes?'
'Yes . . .'

Rat pushed the photographs across the table, with a finger-tip, as if, from another angle, they might tell him more.

'You can say what you like, my boy. That fellow is not a womanizer.'

'What? The Americans seemed to think . . .'

'Oh! There are so many reasons to lay blondes. But you're right: you should put it into the file. But don't use the word "sensuality".'

'What should I put, then?'

'Oh, I don't know. Perhaps "obsessed" . . .'

He gave me a sidelong look. In place of what is known as intelligence he had a sagacity that was not without warmth or, I might say, charm.

'Don't you see, sensuality is a good, healthy thing. It's fresh, French, it doesn't do anyone any harm . . .'

He pushed the photographs away with a tired gesture, his eyes closed, the eyelids almost hemispherical over the sadly swollen ocular globes. His brief foray into clairvoyance had obviously exhausted him. However, I did not resist for much longer the temptation to ask him:

'But, sir, the day-book?'

He opened his eyes, the milky exhausted eyes of an old man. Then, after a while, they seemed to light up again with interest:

'The general has been very good about it,' he said, tapping the edge of the table with the envelope, which he held between two fingers. 'Very, very good!'

As if to himself, forgetting my presence, he added:

'As long as Silbert doesn't summon me tomorrow . . . No, I don't think he will, they're always afraid of acting hastily, that lot.'

His eyes turned back to me. He was assessing me, weighing me:

'But you, my boy, you must show that you've got spunk.'

I spent the evening with Frisquette and I said nothing about marriage.

5

Next morning Malmaison sent another Confidential Note, containing extracts from reports made on Popov by diplomats who had met him while serving. Such phrases as 'a glutton for work', 'the memory of an elephant', 'indefatigable worker', 'encyclopaedic knowledge' set the tone. Suspicions about a double career were almost openly expressed. The Shopkeeper gave me orders for the evening that showed that he had found a way of fixing his own day-book: that meant that he had decided to activate (what jargon!) Culverin.

About five o'clock, Malmaison telephoned me. An officer of the Secret Intelligence Service, who had operated at Beirut under diplomatic cover at the same time as Popov, was in Paris and would agree to see me. He was waiting for me at Harry's Bar. I left immediately and jotted into my diary the word 'neuralgia', because the Englishman's Christian name was Algernon. Mnemonic code is not a highly intellectual exercise.

Algy was sucking a hooked pipe, like Sherlock Holmes's. He had a swarthy complexion, of a sickly rather than of a healthy kind, and green eyes that seemed to be fixed permanently upon a small imaginary theatre placed just behind his interlocutor's head. I caught myself turning round to enjoy the spectacle myself, at least on the few occasions when the expression on Algy's face showed some trace of amusement or pleasure. Most of the time he seemed bored: that shadow theatre of his, he seemed to be saying, was not worth turning round for.

He received me with that distant familiarity practised by the English of his background. His lips, formed into a permanent kiss, produced soft, contented lapping sounds around the pipe.

One felt that if the pipe were taken out, the mouth would continue forever to form a silent O. I came straight out with my question; and immediately the little theatre behind me lit up and Popov seemed, behind the disguise of a melancholy clown, to be in the depths of depression.

'Popov . . . Popov. Never seen him drunk. Didn't smoke.' A glimmer of sly pleasure at the prospect of so much asceticism crossed the green eyes. 'First to see that Israel would get the bomb one day. Good. Very good.'

'Good?'

'Bright, you know. Immersed.'

'Immersed?'

'In the job. Already doing what he wanted at that time. First-class player, knows every game. No need to invent. One victory after another.'

'Typical KGB?'

The typical KGB appeared on the stage of the imaginary theatre; Algy dismissed it with an exasperated flutter of the eyelids.

'Nothing so conventional. On the other hand . . . More like *two* KGB officers. Double ration of guts—and vultures. Perhaps. You know.'

He lowered his voice at the end of each phrase.

'Convinced Marxist?'

His contempt for articles seemed contagious.

'Marx? . . . Leninist, of course. A . . . How do you say "go—getter" in French?'

'Don't know. *Dégotteur*?'

'*Dégotteur*. That would explain some of his rather too spectacular successes. Night-bird hunting during the day as well. His Muslim Women's Liberation Movement . . . If Popov had fallen into the husbands' hands . . .' Grand Guignol, the lips smacked together with pleasure. 'Little jagged knives, you know.'

'Nationalist?'

'Of course, my dear chap. He's a Russian.'

'What does he like?'

'Beethoven, Tchaikovsky, Lenin. A soft spot for Nechaev.'

'A nostalgia for the Stalin days?'

'Not excessively.'

'Expensive tastes?'

'Despises them.'

'In short, nothing of the hero's son who wants to gorge himself.'

On the stage behind me the figure of a voluptuary appeared only to be rejected and replaced by a Knight Templar in armour. I took a large swig of Scotch. I had reached the point that interested me. There was no use letting it show.

'What does he like? Boys? Girls?'

The eyes of the Anglo-Saxons become large, round and, to all appearances hard as billiard balls, at the mere mention of sex. Algy's eyes betrayed no more than a trace of this. He rose in my estimation.

'You see . . . Oh, I don't know. Just gossip. The ambassador lent him his secretary . . . Something of a scandal. She tried on some dresses in a shop. Salesgirl was horrified. Scars all over the place.'

'The knout?'

'The salesgirl said there were toothmarks at the front, scratches at the back, not sure, far from it. Little native girls. Plenty of imagination. Thousand and one nights. Maybe scratches at the front, tooth marks behind. Who knows?'

This time the lights in the theatre took time to die down.

'Did you know the secretary? What was she like?'

'Tall, big.'

'A vamp?'

'Oh, no! Amazon of the Steppes.'

'And Popov himself, did you ever meet him? Talk to him?'

'Often. We used to drink together. At the Normandy. Well, at least, perhaps not drink . . . Mineral water. Him I mean.'

'What kind of a man is he, Algy?' Algy gave a few particularly affectionate pecks at his pipe. He sucked in the smoke appreciatively. He took his time to answer and then delivered himself of a whole paragraph.

'How shall I explain? One doesn't expect a Soviet to be a gentleman, to use the favourite word of those who don't know

61

what they're talking about. A certain density, intensity . . . He knew something about nuclear physics. So do I. I nicknamed him "Heavy Water". Beware of chain reactions. A KGB, you said? A reaction KGB. Know what I mean?'

I left him about eight o'clock.

'Cheerio, old chap.' And, almost imperceptibly, he winked to show me that he was falling back into the character he had created for himself, and even overdoing it a bit.

I was hungry, but I decided to dine later. First I would carry out the Shopkeeper's orders, adding a few touches of my own. I returned by métro, which the hallucinated crowds of dusk had evacuated. At the gate an officer I did not know was difficult about letting me in. I had to show him my card: he would certainly remember me. Before reaching the door of the secretary's office, I examined the key Rat had given me: it was a new, shiny duplicate. With a little dexterity, using Mme Krebs's key—she often left it in the lock—I could have had it made myself. How could I prove that I hadn't if I was caught that evening. If I was caught red-handed by a security patrol? Certainly the Shopkeeper would not cover up for me. I went from the secretary's office into his, using the same key. It is a tradition in the secret services to exercise one's professional talents at the expense of one's subordinates, equals and superiors, if only to keep one's hand in. I had no intention of committing a burglary, however; but it would have been a pity to waste such an opportunity of poking around in my boss's waste-paper basket. It could not contain anything secret (rough drafts had to be burnt under supervision), but I did make one edifying discovery: on a screwed up envelope was written 'Monsieur le Lieutenant Volsky, Groupe d'Etudes scientifiques et techniques, Division du Renseignement, Hôtel des Invalides'. It was to me that Malmaison had been invited to send the notes and photographs, while Rat intercepted them. If the operation turned out badly, I would be neatly framed.

I expected no less of the Shopkeeper: in fact, I was almost relieved to discover that particular dirty trick: it would mean that there would not be any others, except of course, for the new key, which would probably be left in my possession so that, if necessary, it could be 'found' on me.

I went back to the secretary's office and took the blue-grey file marked 'July-August' and the green-grey folder marked 'Ops' from the cupboard. There was very little to put in the Ops file, since all real operations were directed through 144, so much so that it had become something of a hold-all: it took anything that could not be classified in any other category. Anyway, this negligence did not affect our business. I placed the two files on a table. In the day-book, I looked for number 1431 under 3 July. I quote this correspondence from memory, not having taken the precaution of sending copies of all the documents that came into my hands to a Swiss bank; but that, I hasten to add, was a wise step: General S . . ., condemned at the time for insurrection against the State, owed his salvation, it seems, solely to that habit, which he had formed as a young officer, and thanks to which the destiny of so many important individuals was in his hands.

Army General Staff
Intelligence Division
Groupe d'Etudes scientifiques et techniques
No. 1431/GEST/PER/PR/jk
Paris, 3 July
To: General commanding the Intelligence Division
Concerning: Assignment of Mme Jocelyne Paturier, Women's Army Corps
Reference: Your no. such-and-such
I have the honour to inform you that Mme Jocelyne Paturier has been assigned to work on filing with the title of assistant to the head of filing.
Signed: Lieut.-Colonel Rat, officer commanding GEST

I operated the binding system of the day-book—the metallic click echoed in the silence—and extracted the sheet. I did the same with the Ops file, which contained a copy of the same document. I took the cover off Mme Krebs's typewriter and inserted a sheet of paper, with two flimsies and their carbons. I typed out the same heading as on the extracted sheet, then continued with the following:

No. 1431/GEST/OPS/PR/jk
Paris, 3 July
To: General commanding the Intelligence Division
Concerning: Culverin
Reference: Interview of above date
I have the honour to send you enclosed an information sheet
Amyntas 18.
Signed: Lieut.-Colonel Rat, officer commanding GEST
P. J. 1

I placed one of the copies in the day-book, the other in the files, in place of the copies I had extracted. I closed both files, which snapped noisily, and put them back in the cupboard. I covered the typewriter, carefully folded both carbons without staining my fingers, put them in my pocket and went back to the colonel's office. I slid the three papers I was holding (the two copies I had taken out of the files and the original I had just typed) between the yellow, ink-stained blotting paper and the pad: the Shopkeeper would find them next morning. He would no doubt destroy the copies; I did not know yet what he would do with the original. So much for Stage One!

Amyntas was the pseudonym of one of the few agents handled by Rat personally; he had provided no information since his entry number 17, several months earlier: one could get him to say anything one liked in entry number 18. Deep down, I had some doubts as to whether Amyntas really existed: the allowances he was supposed to receive probably went straight into a special account administered solely by the colonel. That was putting the best face on it. There was one problem: the typewriter. Usually the entry would have been typed on Rat's own machine, which, quite by chance, had been sent off to be repaired that very morning. He had suggested that I use my own Olivetti, but I decided to take a little precaution, after all, and disobeyed his instructions on this point.

I went on to the translators' office, to which I was allowed a key, and turned the lights on. It was strange to find oneself at night in a room in which one had only spent one's days, to see all those closed drawers, closed books, closed lockers, empty chairs. Even the smell, which was different from the day-time smell, had something disturbing about it. And that silence . . . It was as if the dazzling lights were trying to break it.

There were three typewriters there (not counting my own), all carefully hooded like so many hunting hawks. Typewriters have always made me feel ill at ease; I cannot believe that they are completely unintelligent. When they make mistakes, especially those that are like spelling mistakes, I am tempted to hit them. It ought to be impossible for them to commit such barbarisms. To see them there, at rest, indulging in heaven knows what literary meditation under their covers, I could not believe that they allowed so many words to pass through them like water through a sieve, without retaining something. Surely, somewhere, they possessed a memory; one day, these machines would be taught to go into reverse, character by character, to the first one they ever typed, yielding up all their accumulated information. What a source that would be for 'novelists' of both kinds! At the very notion of such a discovery, a shiver ran down my back, a shiver of curiosity and desire, the shiver of excitement of a lover (or artist) confronting the indecipherable mystery of others.

At all events, my own machine was out of the question. Quite obviously, the most sensible course would have been to hire one. But—I'm not sure whether I'm making myself clear—I was not thinking of protecting myself exactly; it was rather that I could not resist the pleasure of adding my own little flourish to the scheme, to trick Rat out of a kind of professional dandyism, because trickery is a point of honour with a 'novelist' and because he owes it to himself to miss no opportunity of laying a false trail. On which of my three colleagues would it be best to throw suspicion, however slight? (They could not run the slightest risk: experts have no difficulty in identifying a typist by his or her particular touch.) Divo was the youngest, the one most suspected of initiative, the one most capable of appreciating my little joke. I uncovered his Royal, bought in an American army surplus store, and revealed the jagged, toothless, screeching mouth, worthy of one of Macbeth's witches. A page had been left inserted in it and what was written was something like this:

faithful.

That sly Alona, Grigori reflected with gentle irony, has been right all along.

Now the living and the dead were united in the prayers of the liturgy.

'Oh Mother,' said Grigori, 'so you are here too.'

Quite obviously, this was not the translation of an electronics article. I also noted, with some satisfaction, that there was nothing very brilliant about the style. My own writing, I decided, had more virility. If I took out the sheet, I might not be able to put it back in exactly the same position, and I had no desire to leave any trace or to disturb in any way the only true work of my young colleague. I put the cover back over the witch.

It occurred to me that there would be something particularly pleasurable about using the chief translator's big Japy: he was always so concerned about the opinion of his superiors. No one could ever suspect him of playing a double game! I took off the cover: there, too, lay the beginnings of a masterpiece:

'Ah! My delectable Embolia! How I shall wrap myself in thy incandescent snow! The myriad crystals of thy frigidity will be the fiery needles of my entire acupuncture. Embolia, dearest fairest Embolia, in thy honour I shall stand horizontal and, as on the point of a top, I shall slowly spin, in a majestic revolution of my being around thy axis.'

So, Monsieur de Pudelevich? You too, little goody-goody, you, too, are stealing minutes from the Republic? We certainly were a literary section! No wonder it took us weeks to translate an article. In the end, it was M. Alexandre's honest Remington that served to type something like the following.

INFORMATION
Date: 27 June
Source: Amyntas
Order No.: 18
Quotation: B/6
Information:

66

Igor Popov, KGB major, has been appointed to a post in France. He will probably use a diplomatic cover concerning relations with para-or crypto-Communist movements, such as peace and youth movements, etc. He will probably be entrusted with an Intelligence mission concerned with French science and technology, with particular reference to nuclear physics. He may well be placed at the head of an existing network, which will be expanded accordingly. It would appear from our source that Popov will become the officer controlling the dangerous spy codenamed Crocodile by the Security Police, which has proved no more successful that SDECE in uncovering him.

According to our source, Popov must be regarded as a highly qualified, extremely gifted officer capable of achieving exceptional results, as he has already done in his previous posts (Near East). In particular, he seems to have provided the Kremlin with indications of an advanced nuclear programme in Israel. An orphan, of humble back-ground, a self-made man, a creature of the régime rather than a devotee of the cause, he belongs to the new Soviet élite, which uses its roots in the people to take advantage of the privileges offered by their social situation. However, in his case, these privileges are not so much of a material kind as those satisfying professional ambition. Popov appears to be without any other vice, though, in certain areas, his appetites, conventional enough in orientation, do seem to be rather excessive, and to involve a degree of violence that may be regarded as sadistic. His wife appears to have died as a result of his treatment of her. The authorities seem to place no obstacle in the way of his activities; on the contrary, they provide him with the means of satisfying his obsession by supplying office staff who are physically well endowed. This favourable treatment appears to be justified by a consider-able degree of success.

Comments:

Amyntas is a conscientious informant, who does not indulge in sensational gossip. A discreet investigation carried out at the Quai d'Orsay seems to confirm the above description. A scandal, involving behaviour of the kind described above, appears to have been the object of a cover-up in Beirut in 1960.

Desiderata:

When a request for a visa for Igor Popov is made, make sure that it is approved. Entrust his surveillance to the directly competent body: GEST. In a second stage, plan for an operation whose aim would be quite simply the turning of the person in question who, by his compromising habits, would seem to be susceptible to an attack of this kind.

Advantages: a) the leakage of French secret scientific and technical information will be stopped, with the additional possibility of arresting those responsible, in particular Crocodile; b) the Intelligence Division will enjoy greater latitude in Providing Bureau T with disinformation concerning national research. In the event of success an allowance of 1,500 francs might be made to Amyntas for services rendered.

This pastiche of the Shopkeeper's written style, so different from his spoken style, was both a precautionary measure and a self-indulgence. I tore the rough draft and the three carbons I had used earlier into tiny pieces and then went and flushed them down the lavatory. A tap was dripping in the silence. I tried to turn it off, but it probably needed a new washer. I went back into the colonel's office. I slipped Amyntas' sheet and its copy into the hiding place in the blotting-pad. I then went out and dined at the *Pied-de-Fouet*, a former coal-merchant's premises that had become the rendez-vous of the shabby-genteel Faubourg Saint-Germain on the maid's day off.

Three questions preoccupied me.

1. Supposing we had solved with elegant simplicity the problem of our own day-book, how were we to deal with the problem of the Divisional archives?
2. Supposing that General Poirier was willing to give Culverin a helping hand, what could one justifiably expect of an officer who, after all, was not only honest, but also retired?
3. Supposing that Culverin really took off, where would I find a

volunteer who possessed both the physical attributes and the necessary talent to play the female role? However, if I were to remain at the head of the operation, it was essential that I should recruit my own staff.

6

As a 'novelist' I was a mere novice. Did I really imagine that General Poirier would agree to bend the rules to please his colleague Rat? Not that there would be any great risk attached to it, but all his habits, not to mention his principles, went against this kind of thing. A helping hand to Culverin! Whatever next? The French army is tolerant; one can indulge in any irregularities, provided they are based on human motives (compassion, drunkenness, conceit, sex) and provided they don't interfere with the smooth running of the service. Apart from that, the rule was strict discipline, willingly accepted. It was unthinkable that a French general should allow himself the kind of vulgarity I was expecting of him.

About ten in the morning, I was summoned to the colonel's office, where I found General Poirier awaiting me. Under repeated assaults from the visitor's knees, the desk had moved away from the wall; placed aslant it looked less humble, but it was about to lose its lamp, the flex of which was stretched to the full.

'Lieutenant Volsky reporting, sir.'

The general extended two fingers towards me, in lieu of a handshake, but it was no more than bad manners (like sitting in Rat's chair): it wasn't directed at me personally. Poirier was neither a petty tyrant, nor a demagogue. Silbert applied the usual tricks of command and never forgot that he owed his promotion to the Resistance; Poirier, on the other hand, recalled proudly that he had risen from the ranks, saw in his military career a well-deserved social advancement, and had always behaved as a natural leader. His manners were appalling, but unpretentious. He never gave me cause for complaint.

I found that retirement and loneliness (he was a widower) had not changed him in the way I had expected. He had put on weight and had obviously had some difficulty getting his torso into a double-breasted, navy-blue suit that he had had made while still a captain or major, and which he now wore, unbuttoned, over a grey woollen sweater. The trousers, too, were filled to bursting. But the head, round as a cannon-ball, with grey hair cropped rather than cut, was just beginning to get fatter; over the cheek-bones, marbled with fine red lines, the small eyes, radiating a bluish light, still carved up the world into slices, like two laser beams; the bearing and the gestures were in no way those of an old man who spent his days sitting by his fire-side; on the contrary, there was something about the general, a certain restlessness, that I had not known in him before.

'Ah, yes, Volsky, here I am again. You thought you'd buried me, I bet! I may have white hairs, but you haven't seen the last of me yet . . . How are you, my boy? Rat tells me you're not doing at all badly. Good! The country needs new blood. Never think you're finished. Die in harness. Take me: you thought I was on my last legs, didn't you, ready to push up the daisies? Then, suddenly, here I come popping up again. When you've served for forty-six years, my boy, especially in our Shops, you're never as retired as you look. I've known men who have put on mufti only to take commands they could never have hoped for when in uniform. Right! I see that old codgers like us have to come back and give you youngsters a hand. Silbert's not a bad fellow, but he needs shaping up. Now, what's the problem? Turning a Commie agent. How? A blonde. They're not scarce. As you know, red tape won't keep me out of an operation like this, if the good of France and the army are at stake. When we have Popov up our sleeve, the Allies and the Big House will just have to get lost. If I'd known such a thing was possible when I was here, I'd have jumped at it. So what's the difference? I'm not going to let that bitch of an age-limit stop me. Right; no use telling you what to do. You know the game. Golden rule: Mum's the word, and cover your traces. Step One: antedate Operation Culverin. Child's play. I'll tell you what you have to do. Step Two:

eliminate the competition: get rid of the American girl; identify the Russian girl; get rid of her too. Step Three: infiltrate one of our own wenches. Two alternatives; either she knows the score or she doesn't. It's up to you—it's not vital. Expected result: one of two things. Either Popov's fixation puts him completely in our hands and we'll turn him like a glove—voluntarily—or he'll send us packing: in which case we politely inform him that the girl was one of ours; a few photographs will do the rest. Not that the Commies are as straitlaced as they pretend; but they don't like their majors getting de-bagged like mere greenhorns. He cares about his career, doesn't he? He'd be forced to defect. A big scandal. I'm sure, my boy, you'll have a good time with this one.'

'It's not quite as simple as you think, sir,' Rat interrupted. 'To begin with, this fixation that so excites the Americans . . .'

'Well, what of it? Freud, I suppose you've heard of him? Psychoanalysis does exist, you know. You've got one of the operations of the century in your hands, a young officer who has proved himself, an old fox like me to advise from time to time, and you hesitate?'

I listened to Poirier and I realized how foolish I had been. Here was a man dying of boredom in his retirement: Culverin had brought him back to life. Far from having any scruples at the idea of committing a small breach of the rules to help a friend, he had only one fear: that the last affair he had anything to do with, be it only at one remove, might elude his grasp. He would have had to have been much older, or much, much younger than he was to let slip an opportunity of pulling off one last successful coup. For me, even if it succeeded, the operation would bring no more than a few material advantages; for Rat, it would gild, literally, his two silver stripes and, figuratively, his suburban house; but for Poirier, even if it failed, it would breathe life back into him—it was already doing so. How could he resist the temptation? Nor was there anything surprising in the fact that he had insisted that the affair should be given to me: I would be a more malleable contact than the colonel, who would have preferred to take over the operation himself. Imagine a novelist who is offered characters for the last time: who would have the strength to refuse?

72

Characteristically, whereas Rat was looking around for some way of exculpating himself if necessary, Poirier was giving me clear, unambiguous orders, despite the fact that he was in no position to give orders to anybody: 'You go, you open, you look, you take away, you put in, you shut . . .' I was not taken in by his peroration on fictional retirements, intended to lighten my conscience and perhaps sustain his own self-deception: spending one's entire professional life as an illusionist is bound to take its toll. As he spoke, I tried to control the expression on my face: above all, he must not be able to read any trace of the perfectly reasonable panic I felt when faced by the dream of this former conjurer, who, having spent his life trafficking with reality by means of tricks, expedients, schemes and sleights of hand, was suddenly pretending that he controlled them by magic. I had not yet committed any serious crime; I could still back out. But did I want to? And, in any case, could I fail to carry out the simple, direct, intelligible, categorical instructions of this old man, whose job had consisted in commanding obedience and who, having lost power, mysteriously preserved the authority that went with it? When he had finished speaking, I had made up my mind, or rather, I had stopped striking attitudes, I was resigned to letting myself float on the rising tide. All the same, I asked to see the preliminary budget authorization prepared by the general. He pushed it towards me across the table without turning it over.

Army General Staff
Intelligence Division
No.　　　　　/DIVDOC/EXP
July
To: Lieutenant-Colonel commanding GEST
Concerning: Operation Culverin
You are hereby authorized to charge expenses incurred by the operation by reference to chapter IV article 6 of your budget up to a maximum of 2,500 francs.
　Signed: General Poirier, officer commanding Intelligence Division.

* * *

There were three copies. The original was signed, in blue ball-point, with the crude, simplified, but legible signature I knew so well.

'But sir, there's no number or date.'

Poirier gave me a short, sharp smile, devoid of amusement or warmth, and pointed to Rat, who was sitting in a corner, our 'Expenditure' file on his knees, turning over the pages with his index finger, which he frequently licked with his nicotine-stained tongue.

'One could do this,' he suggested at last. 'Increase of my petrol allowance: 18 July. Silbert won't reduce it, if there's nothing written, will he?'

'Certainly not. That's all done by routine, as you know, Number?'

'2397.'

'Carbons?'

Rat, bending his long body in two, presented two carbons, offering, with the obsequiousness of a secretary, to arrange them as required. Poirier snatched them, slipped them between his copies and, in his own small, clear, hard, pitiless handwriting, wrote in the date and number. We watched him, perplexed. He looked up, an amused look in his eyes. It was the first time in my life that I had seen him with his glasses, which he had slipped on almost surreptitiously, even without my noticing.

'Ah, yes! I always put the number in myself. I'd say to Estienne, "give me a number" and I'd insert it. The date, too, quite often. The secretaries were forbidden to type them. It's quite useful to antedate things. But it mustn't be noticed.'

He snatched off his glasses, which made him look like the grandmother in *Little Red Riding Hood*, crumpled the carbons, stuffed them into his pockets and held out the three papers to me.

'You're quite clear what you have to do? Repeat it.'

I repeated it. He corrected me on one or two details, reminding me of the exact location of a particular drawer or shelf. When he was satisfied with me, I ventured to remark, not so much out of precaution as to show him that I had missed nothing:

74

'But what about the typewriter, sir?'

'What about it?'

'It isn't the right one. They might notice that.'

'It is the right one.'

He had surely not sneaked in overnight into Warrant Officer Estienne's office to use his secretary's machine! I could not conceal my incredulity. I didn't mind playing the cat's-paw, but the clown—no thanks! The next few seconds were embarrassing. Then, because he was a real officer, and conscious of his responsibilities, and because he was sending me on a dangerous mission, Poirier told me the truth.

'It didn't work very well. Too old. There were a whole lot of them put up for sale just before I left. I bought this one.'

I still wonder why he allowed himself such an easy solution; there was nothing wrong in what he had done, of course, but he offered his explanation almost defiantly. He could not have foreseen that it would enable him one day to return to the stage by way of the prompter's box. Had he simply given in to the very French instinct of saving everything, sticking bits of soap together and producing puddings out of stale bread? Had he just annexed the machine? Or should one see in this almost sentimental, almost Adlerian attachment to this typewriter, the indispensable attribute of his function, the privileged channel of his power, one more sign of the double vocation of the 'novelist'?

'You aren't going to walk around holding those papers, I hope,' he said, cutting short my meditation. 'The colonel will lend you a briefcase.'

So far the following 'corrections' had been made to the GEST archives. In the day-book and in the 'Ops' file the copies of our correspondence concerning the appointment of Mme Paturier had been destroyed and replaced by copies of the memorandum referring to sheet Amyntas 18. A copy of this sheet had been inserted in the Amyntas file. In the Expenditure file, the correspondence concerning the petrol allowance had been replaced by the authorization of expenditure for the operation. The corresponding amendments still had to be made to the Divisional archives: remove the petrol-allowance correspondence from the day-book and the Expenditure file, substituting the expenditure authorisation; remove the Paturier report from the Establishment file; insert the memorandum concerning Amyntas into the 'Ops' file and the Amyntas 18 sheet into the Informants' Reports file. But, on this last point, we would have to take an additional risk. Since the file was kept in Silbert's office, outside our reach, we agreed to leave something undone, on purpose. If Silbert noticed that it was missing from the collection all he could do was to ask for a copy. In no way could he accuse us of not having sent it to him, since the memo would be in its correct place in the 'Ops' file. If the worst came to the worst, Estienne would get his knuckles rapped for negligence in the filing. And that didn't bother me in the least.

Rat lent me his briefcase. In the first pocket we put the original of the Amyntas memo and the two copies of the authorization of expenditure. The second pocket was kept empty for the items to be destroyed. We did four rehearsals in Rat's office, which was temporarily transformed into Estienne's office for the purpose; at the fourth I got everything mixed up: Poirier said it was a good sign. At half-past eleven, extending hearty wishes for our success ('Break a leg!'), he took his leave. I imagined him moving with springy steps almost too long for his height along the corridors leading to his Division, recognizing on the way doors, radiators, stains on the wall and other landmarks, smiling, with that special look in the eyes that superiors reserve for their inferiors, at an astonished orderly met on the way, subjected perhaps to a terrifying handshake; struggling with some success against a weakening nostalgia, strutting gravely on before the inevitable spectres of old age and death that came to meet him at the end of the corridors and, finally, there he was, frowning, outside his own door, which had treacherously changed its number. Five minutes.

I then imagined him calmly walking into the office where I had been kept waiting for so long, patting Estienne's shoulder, marching straight into the boss's office without knocking. If Silbert had a visitor, or was away, or if, for some other reason, the plan could not be carried out, Poirier would telephone Rat, conveying his respects to Mme Rat—that was the code. I imagined Silbert hiding his annoyance, his disapproval even, behind his blue-tinted spectacles, and feeling obliged to humour his senile predecessor. How are things? Not too many hard knocks? Couldn't pass through Paris without dropping in. Manpower still expanding? And they're not too worried Up There? Poirier would wink, in the irreverent way of the retired. Silbert defended his secrets like a prude her virtue . . . If by any chance he proved to be more communicative than expected, which would prevent me from acting in time, there would be a telephone call conveying Poirier's respects to Madame. If he talked about Culverin, we would play it straight, of course, but Poirier would refrain from bringing the conversation round to it. Five minutes.

'I say, Silbert, I'd really like to take the junior staff out for a drink at the *Carotte*. We'd talk about the good old days when I nagged at them from morning till night. It's twenty to twelve.' It would indeed be 11.40: we had synchronized our watches. 'I dare say you can spare them just this once. After all, it isn't every day the old boss is here. I won't ask you to join us: it would only embarrass them. The two of us will go out another time.'

It was unthinkable that Steel Wool would refuse. All that had to be done would be to summon Estienne and tell him to drum up the secretaries, typists, non-commissioned officers of the command platoon—some fifteen individuals in all—and, at the same time, say hello to the officers Poirier happened to meet on the way. Five minutes.

And another five minutes for faces to be made up, hair combed and keys turned in locks.

And then five minutes for security. It would then be five minutes to twelve. Alone of all the administration, Silbert would remain at his post. He would not move until the staff had come back, Estienne at least, for the others would go straight off to lunch, but Estienne would come back to shut up shop and Silbert would want to know how long the drinking had lasted. The only danger was that he might come into Estienne's office looking for some paper or other and be astonished to find Lieutenant Volsky there.

'If the cupboards are open, if you feel cornered, tell him the

77

truth. I'll cover up for you. Don't look so surprised. You heard me aright. I'll. Cover. Up. For. You.'

His protection was no longer worth anything; he guessed that I knew this; but the manner, the style of command were still there. Which explains why men had gone to their deaths for Poirier without jibbing too much.

At eleven minutes to twelve, I set out. Of course, I had to pass Tolstoy. He glanced sarcastically at the colonel's briefcase—a cumbersome old thing made of cardboard, covered with black, simulated leather, with a lock that didn't work. It didn't matter. It was not the first time the Shopkeeper had sent me out on an errand with his briefcase.

Corridors, stairs, orderlies. At five to twelve, I turned the handle of room no. 121. My hands were moist, but my head remained cool. I went in as quietly as possible, though without looking too furtive. If by some chance the general or the warrant officer was there, I had come to get some extra petrol coupons for the colonel, from the secret funds. The large room with its window in one corner (the partitions had been set up without any regard to aesthetics) was deserted; the files shut; the padded door leading into Silbert's office closed; above it, the light was red. I suspected Steel Wool was sulking. All the better.

Walk behind the big green metal table used by Estienne. Without putting down the briefcase, open the pencil box, take out the roll of sellotape placed on a multi-coloured pile of elastic bands; from the pile of bands, extricate two flat keys. Try the first in the middle drawer; if it doesn't work, try the other; open the drawer, leave the correct key in the lock, put the wrong one back into the pencil box. In the drawer, lift a metal tray containing paper clips, stamps and other office accessories; find two keys hidden under the tray, one white, the other yellow. Take the yellow key, cross the room, place the briefcase on the polished wooden table (the one I had sat down on with such unconcern), open the grey cupboard, not the green one. From the top shelf take the day-book for July, place it on the table, look for no. 2397, quietly open the binding, remove the document. Open the briefcase, take out one of the copies of the false no. 2397, put it into the day-book in place of the true one, place the true one in the second pocket of the briefcase, close the binding, put the day-book back. On the second shelf from the top take out the Expenditure file, put it on the table, look for the same number, quietly open the binding, take out the document, replace it with the second copy of the false one, put the true one in the second pocket, close the binding, put the file back. On the same shelf, take out the Establishment file, place it on the table, look, under 'Army Female Personnel', for the Paturier correspondence, quietly open the binding, take out the correspondence, put it into the second pocket, close the binding, put the file back. Carrying the briefcase, go back to Estienne's desk. With the key left in the pencil box, open the right-hand drawer. Find there, among a dozen others, two rubber stamps: one saying 'DOC DIV RECEIVED . . .' and the other a date-stamp. Adjust the date-stamp to 4 July. Remove from the first pocket the reference to the Amyntas sheet. Stamp it with both stamps. Put the date-stamp back to today's date, put both stamps back into the right-hand drawer, close the drawer, put the key back into the pencil box. Go back to the cupboard. On the third shelf take out the Operations file, put it on the table, quietly open it, insert the stamped document into the GEST section, among other correspondence received on the same date. Quietly close it, put it back, close the cupboard, bring the yellow key back to the desk, hide it under the metal tray, close the middle drawer, put the drawer key under the elastic bands, with the key from the other drawer, put the roll of sellotape back on top, close the lid. Do all this without hands shaking, without a single wrong move, without sneezing, resist the temptation to check that everything is in order (if one depends on this check one runs the risk of forgetting something). Don't forget the briefcase. Leave quietly. The whole operation should take 210 seconds. I did it.

Before returning to the colonel's office, I wiped the handle of his briefcase with my handkerchief. I had a thirst such as I had never known in Africa. I remember having a vision of whole truck-loads of beer. Then, for weeks, I dreamt that I had made some fatal error: I had hidden the keys in the wrong places, or I had put a document coming from GEST in the Division day-book.

'Passed off all right, my boy?'

I nodded.

'The general?'

'He must be having a drink!' I answered bitterly.

'No: Silbert.'

Ah! Silbert. While I was busying myself in the cupboard, I heard him cough impatiently, then say, with some annoyance, 'Yes'. The sound was so clear that I saw him standing behind me, his hands clasped behind his back, his glasses pointing straight at the small of my back. I turned round suddenly and nearly knocked a file on to the floor. There was no one there. The general was giving free rein to his disapproval in the solitude of his office.

'Silbert? Never saw him.'

I opened the briefcase. Rat checked it. Everything was as it should have been, nothing was missing. We had agreed to meet at a restaurant in Les Halles recommended by Poirier. Before catching the métro, I went into a café and drank two beers one after another. I remember nothing of that lunch. I imagine the wine flowed freely. It was in the taxi coming back that I began to come round. All three of us were packed into the back seat; I found contact with Poirier rather pleasant; his muscular body, his masculine smell, a mixture of dark tobacco and Calvados, had something paternal about it. He gave me a nudge in the ribs:

'This wench of yours, d'you think she'll get cleared?'

'What wench, sir?'

'The one you told us about, of course, your candidate.'

I disguised—with some success I think—my surprise. I had no recollection at all of having mentioned any particular girl to them. I scarcely had anyone in mind myself. Thus characters in a hurry to appear on the stage escape the author's vigilance.

7

Culverin was taking on flesh and blood. In every administration an affair assumes a certain irreversible momentum as soon as the first sum of money is spent on it, and Rat acted as a man of experience when he began by renting a little Citroën 2CV, which was put at my disposal. The expenditure was charged to chapter IV article 6 of GEST's budget, and it had to be accounted for to the Division under the heading 'Culverin' as referred to in correspondence 2397/DIVDOC/EXP. It was a way of testing the solidity of our plaster work while priming the financial pump. And how would the 2CV help me to turn Popov? The answer was not obvious at all, but the car would enable me to run more errands for Rat and to take Frisquette out to the *Relais de Bièvres*. It all went through with only one expected, and desired hitch: Silbert demanded a copy of the sheet Amyntas-18, the original having been lost. This was not surprising: Rat had himself ignited it with his cigarette lighter. How could Silbert have any suspicions? During his friendly conversation with Poirier he had asked him point-blank, with an unconcerned air, where the order to start Culverin came from, and Poirier, laughing up his sleeve, had simply raised his finger to the ceiling which, at that time, said all. Estienne must have been given a real lathering, a notion which did of course give me a certain satisfaction—a feeling for which I have no reason to be proud.

But Estienne, Silbert and the 2CV were not the heart of the matter. That, as in any 'novel', was the relationship between the author (I, as it happened) and the principal character; I was now beginning to see Igor Popov emerging from the internal shadows that precede all creation.

To the photographs, which told me nothing, and to the scraps of gossip passed on to me by Lester, Malmaison and Algy were now added three articles, kindly placed at our disposal by the cultural services of the Rue de Grenelle: and, for the man-of-letters that I must admit to being, those few printed pages—I was not even sure that they had really been written by Popov—had a suggestive power that was quite absent from his biography, his reputation or his photographs.

The first article had been published in a military journal; it argued the advantages of nuclear weapons in rather simple terms. If, scientifically, the argument was too clear to be precise, the style, though didactic and somewhat lacking in elegance, was neither clumsy nor moralizing and, in this respect, differed from the Soviet norm. I was struck by the abundance of such expressions as 'crush', 'pulverize', 'flatten under the weight', 'combine one's small units to form a fist', 'a shock of maximum brutality', 'thrashed with maximum effectiveness', and even 'sweep from the face of the earth'. It was this word 'maximum', so widely used in Russian, in which indeed it has various synonyms, which attracted my attention—M. Alexandre and Puzo having often engaged in Homeric duels over the various ways of translating it. This pleasure in describing strength is neither rare among Soviet writers nor even new in Russian literature—one finds it already in the early epic poems of the language; nevertheless it gave a certain flavour to the author's personality.

The other two articles had appeared in the famous atheistic propaganda publication, *Science and Religion*. They displayed the same ability to locate the target, then to go straight at it with unswerving determination. I thought that it was probably this masterly ability to clear the field that enabled Popov to seduce certain young minds, those who wished to believe that the truth is simple. Unusually, none of these articles was encumbered with quotations gathered here and there from the various popes of Marxism. Only one of them carried, by way of epigraph, some words of Lenin's: 'Fear gave birth to the gods.'

The second article was entitled 'The Last Bastion of God has

Fallen.' It took up the theme enunciated by the cosmonauts who 'did not meet God in the cosmos' and 'did not hear of angels except when picking up the Voice of America'. 'And what if God were infinitely small rather than infinitely high?' demanded Popov, the nuclear physics graduate. 'What if, as is claimed by certain cosmopolitan pseudo-scientists in the pay of American imperialist propaganda, the plan of a rational creation were revealed in the ingenious network of elementary particles?' There then followed a simplified history of the conquest of matter by man, who 'smashed in one by one the successive doors erected against him by the notion of an imaginary creator'. The molecule cracked open under the nutcracker of intelligence; the molecule was followed by the atom. Then, for a time, it was thought that the atom was an exact reproduction of the solar system, but that, too, was a non-scientific superstition: the system exploded and man, having explored matter from end to end, finally arrived at the end of his journey: antimatter rose up before him, symmetrical with matter and, like it, empty of God. 'The Christians were not wrong to say: "Knock and it will be opened unto you." It was enough to knock hard and long, and with clenched fists,' concluded the popularizer.

The third article, the one bearing the epigraph, was the only one to deal with a point of ideology. The constitution of the Soviet Union, declared Popov in short, guaranteed religious freedom. The consequences of this arrangement, though perhaps exaggeratedly liberal, might shock some by their bourgeois-democratic appearance. But this was not their intention. The more believers are free to confess their superstitions, the more the holders of the truth must intensify the struggle. Believers are to be compared with the helots that Sparta deliberately allowed to spread in order to test the virile qualities of its young men. It is in this sense that an apparently easy-going constitution should be interpreted: as a challenge to Bolshevik vigilance. This unexpected turn of thought struck me as being the point at which Popov the 'novelist' first put in an appearance. Nothing is less simple, in fact nothing is more essentially ambiguous, than the novel, and it was the first time that I had surprised Popov making a point of some subtlety. To interpret a measure that owed its existence to the most elementary respect for men's rights as an incitement to repression was typical of the spook mentality. The rest was less interesting: Popov demonstrated that the truth is belligerent by nature, that to know it without propagating it was tantamount to denying it, that to refuse to believe was not enough, one also had to prevent others from believing, if one was not to fall into bourgeois-democratic hypocrisy: 'Cut a worm in two and you get two worms; cut those in two and you get four; but if you go on cutting, you will reach an infra-critical volume beyond which worms are no longer viable. Such is the moral obligation of all who hold to real truth,' concluded Popov, trenchant as ever.

I did not know what role these articles had played in his life. Had a desire for self-expression overtaken him, did he need the money, did he lust after fame? I reached the tentative conclusion (and I believe it was a correct one) that in the Soviet Union, as elsewhere, to have published gives a young man a certain weight in society and that, to the degree that the diplomat Igor Maximovich Popov had to conceal his real professional weight, it was expedient to pour a little lead into the base by means of the printed word. This being the case, and supposing that he had written the articles himself, his personality began to emerge for me, with, above all, that significant preference for the cut over the thrust. Belonging instinctively to the party of the thrust, I looked forward to the singular pleasures afforded by this apparently unequal duel. But I still did not know how in this gladiatorial combat a retiary like myself would catch such a myrmillo.

I was not green enough to imagine that a taste for amply endowed blondes—supposing that it was not a myth—was enough to bring Popov into my net. The fact that his bosses fed his obsession—supposing that it was true—showed that they did not regard it as in itself dangerous. At best, it had to be interpreted as the sign of an internal flaw, and it was in the flaw, not in its symptoms, that I should look for opportunities of turning him. Popov was a professional. He would not betray, on the pillow, secrets that would then give us a hold over him. It seemed hardly less naive to hope to win by showing him that he had compromised himself with a girl working for our services: such a plan was worthy of Rat or Poirier and seemed masterly to them only because it was dirty (a necessary condition, perhaps, but certainly not sufficient for its practical efficacy). Popov was trusted by his bosses; they would know all about his assignations; as for compromising photographs, he could take them himself if that amused him; in short, he would slip between our fingers, as if covered in oil. On the other hand, it was not impossible that his obsession concealed a mystery, nor that exploration of it might prove advantageous.

The need to see my quarry in the flesh filled my working hours and began to arouse Frisquette's jealousy as it spilled over into my leisure time. On sheets of scrap paper, which I then destroyed, my pencil took to sketching long heads with prognathous jaws, parallel wrinkles on the forehead like a child's drawing of the sea, thinning hair ruthlessly combed, cheeks higher than broad, a mouth like an open scar, a bow tie and no eyes, because I did not know how to draw inexpressive eyes. But soon these rituals of evocation—which must have served some such purpose as the cave paintings of bison executed by prehistoric huntsmen—merely served to stimulate my hunger. I felt with increasing urgency that before tackling Popov I had first to see him, actually to set eyes on him. After all, his office was only a kilometre away from mine. We must have trodden the same pavements often enough.

One day, when I was more than usually bored—Puzo was in the Soviet Union with some minister or other, M. Alexandre and Divo were arguing for hours on end about the translation of *tseleustremlënnost'*. I couldn't stand it any longer. I crossed the windy esplanade and, under the suspicious eyes of a policeman who was walking up and down, stared in at the windows of an antique shop specializing in English furniture, a driving school, a very feminine shop selling blouses and skirts, an estate agent's and a second antique shop. I had never seen so many antiques in my life, yet I would be hard put to remember a single piece! This is because, in fact, I was looking at the other side of the street reflected in the shop windows: an anonymous gateway, a gate leading into a Dominican institution and, between the two, my adversary's lair, with its own double gates situated in an oval recess, and a side door, shamelessly flanked by a camera let into the wall at head height. For most passers-by, it was an embassy like any other and, for some, the noble Hôtel d'Estrées. But I came from a world that saw it as the Parisian *pied-à-terre* of anti-Christ. Here men from my side had disappeared, suffocated in cellars, exported in trunks, never heard of again. The bottle-green door, the gleaming bell push, the gaping recess and, of course, the camera, were as sinister to me as certain pictures in children's books. This even extended to the number: 7, symbol of pain, and 9, of multiplication to infinity, which, added together, again produced 7. I admit that I was anxious to move on, though not without feeling a ridiculous temptation to ring, go in, ask to see Counsellor Popov, imprint his face on my retina and his voice on my eardrum.

From then on, I looked for some way of satisfying what was no longer mere curiosity, but already a passion, not unlike, I imagine, the passion that was Eve's downfall and Mrs Bluebeard's salvation. I persuaded Colonel Rat that if we were serious in our intention of turning Major Popov, it was important that I should get to know him as well as possible while remaining unknown to him. Rat was not too convinced of the possibility of a turning, but he was willing to go along with the operation. He sent me off to see one of his friends, a senior police officer.

Late that afternoon, I remember, the clouds were skimming the rooftops; it was raining a kind of liquid ice; in the offices of the Préfecture, all the lamps were lit. Rather pleased with myself, I had decided to wear my cashmere overcoat and was now shivering inside it. I think I had a slight temperature. I was thinking with chilly pleasure that, before long, when I had finished wandering along those green corridors, past those dirty little offices smelling of disinfectant, I would cross the Seine and the rain, and take refuge at the *Pont-Royal*, the warm, quiet, underground bar, as distinguished socially as artistically, that I had turned into my headquarters: a neat Scotch and the urbanity of the large-eared waiter would warm me.

I was asked to sit down. I refused to take off my overcoat; I wasn't going to see it stuck on a hook next to some greasy-collared mackintosh.

'I need a window overlooking the garden of number 79 Rue de Grenelle,' I said, without giving a reason.

The police officer gave me a knowing look. He was as courteous as he knew how, but this courtesy was directed at the card in my wallet; as a human being, I was worth no more in his eyes than some ordinary convict who, holding his unsecured trousers with his thumbs, happened to be sitting on the same chair I was sitting on. He was a small man, with a tuft of hair sticking up over each ear and a typical Provençal face, all valleys and mountains, but he had no accent. No sooner had I said 'seventy-nine', than I imagined him thinking, experienced as he was, about things that would never have occurred to me, perhaps the disposition of the rooms or sewers, or the distance from the catacombs, or some secret installations set up by the Soviets and no doubt detected by our side, or the reverse, a whole network of sordid, but necessary operations that none of the former aristocratic occupants of those houses, the Estrées, the Birons or the Harcourts, would have imagined taking place under their roofs. But who knows? The Duc de Feltre was probably no choirboy, and was not spying the oldest profession in the world bar one?

'You need the Rue de Varenne or the Rue de Bellechasse, on the odd-numbered side, in the sixties. Would you bear with me a moment?'

It was a long moment, but I was not impatient. With that wealth of intuition, that medley of prospects that comes with fever, the choice of priorities being, God knows why, different above 100°, I began musing, in that inhospitable office, that interrogation room in all its horrible possibilities, without books, without papers, almost without furniture, of that man born of woman, closeted on the other side of the Seine, for whom I was laying my nets and traps. Had he, too, lit the lamp in his office? What did he see through the eyes of his body? Through the eyes of his intelligence? (I did not, at that time, think of the eyes of the spirit.) As fever lifted me above the obstacles that intimidate our awakened consciousness, I found myself asking why he was he and I I. Did it mean anything to say that he could have been I and I he? In which case, would he not have been wondering how it was that I was not he and he was not I? I was getting confused. I started again.

I was the hunter; he the prey. I derived a very real, perhaps childish, satisfaction from this fact. I had grown up with the unavowed conviction that *they* had won in advance and that *we* were merely survivors for a time. The very fact of having resumed the offensive—it did not matter why—not only brought me back to life, yes, to life, but also restored my sense of honour—I'm aware how odd the word sounds in the context, but it is the right one, in that those who accept defeat lose it. Let me explain: I had hardly read Marx at all, nor was I particularly concerned about the interests of the bourgeoisie, in fact, I hardly believed in classes as such at all; I was a Russian, but Tsarist Holy Russia seemed quite remote from me; I was French, but the idea of a Panslavist hegemony in Europe did not unduly shock me; of course, I had no hatred in my heart for the likes of Igor Maximovich, and yet I knew—with certain science, as Retz would say—that the pitches had been laid out and the teams recruited even before the match began, and that Popov and I belonged on opposite *sides*. Nobody could be less racist than I: Jew, black, yellow, Caucasian, it's all the same to me, I'm a Daltonian where ancestry is concerned; but I was certain—I still am perhaps a little, may God forgive me—that there were Whites and Reds; that reconciliation between them was impossible; and that Popov was as Red as I was White. If pushed, if asked what I meant by this political colouring, I would not have known what to say. I knew perfectly well that there really were such things as, for example, Red aristocrats and White navvies, White intellectuals and Red bourgeois, but I was quite unable to carry the distinction much further. Nevertheless, if Popov and I had been thrown into a gladiatorial circus, we would fly at each other instantly—it was a question of scent.

But however deep this instinct may have been, what interested me in Popov was the adversary rather than the enemy, the pursuit rather than the pelt. The fact that he was Red and I White served to make the less savoury aspects of the hunt more acceptable, but, if the truth were known, I would have worked with as much skill if not with as much pleasure against another White. This led me to the following reflections: between the hunter and the quarry there are always differences and affinities; the differences were obvious enough, but what affinities linked the Soviet Major Popov and the French Lieutenant Volsky?

To begin with, we had sprung from the same people, and that must mean something: Slav soul for Slav soul, his was worth mine, and mine his. We were both 'novelists', he taken up exclusively with espionage, I trying to straddle intelligence and literature. To within four or five years, we were the same age. That was about it. That evening, as I sat in the deserted office, with its lingering smell of formol, I added that we were both men of pleasure, but I now believe that I underestimated him—and flattered myself. Contrary to what I then believed, pleasure is no joke.

The policeman came back, carrying a handful of sepia-coloured cards, which he laid out in front of him for all the world as if he was going to tell my fortune.

'These are all maid's rooms,' he explained. 'They offer a wider view. Attract less attention. They're cheaper'—he brought his face close to mine and added, in a deferential tone—'and the tenants are generally easier to get rid of.'

The fever must have given me an appearance of impassivity. He must have thought I was cleverer than I really was.

He reeled off a list of names. There was one who was not paying his rent—clearly an aristocrat; there was a young woman who supplemented her income by means of activities which might have been conducted more discreetly; an African who depended on his scholarship and who might, therefore, be deprived of it; an arts student who had obtained a deferment but might still be called up as he was neglecting his attendances at premilitary school; and a few others.

'Which one do you want?'

I may have been a soldier, but I was not a militarist. On the other hand, I've always hated malingering intellectuals. I put my finger on the student's card. A Mephistophelian smile crossed the police officer's face.

'An excellent choice, lieutenant. The military authorities will be delighted to hear from this young gentleman. It will give me particular pleasure to drop a word in at the station to hasten matters.'

He gathered up his cards with the dexterity of a professional sharper. The tufts of hair over his ears stood up as if charged with electricity.

Blinding rain was beating down on the Place Louis-Lepine; behind me, the Préfecture with its windows lit looked like a grid placed over a projector. My feet soaked, I got into the 2CV. Washes of water rolled over the windscreen making it impossible to see through. The sight of my black kangaroo-gloved hands on the steering-wheel was no consolation. I threw myself into the brutal evening traffic with the sense of performing a heroic act. I was sustained only by the hope of reaching the *Pont-Royal*, and, also, I fear, by the memory of my pointed fingernails on the sepia card transforming someone's life. I had exercised my power and as a result some young man, whom I imagined to be something of a womanizer, with dirty feet, not too gifted intellectually, but his head full of radical ideas, would find himself transported from one day to the next to a barracks square, his head shaved, peeling potatoes, snivelling in the quartermaster's stores, rubbing his collar bone, which ached from the unaccustomed recoil of a rifle butt, unable to understand why, among so many irregular deferments, his had been suspended and consoling himself with the thought that at least he'd narrowly missed being bumped off in Algeria.

I parked the car and, hair plastered down on my scalp, my shoes squelching, I reached my haven of grace. I slipped down the stairs, like a lizard disappearing into a crack. That descent towards subterranean warmth, through the dry air and over the thick carpet, was intensely comforting. I entered the low crypt, all leather, panelling and subdued lighting, nodded familiarly to the hieratic barman standing behind his soberly gleaming bar, and saw Olga Orloff, or rather Marina Kraievsky, sitting alone, at the back, just opposite. Her Slav, Gioconda smile spread over—or rather under—her features like a gently gleaming oil, without in any way altering the lines and angles of her face. I say angles . . . Marina did not know what an angle was.

We had broken up in somewhat embarrassing circumstances. If the interests of a clear narrative line demand it, I shall recount them, but later. For the moment, I did not know whether it would be more polite to acknowledge her or to spare her my presence entirely. And, yet, notwithstanding my shirt collar, which must have been in a pitiful state, I walked over without hesitation, as if drawn by that harmonious smile, that gleam in the eyes, that whiteness of the neck—after all, had I not, in better times, called her, among other things, the Eternal Feminine?

I stood awkwardly in front of her table—as far as I remember we were alone in the bar, but I'm probably quite wrong, there must have been other customers, perhaps the painter M . . . with his spinach-green suit and his hair built up as if one were going to place an apple on it, or the writer L . . . with his unkempt look as of a little scalliwag—I stood there, in the middle of a puddle, looking none too good, as Rat would have said.

'Are you alone?'

I spoke in Russian, though French came to us more naturally. There was in that, I think, an admission of defeat, an effort to place our relations on a different level. She gently shook her head. An almost imperceptible dimple ran across her cheek. She had that particular Nordic complexion that gives the impression that it is the derm that is pink and the epidermis simply transparent.

'I'm waiting for someone, but sit down.'

She set the tone. We would treat each other as civilized people. I apologized:

'I must take off my coat.'

I went and hung it up in the cloakroom and came back another man: my suit was dry and a glance in the mirror told me that my shirt collar had stood up quite well. Marina moved over on the seat and I sat down beside her, half turned towards her, holding out the palms of my hands. She looked at me questioningly.

'I'm warming myself.'

She smiled a gently ironical smile, but it was true that on

Mitsuko's spicy waves a sense of wellbeing radiated from her, from her grey-green jersey suit, from the gilt coil that did duty as a necklace, from the whole of her compact presence, very gently, very delicately purring, not so much like a kitten as like a stove when the fire has begun to catch.

She said nothing, but she continued to look at me with perhaps unconscious intensity. As far as I remember, it was because I could no longer bear that gaze and that silence that I launched at once into a subject it would have been better to leave alone until we had got the results of the investigation being carried out by the police. Other, more secret forces were also at work. Perhaps I wanted to surprise her, or impress her? Redeem my all too evident deficiencies by some hidden power? Perhaps I was moved by a certain mixture of shame and satisfaction at the idea that at that very moment, at my instigation, they were ferreting around in her past? In any case, weakness was unforgivable in a young man of my training and pretensions.

'I'm delighted to see you,' I said in French, in an off-hand way. 'For the sheer pleasure of seeing you, of course, but also for another reason. Will you be free at all in the next few days?'

She did not answer.

'The pay would be decent—not like in novels, but still pretty good. All expenses paid, too, of course.'

She continued to stare at me, her eyes full of that familiar warm irony.

'It may be a trifle dangerous.'

She raised one of her golden eyebrows, accentuating the irony without diminishing the warmth.

'Are you trying to impress me?' she asked. 'Or are you really serious?'

'I thought it might amuse a girl like you.'

Yes, there was in Marina a carnivorous quality, a toughness, a taste for gambling that would make up for her professional ignorance. In any case, as an actress at the beginning of a career —advertising films, a bit of television—it was not likely that she would refuse the money.

She still said nothing, and I began to realize that, in the absence of any concrete proposition, I should not have opened my mouth. Without having to be told, the waiter brought me my Scotch with its single ice-cube. I said in Russian:

'It's to do with the Ruskies.'

Slowly, Marina's gaze darkened. At that moment, a man came in and paused at the threshold. He was tall, swarthy, curly-haired, all shoulder and no hips, in a suit of a rather too light blue, what you might call, I suppose, a good-looking guy. Marina raised her left hand in acknowledgement. Her hand was small and chubby; it was fleshy and fine-boned; the three middle fingers were rather too short, the little finger and thumb rather too long: this gave her hand a rounded effect, so that when seen from the front it resembled her face, whose little, flattened-out sister it might have been—a satellite, endowed with its own luminosity, the hand-version of a common subject whose face was the face-version. Each of our cells, they say, contains our whole body *in potentia*: in Marina, this microcosmic homogeneity was evident at a glance.

As she raised her hand in acknowledgement, she continued to look at me. Her Gioconda smile hardly broadened. Sparks swam across her gilded eyes like fish in a bowl. Scarcely parting her lips, she spoke again, this time in Russian, with particular sensuality:

'Why not?'

She then added, this time in French, more abruptly:

'Excuse me. He's waiting.'

I stood up. I helped her to push back the table. As she got up, she opened her handbag and, despite my protests, left two francs beside her tea cup. It was one of her oddities: she paid for herself (and sometimes for others).

The man in blue had advanced a couple of steps. He had obviously no desire to meet me—nor I him. Seeing that he was ignoring me, I greeted him with an urbane, and thereby insulting, indeed humiliating, wave of the hand. But I did not take my eyes off Marina: in those movements that do not lend themselves to grace—rising from a table, leaving money, slipping away—there emerged a singular quality that led me to give her, among other nicknames, that of Little Ripple. Instead of moving like everybody else by successive, hierarchized movements, as in a cartoon, the muscles governing the tendons, the tendons moving the joints, the joints engaging the limbs, Marina seemed to be made up of a single, continuous substance, and the impulses were transmitted through her flesh, as in a liquid or semi-liquid medium by waves. I stood there until she was out of sight, piloted by the arm, submitting with good grace to that grotesque display of male authority.

8

The Popov file was getting thicker: photographs, dates, information sheets, articles, operating charts, press-cuttings, relevant data accumulated. On a large sheet of graph paper I had laid out the time along the ordinate, and along the abscissa five columns: Residence, Acquaintances, Private Life, Cover, Missions; I filled in the squares as the information came in, with, in brackets, a number referring to the file. The third and the last columns still remained empty, but the others were getting blacker and blacker, thanks to my contact with Malmaison and sometimes to other information that the Shopkeeper must have bought somewhere on the cheap. I had been given a safe for all the material relating to Culverin; because there was no room anywhere else, it had been put into the translators' room and Puzo often glowered across at it: I was never able to make out whether he was jealous or simply curious. Of course, I only operated the combination when I was alone. This was made possible by the fact that I was no longer working normal office hours, which gave me a most agreeable sense of freedom. Rat no longer bothered to take first look at all the documents that arrived in the office and it was I who, when I had something new, went and spread out upon his table the sheet of graph paper (which soon had to be reinforced with gummed paper along the folds). He frowned at the empty squares, moving his none too clean finger over the full ones and concluding with his usual grumble:

'Let's have the shadings, my boy, the shadings.'

He revealed his long yellow teeth—a real *memento mori*—when I had cross-checked Popov's musical tastes.

Beethoven or Tchaikovsky featured on the programmes of all the concerts that we knew he had attended.

'That,' said Rat, and the end of his nose seemed to describe circles like a hunting dog's, 'is very good.'

I asked why.

'The fact that Popov likes Tchaikovsky is not very important. What is important is the fact that we know that he does. Don't you see? Carry on, add the shadings. You'll get it in the end.'

I continued my researches, pleased that I was filling more and more squares, but knowing that most of them would always remain empty—unless we appealed to the Big House, and that was out of the question. However, confiding in Rat, I collected the human details, not only to get inside the man's skin, but also because that's the way it was done: it was not so much the rule as the style of the game. Rat, of course, was right: one fights the enemy, but one has to catch the man.

'What's still bothering me,' he would say, 'is that we have got no further than the image he wants to project: the Leninist go-getter, with a touch of the Romantic about him, who succeeds in everything he turns his hand to. We're still scratching the surface. Add the shadings, my boy. He must have made a few blunders in his life. Seek them out.'

But it was he who found one. One evening, when we were alone in GEST, he stuck under my nose a carbon copy (the characters were so faint it must have been a sixth or seventh copy) of what looked like a document, from two or three years back, which began more or less like this:

United Fraternity Front
Yusef Larbi to Dr Si Lachemi Mesrur
    Greetings and Revolution!
    I have had the honour of carrying out the mission you were kind enough to entrust to me. On 22 instant, I was able to penetrate Pseudonym's privacy. I was received with under-standing and I believe I have been able to conclude an agree-ment that will be to the advantage of both parties. First delivery 1,000 Kalashashnikovs (*sic*) and 500 cartridges per weapon. Please request headquarters to work out the

appropriate DZs to be submitted for Pseudonym's approval. Notwithstanding these attractive possibilities, I discommend acceptance of the delivery, reserving an opinion of negative preference as far as the humanitarian developments of the project are concerned. On the other hand, I recommend a complete and immediate cessation of Pseudonym's intrigues . . .

It continued over three pages, in the same heavy, involuted vein. The political implications of this document seem to have escaped the French evaluators at the time. And yet, some fifteen years before the events of 1975, when the Soviet Union was firmly anchored, it seemed, on the other side of the Suez Canal, Popov, in a masterly survey of a still embryonic situation, had already seen what could be gained from an alliance between the Lebanese Muslims and the Palestinian working masses. Brilliant, yes, and it was the same brilliance that made him, in the end, botch an operation that had been worked out so neatly. On first reading I saw that Popov's Bolschevism must have backfired (always assuming that it was he who was being referred to by the author of the document, owing perhaps to some misunderstanding of the coding, under the surprising name of 'Pseudonym'—the dates supported this hypothesis). One never gets away with playing Goliath. Now, in the light of the recent civil war in the Lebanon, I can see much more clearly what happened and I cannot resist the pleasure of imagining the scene.

I don't know where it took place—an office? an orchard? an Arab café? perhaps a Turkish bath with blue and green mosaic walls?—but I can see the characters. Yusef Larbi, a young semi-intellectual with thin-rimmed spectacles, his head buzzing with various ideologies, his sideburns long and tangled, his moustache drooping sadly downwards over a purple mouth. The beneficiary of some imprudent foundation, educated here and there, having learnt to think in *Le Monde* and striving to imitate its style, he dreams of Panarab brotherhood. Having moved in the direction of the left-wing Muslims, he met some who were more Marxist than the rest, and his well-intentioned if

97

not very virile little soul thrilled with admiration before the image of the Muscovite Hercules. He conceived the idea of a Muslim revolution in the Lebanon, in the name of a felicitous marriage between Marx and Mohammed (the fact that such a perversion was doomed to impotence was beyond the grasp of the unaided intelligence): the Palestinians, his fellow-countrymen, would provide the brute force and the military élites; the Lebanese Muslims, the logistic support, and together they would cut the Christian bourgeois up into little pieces. And Igor Popov, fair-haired and white-skinned, his eyes threaded with tiny red veins, carrying behind his high, ridged forehead a first-class computer, endowed with a third eye—who would have predicted that, in the ensuing struggle, he would not be the winner?

There are two kinds of *naïveté*: there's the *naïveté* that believes only in generous causes and the *naïveté* that believes only in self-interest. Most Western historians, having opted for the second, are quite unable to understand nineteenth-century Russian politics, which they persist in explaining in terms of 'the old dream of outlets'. And since it is the current wisdom in fashionable circles to believe that nothing ever changes in Russia, one might be tempted to attribute the same dream to Popov. But, in fact, when one thinks of all the advantages that the world revolution would derive from the first half-red, half-green flag hoisted over some minaret of the Middle or Near East, the opening up of outlets fades into insignificance. Among the Soviet 'residents' in all the Arab countries, there is a kind of permanent race as to who will be the first to declare a pro-Moscow people's republic in the Mediterranean basin. Egypt hesitated, Libya did not go far enough, Tunisia had second thoughts ... Yusef Larbi's idea must have made Popov's mouth water, and he saw himself no doubt as a Hero of the Soviet Union peppered with red stars, perhaps even getting one of the directorates.

The interview between the two men began well. Popov outlined and Larbi accepted the various stages of the subversive operation to be undertaken. During the first stage, social and intellectual agitation would be left to Dr Mesrur's Lebanese

Muslims. During a second stage, there would be a rising of the same, the purpose of which would be to cause as much bloodshed as possible and so provoke brutal repression. During the third stage, Larbi's Palestinians would intervene, coming to the help of their brothers. The Christian conservatives could then be crushed, if only in part of the territory, which would then be declared independent. The fourth stage would see the formation of a transitional government, part-Lebanese, part-Palestinian, part Muslim, part-Marxist. During a fifth stage the new state would move into the Soviet orbit. Agreement was reached on the time-table, which was to be spread over three years. For Popov, everything seemed to be going perfectly. Even the ultimate satellization, which he had feared he would not be able to impose without force, did not seem to shock Larbi: he confirmed it without batting an eyelid behind his virtuous spectacles. After all, he believed in Marxism: he believed it to be both desirable and inevitable, and he didn't want its Chinese version. Anyway, deep inside, he was convinced that Levantine Marxism would be superior to its Russian brand (after six thousand years of history one should be quite capable of improving on the ideas of the useful, but plodding, bear emerging from its Cimmerian mists).

'Agreed!' Larbi concluded, with perhaps unconscious contempt.

Popov, too, was contemptuous, and with good reason. Had he not had it drummed into him *ad nauseam* that in the East all that counted were the salaams and flourishes? He had found it hard to believe, and now he could demonstrate to his masters that the opposite was the case: here, as elsewhere, force was enough. You don't have to kowtow when you're holding a Kalashnikov. They had even gone so far as to draw up the list of the government that would take over at the declaration of independence. Popov, displaying detailed knowledge of Palestinian circles, distributed the various portfolios: Information went to little Mohammed, his hands gnawed by printer's ink; the Interior went to big Mohammed, who was capable of forcing anyone to confess to anything; Economics to Jamal, the trade unionist, nicknamed Nasser; the Armed Forces to Saraf, the 'painless extractor'.

There were no soldiers: soldiers are there to be someone else's cat's paw. Palestinians were everywhere.

'But where?' Larbi asked, when all the posts had been filled, 'are our brothers, the Lebanese Muslims? The star on our flag will have ten points instead of five. They are to be given fifty per cent of the seats.'

Popov, his head thrown back, stared at him with his inexpressive, almost dazed eyes, which inexplicably suggested nakedness (being naked? or stripping you naked?). He cared not a fig for the Panarab dream, which was as utopian as all racisms, and as odious as all religions. 'At bottom,' he thought, 'what these Arabs would like to be is Jews: the real Jews, the chosen of God. Making race and superstition one—what a farce!'

'Your brothers, the Lebanese Muslims,' he said at last, certain of his irrevocable superiority, 'are intellectuals, liberals, conformists of anti-conformism, those whom Lenin called "the worms in the grave of the Revolution" and whom Trotsky . . .' I understand that he dared to quote Trotsky on occasion '. . . condemned simply to the "dustbin of history". You are the true revolutionaries. They . . .'

He swept them away with the back of his hand, confident of being right, confident of success.

'You're surely not going to weep over the intelligentsia?' he resumed, a decided note of disgust in his voice, having glimpsed, in the gleaming spectacles of the young Arab, an unexpected trace of disapproval. 'When you walk over the liberal intelligentsia, you take care not to slip and you wipe your feet on the pavement. Didn't you know that?'

I am not saying that Larbi was not tempted for a moment. It is sweet to link oneself with the expected victor. But to sacrifice brothers who had understood the tragic destiny of the Palestinians, hosts with whom one had broken bread, coreligionists, belonging to the same Obedience? Anyway, he knew very well that the intelligentsia was part of the movement. The bear's flattery had been rather crude: Larbi glimpsed the day when, once the liberals had been forgotten, he, in turn, would be swept aside. Perhaps a second cabinet lay already fully armed in Popov's brain. But Larbi was imbued as much with dissimulation as loyalty. Anyway he wanted to hold on to life and considered it more prudent not to show for the moment that he could not accept Soviet aid at the price demanded and would go and try his luck elsewhere.

He bared his teeth: 'Pity on those dogs? Let them die!' Popov gave a short, sharp laugh.

But he was wrong to laugh. The events of the next few days proved this abundantly. The Fraternity Front suddenly went underground. It was impossible to get anyone to take the funds and receive the Kalashnikovs. Larbi was nowhere to be found. Mesrur was being quite impossible. A rare opportunity had been lost because Popov had applied once too often the method that had brought him so many easy, insolent triumphs.

Did he ever realize the mistake he had made? I don't know, but, ever since, one fact seemed to me to be significant: Popov did not seem to have been punished for his failure, either because he had managed to conceal it or, for some unknown reason, his chiefs were forced to treat him with unusual delicacy.

9

The smell of old Camembert lingered in the maid's room on the
Rue de Bellechasse. The window opened with difficulty: the
student obviously never aired the room. A folding bedstead
occupied one corner. The cupboard had nothing in it but empty
beer bottles and smelled of vomit. The tap dripped into the
rusty, filthy wash-basin. Below, on a square of linoleum, a
yellow pattern on a black background, stood a portable bidet.
The view, beyond a few tiny courtyards and walls, gave on to the
classical garden, badly kept that year, of the Hôtel d'Estrées.
Dead leaves rustled over the sandy paths. A bedraggled-looking
birch-tree, planted by some nostalgic ambassador, fluttered its
remaining leaves in the breeze. A Russian, good or bad, cannot
see a birch-tree without being moved and I, too, reacted according to form at the sight of that being, transplanted, perhaps like
me, before being born. A birch, even a Soviet one, is white; it
cannot be Marxist. I took up my position at the end of the room,
so as not to be seen from outside, and raised to my eyes the
binoculars that I had managed to obtain after weeks of
negotiation.

I kept up my observation for two hours; I saw only a short,
stocky, moustachioed gardener going about with an empty
wheelbarrow, grumbling between his clenched teeth. Indeed it
occurred to me that it would not be much use to see Igor Popov
in my binoculars if I did not know what he was saying. That
merely served to sharpen what, at the risk of being pretentious, I
might call the hunger I had for him. If they already existed at
that time, parabolic microphones must have been the preserve
of the experts. For my part, I had never heard of them. Then,

102

knowing that throughout the civil service, prestige is directly correlated with expenditure, I decided, for once, to perform a good deed: three days later Lev Mikhailovich Lisichkin had a home.

At the time I met him, he was no longer falling into the sins of his second youth, which had consisted in passing himself off as a prince, a guards' officer, a familiar of the court, but he treasured a yellowed photograph in which he was to be seen gallivanting on the back of a jade at the head of a few ragamuffins on foot. He had worn the epaulette; he may have been a hero. He was now little more than a poor, half-starved creature, with a crafty look in his eyes, and that special kind of white hair peculiar to former red-heads. His manner was humble to the point of obsequiousness, his diction heavily laced with saliva, his mouth practically toothless. There was one good thing about him, however: he was as deaf as a post and, since he had never learnt any other language but Russian, he had learnt to lipread it perfectly. Moreover, he was a down-and-out in whom those two irreconcilable enemies, Christian charity and the social services, found a common justification. He ate anything and slept in the homes of old army friends, or under bridges, or even, in winter, in prison, when he saw to getting himself arrested for vagrancy. I may lack humanitarian fibre, but I was delighted at the thought that the poor devil would have a roof over his head—and even central heating—for a time. The security police had already used him once or twice, so there was no need to clear him; I could take him on without too much red tape. There was an additional advantage; an empty room would have attracted the attention of neighbours or of the concierge. Funds were released; I even got a modest payment for old Lisichkin, who danced for joy: the wife of his best friend, Ensign Prince Taratashvili—she ran a small grocer's shop—had just thrown him out for reasons to do with both linguistics and hygiene.

'I hope this mission won't finish before the bad season,' he said. 'Last time, they'd no sooner put a roof over my head than I'd told them all they wanted to know: they threw me out. The cops, you know.'

He laughed, but took great care to keep an eye on me, in case his lack of respect offended me. Seeing that I was amused, he gave full vent to a hysterical fit, which was his way of laughing. He even went so far as to add, with a roguish wink of his left eye:

'If I hear anything interesting'—he always talked of *hearing*—'maybe I won't tell you everything at once . . .'

Suddenly he became serious, fearing, perhaps, that he had gone too far. But, when I showed no sign of disapproval, the poor devil began to shake with laughter once again. He reminded me of those machines that shake you like a bag of nuts under the pretext of relaxing your muscles.

I had always felt ill at ease in his company. I find it natural to respect age; this buffoon dishonoured his. He accorded himself, in an army that had long since disappeared, ranks that he had never held and which were higher than the one I really held in an army that still existed. I was paying him, so he was afraid of me. If I had cared at all for the man he was, no doubt we would have got on better, but I could not see him as anything but an old clown. But at least I could trust him: he drank red wine, without excess, and almost no vodka. I gave him the photographs and the binoculars, and forced myself to drop in at the Rue de Bellechasse once or twice a day despite the embarrassment I felt in Lev Mikhailovich's company and the smell of soused herring that had replaced the room's earlier smell of stale Camembert.

He settled in within hours, aiming at *uïut* (*Gemütlichkeit*, cosiness), rather than comfort. The decoration consisted of soapboxes, a cracked mirror, a razor and its strop, a worn carpet, cushions, ill-assorted books (belonging to libraries to which they would never be returned), bundles of papers (the rough draft of his 'Memoirs'!), signed photographs of moustachioed men with fringed epaulettes and women with hat veils and sad-looking eyes, old cigar boxes stuffed with newspaper cuttings, registration certificates, receipts, money-order stubs of thirty years back and, who knows, perhaps love letters? . . . On the wall was a rather battered reproduction, in faded colours, of Shishkin's famous *Bear Cubs*; over the bed, surmounting a portrait of Nicholas II, was a tiny icon covered by a rather crudely moulded, greenish copper plaque, representing the

Saviour, with the somewhat effeminate features and redness of skin attributed to him by the Russian eighteenth century, in reaction against the symbolic stylization of the Middle Ages and foreshadowing the sentimental interpretation of the nineteenth century.

I unlocked the door—I had my own key—but found my entry barred by the safety chain. Lisichkin ran up, pushed an angry face into the gap, then subsided into a toothless smile, that brought a ripple of wrinkles over its deep pink skin.

'Oh, it's you, lieutenant,' he said in rather official-sounding French, then added in Russian, 'I thought the tovarishchi had come for me already!'

He winked at his own wit in calling those for whom he was a sworn enemy 'comrades'. He then invited me in with much bowing and scraping, which had nothing military about it. I took a few paces into the room, swung around on my heels, and asked: 'So, one might say, you've nothing to tell me, Lev Mikhailovich!'

'One might well say, I've nothing to tell you, Kiril Lavrovich. The ambassador's wife took a turn round the garden with her Pomeranian. Not quite Chekhov's *Lady with the Dog!* More the slut with the bitch!'

He looked at me, head to one side, anxious to know whether he had done well or ill to show such scant respect for the wife of an ambassador accredited to a Republic I served. I left quickly, resisting the fascination exercised over me by those three rows of windows, striped with their opaque blinds, behind which I imagined . . . what? Hell. The idea that, on this side, too, it was hell, had not yet occurred to me. Popov had still not appeared. At least Lisichkin slept in comfort.

One day, however, I received a promising telephone call at my office. I rushed over. Stairs, car, red lights, parking . . . When I got to the Rue de Bellechasse, the chain was on as usual. Lisichkin ran to the door. 'Oh, it's you, lieutenant. I thought . . .'

'Is he still there?'

'He's no longer there, Kiril Lavrovich. When I got back after telephoning you, he'd gone.'

'Did he say anything?'

Lisichkin nodded. I then noticed that he was in the grip of an apparently pleasant kind of excitement. The old man was not far from a certain form of ecstasy.

'And did you understand what he said . . .?'

Ever more enthusiastic nods and smiles of jubilation spread, in successive waves, over his leathery old face. The eyes disappeared as the lower eyelids rose with pleasure.

'Well?'

The old devil was irritating me. At the same time, I was discovering in him something odd that I had never before been aware of: didn't there have to be something of the witch about him to read people's lips at a distance? What semi-occult connection linked this nonentity with the ambiguous forces of the universe?

'Well, Lev Mikhailovich?'

The old gnome was shaken from head to toe by one of his silent laughs, but he still kept his eyelids open a crack to monitor my reaction.

'Ah! The son of a bitch!' he said at last, almost tenderly. 'He may be a comrade, but he hasn't forgotten his Russian. It's fifty years since I've heard the like. Believe me or not, Kiril Lavrovich, it warms an old man's heart.'

'But what? What did he say?'

Lisichkin tried to resume a more military bearing.

'Can't repeat it, lieutenant.'

'Why not?'

'It wouldn't be respectful. The son of a bitch expressed himself in a manner forbidden by the censor.'

I learnt in the end that a half-an-hour earlier, while the gardener was smoking a Russian cigarette in the middle of a flowerbed strewn with rotting leaves, Igor Popov, easily recognizable by his high forehead and his great jaw, had suddenly appeared on the terrace. Walking straight up to the gardener with deliberately long steps ('like a tiger', according to Lisichkin—I was later to learn that this characteristic step derived from the fact that, though Popov had excessively short legs, he took long steps), he had reproached him in lively, picturesque terms, not, as one might have expected, for sabotaging Communist society by his parasitical behaviour, but for having incestuous relations (imaginary ones, of course) with his own mother.

'Ah! Kiril Lavrovich when I *heard* such words at the end of your binoculars, I felt fifty years younger! I was transported back to Holy Russia, on my word of honour! You can say what you like: they still know how to live, the sons of bitches. It's not everybody who can swear in colour. In my own youth, I must admit, I was not entirely devoid of a certain florid inspiration, and when I did let rip, the whole platoon, I mean the whole squadron, stood with their mouths open, and not so much out of fear as admiration.'

I took two steps towards the window. The incestuous gardener had hastily got himself a wheelbarrow, a rake, a broom, a fork and was scattering the brown leaves around him with the energy of a demented Stakhanovite. Now, my knowledge of Popov told me that if, for some reason or another, he had decided to get the garden cleaned up (not that this came in any way under his jurisdiction, but the file had warned me of these sudden, unexpected bursts of interest in the day-to-day working of the establishment, of his excessive love of absolute efficiency), he would not fail to come back to see that his orders had been carried out. So, I spent the morning in Lisichkin's room, reading old numbers of *The Sentinel*, while the gardener ran behind his wheelbarrow with bizarre haste and considerable results. By noon I had had enough and went out for lunch. When I came back Popov was in the garden.

He was standing right at the end, at a spot where the dead, brown, almost black, or violet, leaves formed a thick, and no doubt rustling layer under the skeletal vault of overhanging branches. Over a long torso, he was wearing a jacket of light grey, black-mottled cloth and his dumpy legs were covered with plus-fours of a darker grey. I never discovered whether he imagined that the knickerbockers lengthened the leg or whether he was following some fashion in his own country. For the moment, he was talking to the aproned gardener, who was standing next to him in a reverent posture, ankle-deep in leaves.

107

I snatched the binoculars from Lisichkin and scoured the terrain in search of the face, so often imagined, and now before my eyes. He suddenly appeared as large as life very close, with more hair than I had expected. The eyes, used to conceal everything, had that dazed look about them that I had already noticed on the photographs. The folds of his forehead—they really were like folds, rather than wrinkles: an iron, it seemed, would smooth it all out, a little excess skin remaining on the back of the neck—gave an impression of boredom that I had not expected. The lips were moving forcefully: one sensed behind them a constant mastication of words, a long-held habit of issuing decisions, arguments, orders.

'What's he saying?'

'You've got the binoculars, lieutenant.'

I was fascinated by this dome-shaped forehead in which, at this distance, it would have been so easy to bore a hole 7.5 millimetres in diameter with the help of a sighting telescope and even, for a good shot like myself, without one. I handed back the binoculars.

'Well?'

What he said was of no interest. Popov explained to the gardener what he should plant in the spring, where, how, in what order, what precautions to take. He talked about gardening with as much authority as, no doubt, he talked about nuclear energy. The only expression of any interest—and, even then, pushing it a bit—was 'Everything counts, Fedorich, with us, everything counts', which he said in a didactic way, with a rather incongruous patriarchal severity, for the gardener with the big moustache could have been his father—or grandfather.

I took back the binoculars. This, then, was the rising star of the Committee of State Security, a man who had set up the world's best intelligence network in Israel, Crocodile's new case officer? Being all the same a semi-professional, I did not reckon him also responsible according to our information, for the deaths of at least three French officers—art for art's sake, I insist, is the motto of true 'novelists', rather than the eye for an eye of religions and police forces. On the other hand, I said to myself that he was the resident widower, the Minotaur whom his government provided with a six-monthly supply of blondes to keep him up to scratch. With his sententious air, his dark red tie, shiny from being tied too often, his provincial shoes, there was, I must say, nothing priapic about him. Yet, all the same, that pale complexion, those naked eyes, those hands that clenched and unclenched, punctuating the disposition of salvias and peonies . . . For the garden, of course, had to be filled to bursting with red flowers: 'Everything counts, Fedorich, with us, everything counts.' What a magnificent slogan to get the troops marching: 'everything counts and everything is counted!' I handed back the binoculars.

The gardener said a few words. Lisichkin was amused by his obsequiousness.

'Comrades, indeed!' he muttered.

Popov went off. I observed that odd walk, the legs alone thrown forward from the groin downwards, the trunk remaining erect, the arms hardly moving, the whole body suggesting gymnastics rather than athleticism, probably the rings, maybe weightlifting: the religion of the biceps. A door opened without his having to hold out a hand and closed of its own accord as soon as he was inside.

10

When the results of the investigation into Marina Kraievsky were completed, we held a new council of war, at Poirier's expense, in the same restaurant near Les Halles; this time, however, a private room was put at our disposal. We made a funny trio: Poirier, bundled up in his sweaters, looking like a fairly prosperous horsedealer, putting back double rations of *tripes à la mode de Caen*; Rat, a cream sauce dripping on to his gosling-green tie; I, intensely correct as a subaltern should be, resolutely military, as a soldier in mufti should be.

'Don't be annoyed with me, my young friend,' Poirier said, turning to me, 'if I come and stick my nose in your business. You're the boss—it's all down in black and white. I'm here only as a consultant. Let's see the wench.'

'My young friend', 'as a consultant'! Who did this once-talented 'novelist' think he was fooling? The truth was, he simply couldn't keep his fingers out of the pie. I thought that he had really reached retirement age or rather that retirement age had reached him, but I concealed my facetious perspicacity.

I put down on the table, between the dirty plates and half-filled glasses, the two photographs of Marina I possessed. One of them had been provided by a theatrical agency. It showed Marina in profile, cut off at the knees, bare arms crossed, one shoulder slightly raised, her head full face, a half-languorous, half-sarcastic expression on the shiny lips. That half-smile, both tempting and teasing, contrasted nicely with the almost domestic simplicity of the pose. The other photograph had been given to me by Marina herself at a time when I found new nick-names for her every day. The dedication was written on the back, in Russian, in small, but firm handwriting: 'From Marina', and the date: '19 12/V 63'. It was a close-up. It showed her full face, with, in the foreground, a fur-wrap, in the form of a sloping S, accentuating the fragile nudity of the neck. The eyes had that arrested gaze that many actresses seek without success, the supreme self-assurance of a champion shot, a gentle brightness, a promising gleam (but promising what?—it was not at all obvious that it promised sexual ecstasies). Under the light brown hair (which the Russians themselves call Russian hair), arranged rather too artistically for my taste, the forehead, smoothly convex, invited chaste kisses; the prominent cheekbones made the planes of the temples more affecting; over the mouth played the Slav Gioconda smile; the chin seemed to tremble as if on the verge of laughter—or tears; the almost flat nose suggested those magnificent, open faces of the yellow race, like vases that the potter has finished, but which the painter has not yet touched with his brush.

Having passed over the second photograph, I cringed inwardly. It was not for this that Marina had given it to me one spring morning when we went boating in the Bois de Boulogne.

'Pretty girl,' said Poirier, 'but you seemed to think he liked them rather . . .'

He was looking at the first photograph. Rat, who had already seen it, was looking at him. I was watching both of them. Rat was rather against; Poirier needed working on.

'Yes, sir. That is the American thesis.'

I fished out of my briefcase the photograph of Penelope Barker taken by the Security Police at my request—they were always anxious to help us out in the hope of embarrassing the Big House. It was an enlargement of a photograph taken with a telephoto-lens in front of one of the supposedly secret safehouses of the Central Intelligence Agency. It showed Miss Barker, shoulders back, in order to keep her balance, walking as if on parade in front of the stupefied concierge. Of course, I had chosen the shot that best brought out the idea that one could have too much of a good thing.

'Well,' said Poirier perplexed. 'I suppose some men like that kind of thing—personally, I'd be afraid of getting lost in it all.'

I thrust my hand again into my briefcase. I had had reproduced by our photographic section, on a single sheet, photographs, obtained through Malmaison, of all Popov's secretaries. Since they were passport photographs, one could hardly judge of these ladies' more physical attractions, but the effect was striking nevertheless; all sixteen were blondes, but the hair was variously short, long, straight, curly, frizzy, clean, dirty, well-tended, neglected; all had broad heads, but they were variously round, square, elongated, short; all the faces were fleshy, but some were heavily made-up, others not, some more finely textured than others, some stretched over the bones, others sagging slightly, or firm in their own structure. They had nothing else in common: the eyes were not of the same colour; the shape of the noses was as varied as is possible in working-class Russian noses; the mouths were of every imaginable kind; the expressions went from nervousness before the camera to the placid self-assurance that comes from an investment in sex-appeal.

'Fine lot of cattle!' Poirier commented.

He was right. Beneath the similarities and differences lay a common denominator, which we might not have detected without Lester's indiscretions: victims for the slaughter-house, patriotic ogresses, pulsating females, submissive heiffers, they all possessed an overflowing animality, and I suddenly blushed—with such lack of logic!—at presenting this sample of Russian females to these two drunken Frenchmen. For a moment, these girls were all my sisters and my chiefs, slave dealers. Then I remembered that I, too, was a slave dealer and that my slave was the most expensive of the lot.

'They're all pretty girls, of course,' Poirier continued, 'but the Yankee vamp has got more of what it takes. As for your candidate . . . Well, why offer caviar to a chap who likes liver pâté? You must have felt that.'

Rat nodded in agreement. I then played my master card: an enlarged photograph of a young woman, head and bust taken in three-quarters, from below, by a meticulous and gifted amateur photographer. The light, very fine hair, combed back into a chignon, leaving a few stray locks at the front, revealed an elegantly outlined ear; the broad, open forehead, slightly inclined, suggested an intense life, not so much of the intelligence as of the soul; the pronounced eyebrows, forming a simple, very beautiful line, had something masculine about them; the nose, though slightly thick, was firm and not without nobility, a felicitous variation on the Slav theme; the mouth was sad and seemed to convey to the chin an undercurrent of pathos reminiscent, though in a more spontaneous fashion, of the quiver detectable in Marina's photograph; the neck, round and robust, led to a well developed rib cage, like that of a singer; a collarless jersey, with a low-cut round neckline, revealed a full, tender throat, suggesting motherhood; and all this beauty, all this rather austere plenitude, seemed to be the material transposition of the gaze radiating from the two well-spaced, unusually open, grey eyes. What depths of compassion could be read into those frank, unperturbable eyes! They had all the resignation, all the piety, all the sometimes overwhelming charity of the Slavs. She was Iaroslavna on the battlements of Putivl; Holy Russia weeping over the misery of the world. A painter might have given his Mary this gaze, in a rather sentimental Deposition from the Cross; a film director might have given it to Dostoievsky's Douce.

Rat had not seen this photograph yet. He peered over at it while mopping up his sauce. Poirier put a finger through the knot of his red tie, as if he had difficulty breathing. I was proud of the effect produced, as if I had invented that being. I was afraid that the two old sinners would see her as just another girl like the others, but no, they appreciated her quality.

'Who is she?' Poirier asked.

'The late Mme Popov.'

With my fingernail, as if by chance, I pushed forward the photograph of Penelope Barker. The general understood my gesture at once:

'I see, I see. You don't give skilly to a man who appreciates quail served on a bed of . . . on a bed or anywhere else . . .'

He glanced at Rat, who went on chewing, then he turned his blue, very dense eyes on me:

'You've played your cards very well, my boy. After all, she's an actress, the other one: she must be able to come up with what's expected of her.'

He picked up between index and middle finger the photograph that Marina had given me, and let it drop on the tablecloth.

'We're in the wrong outfit, eh, Rat? I wouldn't have minded that piece for myself at all. What do we know about her?'

'We know nothing about her, sir,' said Rat sombrely.

'Does that bother you?'

All three of us knew that it was very prejudicial to Marina that the investigation had shown that we had nothing at all on her.

'So there's nothing except the cash?' said Poirier anxiously. 'Anyway, Volsky, why would she do it? Have you . . . felt around, if you'll pardon the expression?'

He accorded his bad joke no more than a fleeting half-smile.

'I have had a word with her, sir. Very, very vaguely. She seemed interested.'

I was not criticized for my indiscretion.

'There's always Sacha de Fragance and his advertising films,' said Rat.

'Well, what about him?'

'After all, he's still in our debt.'

'He's already paid his debt three or four times over.'

'We might have forgotten. Anyway, we'd be doing him a favour: a filly like that! He takes her on under contract. She gets used to the high life. She doesn't cost us a franc. Then that's it: Sacha doesn't need her any more. She finds herself back in the street, if not actually walking the streets. With a bit of luck she'll have bought a Jaguar on hire purchase . . .'

'Her second, to judge by the photos.' Half-smile.

'Yes, I suppose one could play it like that. Have you still got a hold on Fragance? He might decide to keep her for himself . . .'

'Don't worry yourself on that score, sir. One has only to say the word "Dubrovnik" or "Dubrov" . . . or even simply "Dub", and he becomes as good as gold.'

'Right. Then how much will you ask Silbert for? Fifty thousand a week, plus expenses, and you offer thirty to the wench, with a bonus of two hundred and fifty at the end? Out of

114

that she'd have to pay her own expenses.'

'We ought to pay her expenses,' I put in.

'He's right,' said Rat. 'She'll cheat on them. She'll be paid to the last cent; that will give us something on her. If she gets awkward, we'll threaten to prosecute her for forging expenses.'

'O. K. When do we approach the Fragance agency? Before the recruitment, or after?'

'As soon as possible, I'd have thought.'

'No, Rat. If she's already got Fragance in hand, she might refuse. Why did she say she would do this, Volsky?'

'For a number of reasons, sir. The money, adventure . . . She hates the Communists.'

'There are politics in this little head?'

'It's not politics. It's a grandfather shot, a grandmother taken away at night from an estate where she had done nothing but good, so they say. It's because she's White and they are Reds.'

The two Frenchmen exchanged glances. I suddenly felt very different from them. Red, White, perhaps you have to be inside it all to understand? But they were ready, especially Poirier, to try anything.

'Let's play it like that then. Before we do anything else we've got to relieve Popov of his present woman.' Poirier gave his fleeting half-smile.

'Who's he got at the moment? Let's take another look.'

The present secretary, the last of the batch, had a sullen, crude look about her, a chin like the prow of a barge, an expression of complacent vanity on her ill-proportioned features.

'What do you think, Volsky, are they just for consumption, or do they have professional responsibilities?'

'They must report back to the special section. But since Popov knows this . . .'

'Right, how do we get rid of her?'

'Leave it to me.'

'Not a "wet business", I hope?'

'No. Nothing damper than a few bouquets of flowers from an anonymous admirer. The special section won't take long to find out. Anyway, the girl will probably report it herself, to be on the

115

safe side. It doesn't matter. When in doubt, the Soviets don't hesitate: they either transfer you or bump you off. They'll transfer her. No more Chantelle underclothes for her! Mlle Turchak will find herself back in Nizhni-Novgorod, or at Vorkuta, a guard at the convicts' camp, which would suit her style of beauty.'

'Not half cunning. I say, Rat, the lad shows promise, doesn't he? Well, now the other one. Has she made contact, this Penelope?'

'I haven't had the resources to keep her under surveillance, sir. Anyway, it wouldn't be worth it. Mlle Barker can't be more than one on a list, at most. With Mlle Kraievsky, I expect something quite different.'

'That he'll really fall in love with her?' said Poirier with heavy sarcasm. But he cut himself short at once.

'Why not, after all? The sadist with the heart of gold. It does happen. All the same it would be better to get rid of the American girl.'

'I'll see to it,' said Rat. 'I'll whisper into the ear of one of Hoover's boys that, five years ago, Penelope took part in a demonstration against aid to Vietnam. The FBI will be only too pleased to put this spoke into the wheels of the CIA. They'll put her on the first plane for Oklahoma City.'

We all laughed, like old cronies, proud of having despatched the respective ladies of the two Goliaths, each in her own direction.

We left after having a last Calvados. This time, Culverin was really under way. I had sold Marina.

11

Four o'clock is perhaps late to rise from the luncheon table. My arteries felt ready to burst. There was no question of going back to the office: to do so would have been regarded as the only sin the French army cannot forgive, namely zeal. I walked back across the Seine, feeling, as usual, that I was going home. The mist coiled and uncoiled over the surface of the river like the artificial vapour used in modern opera productions; it was as if the ventilators were concealed under the bridge. The old houses along the quays looked like an almost too pretty stage set. I veered off towards the Rue de Buci. In some twisted alleyway nearby there was a competent and approachable florist. A single window, taller than it was wide, placed diagonally to save room, formed an obtuse angle with a door, designed it seemed, to keep out the portly; the sign bore the words, in simplified italics, horribly Twenties-style, *Chez Odette*; the feast day was written up on a battered old blackboard (if I am not mistaken, that day was the feast of Sainte-Claudine); the Odette in question sported a fringe of reddish hair and a heart-shaped mouth; but her roses were fresh, velvety, sumptuously odoriferous and I, who had always been very given to giving flowers, went on my way, repeating: 'I can't help it if the Danielle Darrieuxs are more attractive in this hole than at Lachaume's.'

Mme Odette had already run several errands for me; her discretion could be depended on.

'Dear Madame,' I said, taking out a weekly subscription for a month, which I paid for in advance (we had to go through the ignominy of a receipt, for the purpose of expenses), 'I am entrusting you with a delicate mission. You may expect the lady to come and ask you for the name of the sender. You will say that you don't know him. If she sends back the flowers, on the pretext that a mistake has been made, you . . .' Frisquette's address came to mind, but no, I couldn't allow myself to do that. 'Do what you like with them. After the second or third delivery, someone is bound to come and see you about them. Probably a gentleman, perhaps with a foreign accent . . .'

'The husband, M. Cyril? Or the lover? That's not a question, you understand.'

'To begin with, you will pretend that you don't know anything about it. When he has pushed you to your last defences . . .'

'Monsieur Cyril, you do say such things!'

'In the end, you will describe the man who sent the roses. Tall, thin, flushed, receding hair, swept into a duck's tail. Informally dressed. Long legs. Something of the killer about him. Repeat, Mme Odette.'

She repeated it. The portrait might or might not be recognized. If it were, all the better: it was that of Major Cambacérès, the Don Juan of the Service de Documentation Extérieure et de Contre-espionnage, ex-military attaché in the Soviet Union, recalled for incompetence; without doubt he was on the Soviet file. I was discovering my talents as I went along.

I walked as far as the *Pont-Royal*. As usual I did not have to order my Scotch. It arrived of its own accord. I sat down in the place that Marina had occupied the other evening and I said to myself that there was no point in beating about the bush, the fat was in the fire, etc., etc., that I would have to call her. I dragged myself over to the cloakroom. I hoped that she would be out with her man in blue. She picked up the receiver at once, and spoke in her liquid, metallic voice—how many times had I joked about the mercurial resonances I detected in it!

'Hello?'

It was enough for her to say 'hello' in this way to bring back all the esoteric studies I had briefly undergone at Puzo's hand. Mercury, *anima mundi*, *logos spermatikos*, ambiguous, lunar, three-cleft and mediating divinity, locus of fluidities and transmutations, power of the Word, empire of the roads, guide of souls towards their last resting-places, given to successive metamorphoses, from the neutral to the lunar, from the lunar to the solar, from the solar to the absolute. I had laughed; now I would almost see it as prophetic.

I had met her a year before. Puzo, alias Quatre-Etoiles, had organized a press conference in his small apartment on the Boulevard des Invalides. A lot of journalists had been invited: four or five had even come. A Radio Luxembourg tape-recorder was switched on in one corner. The usual crowd of Parisian spongers was abundantly represented. Puzo presided behind a modern table, of Scandinavian design, covered with bottles of port and Banyuls, plus a bottle of Madeira 'for those who like it dry' and small oval plates containing onions, *dolmas*, sprats, anchovies, slices of chorizo sausage, red peppers and, above all, pieces of herring, marinated, salted, smoked, with cream, sour, in the form of rollmops. His round, swollen head, under its circlet of hair, scarcely rose above the table, for he was sitting on a low sofa; his glasses, with their rectangular lenses, glittered among the hors d'oeuvre in an almost surrealist way. Divo, invited like myself, in the capacity of an aspiring author, whispered in my ear: 'I'm afraid of taking one of his cysts for a *zakuski*.'

'Ladies and gentlemen, etc.,' Puzo began, reading in his monotonous, hermaphrodite voice, from a paper in front of him, 'we are gathered here today to speak of erotic literature, a pleonasm that already betrays to what point this meeting is indispensable. For, indeed, instead of taking a stick to us and ham-fistedly driving us back into the ghetto of pornography, censorship, if it had any sense at all, would realize that literature is erotic by definition, that there is no such thing as non-erotic literature, that the only difference between, for example, a mail-order catalogue and a *nouveau roman*, lies in the absence or presence of Eros. In Russian, the very word for novel also applies to what the French call a *liaison* and the English an *affair*. Thus although the bourgeois conventions of Western society have forced poets to transpose their properly erotic inspiration into the hypocritical vocabulary of sentimentality, and even into

119

that of institutions, can one not see that it is Eros who lends his polish to those moons, his movement to those cascades, his wild scent to those flowers, with their stems dripping sap, his post-coital sadness to those yearnings of anticipation, his trepidation to those adventures, his sleep to those couplings? You buy a book of theology, linguistics or nuclear physics, and it is only when finding an insignificant footnote referring, for some reason or other, to the reproduction of the species, that you feel, with a satisfied quiver of your whole being, that you have in your hands a work of literature. In every reading, whatever it may be, we seek, however much we may wish to hide it, a single thing: the more or less direct, more or less disguised evocation of Eros, to whom we owe life, that battery whose energy is transformed into light only by the coitus of those two more or less opposite poles we call the sexes. Two conjoined bodies become, as we know, phosphorescent. To recognize the literary omnipotence of Eros is merely to accept the facts. Yet it takes a certain courage, which was lacking neither in the author of the *Song of Songs*, nor in the Racine of *Phèdre*, nor in the Flaubert of *Madame Bovary*'s hansom scene, nor in the Baudelaire of *Les Damnées*. That the Tolstoys of this world should be hypocritically pleased to denigrate the Eros of art merely confirms what is inevitable, I would even say more nobly, fatal, about it. Eliminate Eros and you will have neither peace nor war; he knew this very well, he, the author of that charter of anti-eroticism, *The Kreutzer Sonata*—a super-erotic work. I beg you, then, to consider that we have met here to demand recognition for so-called erotic literature. Not merely its citizen's rights, but also its letters patent of nobility. Allow me to introduce to you . . .'

He then named the specialist writers who honoured us with their presence: a very dapper old gentleman; a fat, pale-looking woman who had been in turn pickpocket, Dominican nun, and bawd, and was accompanied by a skinny, frightened secretary; an English-speaking, untidily dressed individual from the Near East, exhibiting a chest of hair that would have been the envy of King Kong. Then he named the Chinese representative of a Japanese publisher. Then he presented Divo and myself. Then he asked the journalists to recite their names. Lastly, he turned to a young woman perched on a bar stool, her face in the form of a heart left in the shadow by the dim lighting, her bare knees and gleaming boots struck by the horizontal light, her back arched prettily backwards, her pose both unaffected and unprovocative.

'As for Mademoiselle,' Puzo continued, 'she neither shouts nor writes, she neither commits nor is committed, she is content just to be. And if I have asked her to join us this evening, it is as a pledge of reality or, if you prefer, as an exhibit, so that we might not lose sight of what is the essence of our search, so that, among so much inspiration, inspiration itself should be represented, in short, ladies, gentlemen, etc., as an object, the object *par excellence*, the Sex Object.'

The Sex Object smiled sweetly. Torrents of smoke rose to the black-painted ceiling. It was an unfurling of literary obscenities—less and less literary indeed, as the evening wore on—with detailed borrowings from the worship of Attis, from Hindu or Bulgarian practices, from the history of the Golden Ass, from the *Story of O*, from Aretino, from *Genesis*, from the Orphic cults, from lavatory graffiti, not to mention such diverse contemporaries as Messrs R. P . . ., J. P. . . ., F. F. . . ., de M . . ., and even, which certainly shocked Puzo, from de G . . ., simply because it was impossible not to speak of him.

During the entire evening the Sex Object opened her mouth only once, and then to ask if a window might be opened, which I hastened to do; but since Puzo wanted me to close his heavy black velvet curtains once more, a mere thread of freezing air passed through the assembly, like an invisible razor blade, at neck-level.

I, too, said nothing. I was not horrified, but I felt not a little sick all the same in the presence of this unbuttoned intelligentsia. Divo, lying back on a sofa, a pointed smile on his lips, sipping his Madeira and nibbling a pickle, looked so completely unconcerned, so manifestly above all this mud bubbling around him, that it was indecent. Then, suddenly, he found a systole of the collective logorrhoea into which to interpose, like a small grenade, some half-dozen words, which he didn't take the trouble to explain (he was not, in any case, asked to do so) and

121

which took on, in view of what followed, a meaning that, if I were even more superstitious than I am, I would call premonitory. He had just delicately spat out an olive stone into his fist and, leaning towards the low table to empty the fist into the ashtray, he placed in that fortuituous silence of a second's duration (an angel is passing, say the French, and the Russians: a cop is being born):

'Eros? A door. Nothing more.'

Shortly afterwards the Sex Object decided to leave. I left with her. We walked in the street, breathing in with delight the Paris air, which seemed, by comparison, pure.

I had fallen in love with her, with that freshness of feeling that life gives us only two or three times, with that very strong, very vibrant intuition of mystery and miracle that is every human being, but more particularly every woman, and more particularly that woman. I hardly doubt that love—what we have called love for some centuries—is in reality a sum of complementary feelings (affection, desire, tenderness, friendship, possessiveness, literature) focusing for some reason or other on a single person, but it also happens that, for a limited time, the amalgam appears to be homogeneous, and then one is no longer conscious of components, only of a perfectly successful resultant. Jules Laforgue must have reached something like this conclusion when he wrote that it seemed to him that his English betrothed did not have female organs. I know what he meant and it is a great joy.

A would-be writer and a budding actress share so much: the lust for glory, the showing off, a certain lack of modesty, parallel views on art, an equal passion for words. In addition to that, we shared a common ancestry. We said very little about it, being somewhat embarrassed or intimidated by that sublime race of barbarians to which we knew we were attached; but our internal systems of reference were partly the same, as also were our atavisms, supposing that such things exist.

I picked Marina up at the Buttes-Chaumont, delighted to throw myself for a time into the cosmodrome of showbusiness, and pleased with myself at walking off with this marvel. We dined at the *Boucherie* or the *Charbon de Bois*, we listened to songs at the *Ecluse* or the *Galerie 55*; then I walked her back to her apartment; we parted with a handshake that left my fingers scented. We got on perfectly; she talked little, but was a good listener; what I laughed at, she smiled at; always even-tempered, always on time, always softly gleaming, like a lovingly maintained musical instrument of precious wood, she had only two peculiarities: she would not go out on Saturday evenings, and it was difficult to force her to let me pay for her. To avoid painful discussions, she would pay me back in ties, which I again paid for in flowers from *Chez Odette*: this made everything three times more expensive, and was quite delicious.

One day, I bumped into her at the Russian Conservatoire where I sometimes hung around to brush up my Russian, chatting to the old *grandes dames* I'm so fond of. Between two *pirozhki*, a nonagenarian baroness told me all the gossip about Marina: she was a good girl, of good family, but what a temperament! Morality made no provisions for such a temperament. The baroness herself . . . One has to understand these things: not everybody is born to be a nun. All the same, there are limits, and it seemed that Marina cared nothing for limits. At that moment Marina was moving around at the other end of the drawing-room between two old ladies with whom she was being quite adorable, showing the most attentive deference. I gave no credence to the baroness's gossip (yet there were those mysterious Saturdays . . .), but it did not matter: from that moment the amalgam was broken. To know, even to imagine, a Marina who was not inaccessible unbalanced the proportions of the feelings that I felt for her: desire stood out from the rest, and swept everything before it.

Next time we went out I put my arm around her shoulder. She gave me a look, in which I thought I could read irony, but she did not withdraw. The same evening I entered her room, mad with sinister joy: I had the feeling that I was at last going to revenge myself. On whom? On what? I did not analyse my feelings. And then the unforseeable happened.

I won't go into details. But at a certain moment, Marina said some endearment to me in that common language that we almost never used together, the mother tongue, the language of

123

religion, ritual, spirituality. It was not only the language: the word she chose, however ordinary it may have been, suggested more ineffable links, a relation beyond choice and pleasure. The more she called out to me, the more I found myself incapable of going towards her. When she opened her arms to me, she looked and sounded like my mother: she gave me the body of a five-year-old. What right had she to profane the language of truth, of my truth? Was not French good enough to communicate agreeable, inconsequential matters? Hearing a naked woman speak Russian was close to incest. I beat a retreat, while Marina tried to console me.

Marina lived in a small apartment on the ground floor of a modern building in the Avenue de Suffren. A long, windowless corridor, lit by neon lights concealed behind cornices, with a concrete floor covered with carpeting so thick that one sank into it half-way up one's ankles, ran between the numbered doors. I rang, or rather I buzzed. Behind the spy-hole I imagined Marina's mercurial eye. What concerned me most at that moment was not so much my two-month-old lapse, as my evident need to establish at once those relations of *dressage* without which the contact-informant relationship is not possible. To win trust, to get a hold on, to keep a tight rein, sometimes on the contrary to give extra rein, to pretend to allow oneself to be duped in order later to find occasion to give an extra turn of the screw, to feel enough real sympathy to foresee reactions, but not enough to get involved, to regard the informant as a mere utility and, under cover of human relations, squeeze him till the pips squeak—I had learnt all this long ago, I had practised it on a small scale with some success (little feeling, but not too little; much curiosity about people, but not too much: an ideal motto for an intelligence officer); this, however, was the first time that I was in charge of an operation of such a size and the circumstances were not to my advantage. It was my own fault of course: why had I fixed it in such a way as to get Marina recruited? To see her again without facing humiliation? In the hope of finding an opportunity of redeeming myself without seeking it too laboriously? To compensate with my new authority for an unforgivable fiasco? Or were there other reasons, even more difficult to admit than these? Even after the curetting of heart and brain that is sincere religious confession, I find myself incapable of answering these questions.

She let me in, gave me a whisky, sat me down on a pouf (she had bought it at the Paris mosque), stretched herself, sideways, on the narrow divan that also did service as her bed. In this odalisque-like pose she looked more than ever like one of those dolls that can be pulled about into various sinuous curves—no angles. She was wearing a black jersey and slacks with violet flecks. Little Ripple, Drop of Oil, Slav Gioconda, Eternal Feminine, Olga Orloff, Marina Kraievsky, future spy, she looked at me in silence. The crystal goblet was heavy in my hand.

Two months earlier, I had hardly taken in the décor. This time, I did not miss a thing: my eye ran over the hessian curtains, the rugs on the walls (I don't know much about them, but it seemed to me that they came from Brussels rather than from Bokhara), the mobiles hanging from the ceiling (made of wood, metal, cardboard and silver paper), the small abstract paintings on the doors, cheap presents from painter lovers who had preceded me (with more success) in this chapel, various knicknacks (seven jade elephants, three ivory monkeys, a Spanish doll, a *matroshka*), books with thick, modern, multi-coloured leather bindings, or dirty, well thumbed paperbacks, with notes in the margins (plays), the cheap, modern incense burner, which threw out a sickly-sweet smoke, the fringed shawl dotted with sequins, thrown over the futuristic armchair, the miniature refrigerator decorated with Chinese dragons and, in the corner opposite the door, the mandatory nineteenth-century icon representing the Saviour, face and hands alone visible through the gaps in a solid silver cloak blackened at the folds, but carefully polished and reflecting the reddish light of a lamp placed beneath it in such a way that its crimson shade projected the light on to only part of a low table encrusted with mother of pearl and a part of the rug, the rest of the room remaining in shadow—listing all these details, I said to myself, allows me to avoid the placid, gilded eyes of the Little Idol of the place. However, I had to speak.

Some twenty possible openings occurred to me. But in *medias res* seemed more suitable to my dignity as a 'novelist'. So I made myself as comfortable as I could on that devil of a pouf (Marina did not take her eyes off me) and said: 'I have a business proposition to put to you. It involves compromising a member of the Cheka.'

As I spoke, I imagined the Leninist Popov, with his long skull, his thick ears and his knickerbockers in that starlet's room, scented like a Hindu temple.

'What for?' she asked.

I had always found it interesting and profitable to trust my informants, to give them the impression that they were my accomplices and not my serfs.

'If everything works out for the best, to turn him round.'

'Meaning what?'

'He'll stay where he is, pretend to go on working for the KGB, but in fact would be working for us. If that fails, he may ask for political asylum as the price for coming over. He would then tell us all he knows. That wouldn't be bad either. A third possibility, still quite a pleasant one, would be to discredit him with his chiefs. He's a dangerous man, and it would be very profitable to break his career. Like a viper's back: one blow from the spade, Marina.'

Why did I add this platitude? Marina made no objection.

'You'd take photographs?' she asked.

'Not if that embarrasses you.'

It is good to treat the informant with deference until one has begun to pay.

'I imagined something of the kind. What sort of a man is he?'

'A killer,' I said, gravely. 'Not your honest do-it-yourself killer, a killer by proxy, a man with a great future, perhaps the future boss of the KGB. He's a scientist, too.'

'Is he a member of the Party?'

'Of course.'

I tried to put myself in her place: a White—with that mixture of fear, hate and fascination that the Reds exercise over us; an actress—a part to play; a man's woman—a man to 'possess' . . . But she was also an artist, who had other interests in life than

126

dangerous, dirty operations of this kind. I fired with both barrels:

'He's a Red, Marina and we'll put a price on his head.'

She had not thought, it seemed, about this aspect of the question.

'How much?' she asked, at once surprised and allured.

As d'Artagnan said, it was going to be a tight game. It would be easier to carry out my orders to the letter, but it seemed to me that a little understanding, perhaps even comradeship, might produce better results than the hard-headed cynicism of my two mentors. First I outlined the official terms of the contract:

'As long as the operation lasts, you'll get 30,000 (old) francs a week. If you pull it off, you'll also get a 100,200 or 300,000 bonus, depending on results. It's not a goldmine, but all your expenses will be paid. On top of that you'll get . . .'

I managed to get up off the pouf and take a few steps around the room. I stopped in front of a small mauve and yellow painting, quite well executed, hanging on the bathroom door. I turned my back to Marina.

'On top of that, you'll get a professional engagement which will seem like the chance of a lifetime. I don't know if the role will be of interest to you, but a big international firm will make you a lucrative offer. This will enable you to leave this dog-kennel and take out a mortgage on an apartment overlooking the Bois. You'll also be able to buy on credit a car, furs, a wardrobe, to dazzle other possible producers.'

Marina did not know the habits of the secret service; she could not have guessed that we were trying to get a hold on her, but there were in my little speech five deliberate vaguenesses that she would have to notice if she was to be at all gifted in a job in which everything is done through hints.

I turned round towards her and, in passing, I glanced at the icon hanging over the sofa. What must He have thought of what took place so frequently under his very eyes? I gave a slight hypocritical shudder. The idea that what was now taking place was scarcely more respectable did not occur to me.

In spite of everything that the word 'engagement' means for an aspiring actress, Marina had neither blushed nor paled. She

127

rested her chin on her little fist. She asked me quietly: 'An engagement of the most temporary kind?'

She must have understood what I meant by 'other possible producers' and perhaps even the words 'on credit'. But appearing rather than being, proposing rather than doing? Had she understood that this chance of a lifetime would be better refused? I could hardly go further:

'It would be up to you.'

She changed position, reclined on her back, her hands behind her neck, looking up at the ceiling. Dreamily, like an actress asking a playwright about a character, she murmured: 'Tell me about him.'

I gave her a short history of Popov's career and a description of him. Orphaned as a young child, a hard worker, succeeding in everything, able to see the way the game was going twenty moves ahead. A man of action rather than doctrinaire. Totally devoted to the cause, to the Party, to the Country, which, for him, amounted to the same thing. Indeed, he and his job were identified in his mind. Scruples: none. Humour: none. Indifferent to the *dolce vita*. I stopped for a moment. Should I tell Marina about Popov's sexual proclivities? If I did, I ran the risk of frightening her, but also, unless the gossips were lying, there was a chance I might tempt her. If she were not properly informed, she might mishandle the situation, panic perhaps, when the business was already under way. I was not old enough to play the honest man losing *a priori*. Without embarrassment I went and sat down beside Marina on the divan. She moved over to make a little more room. I opened my briefcase and took out the photograph of Mme Popov: 'His wife.'

With a finger-tip, the actress traced the almost masculine line of the eyebrows, the strong, but feminine line of the neck. Her face took on an expression of overwhelming compassion—some secret, Slav participation in the bringing to birth of the world. She was already playing her part, her chin trembled . . . And then her features relaxed, resuming their usual poise. She handed me back the photograph: 'Sorry, Kiril. I'd have liked to help, but I can't do that to such a woman.'

'She's dead, Marina. Dead of exhaustion. Popov is Blue

Beard, Henry VIII and Ivan the Terrible rolled into one.'

I took out the other photographs: the harem. It was fascinating to watch Marina scrutinizing the sixteen faces one after the other, moulding on their features her own, whose adaptability seemed infinite: her eyes grew bigger, her jaw thrust forward, her nostrils flared, she resembled each of these females in turn. It was as if sixteen masks, at once similar and dissimilar, were being placed over her features *from the inside*, like a dresser changing a shop window. I felt like applauding.

'They took it in turns,' I explained. 'Not one lasted more than six months.'

She looked at me with a trace of anxiety—professional, not feminine anxiety. 'Am I supposed to be like them?'

I did not answer. I showed her the last photograph: that of Penelope Barker, shoulders thrust back so as not to fall forwards. Marina burst out laughing, with one of those childish, yet superior laughs that did not really suit her.

'Who is she?' she asked.

'She', I said, 'is your competitor: Madame Goliath.' Again the tinkling, artificial laughter.

'Secret Agent Kraievsky,' I interrupted, 'we've discussed the money: I think you should treat the matter seriously.'

However pleasantly I made it, this remark sounded pedantic in my ear. But the fear of ridicule is unworthy even in a semi-professional. I could not miss the opportunity, given me by a laugh I did not care for, of asserting my authority. Marina stopped short, as if she had suddenly become aware that today my attitude was different, that I was no longer 'warming myself' at her. Any other girl would have made fun of me. But Marina, too, was a professional. You don't laugh in the director's face. She looked down gravely, as if to apologize for her unseemly behaviour. When she looked up, a moment later, what I saw before me was a quite new face, the blank, vacant face of an actress ready to get inside the part offered.

'Falsies of that size wouldn't look natural,' she objected, without a trace, I believe, of irony.

'You don't understand, Marina. It's not a matter of falsies. The important thing is to get this man to *love* you. He killed his wife and he is revenging himself on all the other women. I'm not interested in your being one of these dolls to be tortured, one of these *dames de voyage*. I imagine he loved his wife: I want you to replace her. Preferably, without dying.'

A trace of fear appeared in her eyes. She was beginning to feel that there was danger in the business, not a romantic danger—kidnapping, Lubianka prison, a bullet in the back of the neck—but a concrete danger in which her health, her physical and mental integrity would be at stake.

'Now, I understand,' she said, in a voice that came from the chest, her Russian voice, though in French. 'I understand you.'

She slid her feet to the ground, sat up, reached for her Russian cigarettes, which lay on a Moroccan table, lit one and smoked it, her hands remaining almost all the time clasped between her knees, in a pose reminiscent both of a well-behaved child and of a sphinx. I did not like her smoking: the Gioconda does not have her lips fastened leech-like on a cigarette-butt. No doubt I could at that point have asked her what she 'understood' about me. Perhaps I didn't want to know. Some sort of hydras stirred in my unconscious—then dozed off again.

'Supposing,' said Marina, 'I get this man to "love" me, though I doubt if he's got the time for that. But, anyway, supposing I did, and I survive. What am I supposed to do? One night of love per atomic secret? Or am I supposed to play at converting him to Western democracy?'

'You gain his trust. For the moment that's all I'm asking of you.'

She stared at me and, for the first time, I told myself that she had the eyes of a serpent! I thought, too, that if Popov really did take the bait, it was more than likely that we could force the choice on him: cooperation or expulsion. Love is an infinitely more powerful lever than sex.

'You will talk to him neither about secrets, nor about politics,' I continued. 'You hardly know that he is a counsellor at the embassy, certainly not that he's a major in the KGB. You will become indispensable to him by whatever means seem to you to be most effective. From time to time, you will report back.'

'To you?'

'To me. Do you think you're able to do this?'

She stubbed out her cigarette and, her eyes fixed on the wall before her, gave a deep snigger, not exactly vulgar, but a bit crude, quite outside her character, already suggesting the sardonic old woman she would one day be.

'Able!' she repeated.

The rest of our conversation was about bank accounts and telephone numbers. As I was about to leave, she asked: 'What's he called?'

'Popov—I told you.'

'I mean his first name, his baptismal name.'

The word 'baptismal' made me laugh. There was little chance that Popov had ever been baptised. Anyway, did she need to know his first name?

I gave it to her. I can now guess the use she must have made of it that evening—not without effect.

12

In Russian there is a three-syllable word meaning 'presentation-of-noblemen's-daughters-to-the-Tsar-so-that-he-may-choose-a-wife-from-among-them'. What a fine language Russian is! In French, we were reduced to talking of 'contact'.

Poirier reappeared and agreed with Rat that it would be better to make the 'contact' at a diplomatic reception, because that was the best place to meet a diplomat. I had a different plan, which was rejected on the pretext that the doctrine forbade the mixing of two quite distinct schemes. I suspected other reasons: Poirier, the old wag, hoped to act as Marina's escort and exercise *jus primae noctis* over her. I respectfully pointed out to him that it was no use Marina meeting him, that anyway an individual as well known as he could compromise everything before anything had been started; his eyes, which had brightened up at the prospect, dulled over again, perhaps forever; I was almost sorry for the old boy when he suddenly accepted my arguments, in a moment of lucidity that was not perhaps solely professional. It was decided that Marina would be entrusted to a certain young diplomat on whom Rat could exert pressure; I myself would witness the 'contact', but at a distance. Poirier was already thinking of setting up a camera in Marina's apartment; Rat dissuaded him from this: to begin with, there was very little chance that Popov would be hooked so quickly, and even if he were, he might prefer to take his conquest to his own apartment; moreover, our budget was not unlimited, and we would already have to pay overtime to the two retired gendarmes who would shadow them.

We then had a heated discussion as to Marina's supposed

identity: Marina Kraievsky, grand-daughter of a Tsarist general? Olga Orloff, young, up-and-coming actress? Or some quite imaginary French girl? I favoured the first solution; Rat, the last; Poirier, who was there only in the capacity of a consultant, insisted on the second:

'If you use her real name, you break the back of the enemy's work. On the other hand, we think we know that Popov has never been interested in anything but Russian meat. For reasons of security? Possible. But perhaps he's only turned on by Russian women. Personally, I think we have to play the Holy Russia line. What's more, Orloff really sounds like a princess: perhaps that's what this *mujik* would like.'

'We could dress her up in Russian costume, complete with bandoliers,' said Rat.

I told Marina of our decision; she seemed surprised. A reception is not a masked ball. But what actress could refuse a disguise? Instead of bandoliers, she suggested a red *sarafan* and a white blouse embroidered with cross-stitch. I reported back; Marina's suggestions were not well received. The West is full of informed Kremlinologists, but as far as Eternal Russia is concerned, one is still at the stage of samovars dispensing vodka in the shade of cranberry trees. General Poirier could have recited from beginning to end the roll-call of the Central Committee of the Communist Party of the Soviet Union, including their patronymics, but he'd never heard of a *sarafan*: for him, a Russian costume was a toque, a fur coat and, underneath, a black, tight-fitting tunic, with bandoliers—of course.

'Even for women, sir?'

'Don't try and be clever. A Russian costume is a Russian costume.'

I reported back.

Marina agreed that the costume could be pleasantly stylized, that in fact there was no reason why Olga Orloff should not appear in the cranberry genre, and we worked out a rather successful compromise: a toque of beige riding cloth fringed with white rabbit skin, a close-fitting coat of the same, over a black fancy *cherkeska* forming a dress, white muff and, of course, boots, high-heeled red boots. In lieu of a personal inspection,

Poirier was allowed to see a photograph, and found 'the bridal dress' to his taste. He gave a fleeting, rather nostalgic smile.

I collected Marina to take her to her meeting with the young diplomat, who was a baron of sorts, I think. We walked there. From time to time I glanced in the direction of the pink profile under the white fur and admired its calmness. The air was cold. A purring Citroën DS was waiting for us at the rendez-vous, and its driver was shivering politely on the pavement. I hoped Marina would lean on my arm so as not to slip in the ridges of frozen mud we had to cross, but she stole away from me with significant haste. I did not insist: I, too, wanted to avoid the vulgarity of an ambiguous relationship; I was the case officer and I was supposed to 'manipulate' her only in the figurative sense.

'Here's the parcel,' I said to the diplomat, glancing at his red nose.

'The p-parcel?' he repeated blankly, stammering with cold, obviously already tamed by the toque and what was under it.

I gave a brief nod and walked away. I reached the *Lutetia* a little later. The usual crowd was there. I saw a hundred people I knew, including Puzo, flitting and spinning round like a fly, through whom I was introduced successively to Ambassador Z . . ., a little old gentleman of the *ancien régime*, with a rather squeaky voice, and to two cosmonauts, one male, the other female, the second of whom grasped my hand in the most merciless way. I then moved around among the different groups, looking either for Marina or for Popov. I saw her first, surrounded by a swarm of actress-hunters. It was impossible to remind her of her obligations; I gave up. Lastly, on the landing, between two potted orange-trees, I found my Popov, in conversation with a rather well-known physicist. It was the first time I had seen my game so close. I could have touched him, spoken to him, looked him in the eyes, breathed in his smell (I have a remarkably developed sense of smell); I immediately withdrew, so as not to be noticed.

He was wearing a rather too long navy-blue jacket, rather too short grey trousers, a white shirt with fine beige stripes (the points of the collar being slightly turned up), a blue tie with a white pattern on it, big red shoes gleaming with polish.

His left hand was stuck in his jacket pocket with the thumb outside; his right hand was gesticulating, independent of his body, fingers stiff as in karate. For every sentence spoken by the French scientist, the Russian discharged twenty, with that technique of verbal cataract that we have already noted. Unfortunately, my ear is not as good as my nose: I could hardly hear his voice in the surrounding hubbub. But I could see very well what was happening: one of those hard sells that deserve to fail, but which, indecently, succeed once out of ten. The physicist's *Weltanschauung* was beginning subtly to change . . . Bravo, Popov! I looked for the eyes under the domed forehead, with its excess of skin that he moved up and down in folds, and found them more quickly than I expected. Were they actually looking at me, by any chance? Had I sought them out? Had they registered me? I still did not know, and this very ignorance brought home to me his superiority over me. Until then no such comparison had occurred to me. But in that single, perhaps distracted movement of the eyes I read a message—which, indeed, I hastened to forget: the message was that I had before me an incomparable professional, whereas I was no more than a dilettante of average gifts. Indeed, this did not make much difference to the stakes: in our job, a little luck, or a little intuition, sometimes compensate for a vast difference in merit. I concealed myself behind a favourable back.

The temptation to get myself introduced by Puzo—who, no doubt had already met the new counsellor (they had nuclear physics in common)—came and went. Rather than run the risk of being noticed a second time, I decided to leave altogether. After all, no one needed me. I returned to operational head-quarters, prosaically set up in my apartment: this gave me two telephones on my bedside table.

'Well, we *have* become important!' Frisquette remarked, with heavy irony.

'It's a direct line to the Elysée,' I retorted.

She pouted. She didn't fancy the President of the Republic.

The telephone rang. Shadow 1 reporting back: the man had returned home to the Rue Barbet-de-Jouy. The telephone rang again. Shadow 2 reporting back: the girl had arrived back at her home in the Avenue de Suffren. Should he hang around? It was damned cold out there. No, no, go home. (Extra hours ate into the budget.) The telephone rang again. General Poirier wanted to know how far we'd got. I knew nothing myself except that the two parties had both got back to their respective homes. We surely weren't expecting love at first sight, were we? The telephone rang: Marina. At last.

Apparently the young baron with the red, turned-up nose had not comported himself too badly. He had cornered the Soviet diplomat on a staircase and, propelling Marina in front of him, and hurled her, so to speak, at the target:

'Ah, Counsellor Popov! Congratulations! Delighted to see you again! What's the weather like in Moscow? Monsieur Igor Popov. Mademoiselle Orla Ogloff. I mean Olga Orloff. Must have seen her in the cinema. Drugstore advertising. Capitalist methods, but a pleasure to the eye . . .'

Marina had been surprised by Popov's build. She had imagined him tall, and there they were, their faces almost on a level. His exaggeratedly developed torso made him seem taller at a distance, but shorter close to. And those shoulders! (Parallel bars, of course, and the rings). Arms that almost filled the sleeves of the jacket! (The horizontal bar). He had not taken his eyes off the girl's face as he absent-mindedly shook the young man's hand. Then he took the cigarette out of his mouth—so he smoked? Since when?—and, blowing out the smoke without too much regard for the young woman, he had merely said, 'Oh, yes?', in an indifferent tone of voice.

One felt oneself becoming insignificant, Marina said, in face of this self-assurance, those badly ironed collars, the vigilance of that inexpressive gaze. Having taken his time checking the visible part of her charms, which had done so much for drugstore advertising, the counsellor stuck the cigarette back into his mouth, accorded them a collective nod and forged ahead.

One would have had to resist him physically to stop him leaving. Marina and her young diplomat had thought it best to stand aside.

'But it might be a feint, Marina? He might get in touch with you later.'

'I'd be very surprised if he did.'

'Will he recognize you if he sees you again?'

'I don't think so, Cyril.' (What affectation! She always used the Russian form, Kiril). 'He looked through me as if I was painted on glass. I had no reality for him. No weight, no colour, no sex.'

'You can't be so sure.'

'But Cyril, one can feel things like that,' she said wearily, as if she had already told me twenty times.

It was nerves. I sent her off to bed. I wondered whether I should give up the whole idea of Culverin. Such discouragement was ridiculous. Was it my nerves, too? Hadn't I just told the general that we never expected love at first sight? I telephoned Rat. Let him call Poirier if he wanted to: I had no accounts to render him.

Rat did not hide his disappointment. But I had been disappointed before him and I attacked him roundly. To begin with, Popov's secretary had only been recalled the week before. Secondly, I had always told him that a contact made in full view of the entire diplomatic corps and the Tout-Paris could not have any result. However strongly Popov might have been impressed by Marina, Rat could not expect him to leap at her in the middle of the *Lutetia*, could he? My recriminations worked: in the end, Rat muttered between two clicks of his false teeth: 'Well, my boy, you think we should go back to your plan?'

'Unhesitatingly, sir.'

'But what if he recognizes her?'

I told him what I had in mind.

'Ah, yes!' he said. 'That might come off. It's dirty enough. But the chap is a pro: he cannot but be suspicious.'

'Let him be suspicious. So long as he doesn't break off the whole thing . . . That's all we have to be afraid of.'

'And you think the girl . . .'

I hung up half-an-hour later, exhausted and relieved: Culverin was still on the rails and I was more and more its master.

13

I telephoned Moutins at his office. We arranged to meet the following Thursday at five. The Tuesday before that, at seven o'clock, he was waiting for me in a café on the Place d'Italie. Moutins was mine. I had brought him into GEST. Tolstoy had tried to filch him from me, but I had managed to keep him by using him to Rat's direct advantage. He didn't bring us much: all the same, the names of young militants were welcome currency to Military Security. They came into the army full of generous enthusiasm for tossing a spanner into the works; they were given time to start a cell, then quietly netted. Given the prolonged interval between the time they had said their manly, but moving farewells to Comrade Moutins and the time they found themselves in the glasshouse, no suspicions had yet crossed the Party's own intelligence section. One day, Comrade Moutins might get a few knives in his belly; meanwhile, he had his uses.

He stood up when I came in. An athletic body; a small, square, angular head, the bone structure showing through the delicate pink skin; fair, smooth, rather long hair; clear, wicked-looking eyes behind gold-framed spectacles, with a double bridge. Unclassifiable. The delicate glasses suggested an intellectual; the green overalls, with slanting pockets over the stomach, a foreman; the voice was rasping, the inflections working-class, the vocabulary carefully chosen from the serious newspapers. In fact, Moutins was a former sergeant-major who, given a reasonable education, could easily have become an officer, though perhaps a somewhat unsavoury one. But 'natural' parents, his own natural laziness, and gifts more suited to brawling than to mathematics had condemned him to non-commissioned insignia forever. He suffered from it to a degree unimaginable for a civilian. His behaviour in public was correct, but in private he treated the top brass as old fogies, the reservists as dead-beats and the shavetails from the Military Academy as hopeless cretins. He always travelled in mufti and at his own expense, so that he could travel first class. Unlike his peers, he drank little, but when he did drink it was expensive whisky and Champagne (*brut*). He belonged to book clubs and even read the books he sent away for. At first, relations between us had been rather strained, largely because he regarded me as a desk officer and I wrote him off as nothing better than a hatchet-man. But subsequent events put him at my mercy, or at least I made him think so. During the Algerian war, he had deserted to throw in his lot with the Secret Army Organization (OAS), not so much on principle as because he hoped it would provide him with more frequent opportunities to satisfy his thirst for killing. Captured almost at once, he did not have the leisure to bag anything more than one useless old Arab and a busybody civil servant working for the riot police. The army would have been delighted to let him escape and even rejoin his unit, with no questions asked. The negotiations were entrusted to me. I was making plans for my own return to France and I found the opportunity full of possibilities. I politely explained to Moutins that he would be court-martialled and shot if he did not agree to work for the special services. He agreed enthusiastically: he was ready to make mincemeat of whatever was sent his way. Unfortunately, I did not find much for him to do. I brought him as part of my dowry, as it were, to GEST, and he was ordered to infiltrate a para-Communist organization, which made him an agitator specializing in youth movements. He was bored. To keep him quiet, we gave him to hope for a transfer into our Action section—which, of course, did not exist.

'Good evening.'

In mufti, he took great pleasure in violating the normal military courtesies under the pretext of secrecy. And, of course, it would have been too much to ask for him to call me 'Monsieur'!

'Good evening, Monsieur Moutins, good evening.'

I sat down opposite him. He imperiously summoned the waiter and asked me what I'd have. I shook my head (the same scene took place every time I saw him) and I asked him what he wanted to drink. Whisky. The waiter was sarcastic. No whisky here. (Oh blessed time, when something of our amour-propre remained!) Moutins then raised his shoulders, obviously horrified: what else can one drink? And you, what are you having? I ordered, as always, a glass of Beaujolais. Moutins resigned himself to doing the same, on one condition: that he would leave his glass untouched.

When our drinks had been brought, he leaned over towards me—the exhalation from some expensive aftershave reached me from his pink cheeks, meticulously smoothed over with a safety razor—and gave his report. Evening classes in Marxism-Leninism; a handful of Monarchists duly wallopped in the Latin Quarter; a dialogue opened with a parish priest in Boulogne-Billancourt. ('He's not a bad old boy, he lent us the church club projector and in exchange we stopped breaking his stained-glass windows with our sling-shot—don't worry, they were artistically unremarkable'); a certain Emile Santon, who had just got his travel warrant, duly loaded with pamphlets concealed in the false bottom of a harmonica case ('and here's my advice: some blithering non-com shoves his great hoof through the case "by accident", or I'm done for.')

I listened to him and I told myself that his fidelity was not unshakeable. He loved the army more than anything in the world, of course, but given his capacity to love, that meant nothing. Moreover, he also hated it for having refused him the ennoblement of the epaulette. It was not out of the question that the Communist apparatus might seduce him by its total pragmatism. There, too, there were brawls and regimentation, but one didn't have to pay one's respects. There, too, there was idealism and action, but the one didn't exclude the other—on the contrary. It could only be a question of time. One day, the Emile Santon he would give me would have been deliberately sacrificed by the authorities of the Party to maintain contact and to set up a deception channel, the ultimate weapon of modern times. Meanwhile, Moutins had not yet forgotten one of his friends torn to shreds in Indo-China because the munitions case he opened had been booby-trapped by Communist women workers. And it might be good to remind him that the forces of order still held him at their mercy. So I moved the conversation round, alluding in sympathetic and yet cynical terms to one of the OAS killers who had just been shot by the security police.

'It's always the same, Monsieur Moutins: the bosses get out and it's the little fellows, like you and me, who get caught. Our best policy is to do as we're told. Neither to the right nor to the left, as the natives used to say.'

To humiliate him with my self-possession, I ordered another glass of Beaujolais.

'I don't know how you can drink that stuff.'

'Monsieur Moutins, I don't have your refined tastes.'

I then explained to him what I wanted him to do, without telling him why. He agreed without asking any questions. We were about to take our leave of one another, standing on the pavement, in the cold, when suddenly, as if on an after-thought—he considered it elegant to deal with serious subjects in this fashion—he said:

'By the way, I've just been sent a new member who seems a bit suspect. You will not be unaware that the Party has set up a permanent system of surveillance and denunciation. It wouldn't surprise me if this bird wasn't there to grass on me.'

'What do you find suspicious about her?'

'She's altogether too willing to be of assistance—with the filing, secretarial work . . . If I listened to her I'd leave all the methodology to her. And at the address she gave me—a big block of working-class flats—nobody's heard of her.'

'What's her name?'

'That too. She's got a Russian name. Now the Russians are either Red, in which case they stay in Russia, or they're White, in which case what's she doing in my outfit? I questioned her about surplus value and the three rules of the dialectic and she hasn't a clue. She bored the pants off me with stories of the injured and the insulted of the earth . . . What I usually get are girls who want guys and guys who want to play with balloons

141

without paying for them if they burst. It's my job to paint for them in lively colours the climate of social injustice in which they live (it's true, in fact, there *is* injustice).'

'What's she like?'

'A chassis like that! Her boyfriend must have his hands full.'

'Doesn't she turn you on?'

He shook his head.

'It's against their principles. Relationships between militants must always be above suspicion. Noses to the grindstone.'

'Does she have a job?'

'She put down "student", but she doesn't seem to do much studying. At meetings, she turns up before anybody else and she's always the last to push off. While the speaker's shooting his line, she hangs on his every word, as if he was revealing the eternal verities, and yet there are plenty, I'm telling you, who are not much cop at public speaking.'

'Does she talk to the other kids?'

'Not too much. She calls them "Comrade". They don't like it.'

'Why not?'

'They think it's too formal.'

'How does she dress?'

'Jeans, red plastic jacket. Like the others. But she doesn't wear them like the others. And she has a funny accent . . .'

'Russian?'

'No. Suburban working-class. I don't know . . . she's too good to be true.'

'What's her name? I'll try and find out if there's a file on her.'

'Kraievsky, Marina.'

Too good to be true! He had no idea how right he was. The character created by me, a 'novelist', and played by her, an actress? Marina could not fail to have that excess of being and that dearth of existence that Moutins had observed. Anyway, his suspicions did not worry me, on the contrary: if he saw her as a spy sent in by his bosses to keep an eye on him, he would be all the less likely to make any connection between her presence and the little job I had just given him.

He reported back two days later.

He had arranged a meeting, waited twenty minutes in a drawing-room resembling, if he is to be believed, the foyer of the Opéra and stinking of polish, then had been firmly piloted by a big guy in civilian clothes along several corridors and two flights of orange-painted stairs to a white cube of an office. The door was opposite a square window looking out on to a garden. Its back to the window and facing the door was a dark, polished work-table, covered with a sheet of glass; on the glass was a black desk-pad containing a sheet of pink, immaculate blotting paper. Behind it, a black plastic and chrome chair. To the left of the visitor was a bare wall, at the foot of which was a chair similar to the one behind the desk. To the right, a wall with another door; on this wall was a calendar representing a combined harvester in a corn field; below that, a metal filing cabinet. Curious, that combined harvester in the middle of winter. In front of the table was another plastic and chrome chair. Behind the visitor, to one side of the door, was a map representing, from white to black and intermediate greys, the progress of atheism in the world. Moutins, who did not read Russian, had first believed it to be about the progress of Communism, but Counsellor Popov had obligingly explained the difference. The Soviet Union was almost entirely white; France, grey; the United States were almost entirely black, oppressively so, with just a few pockets of innocence in California and in the state of New York. I had asked Moutins to observe everything most carefully, not with any particular purpose in mind, but because I wanted to imagine my adversary in his lair: that, too, was part of the prehistoric technique of bison hunting, through the image, another similarity between the master-spy and the novelist. No portraits? Only a combined harvester? That struck me as incredible: there must, at least, be a picture of Lenin somewhere. No, no portraits, but on the table a black bronze statuette about a foot high representing . . . 'It may strike you as being *exoteric*, but I swear it's true . . . a crouching monkey holding a human skull in his hand.' I was delighted with this detail: a similar statuette had stood on Lenin's desk in the Kremlin, and it was in contemplating this that Popov got his political inspiration. Better than a portrait, a symbol: it made the man that much more interesting.

The counsellor in charge of relations with youth, women and the peace movements—Moutins, of course, knew nothing about Popov's secret functions—made an excellent impression upon his visitor: 'If French Communists were like that . . .' (Yes, we would have to get rid of Moutins soon one way or another, I thought.) No hot air, none of your woolly-minded optimism. A mission, means, a tactic: there was a man! When Moutins had politely explained that in approaching the embassy directly, he was not trying to short-circuit the French Communist Party, Popov said, without a trace of emotion: 'Why not?'

And then, as if suddenly a machine had purred into action in the domed case of his forehead, he started to sermonize in a style that was already beginning to become familiar, though I had never heard it with my own ears.

'With us, efficiency alone counts. The French Communist Party is the instrument—an instrument—of the Party full stop. Now wait for it: I don't say "of Moscow;" I say "of the Party," the Party as a united movement. Moscow may bungle things. Paris does so more often than not. But the Party cannot, because the Party is history and to say that history's got it wrong is meaningless. History is speeding along on its rails, and the Party in its unity is the driver, covered in sweat, shovelling coal into the boiler so that we'll get there more quickly. I'm very fond of the French Communists, they do what they can, but they aren't of much interest to me. What interests me are guys like yourself, those who aren't members, those with energy, those who work for the future, those who couldn't care less about the Paris commune. I know the leadership of the French Communist Party: they're petty-bourgeois. I don't need to tell you that *L'Humanité* is a paper for convinced old popinjays. I've nothing to do with them and their convictions: they've resigned themselves to petering out quietly in capitalist society. What I need are guys who don't mind slushing about in the slime, quite determined they won't drown. I need the people's commissars of tomorrow, and you are going to get them for me. If it means treading on the toes of some boyar comrade, then too bad! I'm not interested in some rosy future; it's the battles to come I'm interested in.'

He spoke excellent French, full of idiomatic expressions and subtle hints—perhaps too full. He even had the right gestures. One would have thought that he had been born in France, but one would not have known in what province or precisely in what milieu.

'So what can I do for you?'

Moutins began to stammer: lectures, film-shows, collective farms . . .

'No, I don't want to talk to them about collective farms. They're bored with collective farms. So am I. To begin with, they don't work that well, because our peasants are as stupid as yours . . . ('Did he really say that?' 'And how! He can't stand the bumpkins!') . . . And anyway, what can tales about Russian peasants mean to French workers? No, I'll talk to them about Fidel, and about one of his pals, called Che. I'll give them a lecture on urban and rural guerrilla warfare. You can call it whatever you like so as not to frighten the true believers. For example: "Class relations in urban areas of semi-capitalist type." Yes, put that. But I'll talk to your young people about Molotov cocktails: it's more exciting that the *sovnarkhozes* of the same name.'

He agreed to give two talks, on successive Saturdays, which suited my purposes nicely. Moutins did not venture to ask me the point of the operation. I gave my instructions to Marina, who was keen to make up for her humiliating failure at the *Lutetia*, and I reported back to Rat. Stroking his pursed lip with his forefinger, he said:

'It may work or it may not. So far, I must admit that you have piloted your ship very well. As far as the filly is concerned in any case. She's just agreed to join Fragance, without a contract. Bravo!'

I did not really deserve his congratulations. Learning that Marina had not cottoned on, I almost betrayed my annoyance. Then I shrugged my shoulders: if the silly goose, blinded by ambition, was incapable of forgoing a dangerous opportunity, so much the worse for her—and so much the better for my reputation as a case officer. Perhaps she had not grasped my advice, perhaps she had chosen to take the risks, perhaps she had coldly

145

decided to exploit us (after all, until she contracted debts we didn't really have a hold on her: it was up to us to give her expensive tastes, and up to her to resist their temptations). Her real motives never occurred to me.

The following week dragged slowly by, I remember, with exhausting translations to be done in the field of pneumonics. Again and again I was tempted to go to Popov's talk, not so much to listen to him as to see him, to make our relationship in some sense less Platonic. I had not forgotten that blind look that he had thrown in my direction and which I still felt as a trace sticking to my face. It disgusted me and I was asking for more. But I resisted the temptation: I wanted neither to risk being recognized, nor to rouse Moutins's suspicions. The Saturday came. The two ex-gendarmes took up their observation posts and I settled in at home, having forbidden Frisquette my door; she was half intrigued and half annoyed.

'I hope she has a gift for it at least!' were her parting words, accompanied by a scowl.

14

Billancourt. Not Boulogne, no, the real Billancourt, with its prison-like factories. The factory is a cathedral, Malraux once suggested. Perhaps he had never been to Billancourt—though he didn't live far away. He lived at Boulogne. As if to make the uniformity of these long horizontal halls, painted grey, orange or green, walled in by the fairy Electricity, more dispiriting still, there crop up, here and there, little old houses, squatting at the end of their little front gardens, and charming little hovels with windows replaced by newspapers, the only vertical, the only rebellious things in sight.

The school, too, was older than the factories, an honest school of the old school, resembling a prison, not a centre for community multisex recreational activities; it was built out of good grey stone, with black wrought-iron railings over the windows and, on the outside walls, a belt of fading inscriptions alluding to obscure laws passed in 1881. Inside, that irreplaceable smell of children's sweat and chalk dust, the smell of our communal schooldays. Fears that nothing will ever exorcise still lurk in corners (the headmaster's study—the broom cupboard), yet how brave and free one feels when walking as an adult along those nauseous corridors, with their multifarious traps (clouts administered at random around one's head by the teacher, big boys sticking out a foot to trip one up); how blithely one sits at these Lilliputian desks, how one searches, among the violet ink-stains and the carved initials, for one's own name, even if the classroom was another classroom, perhaps even the school another school—but there has never been but one single school in the world.

Popov's arrival was greeted with applause: he had arrived straight from Paradise, and the faithful, despite all their hereditary distrust (their honour), responded to prompting. Shouts broke out: 'Long live the Party! Long live the USSR!' Popov, still in profile, a leg still raised, muttered over his shoulder, half-joking, half-serious: 'Belt up!'

Then he faced them. His hands in his trouser pockets, and a jerk of the chin: 'Sit down.' In front of him I imagine a collection of young people, three quarters boys, a quarter girls, faces prematurely hardened, prematurely envious, giggly or querulous, on the defensive, successfully hiding a purity still almost intact, I think, which was of no interest to the KGB officer and would not have interested me either at that time. Among those forty or so chiselled, young French faces, was an oriental, smooth, polished, silky, gilded face on which, instead of their cynicism, masking their hesitant, chaste hope, there glowed a Nietzschean, Nichevian, Nechaevian faith, one of those faiths that move mountains—with the help of a little dynamite; a face like an oil-lamp, shining steadily among the shadows and incoherent sparks.

Breaking the silence that fell at last, Popov went on:

'There's this story in the Bible. This guy St Paul arrives in a village and performs a pseudo-miracle. The local bumpkins, who still believe in the gods, want to make him a god just like that, hey presto. But he wasn't so daft and said, like I did just now, "Belt up. There is no god but God." Well, you, who know that there is no God at all, have no excuse. You think they perform miracles where I come from . . . of course they do. But you don't need gods for that. All you need is men. One of our writers, Ehrenburg, tells in his memoirs of a Burgundian winegrower who believed that in Moscow they had better wines than in his village, because the Bolsheviks had won. If you believe that, you still believe in the gods.'

The reports came in and filled in the picture. According to Moutins, the young people had been struck at first, pleasantly enough, in fact, by the severity, the intransigence of the speaker. 'He's a strict one, you can tell,' they said afterwards, admiringly. Moutins himself had been more interested when he

148

turned to urban guerrilla warfare, with its three phases—provocation, intimidation, consolidation—and, above all, by the technical details of kidnappings, the systems of levying, the bank raids . . . and the summary executions, the nails scattered in front of the mounted police, the oil poured in the path of the motor-cycle police, the petrol bombs thrown at armoured vehicles. Marina—she showed me the notes that she had taken in an ecstatic handwriting—had recorded a large number of blasphemies, an excessive number, I thought: if she was to be believed, Popov thought it was more important to seize a cathedral than a telephone exchange. In Latin America, perhaps; as far as France was concerned, I could not help but see this as a somewhat hysterical distortion of political perspective. Anyway, his listeners' attention had wandered when he turned more particularly on the Jesuits (his information was rather out of date on this point), and was won back only at the end:

'That's all I have to say to you, this time, anyway. Next Saturday, we'll talk about rural guerrilla. First, exploit the kulaks; then dekulakize them. Those who want to come back, come back, whether you are Communists or not. Now, a word for the fellow-travellers. It's all very well coming some of the way with us. It's all very well coming and sniffing under our tails. But I'm warning you: limping fellow-travellers with blisters on their feet, who need a drink every ten minutes, we can do without them. We march with a spring in our step. And after one or two excursions, you have to make up your mind: either you become like us, or you turn against us. And if you turn against us, we will mow you down.'

He had tried, with his usual style, to disgust the less good and to light up the hidden fires in the others. He worked on two levels: from among those whom the agitator had inflamed, the master-spy might later choose collaborators.

He had each of his listeners introduced to him individually, answered their questions with feigned bad temper, calculated to inspire respect. When Moutins suggested that they repair to a nearby café, he replied contemptuously:

'I'm not interested in idle café talk.'

He moved off, alone, goose-stepping his way along the

pavement, when Marina caught up with him: 'Comrade?'

He did not stop.

'What?' he asked, his head barely inclined towards her.

This was it. An enterprise set in motion four months earlier was at last reaching the start of its active phase. Ah! How I would have loved to have been there, but the novelists of reality do not enjoy the privileges of fiction. In fact, I still don't know whether this scene took place as she described it. How would Balzac have borne it if Grandet or Rastignac had been his sole sources of information? And how would he have evaluated their information, I wonder?

To begin with, I had no way of knowing whether Popov would recognize the Olga Orloff he had glanced at for a few seconds, three weeks earlier, wearing make-up and costume as different as could be from what she now wore. It depended on his eye, which I had no means of judging. I did not want to gamble either on his recognizing her or on his failing to do so, therefore I worked out two different tactics: Marina was to choose as appropriate. I could only hope that she would mislead neither herself nor me. Popov, she told me, went on walking, glancing at her with his glazed eyes from time to time, without betraying the slightest trace of recognition.

'Yes, you were in the front row. Well?' he snapped impatiently.

She was not used to being treated in this way. The arrogance of impresarios, the wandering hands of assistant assistant-directors, the handkerchief occasionally dropped by the great panjandrum himself, which has to be scooped up in haste without knowing whether the contract would follow—that she knew. I don't suppose she minded, she may even have liked, the feeling of being weighed up by the whole rabble of agents, press attachés, photographers, cameramen, boom operators, seedy reporters. But these 'whats?' and 'wells?' this way of stripping her of everything that had such value for others, could not fail to unnerve her. If she could at least have believed that Popov didn't care for women! . . . She felt the tears pricking her eyes. Fortunately, the theatre teaches one to reject self-pity and to put up with any audience. She would play for this Red boor with as much care and integrity as for a Royal Highness or for M. Gautier. She came off well. I had provided her with the scenario, but she had to select the quotation herself. Trotting along beside him, she poured out to him with that absolute lack of modesty possessed by *monstres sacrés*:

'You've no idea what it meant to me to hear you say: "the revolutionary has neither father, nor mother, nor job, nor property, nor wife, nor place to lay his head: the revolutionary has only the Revolution." You have said with your Russian voice what I have always felt at the bottom of my Russian soul.'

All that, which sounds grotesque in French, comes off quite well in Russian. No author can resist someone quoting him. As for the change of language, had I not myself experienced its magical power? And it was natural that this magic, so full of inhibitions for me, because I saw Russian as *the* sacred language, should, on the contrary, release Popov of his, because he had always used it to speak to his women. The effect that I had anticipated did not fail to come about. Popov began to relax. Besides, to speak Russian in Boulogne-Billancourt was a complicity in itself.

'You went for that?' he asked abruptly.

He was walking faster and faster. She started panting—seduction is not easy when you are out of breath. He suddenly stopped at an intersection: 'You go this way. I go that way.'

She put her hand on his sleeve: 'But I'm going that way, too. No, really!'

He recoiled and snapped: 'No. You go this way.'

It was an order, given with excessive brutality, and therefore comic. But the character Marina was playing could not burst out laughing, she could only accede, bow out, literally, from the waist like a real Russian woman, and let Popov move away towards the métro with his characteristic step, redolent both of the conquistador and of Groucho Marx.

He went underground at Marcel-Sembat, took the Montreuil train, changed at Molitor, then again at Duroc, got out at Varennes, and walked to 79 Rue de Grenelle. It was Saturday afternoon: most of the offices were in darkness. Guards disguised as orderlies stood up as he passed. He paid no attention to

151

them. He crossed half-lit drawing-rooms, whose marble door-ways, over-decorated candelabra and glowing mirrors gave to whoever moved through them the illusion of staggering into the night of time, the night of history, towards a bright window at the far end. He reached the pool of light and climbed the small modern staircase—orange-coloured, fitted carpet, bare walls, white wall-brackets spreading a harsh light—which led to the reassuring efficiency of the third-floor offices. An orderly leaned over the bannister, arms outstretched, suspicious.

'Good evening, Igor Maximovich,' he said obsequiously.

Popov let himself into his office with his own key and turned a switch, which emitted a dull sound. The room was flooded with light: Popov loved watts, a lot of watts. He shut the door behind him and went over to the metal filing-cabinet, which he opened with another key. It was there that he kept his Secret files. The Absolutely Secret files were kept in a strong-room. He picked out an empty yellow folder, an unused pink form and took them over to his desk. He took out a fat royal-blue thick-nibbed fountain pen from his pocket and unscrewed the top. He reflected for a moment, then, on the outside of the folder, in the top left-hand corner he wrote, in thick Nile-blue letters, *Zmeïka*. Then he opened the folder, and put in the form with only the first items filled in.

PSEUDONYM: Zmeïka
NAME: Kraievskaia
FIRST NAME: Marina
PATRONYMIC: (he left this blank)
NICKNAMES: Orlova, Olga
RECRUITED: (he filled in the date)
FUNCTIONS: Informant
SPECIALITY:

After another moment's reflection, he wrote quickly: 'General information, the psychology of the fellow-travelling intelligentsia, prospection of possible recruits'. Then he closed the folder and, returning to the filing cabinet, placed it under the letter Z, the eighth of the Russian alphabet.

15

Marina reported back her second failure even before the shadows had called me. I took a deep breath. A volley of reproaches rose to my lips, but I controlled myself: 'You still have next Saturday.'

I heard myself say that in a flat, hollow tone, like a child trying not to cry.

'I'm sorry, Kiril,' she replied, contritely.

And then, after a silence that I refrained from relieving, she continued, in a voice that was already livelier: 'Shall I be free for this evening, then?'

'Yes, yes, run off to the cinema and see a spy film.'

Still her mysterious Saturdays. I sent the two shadows home and waited some time for a call from Poirier: it did not come. I should have expected as much: the toy that he had not been able to wind up was already beginning to bore him. I called the Shopkeeper. I told him that the plan was being carried out as arranged, that contact had been made, that no recognition had been indicated, that the 'client' and the 'interested party' were to meet the following Saturday at the same time.

'Which of them asked for the date?'

'They will meet again at the client's talk, sir.'

'So phase B hasn't begun yet?'

'Oh yes. They spoke Russian.'

'Did she get things moving?'

'Unfortunately not, she didn't have time.'

'Why, was there a fire?'

'The client made off. He seemed in a hurry.'

The sound of salivating.

'Look, my boy, you know how I have trusted you . . .'—he trusted no one—'But look, here we are today already . . . your protégée had better make her connection next Saturday, or else . . . Silbert is getting impatient: he wants results. I explained to him that in this job, it's not like in guerrilla warfare: one can't go into the village and kill off a few old men in time for the report to HQ, but you know what he's like: when he says results . . .'

I knew. My protégée did have an interest in getting things moving and I had an even greater one.

This week was no less tiresome than the previous one. Tolstoy looked at me with a sparkle in his ocular icebergs:

'Well, Volsky, we seem to be writing fewer reports? Less bla-bla-bla, anyway. Take care: your pen will rust. We haven't decided to become a man of action, by any chance, have we?'

And his eye nailed me to an invisible board decorated with a baroque scroll surmounted by the well known motto: 'A fizzling spook always turns into a hack'.

I hung around in Mme Krebs's office: she was attacking her national Japy with her cerise-coloured fingernails: 'Ah, Mme Krebs! How I would love to be your typewriter!'

She swelled up inside her mauve or brown bodice; she looked as if she might burst like an overripe plum: 'It would be good for my spelling, lieutenant.'

I went into the translators' office. Puzo, just back from the States, assumed airs of pained virtue. When asked what was the matter, he sighed deeply, shook his round head, and finally revealed in a murmur that the Allies did not appreciate the Head of State.

'I'd have been astonished if they had,' M. Alexandre remarked in his *basso-cantante*. 'They put him in the saddle once, he falls off. They put him back, he sends them packing.'

Divo could not resist adding: 'Do you know the story? Kennedy lands at Orly and says to him: "Fine weather you're having here." And he answers: "Thank you".'

Puzo looked up to his closed cupboard. It was as if his eyes had turned into a blow-lamp, pierced the iron door and met the centre of the brain, the ego, the self, the very kernel of his idol, in order to make his pathetic excuses. All this seemed to me rather foolish at the time: I'm not proud of the fact.

I also had for that week a 'toothache' in my diary, indicating that I had my periodic lunch at the *Cuisse de Grenouille*.

'Well, boyo, what's cooking?'

Lester looked out of sorts. I allowed myself the pleasure of attributing his mood to the recall—obtained at last—of Penelope Barker. With his plaid jacket (red, orange, brown, no green), with his winks directed at the legs of every girl that passed—sometimes he made a mistake and eyed the dignified calves of some respectable matron, then, realizing his mistake, he would give a dismayed whistle and throw me a contrite glance—and with that kind of hypocritical sincerity and sincere hypocrisy that constituted the secret of the character, he aroused in me by turns irritation and a kind of envy. What must it be like being, not a tight-rope walker, a dilettante of the balancing pole, but a Texan, who had scarcely scraped the mud from his boots, a sorcerer's apprentice waving his broom in the air, and to feel behind the least, or greatest, of his blunders, two hundred million men, the richest, the strongest, the most innocent in the world! I have changed my tune since then: America—and good luck to her—is not so simple, but at that time I envied its Goliath complex. We joked as usual about the exploits of our respective star agents.

'How's Popeye, Major?'

'Popeye? Still popping. And Greek Fire?'

'Still firing.'

I avoided talking about anything to do with Culverin, but Lester, between the camembert and the compôte, his head bent over his plate, raised his eyes to ask me, between chews:

'Anything new on the Russky counsellor?'

'I . . . Ah! You mean Popov. Well, as you know, C. E. isn't really our job. I caught a glimpse of him the other day at the *Lutetia*.'

'Impressions?'

'He's no beauty. Short legs, a gymnast's torso, sugar-loaf head. Are you interested suddenly? I thought you knew everything about him.'

'You never know everything about a Commie. Especially a

comic Commie like him. Ha!'

He dropped the subject. I concluded that our Allies hadn't abandoned the trail. Perhaps they had wheeled up a Penelope Mark II. Would that explain Popov's indifference to Marina? I didn't think so. I don't know why, but the myth of an omnivorous Popov seemed to me more and more simplistic. I might not be pulling it off, but I really believed I was going about it the only possible way.

That Wednesday I went to see Marina for a last briefing. We had seen each other several times during the period (I no longer have the dates) and I detected a certain formality in the way she treated me, which I interpreted as an actor's sense of discipline: it was something else, of course, but how could I have seen that, I who knew no other judge but myself?

That day she was wearing jeans and a man's shirt tucked in. I asked her how she had been feeling since her failure some days before. It is good to humiliate an informant sometimes, but one shouldn't exaggerate.

'I feel,' she said, 'even more firmly harpooned. Deep down inside me, that's what I really like: being ill-treated, rejected . . . Slav masochism. My little decadent aristocratic admiration for the brute force of world Communism as represented in that muscled plug-ugly simply increased when he spat on me. He's got me on the end of an elastic: the harder he pushes me away the faster I come back.'

She was eloquent, almost chatty, when she talked about her roles.

'Yes, Marina: your role. But what about yourself, aren't you afraid to confront him again? To look him in the eye? Think about it.'

She looked surprised.

'It's not like that. At those moments, I'm her.'

'So Diderot was wrong?'

'Oh! There's always the one who observes, but that one has no emotions. Diderot had not read Stanislavsky. Don't worry, all that's part of the job. I'll roll around on the pavement at his feet if necessary.'

'And physically? Do you find him attractive? He doesn't

repulse you? That might explain his . . . lack of enthusiasm.'

'Physically?'

She thought about it.

'I wouldn't say he attracted me. But if I understand your analysis of the character aright, he only likes to crush people. *His* attraction must be in inverse ratio to that of his partner.'

She paused, then went on: 'Have you any other stage-directions to give me?'

It was a way of getting rid of me, without even offering me a Scotch. She was humble, and therefore beyond humiliating. I left.

Back in the street, I shivered, penetrated by the damp more than by the cold. Mounds of dirty snow were piling up at the side of the pavements. I was overcome by that lassitude, that very special discouragement that every kind of 'novelist' knows when his characters cease to function according to the programme laid down for them. One has a strike, a mutiny, on one's hands; the plots themselves seem childishly contrived, the dénouements improbable and one feels quite small, quite inadequate, before such a titanic task. Yet Marina had not refused to obey; on the contrary, she seemed fascinated by the part that I had given her and which was growing and flowering inside her with perfect coherence, our author-actress relationship having found this piquant form of expression. Who, then, was disobeying me? It took me some time to discover what was really obvious enough: it was Popov.

We would see on Saturday. I called on Frisquette.

But Frisquette was beginning to irritate me. She had a perpetual gaiety, subordinating everything to love and pleasure, which, at first, had enchanted me, but which now I found tiring. This was because I only played at being liberated, while she really was one of those delicious, innocent, natural, eighteenth-century libertines which, of all the European races, the Latin is alone capable of producing. Towards the end of the evening she was finding me an old stick-in-the-mud, and I went back, I think, to sleep in my own apartment.

Thursday saw a welcome comic interlude. Puzo arrived at the office later than usual. He paused in the doorway and, when we had all looked up and taken note of his mandarin's figure, his legs slightly apart in their over-wide, skirt-like trousers, he declared, finger raised: 'Tonight, we celebrate!'

The glaucous depths of the eyes seemed mysteriously disturbed—'The siren eyes of our national Puzograph,' M. Alexandre called them. That day, all the monsters of Loch Ness seemed to be swarming in those liquid eyes. Puzo slumped into his chair.

'And wherefore, young man of the fair curly hair?' M. Alexandre enquired.

Puzo's grey hair was straight and thick as macaroni.

To Divo, who had turned his keen bevelled gaze upon him, Puzo replied: 'It's the happiest day of my life!'

He took out of his pocket a sheet of expensive-looking writing paper, unfolded it and read the contents *sotto voce* (his lips moving as if in prayer), folded it, put it into his wallet, then hastily withdrew it again, smoothed out the creases and put it back into his jacket inside pocket. Of course, we were cruel enough not to ask him to share his secret with us. With one accord, we plunged back into our translations and, since Puzo began the same ceremony some twenty times over and since we feigned indifference as often, we got more work done for GEST that day than in a normal week. It is true that Puzo's idleness compensated to some extent for our activity. Every quarter of an hour he rushed out into the corridor after somebody else to invite to his 'celebration'.

'Anyone would think we were going to the Rich Man's Banquet,' remarked M. Alexandre.

He was more right than he realized: many of those invited were in a hurry to get home and refused the honour. Puzo, on the verge of tears, pleaded with Tolstoy: 'Captain Tolstoy!' The title filled his mouth like a meringue. 'This is the happiest day of my life. I can't get sloshed all by myself.'

Tolstoy, who, generally speaking, avoided him, had pity on him, or perhaps his rather cruel sense of humour was responsible for the following stratagem: 'All you have to do is tell them who the letter is from and they'll be falling over each other.'

158

Did Tolstoy know, then, who the letter was from? I did not note this detail and the fact is that at a quarter past six the little apartment on the Boulevard des Invalides was chock-a-block: from the lieutenant-colonel to the peons, the whole of GEST was there. Only Tolstoy had excused himself: a meeting at the Division! Glasses in hand, we fell silent, stifling our nervous giggles. Puzo began in his flat, unmusical voice:

'Colonel, sir, officers and engineers, ladies and gentlemen.' (This time, there was no 'et cetera'.) 'Today, as I think I have already told you, is the happiest of my life. I serve France to the best of my ability.' ('Only dirty foreigners like us would venture to speak of serving France,' Divo whispered in my ear.) 'But it is not to the insignificant services that I have been able to render my country that I owe the honour that has befallen me today. There is a side of me, an important side, that some of you are still unaware of.' ('That would be difficult,' M. Alexandre, seated behind the speaker, whispered to me.) 'I am not only a humble translator, a modest interpreter . . .' (he was the second-best, if not the best in the country), 'I am also a man who receives' (in a theatrical gesture he plucked the paper from his side pocket, where it had been carefully placed within reach of his right hand) 'letters like . . . THIS!'

He unfolded the thick and still slightly crisp sheet of paper. He put on his spectacles. His face reddened slightly. He read (I quote from memory):

My dear Pudelevich,

Thank you for sending me your latest work, *La Camisole de Chasteté*.

Although it belongs to a genre for which I do not feel much affinity, I have followed with interest the misadventures of your Y and note with pleasure that the loyal companion of former days now has a perfect command of our beautiful . . .

(Puzo turned the page.)

. . . French language.

In particular, I was very touched by the few words that

159

you were kind enough, my dear Pudelevich, to inscribe on
the fly-leaf.

> Your very devoted . . .

Puzo pronounced the name in an inaudible murmur, his breath
escaping with reverent economy. Then, in an emotional voice,
he returned to the more intimate passages of the letter. *My dear
Pudelevich*: he was called dear . . . twice! *Thank you*: to imagine
that *he* should have any need to thank him. *I have followed*: a
number of minutes of that precious life had been devoted to
him. *The loyal companion*: he was accepted as a brother-in-arms,
his unshakeable loyalty was recognized. Ah! Truly, this was too
much glory, too much joy! Tears formed like lenses magnifying
the poor man's eyes. *Our French language*. Was not this 'our' a
certificate of naturalization? (For my part, I read it as precisely
the opposite.) So he had not forgotten the day when abuse was
heaped so mercilessly—but so benevolently and so deservedly
—on some insignificant secretary for his phonetic spelling! *I was
very touched*: 'I, Pudelevich, a miserable expatriate, a poor little
scribbler who am not worth the mud on his boots, I touched
him!' *That you were kind enough*: what sensitivity! What delicacy! As for *your very devoted*, 'I know it's only a formula, but
note that he put *very*. Indeed does not the rest indicate that this
apparently empty formula is in reality crammed with sincerity
and truth?' And the handwriting! 'Just think, written with his
own hand. His fingers have touched the sheet of paper . . .'
I was incapable at the time of grasping how holy such a
passion was. Like most of us there, I could hardly hear the
words 'the mud on his boots' without wanting to shout out in
exasperation, or to roll about laughing. But make no mistake:
for soldiers and civil servants there was no question of doubting
publicly the true content of these dithyrambs. As for the form, it
should not be forgotten that distinguished spirits had opened
the way. The Head of State himself had pointed out to one of
these biographers that Joan of Arc did not have as much merit as
he, and a Catholic writer, comparing the president of the
Republic with Jesus Christ, opined that the former lost nothing
by the comparison. I had recourse to tickling the back of Mme

Krebs's neck with the end of a plastic straw; Rat coughed on his cigarette and, in order not to catch anyone's eye, stared at the little surrealist and pornographic paintings on the walls. 'The sincerity, truth . . .!' From a man whose motto was 'I feign to feign all the better to dissemble'! Suddenly I caught Divo's eye and looked away at once because we had just guessed the same ignoble temptation in the other. The Head of State read everything, wrote to everybody, it was well known (one even wondered how he found the time to govern us) . . . Was not an inflated dedication on the title page of a first novel a way of short-circuiting glory? *'Françaises, Français,* I should like to draw your attention to a young author who writes with admirable style. His name is . . .'

Nothing happened on Friday.

16

On Saturday at three o'clock in the afternoon (yes, I felt dizzy, I won't deny it), I had arranged to meet my two shadows in front of a café at the Porte de Saint-Cloud. The terrace windows were steamed up. Bourjols, a red-faced Burgundian with laughing eyes peeping from behind ramparts of pale fat, offered me some chestnuts he had just bought: we burnt our fingers on them. Planacassagne, a skinny southerner, his skin stretched over flat bones and dotted with the shadow of a beard, a beret pulled right down over the tops of his ears, panted with excitement: 'Yes, sir; right you are sir.' Our mouths exhaled swirls of vapour: add to this the onomatopoeias and we could have been taken for three conspirators from a strip cartoon.

'You understand, Sergeant Bourjols. You'll take up your post at the intersection. You, Sergeant Planacassagne, will stay at the Point du Jour fork . . .!'

'Right you are, sir.'

I called them both 'sergeant' out of ignorance of the gendarme hierarchy and because they were retired; they seemed grateful for it. We left each other fairly early to give them time to find somewhere to park—Bourjols had a Simca and Planacassagne a Honda motorbike. (They used their own vehicles, and we reimbursed them for the petrol and an agreed sum for wear and tear.) Knowing that nothing would take place until after the talk, I no longer resisted the desire to catch a glimpse, if only at a distance, if only for a second, of the game I was tracking: it was like the frog hypnotizing the snake. I found a tiny space not far from the school and displayed my virtuoso abilities at parking by squeezing my 2CV into it. I had warned my two shadows that this was not to observe them, that I would leave them a clear run as soon as the client had arrived (it pays to show some regard for one's subordinates). I did without heating so as not to attract attention by having the engine running. There were very few passers-by. Above the grey wall of the courtyard, the bare branches of the plane trees rose to an overcast sky.

At half-past three, Marina appeared enveloped in a rough, goatskin coat, white flecked with black, that she must have found at the Flea Market; one isn't a Stanislavskian for nothing. Below protruded the worn legs of her jeans, ending in square-toed, black, shiny plastic shoes. On her head was a red and blue woollen bonnet, topped by a pom-pom. She had thought about every detail, right down to her walk, which was both provoca-tive and tomboyish. For a moment, I forgot which of the two superimposed characters she was supposed to be interpreting, and I thought she was exaggerating. But no: in phase C she became once more an actress. It was all as planned.

Moutins arrived next, his shoulders hunched forwards, his hands stuck in the slanting pockets of his green wind-cheater. One could sense the blood rushing through the veins under the thin pale skin; his lips were pressed together as if to whistle.

The 'youngsters' began to emerge from the walls. I find it difficult to admit it, but their thin forms, their pale faces turning blue in the cold, their angular features, their ungainly gestures, that kind of ill-bred insolence they displayed, while demanding to exchange it for the first half-way demagogic discipline they met, all this repulsed me: it was not the panic of the conformist bourgeois, but a mere shudder of contempt that I won't try to justify. Since then, I have learnt that only love is able to deal with that kind of sterility, but, at the time, I felt not the slightest sympathy as I watched all those pullovers, upturned collars, scarves, mittens, balaclavas, duffle coats file past: the poor are obsessionally susceptible to cold.

Suddenly, I saw Popov's back. He had arrived behind me, on the other pavement, and crossed the street between my 2CV and another car. *He* did not feel the cold. He was wearing a jacket over a turtle-neck sweater, no gloves, no overcoat. Of course, after 'Leningrad', he must have felt as if he were on the Côte d'Azur. One of the young men gauchely held the door open for him. He went in without thanking him. That was all I saw. Again I thought of going and listening to him, but less than ever could I allow myself this imprudence: this Saturday was our last chance. I drove off; a welcome blast of heat rose to my calves.

That day, Popov talked about Angola, Algeria, Cuba and the Russian civil war; he mentioned neither Greece nor Spain and he talked as if Mao tse-Tung had never existed. Indeed, his doctrine differed from that of the Chinaman in a number of respects: to the guerrilla who lives in the population like a fish in water (Mao), he preferred terror considered as a means of government (Lenin). For him there could be no true symbiosis between the revolutionary and the peasantry: temporary alliances, based on the logistics of one side and the greed of the other, yes. No more. 'From a revolutionary point of view, the only advantage offered by the peasant class is that, dispersed as they are over the terrain, the forces of law and order cannot effectively guarantee their protection.' In this, he was in full agreement with his audience, the hatred of the peasantry being essential to the class-consciousness of the French proletariat.

He stopped at exactly five o'clock without a conclusion. Spontaneous applause broke out. Each of these fine young fellows was longing to go and dekulakize the Beauce. Images of woollen stockings filled with *louis d'or*, haystacks dotted with semi-recalcitrant farmgirls, stirred in their brains: should they not repay themselves for their work in the emancipation of the agricultural workers (a work force whose labour was most readily exploitable)? Moutins offered a round of drinks, of course. Popov, of course, refused. He was still gathering up his papers when Marina approached him.

'Comrade, I'd like a word with you.'

'Well?'

'Privately.'

'Walk with me to the métro.'

They left together, under a barrage of scornful and hostile looks. Marina had been rejected by the group as, be it said in passing, I had expected and hoped. Bourjols and Planacassagne followed without difficulty. Planacassagne called me at home half-an-hour later. With his rugged accent—it was like a tipping lorry unloading gravel—he said:

'They're walking along the quays together, talking—anyone would think it wasn't ten degrees below. Bourjols is O.K. in his car, but on my Honda I'm freezing my balls off.'

'Where are you calling from?'

'I'm in the *Café des Sports* to warm up a bit.'

'Put it down to expenses.'

'The brandy too?'

'If you knock it back right away.'

'Right you are sir. I'll go back at once.'

'I don't want to teach you your job. You're following them in echelon?'

'Right you are, sir. We might have a bit of luck today. Maybe he'll decide to get himself a piece all the same. Not very hot-blooded, these Russkies, it seems . . . Oh! What am I saying? Excuse me, sir. I always think of you as being as French as I am.'

Fool! I hung up. I could imagine the scene. The sky heavy with snow. The river dark brown. Deserted streets. Dusk already. Two shadowy figures, sometimes overtaken by a motorbike, sometimes by a car. Was this really going to work? How I'd love to have been there myself!

Marina had begun to speak Russian at once, her very correct, rather affected *ancien-régime* Russian, but with a tone that came from the chest, an innocent volubility, with breaks in the voice: like a performance of Chekhov.

'*You* don't know what exile is. You even get to the stage of wondering whether the country you come from really exists, whether it isn't one of those imaginary kingdoms, like in fairy stories, situated three times nine countries away. If you come from Nowhere, you don't exist. You resign yourself to becoming someone else. You eat cheese at the end of the meal, even at home, and your bread over-baked, and you drink your tea very black and you ridicule everything, and you believe in nothing but intellect. But, deep in one's heart, the truth remains, like a blood-clot . . . In becoming a foreigner, you have become a foreigner to yourself. You only speak that other language, and

165

with the tongue only, not with the throat and chest, as Russian is spoken, you hardly nod, you count your small change and you are deeply moved less and less. But it's so sad . . . What is your first name and patronymic?'

'Igor Maximovich.'

'It's so sad, Igor Maximovich. Like some dear friend who begs you not to drown her with your own hands—and this friend is the real you. I've worked really hard to make myself French. But I only have to hear three notes of a Russian song to burst into tears. I see a birch tree and it's as if my entrails were being pulled out of me. A country I've never been to, where even my parents hardly had time to be born . . . There must be something very special about our Russian Truth. As soon as it gets a bit cold, like today, I feel myself coming back to life. Do you know what I feel when they serve some of our Russian caviar at a party? They may say that the Iranian is better, they may laugh and make a noise, but I just sit quietly in my corner, slowly, respectfully eating my caviar. I don't know whether it's good caviar or not, I'm too busy trying not to cry for joy. I feel even more moved when it's something more ordinary: good black bread that has germinated and grown in our black earth; I wouldn't lose a crumb of it. Or the little fish from our own seas, sprats, you know? I eat them and I say; "Good little Russian fishes, you're lucky all the same, it's Russian flesh you're feeding. Foreigners might well have bought you up." And then you come, from the Other world. I speak to you in our language (sometimes I used to think it was as dead as the Egyptian of Rameses) and you understand me. You have a first name and a patronymic. You tell me that the Golden Cockerel and the Grey Wolf from my childhood really exist. You tell me that the mother I was mourning is still alive. But then everything is alive, Igor Maximovich, everything is immortal.'

'Not exactly,' said Popov. 'The nation is more alive than ever. The Golden Cockerel and the Grey Wolf never existed and still don't exist. In their place, we have bulldozers.'

'Ah yes, bulldozers! You, too, Igor Maximovich, you are a bulldozer. Just now you talked about how the countryside is enslaved in capitalist countries and what has to be done to emancipate it. "The land in chains", you called it, and I thought of the emancipated land in our country, our damp Mother-Earth, who breathes freely through all her pores, who produces freely the good things she carries within her. All she needed was to flex her muscles a bit to crack the boundary fences. Tell me: do you think I could get a passport and go to work in a *kolkhoz*? The Jews have their *kibbutzim*? Why couldn't I do like them? That's what I wanted to ask you: get me a passport. I want to go *home*.'

Phase B had reached its zenith. Marina seemed to have found in herself the dispersed elements of the character that she had newly created. I was rather surprised that she had been able to exploit herself in this way without feeling that she was committing sacrilege. I attributed this to an actress's lack of scruple; for an actor, anything will serve, whether for mere ambition, or for artistic integrity.

'*Home*?' Popov repeated. 'And pray, why did you leave home, your ladyship?'

'I didn't leave. It was my parents! My grandparents!'

The White blithely denied herself, even with a certain surreptitious pleasure, I like to think.

He laughed and replied with a proverb: 'The cat knows who it has taken the meat from.'

At first, she said nothing. She was busy forcing up her tears. When her throat was sufficiently tight and real tears were on her eyelashes, she stammered out: 'Will there never be any forgiveness, then?'

They walked for some time in silence. Suddenly Popov said: 'You have a chain round your neck. What is on it?'

I reproached myself bitterly for not having taken it off her. A fine sight she'd have been in Popov's arms, with her baptismal cross. She answered, almost in a whisper, knowing that her character would be seen as no less plausible, if less likeable: 'A cross.'

'You believe in God, little girl?'

She looked up sharply. 'Freedom of worship is guaranteed by the constitution of the USSR,' she said. Then she placed a white woollen mitten on his sleeve and continued, imploringly: 'Get me a passport.'

167

He thought before answering. His Russian, she told me, was didactic, highly rhythmic, with exaggerated musical intervals.

'I see what you'd get out of it: the severed branch weeps for the native trunk. But what does it do for a body to graft a gangrened limb on to it? You carry gold crosses under your bodices, you ask with tears in your eyes if there's no forgiveness. Forgiveness is one of those meaningless pseudo-words invented by your people to brainwash mine. One cannot forgive. One can punish or not punish, that's all. As long as you held the upper hand, it was in your interest to make us believe that forgiveness exists, because it gave a metaphysical dimension to our slavery: when you refused it, we shook with fear; when you gave it, we suffocated with gratitude. And now that you are being pushed around yourselves, you come to us and ask for it. But we don't know what it is. If it's more advantageous to punish, we punish; if it's more profitable to reprieve, we reprieve. What would we gain, tell me, if we let you milk cows or shift manure at Skotoprigonievsk? (Yes, I read Dostoievsky too.) Would your output be worth the trouble of getting you a passport, not to mention the surveillance we'd have to keep you under for some years? Our people believe quite simply in a simple truth. You really don't imagine that we will let you bring back with you the germs of religion or doubt into those pure souls, do you?'

'I ask only one thing,' Marina said firmly, 'to shift my homeland's manure. I could take a vow of eternal silence, if you liked.'

Popov did not notice the incongruity of 'vow'. He explained patiently (he liked explaining things):

'You imagine now that just to breathe the Russian air would be enough for you. In six months—or six minutes—you will realize that all these luxuries of Western life, which you think you hate, have entered your very soul; that the Russian air cannot be breathed with your little Parisian's lungs; that you are incapable of living as part of a team, of systematically forgetting your ego in the name of the collectivity; that your paltry bourgeois freedoms are important to you; that manure, even patriotic manure, doesn't smell as good as Coty.' (He took Coty for a great perfume manufacturer.) 'Then you'll remember that you haven't lost your French nationality. You'll apply for repatriation. You'll alert the world press and your pretty little face will appear on their front pages, and you'll have done grave harm to a country to which you thought you wanted to do good. In fact, all you want is to do yourself good. Over the centuries you've learnt the habit of exploiting, and now you've found a new means of exploitation. You want to live off the people not simply as people, but as people now emancipated from you. That much said, you are entitled to lodge an application. A decision will be made.'

If Communism ever perishes, it will be through its own rhetoric.

'But it's not true, Igor Maximovich!' Marina cried. 'There must be salvation for us too! After all, Lenin had some noble blood, didn't he? You can be a determinist if you like, but you can't be a fatalist. It was we, the nobles, the intellectuals, the bourgeois, as you say, who set your snowball moving. You proletarians jumped on the waggon after it had started rolling. Between the two of us, you and I, it is I who believe the more strongly in the Revolution.'

She paused, then continued in a voice still that of a studious school girl, but now trembling with rage: 'A revolutionary must apply all his strength and all his energy to increasing and intensifying the ills and misfortunes of the people until their patience is exhausted and they are led to a general uprising . . . Hatred and abuse are useful to the extent that they drive the masses to revolt . . . The revolutionary detests and despises existing social morality in all its manifestations. For him, whatever contributes to the Revolution is moral. And everything that stands in its way is immoral and criminal.'

He looked at her, amused: 'Have you read Nechaev?'

I had carefully chosen those extracts, knowing through Algy of Popov's weakness for the little ancestor. She went on: 'Society consists of six categories. 1: Those to be killed off. 2: Those who "must be temporarily spared so that, through a series of monstrous actions, they lead the people to inevitable revolt." 3: The pigs who are running things: their guilty secrets will be systematically exposed in such a way as to transform them into slaves and to use their power to our profit. 4: The liberals—they will be compromised and used to create disorder in the state. 5: The frauds—they'll be encouraged to take up catastrophic positions and they'll serve as lightning-conductors. 6: Women.'

She stopped for breath.

'Well? The women?'

'Divided into three sub-categories; the frivolous, to be treated like the pigs and the liberals; the over-emotional to be treated like the frauds; lastly, the true revolutionaries whom "we must regard as the most precious of our treasures: without their help we will never succeed." I'm one of them, Comrade Popov,' she concluded, raising her head. 'Without me you will never succeed.'

Popov laughed without opening his mouth.

'You don't know what you're talking about. You've lived a cosy life behind walls of books, battlements of little scent bottles. You've never been cold or hungry; you've never punched anyone; and you dream, I suppose, of bombs. You're a woman: you want to strip, show yourself off, that's all. The Revolution, in your case, is merely an abuse of French sensuality. When you think of the Revolution, you must imagine Delacroix's bare-breasted woman promising agreeable evenings to the crowd of drunken bourgeois chasing after her skirt.' Marina thought she could detect some darkening of his eye, some suggestion of anger in his voice: illusions, probably. 'Or Princess Volkonsky following her husband to Siberia. But the Revolution, my dear girl, is neither the distinguished, oh! so distinguished twilight victim of December nor the tart of July. The revolutionary woman thinks neither of her noble husband, nor of having a good time. She's chaste, thin, lack-lustre, buttoned up to here, she has calloused hands, she works twenty hours a day, she's given herself up to the Revolution like a nun to her priests. It is not, believe me, a very comfortable or romantic life.'

'If there's anyone who has no right to talk like that it's you, a Communist, a Russian Communist!' she protested. 'Have you forgotten Zasulich? And Krupskaia? And Stassova? And all the others? How do you know I'm not as good as they? You are in charge of the women's movement and, at heart, you're nothing but a patriarchal mujik. I've a good mind to write to the ambassador!'

The ambassador could not have inspired much fear in this Chekist, but for the moment, Marina was supposed not to realize his true position. If he was to play the game, the patriarchal mujik could not allow himself to be accused of anti-feminism.

'It is precisely because we have had such admirable women that we know what we're talking about. They were not little flibbertigibbets, puffed up with a few exalted ideas and curious to get themselves laid, for a change, by real men.'

Communist puritanism had merely exacerbated Russian Victorianism. I had Marina repeat this sentence to me several times: it seemed to me that it marked a certain loss of control—one trick to me. Popov was, however, not slow to recover.

'I *venerate* women, but this *veneration* has nothing *venereal* about it,' he explained, using French words to clinch his pun. 'The instincts are one thing, we all have them. The Revolution is something quite different. The Revolution is a pure, sacred thing from which all ambiguity must be eliminated.'

Marina had found her way: 'That is precisely why I deny you the right to suspect me of base motives. Revolution: you have only to say the word to feel purified. You accuse me of having led a bourgeois life. Really! What do you know of my life? I went to school with holes in my socks. My mother could darn them twenty times over, they still got holes, either in the same place or in new ones. It drove her to tears: "How can you do this to me, child?" she used to say. My shoes had holes in them and the heels were worn down . I daren't kneel down in church for fear of showing the soles of my shoes. When we had soup at home it was a feast, because we could have as much as we wanted, or almost. Cold? In winter I did my home-work without taking off my mittens: if you think it's easy to hold a pen with those on! I studied without books because we had no money to buy them. I wrote on the cover of my exercise books in order to save a sheet of paper. You talk about punches, but if you're aiming at shins

171

feet are more useful than fists. "Hey, Russky! What did you eat last night? Turnip tops?" Bang, a kick on the ankle from my studded shoe. That shut them up. Even now, in the métro, I can still do it.'

I am, of course, reconstructing, abridging. Where did she get these moving little details from? Authentic experience? I don't think so. She must rather have found them in herself, harvested in those immense fields of unused potential that all artists exploit. One explores the parallel worlds in which things might have been *a little* different, and feeds one's work with them. The myth of the pelican is true, except that it relates to a parallel pelican. That is why, perhaps, one can use neither raw reality nor pure imagination: what is needed is exploration, that is to say, both a distance that dwindles and a knowledge that increases. The actress can die wonderful deaths every evening because one day she will really die. We cannot play a role or tell a story that is totally alien to us. Fortunately, *humani nihil a me alienum* . . . I often wondered where the real Marina was while this other Marina became sad, rebelled, plotted, argued . . . Offstage, in the wings of the soul? But surely it was the real Marina who handled, like an incandescent piece of forged iron, the unpremeditated inventions of her conversation with Popov. It was the real Marina who risked her physical presence at the side of this wild beast? She gave me a perfect account of the conversation, full of cool insight and precision: I got nothing else from her.

They walked upstream along the left bank of the Seine, through that icy setting that went so well with the images of Russia, poverty and revolution that they were evoking. Warmed up by a brisk walk of almost an hour, they reached the Pont Mirabeau, beneath which, as an observant poet has remarked, flows the Seine; here they turned and started to cross the bridge. Popov had lit a cigarette. He smoked with a sort of anger, holding his cigarette between his thumb and forefinger, dragging at the butt till it burnt his fingers, lighting a second cigarette with it, which he got through at the same rate. They leaned over the parapet and looked down at the water swirling around the feet of greenish bronze nudes that seemed to find the weather to their liking.

'It's funny,' Marina remarked, with Chekhovian playfulness, 'they don't even have gooseflesh.'

And, deliberately, feeling that the moment had come to begin a new movement in their relationship, she flashed a smile at Popov—her first. She did the smile again for me. It was a very Russian, very contemplative, barely feminine smile, more in the eyes than in the lips—the smile that the late Mme Popov might have had.

He threw his cigarette end into the river.

'So you don't understand,' he declared with a mixture of weariness and enjoyment, half closing his eyelids to protect his eyes from the smoke. 'You're nothing more than a fag end. You and your sort are just fag ends. Barely worth crushing under foot to avoid a fire. You talk about the privations of your childhood. All right, so maybe you *were* poor. But it hasn't made any difference. Understand that anything you can do, one way or the other, for us or against us, doesn't matter a jot. You were telling me you feel you don't exist. Do you know why? Because it's true. You have been vomited by history and, as such, are insignificant. This river cannot stop itself flowing; these bronze women cannot follow it. It wets their shins and passes on. What does it matter whether they want to stop it or throw themselves into it? You are the parings of Truth: there's no way you can appear on the table. You're like a watch that has stopped and imagines that time should stop too until it's ready to start again. Dud watches should be thrown into the dustbin! A White émigrée? But what are White émigrés? Clowns walking the tight-rope between cocaine and suicide, just good enough to drive Western bourgeois around in taxis or to get their bourgeois women dancing in pseudo-gypsy cabarets. Our intellectual cleanliness forbids us to touch you. We mowed you down fifty years ago, and now your exposed entrails disgust us. You're nothing more than carrion.'

He spoke with natural lyricism, a cool violence, looking straight ahead of him. Was he hamming it up just a little bit? I don't think so. There was not even a trace of hostility in his voice, just the certainty of absolute superiority. If he was

173

playing a part, he too was playing very close to the truth.

He turned to Marina with one of his joyless smiles:

'What do you think Communism is? "Power to the Bolsheviks plus the electrification of the countryside"? You think the state, made redundant by equality and universal social justice, will suddenly, one fine day, crumble into dust? You believe that then "all men will be happy" and "all women will give birth without pain"? You think that's how it has to be, but that it's also a good idea to stoke up the boiler so that we can get there more quickly? In short, you've been reading *State and Revolution*.'

Marina had contained herself when he was tearing the émigrés to pieces, but she failed to notice the second trap. Yet I had warned her that Popov was not exactly a run-of-the-mill Communist. I remember putting it to her very neatly: 'He's a Communist squared.' Her head was bowed under the insults. Now she looked up.

'Yes, I believe in all that,' she cried, her shining eyes fixed on the horizon, which was getting darker every minute. (I can see her from here: she was Irina, 'The Seagull' . . .) 'I believe that the golden age will come the day after tomorrow and that it depends on us to hasten its coming. I believe in a radiant future for the whole of mankind. I believe that we only have to give one mighty puff, and the whole mildewed social order we now have will collapse like a house of cards. I'm ready to sacrifice my life if it will bring it an hour earlier.'

He looked at her out of the corner of his eye, apparently satisfied with the trick he had played on her. Then, protecting the flame of the lighter with his two big hands, he lit a new cigarette. He shivered slightly—not with cold—and began to speak in a pedantic voice that scarcely concealed his internal delight. The vapour that came out of his mouth mingled with the smoke rising from his cigarette. Marina stood, hanging on his lips, freezing from the end of her nose to her feet, secretly triumphant: she was going to carry off her mission. The sky and the river had assumed the same blank darkness. The water washed against the piers, resounding under the arches. Suddenly the violet street-lamps came on over the bridge and gave to the whole setting an air of some ghostly festival.

'Have you ever thought about the word *Bolshevik*?' Popov began. 'For your information it means "member of the majority at the social democratic congress of 1903", but, apart from the fact that the majority seems, fortunately, to have been trumped up, we must look at it more deeply. Stalin—you may denounce me to the ambassador for having mentioned the old father—said: "Bolshevism and Leninism are one and the same thing." Ostrovsky draws our attention to the word: it is muscular, dense, one can bite into it. For me, it's a deep red word, nearly brown; a heavy word, suggesting heavy artillery and heavy industry. It's a word like *bombardier*, like *steam-hammer*; a word to inspire both fear and warmth. As a little boy, I dreamt of nothing else—to have the right to say: "I'm a Bolshevik." I dreamt about it more and longer than a cadet dreams of the epaulette or some American telegraph boy dreams of Carnegie's millions. I followed the thread: Pioneers, Komsomol, Party candidature, the examination in which one lays one's soul on the operating table . . . I was given my ticket. That was it. You're nothing but a decadent little Westerner if you imagine for a moment that I was disappointed. On the contrary: the initiation went beyond my wildest dreams. When I looked at myself in the mirror, pointed to myself and said, "There's a Bolshevik!", I felt I had upgraded myself. But, meanwhile, I had gradually learnt the real meaning of the word. A Bolshevik isn't a protector of widows and orphans, as you think, nor a fighter against the forces of darkness, as I once thought myself, nor a more conscious proletarian, nor a better informed economist, nor a more clear-sighted prophet, nor a more logical dialectician. These images come out of one another like our Russian dolls: all in the image of the truth, getting closer and closer to it, and therefore all true and all false, till you reach the last one, the one that no longer opens, the kernel under the flesh, the unfissionable particle, the very truth. I had wanted to become a Bolshevik, now I was one, but it was not as I expected: it was better, infinitely better.'

He smiled nostalgically, almost fondly, while continuing to look at Marina, with, she said, 'a shy, collusive, rather charming expression':

'I burst into tears. I'm not ashamed to admit it.'

He became serious again, and drew on his cigarette:

'Bolshevik doesn't mean someone who is in the majority, but someone who always wants more, whether of a majority or of anything else. When he has reached B, he sets his sights on C, and so on. Fools accuse us of changing face the way they change shirts; they do not understand that our face is precisely that: change. The *bolshak* is the highway and the Bolshevik is the one who takes the highway. We are accused of opportunism: it's like accusing the sun of shining. As you move forward, the landscape is bound to change. That's why Lenin is the greatest genius of all time: because, in fact, there is no such thing as Leninism. Marx is encapsulated in Marxism, Engels in the dialectic: they may be superseded; Lenin bloweth where he listeth. He wrote *State and Revolution*, but he also organized terror—and he also organized the NEP. The truth is that there is no truth. It is difficult to understand, it is sometimes bitter to digest, but once one has accepted it, it's magnificent. The truth is what I find in my daily paper. Yesterday's paper lies—always. Today's tells the truth—always. That's why *Pravda* is called *Pravda*. The truth is daily bread to us Bolsheviks, and just as you don't eat yesterday's bread, we refuse to eat the dry crusts of history. If there is no truth, we can impose our own. Please note, I don't say "mine". The "I" hardly exists, the "we" makes itself felt. The "we" is already a step forward, it is already a Bolshevism. We were wrong to take the word Bolshevik out of the Party name: it made some people think that Bolshevism was a form of Marxism, whereas the opposite is the case. "One can become a Bolshevik only after enriching one's memory with all the riches amassed by mankind"—Lenin. The only truth is addition. Not what one adds: the act of adding. Whoever subtracts himself from history is subtracted from history —because the only truth is history, which is a permanent addition. As one comes to each new stage, one finds oneself a bit bigger. That's what Bolshevik means: growing bigger. It's to breathe ever more deeply; to feel that one knows how big the world is and that the world has no limits. I know, you won't find that in our books, not in so many words. It's not that we were trying to disguise or encode anything, but because there are things that are worth saying only to the initiated. At each stage of initiation one sees the face of things change until the last metamorphosis, which is the right one. In fact, we reveal everything every day, in many different ways; the bourgeois don't understand, so much the better. To you I explain this without parables because you add up to nothing, because you might as well never have existed. Whatever is not more is condemned to being less. We reach towards the all, the rest of the world reaches to nothing. Believe me, it's worth every sacrifice, every vexation, what others call every crime, to find oneself on the ascending line and to know that, in the end, one cannot but win, since, by definition, we are the winners. It is not us who are the winners, it is the winners who are us. You see why the "we" is essential: *I* may get bumped off; *we* can only succeed. With every instant that passes, we come closer to the end that we shall not reach, just as the hyperbola does not reach the axis: our greatness is to be found precisely in that fact, which you, and of course many of our own doctrinaires, cannot understand. We are nourished not by the *plenty*, like you self-indulgent Westerners, but by the *more*. The bourgeois make fun of our vision of heaven on earth. They're right. Our heaven is as ridiculous as their golden age. Heaven is impossible; what is possible is progression. Not progress, progression. We are not the sum, we are the addition, do you understand that? We are not affected by the + sign, we are the + sign. It's the + sign we bear on our flag, disguised as a hammer and sickle, because it's a romantic, folksy century.'

He paused for a moment, then went on:

'You think I'm really interested in the happiness of the people? Do you think I really believe in the nobility of work? The people: I've scented them from close enough: if your intellectuals, who lament the fate of the lower classes, had spent as many days as I have on building sites and as many nights as I have in shacks, they wouldn't be so affected. Every people has the fate it deserves; it's the lachrymatory sequelae of Christianity that have made the populist jeremiahs fashionable. Poor little bearded mujiks. Dirty reactionary kulaks, yes. But so

177

much the better: it's all grist to our mill. Have you never noticed that there is no society more selective, more elitist, as they say, i.e., more aristocratic, than ours? That is because we never sacrifice an opportunity to an idea. Julius Caesar, too, was a Bolshevik.

'You must understand that we are the Tsars of the future. There is nothing more beautiful than strength, except more strength. You have only to look at our muscle budget. Have you ever amused yourself comparing two maps compiled twenty years apart? That red area that is spreading, those pink areas turning redder. There's not a single country in which our yeast is not working, in which our dough is not rising. The struggle is unequal between us because you have no yeast, no leaven, nothing but the boring *status quo*. Trotsky was mentally retarded: he wanted to declare war on the bourgeois. To what purpose? The bourgeoisies are maturing and decaying of their own accord. Their termite-intelligentsias gnaw away at them from the inside, teaching them not to love themselves. But what kind of a collectivity is it that does not love itself? Once you have really beaten yourselves, all your fine, prosperous economies, all your pretty, refined civilizations will fall into our mouths like roasted larks: *yum*! You're still sweating over problems: we have the master's book and we have seen the answer on the last page. I'll confide it to you under the seal of secrecy: *the Bolsheviks have gobbled up the world*. And that's good, that is beautiful, because it is good and beautiful that the strongest should be the most powerful. Historians go on and on about absolute monarchs; but Ivan and Peter did not have the least idea of the power that we shall hold, that we already hold. What they merely glimpsed, all your popes and emperors, your Charlemagnes and Charles the Fifths, the whole world held in a single hand—what they saw was a vision of our future.'

His left hand, clenched, was stuck into his jacket pocket with the thumb outside; but he raised his right hand in front of his chest, palm upwards, his fingers clenched round an imaginary sphere. He had a big hand, with nails cut so short they seemed to be printed on to the flesh. The wrinkles of each finger-joint were deep, the wrist thick. ('A marvellous hand for an actor, Cyril.')

'Nations will be broken up, races mixed, religions abolished, differences forbidden, and the whole of mankind will be served to us on a platter like the head of your John the Baptist. A head-cheese, my dear girl, as the French say, that's what mankind is. Oh, yes, meanwhile, all this has to be expressed in terms of surplus value and alienation; we have to apply the three rules of the dialectic, and queue for hours in front of a porphyry mausoleum that is fortunately quite simply a fraud. Didn't you know? Ilich's body escaped piece by piece the alchemists of the apotheosis. The entrails had already been thrown away, as they have to be. The toes then began to stink; they were replaced. Gangrene attacked the legs; others were put in their place. Then the fingers; they were redone, pink as a child's. The abdomen became infected; a synthetic abdomen was stuck in its place. The face became terribly marbled; the flesh was taken off and the skin stretched over a mask. The skin itself began to peel away; wax was applied. Now there's no longer a single particle of Lenin's flesh in the glass coffin. What they are now venerating is a Snow White from the wax works. He skipped off without saying good-bye, did father Ilich. It was his final and heartiest joke. Several embalmers were hanged because they failed: they should have been impaled for trying. Making relics from a Bolshevik's corpse! Disgusting! Did they not understand that he was decomposing in the flesh only to be reconstituted in light? It was no use working on him—he slipped away between their fingers. Lenin finally rid himself of the unclean instrument he left us, and which should have been thrown on the refuse dump. You see, it was the last examination he submitted us to—you know how he loved checking, controlling, testing: he left us that filth, and we did not understand that it should have been dropped into the sewers. As if in collusion, the sewers then flowed into the mausoleum, but we have refused to interpret this sign; saturated with Christian idolatry, we continue to venerate the Carcase. Lenin died too soon: he hadn't taught us enough.

'Having failed this examination, we must draw a lesson from it. Just as Lenin cut himself off from himself to conquer the world, just as the snake sloughs off its old, worn skin, and the lizard leaves his tail to whoever wants it, and grows another one, and the fox caught in the trap cuts his own paw free with his teeth, so we must treat our own past, individual and collective, with lancet and TNT. All our past. Freud got it all wrong: Oedipus would have been a happy Bolshevik if he'd been content to liquidate his little dad as a hostile social element, but he went and complicated it all by bringing in his mother. The pilgrimage to the sources is incest *par excellence.* Life is a constant plucking out. The world is sticky: everything sticks to me, habits, objects, people, the earth, everything sticks to my hands and to my feet. One has to free oneself, even if it means leaving behind bleeding pieces of oneself. And, of course, one must not hesitate to break the creepers that bind one, the brambles that catch one's sleeves. Your close ones are your enemies. Each pause is a burial. We walk on quicksand: the trick is to walk fast enough not to be sucked down. And you, what do you do? You live among forests of mummies, kept standing artificially. You're necrophagous, and you imagine you're living?'

He paused again, before continuing:

'You can't imagine, I'm sure, the offensive stink that the West puts under our nostrils. You laugh at us because we lack this or that. But don't you know how much better it feels to go without something than to vomit? How much lighter one feels if one is thin instead of paunchy? You yourself coined the phrase "consumer society". But it's worse than that. To consume, after all, is to make something disappear, that is still relatively clean. You are an excremental society! You don't produce to consume, you consume to produce. You're like some crazy machine that cannot stop disgorging useless goods, like a woman who can no longer stop producing monsters time and time again, endlessly. It's not in production, my dear girl, but in consumption that you fall down: your garbage cans are full of crusts of bread and meat fat; soon you'll be throwing away croissants and steaks. The whole West is nothing but a gigantic garbage can full of inverts, perverts and converts. You beget children for pleasure, you produce criminals by platitude, and when they rape you and kill you, you don't even have the gumption to shoot them. Haven't you grasped this one simple point: *the West has cancer . . .?*

180

'Oh! We'll deal with you one of these days. We'll arrive with our surgical equipment. Unfortunately, it will be too late for the scalpel, we'll have to use the saw. But don't worry, the anaesthetic is already operating thanks to your etherized intelligentsia ... Pah! You're Mensheviks, that's what you are, and menshevik means minus. You're the froth on the menshevik culture proliferating to the point of disgust. Now, I ask you, can you bear to look at your own representatives? When you look at them, don't you see how shoddy you must be yourselves? Well? Look at your capitalists, fat as white worms, swimming in their sauce and having, apart from their natural functions, only one way of being in the world: sheer funk—they're scared witless, knowing that the axe is laid to the root. Look at your rulers, who know only how to wallow in front of you to get your votes and who, once they are elected by the left, rule on the right and vice versa! Look at the President of your Republic, a quixotic Münchausen, a petty tyrant, a tyrannosaurus, a walking anachronism! Your soldiers, dressed up as civilians! Your Picassos who take a rise out of you —by your own choice! Your intellectuals perhaps! Ah! I wonder how they don't make you sick, those professional incense-burners, those prostitutes of intelligence, those unremunerated thurifers motivated by the unavowed desire to be impaled by us! All your Russells and all your Sartres, kneeling in the filth! D'you imagine we don't want to kick in the ecstatic faces they hold up to us? We accept their homage with handkerchiefs to our noses. And you know what they worship in us? The Bolshevik, mademoiselle, who has only to crack his whip to have them come and lick him between the toes. Ah! How gaily we'll slash them down to right *and left* when the time comes! A collectivity that does not like itself must disappear: it's scientific and what's more, it's just.'

He raised his big hand, more used to grasping the horizontal bars, and brought it down on the back of Marina's neck, forcing it down towards the parapet, towards the river. She felt his fingers searching out her vertebrae. It was not, she admitted to me, an entirely disagreeable sensation. He went on:

'Don't think I'm advocating some childish voluntarism of the vicious boy-scout kind, like Nietzsche or your Gide. It would be easy enough to tip you over into the Seine.' He said that between his teeth: Marina thought she detected a certain sensual pleasure in his tone of voice. 'But what's the point? Whether added or subtracted, you are a negligible quantity. What in chemistry is called a "trace". You don't belong to the Plan. The Plan! Don't you hear how regal that sounds? We don't draw up plans on the comet, but on the planet. We are going to put a bit of order back into the rickety creation you Christians have the cheek to attribute to God. To start with, a clean sweep, then we'll put mountains where there should be mountains, seas where there should be seas, leaders where there should be leaders, and scullions where there should be scullions. We shall rationally exploit the collective capital received from nature. We shall wash off the placenta of civilization bequeathed us by the bourgeoisie. And we shall construct the future on new foundations.'

It was the first cliché he had uttered. Marina set it down to tiredness. Dying of cold and wanting to get things moving (it seemed to her that if she did not intervene, Popov would stay there talking away until the next day), she leapt into the breach:

'Igor Maximovich, what you say is exactly what I think myself. Only you express it so much better. Lacking your political knowledge, I tend to think directly of men's happiness and dignity. You, on the other hand, have grasped the intermediary stages that must be crossed. Your clean sweep, your new foundations , your Plan would have no meaning if the salvation of mankind were not at the end of them. We are talking about the same things in different terms. And that's why I'm asking you once more to let me help you.'

Her mouth was so frozen she could hardly pronounce words in an intelligible fashion. Popov lifted his hand from her defenceless neck and replied in French:

'Just as I thought. You've not understood a thing. Then understand this at least: there is no way in which you can help us. We let the dead bury the dead.'

He threw away his cigarette—a shooting-star falling to extinction in the water—and, both hands in his pockets (perhaps he, too, was beginning to feel cold), he moved two steps towards the left bank.

Marina was tempted to let him go: she thought only of warming her petrified feet, her frost-bitten fingers and her face, which felt as if the wind had placed it in a vice and was filing it down. To initiate Phase C at that moment seemed to her to be superhuman. Where did she get the energy? In her soldier's blood, in her actress's stamina, in the secret decision that consumed her? She knew very well that if she let Popov go, she would never catch him again. She called out to him (which, in that temperature, was heroic enough in itself).

'Comrade Popov! You're wrong. I *can* help you.'

He stopped. But he did not turn round.

'I have been recruited by the French secret service to attract your attention.'

He half turned his head.

'Then understand that you have not succeeded, ' he snapped, sarcastically.

'I'm putting myself at your disposal. If there's anything you want me to report to the French . . . You will write my reports yourself.'

It is understandable that the proposition could not fail to be of interest to this professional. Whatever his delusions of grandeur, he was not unaware that the war between them and us was not yet over. He might not trust, but he could not reject, this dagger that I was politely offering him, handle first. He came back to Marina and took her chin between his thumb and forefinger; he squeezed it painfully; their eyes were at the same level, but she felt as though she were looking up at him. My only fear was that he would refuse, in all sincerity, to believe her, that he would see her as no more than an adventuress endowed with a little imagination. It was a vain fear.

'Do your chiefs think I'm blind?' he asked. 'Do they imagine that I can't recognize a face whatever sauce it is served up in? And that I don't have the means, Mlle Olga Orloff, to get whatever information I want? And do you think I haven't identified your ever so discreet, half-frozen motorcyclist? And why do you think I've spent all this time listening to your nonsense?' In fact, he had not done much listening, for obvious reasons. 'As a personal favour? I don't know whether you're betraying out of stupidity or on orders, but you can tell your employers that I have nothing to gain from disinforming amateurs like you, that the correct procedure is to use two shadows, that I am told every day what they have for lunch and what they have for dinner and that one day . . .' He searched for some insulting expression and—no doubt because of exhaustion—fell back on one of his favourite formulas: 'I shall mow them down.'

17

Marina had never been to my apartment. That evening, she dropped in on me unexpected (I had been expecting only a telephone call), her eyes the colour of tin, her lips blue, her teeth clenched to stop them chattering. I took off her wretched coat, which smelled of goat, my arms encircling without touching her stiffened shoulders: I got her to sit down in my corduroy-covered armchair; I stuck a glass of brandy in her hands; I turned up the radiator, which boomed out hot air. One has to look after one's men (and one's women).

I lived in a rather shabby one-room apartment, decorated and furnished in the style of the 1920s, with maps on the walls to give a military air, and never a care for the drawing-pin holes; it suited me all right, but I hardly ever invited people in. I felt embarrassed at receiving a caller here. The idea of taking the opportunity to right the wrongs committed the other day did occur to me, but I rejected it as beneath me. Several times Marina tried to speak; despite my impatience to know what had happened, I generously advised her to warm herself up first. Slowly, the blood came back to her lips; then, her teeth sometimes striking the edge of the glass, which she held in both hands, she told her story.

There are at least three of us who have had a hand in altering the speech delivered by Major Igor Maximovich Popov that evening on the Pont Mirabeau. First, Marina, whether she liked it or not; then my memory—for memory does not retain, it reconstructs daily; lastly, myself, the novelist, who put into Popov's mouth words that one can swear he never actually uttered. At best, I am reproducing here not the letter but the spirit of what Marina said that Popov had said to her: I am under no illusions on the matter. However, as far as possible, I have tried to reconstruct not only the content of Popov's thought (such as Marina transmitted it to me), but also the element of his motley, baroque style. For example, I have added to what he said the correct dose of biblical references, not that these references came as a surprise to me—they are to be found on any page of *Pravda*; in Russia, the general culture is essentially Christian, however anti-Christian its representatives wish to be. For the rest, I was well aware that Popov had said only what he wanted to say: if he had betrayed himself, however little, it could only be in the style, not in the content. He presented himself to Marina—or he was presented by Marina—as a kind of poet caught up in the vortex of a metaphysical dream. This did not contradict what we already knew about him. 'Conqueror's son', Rat had called him. Was that what a conqueror's son was like? Between appetite and vainglory he had chosen the product of the one by the other. It remained to be seen why he had given into the temptation of spouting nonsense. It seemed clear to me: a dream under such pressure had to have an outlet. Even Communists are, to some extent, human, and they must feel the desire to confide their soul-searchings to other human beings (for all that they deny the soul's existence). And who could Popov speak to? Not to comrades, not to someone outside the Party, certainly not to a foreigner. He could allow himself to be sincere (supposing he had been) only with an enemy, for an enemy, *a priori*, does not tell tales. Add to that Marina's velvety femininity, the contemptuous attitude Popov seemed to have to women in general, and his habit of using them as tools: that outpouring, that ferment, that disgorging of excessive ambition was unavoidable. Of one thing I was no longer in doubt: Popov detected in himself the raw material of a second Lenin.

In view of that, what was the significance of the attitude he had chosen to adopt to Marina's confession? What was the significance of his allusion to our eating habits? Pure bluff, no doubt. But why had he rejected this opportunity of forming with us one of those ambiguous connections on which, through a kind of mutual vampirism, our services feed each other? He had recognized Olga in Marina, he had remembered her real name, he had detected half at least of the surveillance we had placed on him. None of this upset me, since we were in Phase C and I was hoping to catch him with the bait of his own perspicacity. But I would like to have known if he was merely pretending that he had not noticed the Simca or whether Bourjols had really escaped his vigilance. The utter despair which, I admit, had gripped me when I had opened the door and seen the livid ghost of Marina on the threshold gave place to a bubbling mass of various hypotheses. As she told me how he had moved off towards the left bank, his hands in his pockets, his back arched, his legs pacing out against the wind like those of a horse, and how she had left, running and stumbling, towards the right bank, how she had been unable to warm herself up in the taxi that had brought her here, I noticed that her body was gradually resuming its natural, unctuous elasticity and, showing more intuition than compassion, I questioned her again: 'Is that all? Nothing else?'

She looked at me for a long time before speaking. The golden flecks had come back into her eyes as the heat liquefied them. She moved her legs without beginning to shiver. She moved her little snake's tongue over her lips.

'I don't know,' she said. 'As he left, when he let go of my chin—not the chin exactly, he gripped me by the skin underneath, it hurt . . .'— that same obsession with precision that the actors of certain schools possess. 'He let his hand drop and, as if by chance . . .'

She imitated the gesture. I wanted to know the precise attitude of his hand. Marina wasn't sure; it seemed to her that it was turned out and open, that the entire palm, followed by slightly curved fingers, had slid over the rough hair of the goatskin . . . If she was not mistaken, what might seem definitive failure might also prove to be the beginning of a foreseen, but unhoped for, success.

Marina was afraid to go back into the cold, I felt. I put clean sheets on my bed, after warming them over the radiator. I took out some well laundered pyjamas from my chest-of-drawers, I prepared a grog (my culinary talents went thus far, if not further), and went off to sleep at Frisquette's.

On the Monday morning, I had no sooner arrived at the office than Mme Krebs came looking for me on behalf of the Shopkeeper.

'He doesn't look too pleased, sir.'

'I wonder, Mme Krebs, what you have done to him, or rather what you haven't done.'

'I typed *appreciate* with one *p* again, but I don't think that . . .'

Rat looked at me over his glasses, with his weary eyes:

'Volsky, my boy, it's curtains. Culverin is finished. Aren't you pleased? It's a pity. With my budget I can't go on paying for an operation that in three months has not produced that . . .' He clicked a thumbnail against a false, yellowed incisor. 'I pay for your lip-reader, I pay for his room, I pay for your 2CV, I pay for your two shadows, I pay a fortune for that filly of yours, and what for? I let you take the devil of a risk when I let you give the signal "Shoot me". I don't see that it's come off. Anyway the whole scheme was pretty crazy to begin with. Perhaps if Tolstoy had taken it in hand . . . As it is, we'd better drop it before the high command realize what's happening. As it is, we look none too good.'

To look good was the ideal of his life. I noted that he did not reject all responsibility for the operation and I saw that as a good sign.

'I'm asking you, sir, for one more week,' I said tragically.

'Refused.'

'But, sir, Popov has confided information to the informant.'

'That crazy rubbish you told me about over the telephone? Do you want me to give that to Silbert? You must be crazy yourself.'

'That rubbish will do very well in a report.' In the army, one is damned by cost-effectiveness and saved by reports. 'Popov has more or less said that he does not believe in Marxism-Leninism—and he a major of the KGB. That doesn't strike me as too bad for a candidate to be turned around. On top of that he made a pass at her.'

'A pass . . .! Your KGB major must have drunk a bottle of

vodka for breakfast. You know very well that his chit-chat isn't worth a damn.'

'Not the chit-chat itself, but the fact that he felt the need to talk. And even more, that he refused the services of the informant.'

'Well, so what? He doesn't trust double agents. He's right. Neither do I. He treated her with contempt.'

'Precisely: he treated her like dirt on purpose, both as an informant and as a woman. He recognized her, he had got information about her, he had detected Planacassagne; applying the method of absolute contempt, he thought he had forced Marina to unmask herself. He must be congratulating himself: that's the moment—as you know better than I do, sir—to grab a man like a trussed hen. By a kind of professional reflex, he suggested that Mlle Kraievsky was betraying on orders. But he doesn't believe a word of it: he thinks she's been bulldozed by his charm. His great monologue may have had no other purpose than to persuade Mlle Kraievsky that he was superior to everything, even her own image of him: hence his threats to us and, simultaneously, that expression of sexual interest: he put his future victor's hand on our emissary. Attila is hooked, sir. So much so that, if we had the time, my opinion would be that Mlle Kraievsky should stop seeing him: I bet he would find a means of renewing contact. However, since Steel Wool is getting excited, I think we can risk a little extra initiative, for which Popov himself will provide an opportunity: note that he hasn't finished his lectures on guerrilla warfare.'

I was sitting quite close to Rat, our heads were inclined towards one another: two 'novelists' writing the same novel, debating the psychology of the characters, suggesting a touch here, a bit of trickery there. Popov, Marina, Silbert belonged to us. Rat put his hand into his mouth, probed the gum, brought out under his nail some piece of detritus, which he examined carefully, then, with a flick of the finger, he sent it flying across the room. He sighed deeply with his old, flabby lungs.

'If she hasn't got herself laid by next Saturday,' he declared, 'Silbert can ask me for your head on a plate: and he'll have it.'

I would have felt less sure of myself if I had not had up my sleeve an additional element that I had thought best not to divulge.

On the Sunday, I came back early from Frisquette's and found Marina making coffee. She offered me some and we drank it together, sitting opposite each other across the blue and green checked wax cloth of the kitchen table. It was touching to see the Eternal Feminine officiate at so humble a meal as breakfast; it was touching to make out the warm swelling of Little Ripple under the masculine costume I had myself worn so many times—the pyjama top, stuck into trousers, formed a blouse and there was something particularly touching in the sight of the buttons on the wrong side for her. Rested, warmed, once again all golden, once again the Little Drop of Oil that I had been in love with, she inspired in me an all-powerful sweetness that nearly made me do something very odd. It would not have needed much for me to hold out my hand across the wax cloth and say: 'Don't get involved in this filth, Marina. We get on so well together. Let's marry instead.'

It would have been easy for me. Quite spontaneously, we had begun to speak Russian (Would you like some coffee?—The sugar is on the right of the top shelf) and it is easier to say simple, serious things in Russian than in French. But I held off. Give up Culverin? Resign? Abandon a game I had begun—and begun not too badly—against a worthwhile adversary? It was out of the question. I then gave myself a valid reason to maintain the *status quo*: was not Marina ready to prostitute herself? Does one marry *that*? I was seized with anger, and resolved to continue my operation to the end, whatever the cost. Once Popov was wrapped up, once Marina was reduced to the level of a tool somewhat blunted by use, somewhat dishonoured by her own function, once she was totally subjected to his will, perhaps I, too, would treat her as I liked, at a reduced price: she would be in my hands, she would have to put up with me; if it was without pleasure, then my triumph would be all the sweeter. I suddenly brought the conversation back to the events of the day before and she, interrupting herself in the middle of a sentence (she was talking, I remember, of how she loved playing in the snow: 'Not as a skier, you know, skiers are almost as pedantic as horsemen, but throwing snowballs, making a snowman, giving him a carrot for a nose'), she began to answer my questions with exemplary docility. This both pained and pleased me. It was almost as if I were beating her! If, below the docility, there smouldered a hidden enthusiasm, I did not detect it. She described for me in great detail Popov's 'equivocal' gesture—why, indeed equivocal? Would it not be better to say, whatever it was worth, that it was simply an initial caress?—and added what seems ridiculous in the repetition but which, increasing my own excitement, also increased my hope: 'Then his white eyes became small and dark.'

It was no use trying to get her to contradict herself, claiming that she could not have made out such a mutation of colour in the darkness, but she maintained her position, even with a touch of irony: 'Didn't you know that women can see in the dark, Cyril? At least things like that.' In the end I accepted the idea that even if her literary taste was not impeccable and that, consequently, her descriptions had something of the bogus picturesque about them, she was not inventing this change in Popov's attitude, and that such a change was in the desired direction. I went so far as to consult her as to what we should now do, and I saw that our feelings, to some extent, coincided: she thought that although the KGB major was in no way interested in her, the male was caught. I admitted to her that, the previous night, I had thought the whole thing was over.

'Poor Cyril! I did, too, but only for a moment: just before admitting to him that I was working for you. But immediately afterwards I felt I had him. I was even sorry that I'd told him.'

'Don't be sorry: if he really is caught, your confession will give him an excuse to see you again. Both from his own point of view and from that of his Shop. My only fear', I added out of weakness, 'is that he is not as badly bitten as you think.'

She smiled: this time it was not an ironic, but a frankly sarcastic smile.

'Don't worry yourself about that. I know what I'm talking about. He'll have his way with me. And you'll get what you want.'

She looked at me; I remained poker-faced. She added:

191

'Yesterday he was already enjoying my debasement. On stage, he would have to speak the political monologue as if he had no other aim but to dazzle the little woman.'

'You think that's what he was trying to do?'

She shook her head: 'No, but it would be more stylish.'

We planned what she was to do next; she struck me as passionately keen to continue the mission. I did not tell her that everything still depended on Rat.

I summoned Roger Moutins in the usual way and we proceeded to the usual little game: whisky, no Beaujolais, how can you, etc. I explained to him what I wanted him to do. He seemed to have in his head some idea that was as murky as it was fixed.

'Listen,' he said (the 'sir's leaving audible blanks in his conversation). 'I'd like you to come clean with me about your secret motives. You see, I'm in the firing line. If you're planning to do him in, I'm finished. So . . .'

'M. Moutins, it is simply a matter of inviting the counsellor to complete a lecture that he has himself left unfinished. I can assure you that we have no designs on his life.'

'Ah! . . . you don't understand,' he said, stubbornly.

I found him changed: thinner, bags under his eyes—in the nineteenth century, one would have diagnosed that he was in love. He toyed with the base of his glass, fingering it with both hands; he leaned forward, staring at that red glass as if it were a crystal ball. I said nothing: I had to give him time to find the words to express what it was that I did not understand. After a while, he spoke again, the spectacles still inclined downwards—a lock of his greased hair had detached itself from the mass and, hanging like the wing of a dead bird, tickled his forehead:

'If you intend doing him in, either one way or another, I'm finished. So, while we're at it . . .'

He raised his eyes without raising his head, which made him look both cunning and naive, like a naughty boy who has found what he imagined to be an irresistible way of asking for a sweet. He lowered his voice: 'Give him to me.'

I pretended that I did not understand and he went on almost at

192

once, with a gesture of the hand, demanding indulgence, like an alcoholic or a smoker: 'Leave him to me.'

The lives we lead are so innocent on the surface that it is always a shock when, in a café on the Place d'Italie, an inveterate killer asks you to help him satisfy his mania. This time, it was more than that: it was a matter of assassinating a foreign diplomat, a Communist, in the middle of Paris . . . Pure blood and thunder stuff. I took the shock with all the elasticity I could muster and made an effort to analyse the proposition as if it could have been taken seriously. One day I managed to arrange, under false pretences, to have sight of the report made on me as an officer. Among others, I read the following note, which I found highly flattering: 'Has the rare merit of believing in the incredible and exploiting it before it becomes credible and others get hold of it.' It is not quite credible that a man with whom you are drinking a glass of bad Beaujolais can no longer do without killing and shyly begs you to help him out, but it can happen, and it's better to be ready to take advantage of the unexpected rather than to deny it. Having taken my time, I replied simply:

'M. Moutins, for the moment there is no question of eliminating him. If it comes to that, I'll think of you: that's a promise.'

He nodded by way of thanks, frowned, looked into the distance, full of unknown desires, then came back to me, alert, ready, the exemplary young NCO.

'At your service, *sir*.'

He had said it! He blushed, but I was generous enough to pretend that I had not noticed his lapse. He was not too dissatisfied with me, I think: he showed a gaiety, a *joie de vivre*, that I did not know him to possess, but which I recognized; it was a mood very much like my own when, after a period of chastity, I was on my way to some promising rendez-vous.

18

For the rest of the week I walked around like a ghost. The hours dragged on interminably; the days passed fairly quickly; the week as a whole flashed by. The blanket of snow that continued to cover the esplanade gave the weather a strange quality. In the translators' office, we turned on our desk lamps early and we worked or daydreamed under our respective cones of light, calling across to one another, from island to island, through the gathering dusk. Behind the door, the corridor, inundated with its lilac-white neon brightness, seemed to belong to another, science-fiction world, contrasting with the noble old courtyard disappearing behind the window and in which, by a kind of mirror effect, our lamps, our books, Puzo's glasses, M. Alexandre's bald head seemed to float, immobile like jellyfish suspended in hyper-space.

The others, taking advantage of that atmosphere of urgency that snow brings with it (at least into government departments), left even earlier than usual, but I stayed on, skirmishing with my hepta-glot dictionaries or rereading my report of Marina's revelations. Often I stopped working and thought that some thousand yards away Popov was no doubt sitting under his lamp, in front of his monkey and skull, busy laying traps for us as we were for him. Perhaps he had just got back from a meeting with Crocodile, as I had just got back from meeting Moutins. I tried to imagine the stratagems forming in his head; Western defeatism, or, at a deeper level, a kind of collective *Todwunsch* convinced me that they must be infallible; I saw a smile hover over the inexpressive face of the conqueror of the future. Two men, doing the same job, each in his office, suspended in the night, surrounded by interchangeable office equipment . . . A strange dizzy feeling came over me. Was I not saying to myself: '*I* would like this, *I* would do that'? And was he not saying on his side, '*I* think, *I* predict, *I* order'? Who, then, was *I*? Was it he or I? Or rather why was I I and not he? Always supposing it meant anything to say, 'I am I' for he, too, said 'I am I': it was like those badly formulated sets of equations at the end of which one discovers the incontestable truth that $x = x$. I, the French I if you like, Frisquette's I, Rat's I, could it not also have been born at Vladimir, and become a Soviet spy, and found itself at that moment on the second floor of 79 Rue de Grenelle? Could not the I of the Rue de Grenelle have been born in the 15th arrondissement, fought in the Algerian war and contemplated at the same moment its own reflection against the darkening office, with the lampshade lowered, gleaming reflections from the cupboard, shelves of bound reports, piles of papers, through which showed, as in a second negative taken on the same film, old cannons lying on their bellies on the paved courtyard, pyramids of cannonballs and slender windows, with small panes, all dark except for one, at which, below the corner of a wooden table a mottled uniformed trouser-leg was to be seen, with the officer's stripe down its side, ending in a large brown shoe? Why had not this face reflected in the glass a high wrinkled forehead, white eyes, a heavy chin, but on the contrary features that I like to think were well proportioned and eyes of a fine grey? But what did I mean by these 'I's that I superimposed one upon another? Was I already imagining individual souls, the targets of divine love? I doubt it. It's just that I could no longer understand why we, he and I, were confined within our own limits. I remembered how as a child I had often asked myself, with unbearable anguish, why I was Volsky and not some friend or other (the boy who always had ink-stains on his hands, or the one whose brown pullover gave off that sweet smell) and, when older, every time a plane passed overhead, how was it that I was on the ground imagining the passengers, yet when I too flew in an aeroplane I imagined the crawling creatures over whom I was flying. 'I' is in the plane, but 'I' is on the ground; who is 'I'? Could there be several 'I's? Could there be other 'I's than the divine 'I'? Should we not interpret the name Yahweh as signifying not 'I am who am' but 'I am he who is I'? A rather free-wheeling Hebrew, perhaps, but to what extent did I have the right to say 'I am Kiril Volsky', when there was a man who said 'I am Igor Popov'? I was in the grip of a confusion similar to that of Major Kovalev or, to be more precise, that of Major Kovalev's nose at the moment when it, too, becomes an 'I'. I would get up, go out and walk up and down the Rue Barbet-de-Jouy, in front of the building in which Popov lived. One day, unable to bear it any longer, I went into the entrance hall; an *ancien régime* concierge leapt out at me and asked me what I wanted; I was petrified; I couldn't think of a single name; in the end, I asked in a stammer whether M. Barbet de Jouy lived there. It was not all that absurd: the benefactor of the city of Paris might still have descendants living in his district; but I was shown the door with more firmness than politeness. On other occasions, I imprudently paced up and down the Rue de Grenelle, alternately hoping and fearing that I would meet this 'I' who was so little like me, yet was becoming my double. At certain moments, the same metaphysical vertigo assumed a more down-to-earth form, well known to those who have practised my profession: an almost uncontrollable desire to pass to the other side of the mirror, to step over the threshold separating the two opposed and superimposable camps. This hypnotic power exercised by the symmetrical nature of the adversary has produced more double agents than the bait of lucre. For my part, though I have never been a traitor, I have recognized the feeling that treason must be the most voluptuous of pleasures. To become another while remaining oneself! Think of the pleasures of reproduction, then imagine the delight that this proliferation of self, this internal scissiparity must procure! I saw myself ringing at the infernal door; I'd walk through a clicking of cameras, moving as in a dream, without touching the admirable parquet floors; if I was questioned or accompanied, it could only be by semi-invisible beings (the snouts of hippopotamuses, cloven hoofs, the tip of a stag's antlers stuck through the panelling); flying above ground level, I'd cross the reception halls, climb the little orange staircase and

196

reach at last the gleaming cube in the midst of which would sit Popov, his forehead wrinkled in folds from top to bottom, his mouth half open as if to gobble me up. I'd stop in front of him without being able to break the terrifying silence. At last, without emitting any sound, my lips would manáge to convey in the language that formed the only real bridge between our two 'I's: 'I have come.'

Examining me attentively from head to foot, he'd answer like a grand-master seated on a throne at the centre of the labyrinth in some masonic novel: 'I always knew that you would come.'

I'd look at this man-vortex, with that crescent of shadow between the teeth, and remember how as a child I had thought the Bolsheviks were literally red, that they had red clothes, red skins, red hair, red irises. This pale figure with his white sweater and grey jacket would reassure me. He was not a Bolshevik; he was a man. I'd tell him that I wanted to work for him. He would reply ironically that I was already working for him, that the whole world was already working for him: 'The very tides,' he'd say, 'carry their shingle for me.'

I'd then try to explain to him what he represented in my world.

'You are,' I would declare, 'in every sense of the term, *the other*, the diametrical opposite, the reverse. You have a maximum coefficient of otherness and you are also, as in folklore, the Other. The Evil one. The Red. The Prince of this World. The ancestors thronging in my blood abominate you, and my whole upbringing, everything I have done with myself until this moment, make you my irreducible Enemy. Nevertheless, I have succumbed to your fascination. Having been fully what I am, I now wish to be fully the contrary. What must an algebraic factor feel when its sign is changed! That's what I want to feel.'

My mathematics were as haywire as my Hebrew. Popov would still be observing me with that air of superiority.

'Symmetry does not exist,' he would comment at last. 'The galaxy is flying in one direction only.'

That was the nub. My world was pagan and symmetrical; his, pagan and directional. But, for the moment, what fascinated me

197

in this exchange of views was simply that it was possible, and, in my wish to place Popov before me, to circumscribe him, to strap him down on the laboratory table, I'd go on:

'Let us forget symmetry. You have one unusual quality for a Communist: you don't exude boredom. The idea of changing camp and face had already occurred to me, you see. As an adolescent, when I saw the Communists winning on every side, at every level, I wondered if I might not do better to go and join them. For a start, it's more fun to win than to lose and, anyway, I never believed much in ideas. However, I thought it was perhaps my duty to grasp the right end of the stick today as my family has done for some generations. So I opened your books and your newspapers. The ugliness of your typography began to repel me; then it was the childishness of your agitprop, your contrived statistics, your edifying postage stamps, the academicism of your painting, the ugliness of your postcards, your innumerable insignia, medals, stars, badges, your obtuse faces in your magazines printed on bad paper, your tireless parroting of mawkish commonplaces. I saw clearly enough that I could never get worked up about maize plantation or tractor production, never think in stumps of words stuck together (kol-khoz, gor-kom, kom-div, gos-kult, prosvet-izdat), never give my life for a string of initials, never learn by heart quotations that managed to be both maudlin and bureaucratic, never applaud for hours on end truisms trotted out by men of straw, never write articles to demonstrate for the hundredth time what others had already demonstrated a thousand times before me. Nothing's more tedious than the bourgeois style, comrade, except the proletarian style.'

'The West will die of frivolity,' he'd reply. 'Seriousness has its virtues.'

I'd retort, with what I thought was subtlety, that seriousness was not serious, and that he was himself a shining example of the truth that genius did not have to weigh a ton.

'You have not yet treated me to a single quotation from a Party Congress, a single directive from the Central Committee. You are attached to none of those fetishes the mere mention of which makes me yawn; in fact, you ride Communism instead of letting yourself be ridden by it. From this point of view, old chap, you are a man after my own heart. I know very well that I was born in the margin of history, but that is not necessarily irremediable.'

I'd now begin walking nonchalantly up and down, sometimes gesticulating, sometimes clasping my hands behind my back.

'You have vigour,' I'd go on, 'but I have lucidity. There's nothing new in that; nothing has ever been achieved without force, and I would not pretend to disdain it. I'd like to tap electricity from your pylon, or rather throw my tepidness into your volcano. You are, I do not deny it, the man of the future, and it is my ambition to accompany you there.'

He would not have offered me a seat, which would both annoy and impress me: I'd be Talleyrand-Périgord before Bonaparte. I'd suddenly stop in front of him and add, with a touch of oily obsequiousness: 'And may I be so curious as to ask what I am to you?'

He'd look me up and down, contemptuously, blowing out the smoke of a cigarette he had lit without my noticing. He'd then obligingly answer: 'You are the parings from my fingernails.'

This remark would irritate me, but I'd think it more prudent not to show it. As one of history's parasites, I'd even give a little amused chuckle. The great man was taking the trouble to speak to me. I discovered in myself a courtier's soul. Nevertheless I'd be weak enough to change the subject. I'd flick a finger at the pate of the bronze monkey; then I'd ask the meaning of the man's skull in its hand and that perplexed expression in its large questioning eyes.

'What do you think it means?' Popov would look amused.

'I think,' I'd reply with some pedantry, 'that this sculpture, of deliberately evolutionist inspiration, might be called *The Poor Relation*: a monkey finds a man's skull and asks himself why it was not his family but his neighbour's that underwent the Great Mutation. "All my ancestors needed," he says, "was to be born with a twisted chromosome for me, at the present moment, to have a cranium of such capacity. It's unfair." One might also call this masterpiece *The Lost Opportunity*, and see the monkey as a bourgeois who has missed the boat, and the possessor of the skull as a triumphant Bolshevik. In which case, the bourgeois is

199

saying, "Better to be a living monkey than a dead Bolshevik."
Since this hypothesis does not follow the direction of history, it
would be preferable, I suppose, to see it as an allegory of time
flowing backwards: if one of the two characters is alive and the
other dead, and if one is the ancestor of the other, it is clear that
it is the dead who has engendered the living: one would then see
this as an expression of the temporal paradox dear to science-
fiction, or one would admit that monkeys are in reality degener-
ate men and that the more *progressive* we are, the more rapidly
we will evolve towards four-leggedness. In which case, we must
take it that the skull belongs to the dead bourgeois and the four
paws to the living Bolshevik. This hypothesis, my dear Popov,
doesn't seem to please you? Well, we might see your sculpture
as a somewhat irreverent illustration of the famous "Alas! Poor
Yorick!", or if you prefer, a caricature interpretation of
Soloviev's famous witticism. Mocking the liberal, atheistic
intelligentsia of his day, who were still struck with Darwin, he
attributed the following slogan to them: "Man has descended
from the monkey. That is why we must love one another." '
My courtly wit would not seem to be very successful. Popov
would wriggle on his chair and become, by perceptible degrees,
grey, dark grey, black. At that moment, I'd become aware of the
map of world atheism on the wall behind me. I'd see it as clearly
as if I had eyes in the back of my head. This map would be ani-
mated: the shaded surfaces would be contracting with every
moment, the white areas, shining with the purity of the void,
would be rapidly spreading. Although I was not very religious, a
shiver of fear would run down my spine: I had never seriously
considered that Christ could lose. Not that I was very attached
to him at that time, but he always seemed to me to represent the
most secure, if not the most attractive, value. I'd suddenly feel
very angry: he had no right to lose. 'I have conquered the world
. . . the gates of hell shall not prevail . . .'—appropriate quotations would rise up from an almost forgotten childhood and I'd
discover that the mutation I had envisaged was impossible.
Symmetry for symmetry, something held me to my place.
Popov and I were as close and as dissimilar as the monkey and
the man in the sculpture. Indeed, Popov would be grinning, his

lips protruding to form a great black sucker, his eye dark and mischievous.

'What does the group mean? I'll tell you . . .'

He'd then whisper, with a suggestive grin on his face, the Russian proverb that corresponds to 'a little more than kin, and less than kind'. It was enough to pull me out of the unhealthy daydreaming in which I had been plunged. I found myself once again on the gleaming pavement, I looked across the dirty snow to the door that one imagined would be reinforced, barred, locked, protected by cathode rays and laser beams, surmounted by an invisible scroll bearing the famous inscription that Dante found on the entrance to hell, and I concluded, regretfully, that I would not succumb to a temptation that had come to me like a spasm in the entrails, but which I had entertained for so long only out of a morbid taste for the impossible. There was no tunnel of the consciousness or of the unconscious that could lead me to Popov. We were different, he and I, by virtue of the non-fissile, primordial elements in us. I was condemned to fidelity. The I, whatever its mystery, exists.

19

In the past I had enjoyed some success in shooting competitions (I suspect that Tolstoy begrudged me my success) and I felt that, in order to win a closely fought match one has to approach it with a particular psychosomatic attitude, a perfect and deliberately precarious balance between appetite for victory and indifference to defeat, something of the acting without acting of the *Bhagavad-Gîtâ*, the paradox of holding and detachment. I never learnt how to cultivate this attitude: it is given to me or refused; but I know how to recognize it by the specific sense of wellbeing it creates in me. On awakening, that secure tranquility, that vigilant gaiety, that pleasure in life grasped as a rationed commodity, tell me that whatever depends on me will pass off well, and even that, to some extent at least, luck will be with me. Dogs foresee storms, onions the cold: there's nothing surprising in our elementary nature knowing how to unroll some part of the wrappings of the future. I woke with that mood on the following Saturday and, by way of recognition, instead of making myself a bad Nescafé on my filthy old gas ring, I went down to the corner café and had a large white coffee and croissants. Milk—for once I want to descend to clinical details— is usually the enemy of my stomach, but, at certain moments of grace, I can drink a moderate quantity of it without any unpleasant consequences, and I feel a childish pleasure in seizing these opportunities to triumph over myself. I then went to the office, where Rat had arranged to see me for a last briefing, which, though perfectly useless in itself, stressed the solemnity of the day that was to be our last chance.

Fresh snow had fallen during the night, and it was pleasant to

Besides, it wasn't really cold. I saw Marina arrive first. On my orders, she had changed her costume. Moutins would be flabbergasted. As for the others! Skin-tight black trousers, short, high-heeled boots, very Central Europe, a sable jacket, a saucy cap perched on bouffant hair: she had burned her boats. Then Moutins turned up, with that look of a dreadnought bearing down on a submarine. Then the boys and girls: a rout in reverse, as in a film played backwards; a reconstruction of the shattered fragments of hope. Lastly, Popov, and this time, since luck was with me, I saw him from a distance, walking towards me, wearing a brown sheepskin (he had finally come round to believing in the cold, inopportunely), a light vapour emerging from his mouth, his lips pursed as if to whistle. I wanted to sink lower behind the windscreen, but I stopped myself making any movement, and Popov did not seem to notice me. As he was passing, I felt an impulse to open the door and, like a jack-in-the-box, leap at his throat or into his arms, I don't know which. I merely turned my eyes slowly, just my eyes, to follow him as long as I could.

The wait that followed did not weigh heavily upon me. I like the long patience required of stalking. I like to get to the theatre in good time. In less than an hour I was surprised to see the catechumens emerging. I looked into their faces for some reflection of the sermon, but I could see nothing: like most young French people today, they looked more disgruntled than facetious. Their intelligent eyes expressed an *a priori* sense of superiority that was addressed not to what they had just heard, but to the world in general. In France—and I smiled at the thought—a political commissar would soon become as ridiculous as a parish priest. Popov and Marina soon appeared, he walking on the inside, holding her firmly by the arm, she trying to keep up with him. First they tried to walk on the right-hand pavement, but the herd slowed them down; Popov then looked quickly up and down the street to see if it was free and they crossed the roadway at a slant. I turned on the engine. When, on the left-hand pavement, they had reached my limit of visibility, I moved off. I started to follow them in second gear, hoping that my slowness would not create a traffic jam behind me. I was not surprised to see that I succeeded perfectly in my undertaking: my good mood of the morning had promised me as much.

The couple walked briskly, without trying to hide or to give the slip. Planacassagne's exploits, riding backwards and forwards on his motorcycle, must have taken up all the professional attention Popov was capable of. I only saw Bourjols myself once, at a red light: the operation was proceeding with flexibility.

Avenue Jean-Jaurès. I turned the corner on the amber light, which made me nervous for a few seconds, but since everything continued to proceed as planned and the motorists were not hooting behind me, my calm returned. I overtook the couple, spotted a space to park in and waited for them. Having let myself be overtaken, first by Bourjols, then by Planacassagne, then by Popov and Marina, I made somebody happy by leaving my place. The snow was melting; sheets of rain fell at intervals; the mud made the road and pavements slippery, but it was a gay mud, heralding the spring. Catching a glimpse from time to time of Popov's rectangular back and Marina's silky one, with that large gymnast's hand now upon it, I began to envy him, but in an almost kindly way, as if he were a brother going off to some party, and already, the lucky fellow, having a good time. I reached the Place Marcel-Sembat; I watched them walk towards the métro and disappear from view without Popov once looking back; Marina turned round for an instant and he pulled her quickly by the arm. He seemed to be in a hurry.

I left the 2CV between the studs of a pedestrian crossing. It was Saturday afternoon: the métro would not be too unpleasant. Marina, providentially, did not have a ticket; Popov wanted to get her one; she had to insist that she buy her own, as she usually did; that held them up and gave me time to arrive. I was prepared. Then I lost sight of them, but I betted on the Montreuil direction; I won, of course, and found them on the platform. Planacassagne was already there. Bourjols, calmness itself, was the last to get through the barrier before it closed.

The train pulled in. Popov was pushing Marina in front of him, the deep fur half closing over his widespread fingers. They got into first-class, which I never did. However, I felt I had to follow them. Planacassagne and Bourjols, more experienced as shadows, separated and went into the second-class carriages on either side of it. The train moved off.

Standing, stuck between a support and a window, I pretended to be passionately interested in the 'landscape', hoping, by this ostrich-like policy, that Popov would not see me. But it wasn't Popov who worried me most: I was terribly embarrassed at the idea that an inspector might ask me for my ticket and that I'd have to present him with a buff one instead of a pink one. Respect for uniforms had been bred in me with my father's blood and my mother's milk; it is not for nothing that Russians were commanded by Prussians for two hundred years: I totally lacked that natural spirit of independence innate among the French; any government employee, however menial, was for me an *oprichnik*, a Tsar's man. Crazy solutions came into my head. I would show him my card. I would pretend not to understand French, or to be deaf. I would have an epileptic fit. In the end I decided to get out at the next station and take refuge in a second-class carriage, but since no inspector got on at the next station, I forced myself to stay put, at the risk of seeing him arrive from the next carriage. A little calmer than before, I threw a glance at my quarry.

They, too, were standing: he had his back to me and completely obscured my view of her. The sheepskin coat, with its square shoulders, suggested great strength. This irritated me; I was not built to take on this athlete in physical combat. His nut-brown hair stood out in tufts over his collar. His right hand gripped the support; his other hand lay on the mound of fur in front of him. In fact, rather lower than the shoulder. Not typical Soviet behaviour in public . . . But he was in Paris, after all. The two faces were close to one another and I imagined that Popov, who was talking volubly (about Lenin?), was breathing on Marina's cheek. I felt a moment's revulsion: I imagined such a thing would be disagreeable to the Eternal Feminine. Then I almost giggled at my inconsequence. Should I not, on the contrary, congratulate myself on my plan's initial success?

I then saw this plan in all its improbable richness; I felt dizzy at the prospect. In that long narrow case, borne on those rails, among the other passengers, the seats, the adverts, the 'No Smoking' signs, all equally important, I held captive a quarry, as deliciously edible as it was dangerous, an elephant, if you like, from which I hoped to derive meat, leather, ivory, but in the presence of which I felt infinitely weak, my inferiority in his regard being compounded in a sense by my evil purposes. This quarry, incredible as it seemed, was a counsellor at the Soviet embassy, a major of Bureau T of the KGB, Crocodile's case officer, a walking treasure of unimaginable value. And I had a hold on him. It was no longer quite unthinkable that he was mine. I was under no illusions: Popov might still not become Marina's lover, or again he might and still elude my grasp. But these two unfavourable possibilities were by no means sure; he might become attached to my Slav Gioconda (in whom he was to see, in a reversal of determining-determined order, a Slav with a Gioconda face) and wake up one morning at my mercy: in my hand, like an orange; between my thighs, like a horse. This dream was so unbearably attractive that I almost wanted to stop our common race to the final test: it wouldn't take much for me to pull the emergency cord! I shoved myself deeper into my corner; I deplored the absence of camouflage. I had only one fear: of catching the eye of Marina who, of course, would recognize me, or that of Popov, who, naturally or supernaturally, might also recognize me.

At Exelmans, one passenger alighted, two got on. The doors sighed before closing. Suddenly, in an explosion of strength and velocity, Popov threw Marina across the width of the carriage and on to the platform, flung himself after her, caught her in mid-flight, pressed her to himself and, swinging round, his legs thrust apart for greater stability, watched (with a look at once wild and amused) the increasingly trapezoid windows slip past. I had the presence of mind not to move and I myself passed by that long, bony head, separated from me by a pane of glass and little more than a few inches, and inside which I glimpsed—I like to think—labyrinths, blind alleys, secret dungeons, short-circuits, a whole internal underground railway, a nightmare termitarium, a gnawing of which he himself was hardly aware.

I also saw Planacassagne, who had time to jump off at the last moment and stood on the platform, somewhat amazed and even more annoyed. It did not matter: he was already known to Popov. But what to do now? Where was Bourjols? A moment of panic: had we lost them? And then my serenity returned: in any case, this surveillance, whether successful or not, would not affect the outcome. Only professional vanity demanded that the lost scent should be found again.

I got off at Molitor; I went and sat down on a bench, relieved at no longer being in contravention of the regulations. Why had Popov performed the classic number of the emergency escape? To shake off his shadows? To identify them? To show Marina that he would let himself be followed only if he wanted to? Supposing he really did want to get rid of us, he would set off in the direction of the Porte de Saint-Cloud and get a taxi or a bus. But what was the point of playing these little games when he knew already that Marina was working for us? More likely, it was no more than a demonstration of competence and, after giving himself the pleasure of making Planacassagne look an ass, Popov would calmly board the next train.

The distant rumble that announced its arrival could already be heard. I positioned myself at the head of the platform. The ever-sinister cat's eyes of the first carriage appeared in the tunnel and the swaying train, the doors opening like valves, moved into the station with the usual squeaking and whining. Bourjols was the first passenger to get out. I ran up to him.

'Well?'

The cunning old rascal had been getting off at every station and getting on again last: that's how he had managed to remain in contact.

'Be careful, sir, they're just behind you. I think they're going to change here.'

We let them pass.

'And Planacassagne?'

'Plana, sir? What a joke!'

At Exelmans, when Popov and Planacassagne had found themselves a few feet away from each other, the professional had walked slowly up to the bungler, his blank eyes fixed on him, his legs thrown forward as if on parade in front of the mausoleum;

Planacassagne, moving back, step by step, hardly daring to look at his opponent, had very nearly fallen on to the track. Popov then got within arm's reach of him, raised his left hand to shoulder-height, the thumb erect, the forefinger extended, the other three fingers folded in, raised his right hand to the same position, slipped his left thumb into his right forefinger, closed his left eye, aimed his improvised revolver at Planacassagne's temple, and, with the right thumb against the second finger of the same hand, made a noise that was a passable imitation of an explosion. He burst out into a peal of laughter, and went back to Marina to receive her admiration for his prowess, as if he really had laid this man out at his feet. Grabbing her by the shoulders, he urged her with vigorous gestures to observe the inglorious flight of the vanquished opponent. 'He behaved as if he was drunk,' Bourjols remarked. I wondered if this childish display was to be taken at face value or if, on the contrary, Popov wanted us to think that he thought that he had thrown us off his track in order to observe our surveillance more effectively. It is this infinitely binary game of the object and its reflection that is one of the most perverse charms of my ancient profession. Once again, my present profession does not differ very much from it: every self-respecting novelist owes it to himself to remain ignorant at all times as to whether he is grasping the reality of his characters or merely the shadows they cast. Otherwise writing becomes little more than canned literature. In both cases the real beauty is perceived in the palpitating element of risk. At all events, Popov and Marina had boarded the next train as if they had not a care in the world.

We took the Austerlitz direction, our quarry entering a first-class carriage, either because Popov had petty-bourgeois principles about the respect due to ladies; or because it is easier to detect possible shadows in first-class. Bourjols got in the carriage ahead; I, in the one behind. Through the two glass panes that separated us I could see quite distinctly the entwined man and woman I was tracking. She, propping her back, had placed her little gloved hands on his vast chest, perhaps to protect herself with her elbows. He, crushing her defenceless sides with both hands, was talking animatedly and, from time to time, laughed in quick, sharp bursts, as if laughter were rationed or he needed to replenish before the next salvo. It did not look as if he was kissing the captive. Perhaps Soviet strait-lacedness still held him back on this point, even in Paris; perhaps he did not go in for kissing: it does happen. The file had nothing to say on this point.

I did not know if Popov—supposing that everything worked out as we hoped—would take Marina to the Rue Barbet-de-Jouy, as prudence should have suggested, or whether he would let himself be taken to her apartment in the Avenue de Suffren, as discretion might dictate. It was unlikely that he would risk going to a hotel on account of his diplomatic position. For us, there were minor advantages in either course: in her apartment, it would be easier to set up an electronic surveillance apparatus later; in his apartment, it could be useful to us if Marina had obtained right of access. Whatever their destination, they could either stay on the train until Duroc, or get off at La Motte-Picquet-Grenelle, which is what they did. So we mingled in the flow of passengers that surrounded them, convinced that they would immediately leave the métro station unless they changed to the Invalides direction and made for the Champs-de-Mars. Result: we nearly lost them, because they took the opposite, Place Balard, direction. I had no experience of shadowing. I had felt calm as long as I knew where they were going; now I had a moment of panic: I'd been tricked! They couldn't do that to me! Fortunately, Bourjols, serious but not anxious, both detached and concentrated, was already close on their heels. I let him get a bit ahead of me, moving in echelon. Somewhat reassured, I told myself that perhaps Popov had a secret bachelor flat somewhere, or was in the habit of using a *maison de passe*, and that this would read very well in the report.

There are a number of tricks one can play on shadows in the métro, but either because Popov did not suspect our presence, or because he didn't want to waste time, he made no attempt to use them. Marina and he simply got off at Lourmel and proceeded up the stairs without even so much as a glance behind them. Outside, night was falling. Something had changed in the seduction relationship: whereas, in the métro, the initiative had clearly belonged to Popov, it was now Marina who seemed to have the advantage. He would push her by the shoulders in one direction, but she, laughing, grabbed him by the hand and pulled him in another. He would obey at once, catching up, going beyond her, almost carrying her to help her follow him, then suddenly, with some difficulty, she would stop him and drag him into a side street, where once again he would forge ahead. It was pathetic and slightly repulsive, this obvious haste, this feverishness. I thought of the rape of the Sabine women, which had so intrigued me, in my schoolboy Larousse; this time, it was almost the rape of the Roman.

Bourjols had fallen back; it was now my turn to follow close. Surprised by this unforeseeable itinerary through a district I did not know well, I found myself at one point quite close to the couple. As they suddenly emerged from the enveloping greyness of dusk into the light from a baker's window, I caught a glimpse of the two profiles facing one another as on a medal. Not only on Popov's face, screwed up into an almost tetanic hardness, but also behind Marina's, superficially mischievous and promising, I thought I could read similar expressions, at once wild and almost solemn, though it is perhaps wrong of me to pretend to a divinatory power that I did not possess. I slowed down in order to escape notice. Once or twice I saw Popov look up to read a street name: so he didn't know where he was going? Suddenly they disappeared to the right, into a doorway.

I arrived at the doorway and stopped.

The branches of a tree, theatrically lit by the window of an adjacent building, overhung the wall. The door, dark, narrow, low, was more like a postern. I looked behind me: Bourjols, a typically Parisian, big-bellied shape, arrived, without haste. The postern was ajar. I was invited to enter. I pushed it. I found myself in a corridor leading to a few steps, which in turn led to a raised courtyard. Half-memory, half-imagination, an idea came into my head about the place in which I found myself; I rejected it. I followed the corridor and climbed the steps. In the polygonal, walled-in courtyard were stuck a lamp-post and two or three sickly-looking, but indestructible trees. Whereas in the street the snow had been entirely washed away by the rain, here there were still virgin patches, white and mauve, dotted with irrepressible weeds. Before me stretched the side of an old, rather dilapidated, rather shapeless garage with a glass roof. I could not see the front of the garage, which must be on my left, opposite a doorway that I could see and which opened on to a street perpendicular to the one I had just left. Higher up, between two old buildings that seemed to sway towards one another, and whose balustrades, meat-safes and window-boxes ate into the courtyard, a very blue night sky, decked out with big yellow stars like pom-poms, suggested an early spring. Now I knew where I was, but I still did not know what we were doing there. On earlier occasions, I had gone in through the main doorway. The situation struck me as so absurd that I clung to a hope that was more likely than the truth. On either side of this courtyard were steep staircases leading to innumerable more or less wretched rooms, one of which, for some reason or other, financial or romantic, might serve, as it were, as Marina's 'bachelor's flat'. Perhaps she was anxious to preserve her respectability at the Avenue de Suffren, or perhaps she found it exciting to hide her debauchery in these lower depths of the Russian colony, in a family setting, so to speak, in a place where the records coming full blast through the thin walls and the dirty old visiting-cards stuck to the doors (colonel, countess, imperial procurator) must remind her of a relatively innocent childhood? Yes, all this was possible, but I already knew deep down that it was not so.

I crossed the five or six yards of the courtyard. A side door gave on to what had once been a garage; I had never been through this door, but I knew it, because I had seen it from the inside. I knew that the handle would squeak if I turned it and that the hinges would whine if I pushed the door open. Such are the tricks of memory: I could already hear that squeaking and whining. I also knew that *odour of sanctity* that rose in my memory a moment before the smell actually reached my nostrils.

I glanced over my shoulder. The courtyard was empty. Bourjols must be waiting for me in the street.

The handle squeaked, the hinges whined, the smell rose towards me. I quickly went in.

20

The premises had the shape of an unequal-sided quadrilateral narrower at one end than at the other, taken, not along its axis, but laterally, obliquely. A largely reddish darkness, striped vertically with pale, thickening candles, thin and pliable as a child's finger, or thick and rigid like walking sticks, caparisoned with a crust of dripping wax, stuck in copper candelabra, in wooden candlesticks, in sheets of beaten metal, in red glass containers suspended from chains: one here, two there, further on a burning bush, humming with a dim light and warmth. The glass roof had long rectangular panes stuck in masses of thickly applied mastic, some transparent, others daubed with blue ink; through them, one caught glimpses of branches moving to and fro, sometimes clearly detached, sometimes bunched together, sometimes invisible, driven by a gust of wind that heralded the spring. The walls were bathed in shadow, with reflections from polished wood, gold, silver and brass. At first sight, there seemed to be no furniture, but here and there heavy screens, with lace fronts and twisted columns, covered with chiselled metal foliage, surmounted by long brass poles from which hung squares of fringed brocade, and barricaded with round chandeliers bristling with candles, some just lit, others almost out, surrounded a tall white cylinder, crowned like a lighthouse with a red snuff. Eyes everywhere: it was as if a gigantic peacock's tail was spread out on all sides: the eyes were badly drawn, in fact, and looked nothing like eyes, but rather like boats or leaves or insects or olives or daggers, all run through the middle by the same thick, hollow, black needle that served as a pupil; monstrous eyes painted in fresco on the wall, miniature eyes drawn with a fine brush on wood or enamel, some encased in corsets of a more or less precious metal, others covered by squares of glass that blurred the view; embroidered eyes, pearly eyes, hypnotized-hypnotic eyes, leaden eyes, alert eyes, throwing as if by stencil over different surfaces the same inevitable, majestically squinting gaze. A veritable bank of eyes. And, in the middle of all that, another gaze, neither painted, nor woven, but real: that of Marina Kraievsky. She mysteriously bowed her head, smiled and, in an angelic gesture of her outstretched hand, which resembled her face, she proudly presented everything around her, all that wretched plenitude, all that picturesque trumpery. Her own eyes swelled with an overflowing, secret triumph: she could not contain her joy at the idea of having so admirably pulled off her *coup de théâtre*. She was smiling broadly, but not enough to show her teeth. What unction and what sarcasm in the gesture of the chubby hand! What contempt, what damning severity in the features! Suddenly her lips parted a little, and she whispered distinctly, experienced actress that she was, without losing her serpentine, courteous smile: '*Dobro pozhalovat*'. Welcome.'

Then, after a moment's silence, with a strange broadening of the gaze, her shoulders in profile, she slipped over to the right, towards the far corner of the building and, moving between two lighted, sputtering candlesticks, which stood like two protective angels, she disappeared into the darkness that reigned behind them. The warm waves that rose from them made the air curve inwards and shimmer like a curtain.

The music began. But for the lover of Beethoven and Tchaikovsky, it was not real music: there was neither harmony nor unison, just the feeble voices of old women chanting atonal melodies and, from time to time, the roarings of a wheezy old lion, which could not even be called out of tune because they were toneless. Incomprehensible words, but one guessed that they belonged to the same hieroglyphic universe as the mottoes, quotations, epigraphs, monograms and symbols that were displayed unintelligibly on all sides, with their characters overladen with tildes, accents and various flourishes, surmounted with crowns and illuminated with tails.

Then there was the smell! An ever more intrusive smell stirring in the memory a whole convoy of images long since liquidated, liquidated but not liquefied, still solid, granular, presenting themselves with all the vertiginous concavity of an undischarged liability.

The airvent through which the smell . . .

Block up the memory.

Then, in that misshapen space, gently undulating with warm air, lightly coloured by the haze of a thin cloud, a thick black form stood out from the wall, rolled across the concrete floor covered with a red carpet, danced from one candlestick to the next, moistened her fingers in her mouth, squeezed between the thumb and index finger the wick of half-burnt candles and, after a final and satisfying pfft, snatched these candles and dropped them into a cardboard box on the ground, where they landed with a still more satisfying and definitive plop.

Babushka. Pfft. Plop!

There were other babushkas there. Interchangeable. Prostrated behind the candlesticks, stuck together in groups, packed together at the foot of walls on invisible benches, wobbling on their old, varicosed legs, their stockings rolled down below the knee, grey shawls or white straw hats on their heads, black crocheted mantillas, lace bleached to a sepia, their colourless hair showing glimpses of the pink skin of their heads, one of them a grotesque with the bloody mouth of a vampire, the others, on the contrary, decent, well-behaved, molluscs in the process of turning to mineral on the hull of a ship; one more, one less, it did not matter.

There were not only babushkas there. Other forms could be made out against the candlelight, an old man with a moustache, stiff in a kind of frock coat, green with age, a chubby little girl holding the hand of an ample-bosomed young woman with voluptuously regular breathing, a fair-haired young man wearing a long, black robe pulled in at the waist, with a chalky face, a hard eye, a bearing more military than religious, so slim that he looked like one of those flat silhouettes used for target practice. He was devoting himself to a whole specialized gymnastics: kneel down, forehead touching the ground, stand, kneel down—he seemed to like it.

The overall plan gradually became clearer. The narrowest end of the building was concealed by a wall of images arranged on a platform covered by a carpet. In front of this platform, on either side, were projections, like wooden bastions, also illustrated with images and bearing banners and standards. Behind the right-hand bastion, on the platform, was hidden the choir—which was all to the good! This bastion consisted of a painted wooden carving representing the crucified Christ, flanked by a woman and a man, Adam and Eve, perhaps, but they were wearing clothes. The Crucified did not seem to be suffering; he seemed rather to be floating in mid-air. There was no sense of the weight of his body pulling on his arms. His face was sad, but did not express the physical suffering that he must have been feeling. So much for realism! The man and the woman, too, fixed in their artificial poses, their heads raised obliquely, had been drawn by an amateur. The stones at the foot of the cross looked like anything but stones: the artist should have taken lessons in perspective before making himself ridiculous. In anatomy, too: a body nailed by the hands would not stay hanging for long, since the nails would have torn through the palms. And in balance: a cross of that size stuck among those few pebbles would have fallen down at the first hammer blow. In front of the carving was a small metal table, with holes for candles: there were four candles and at least forty holes, a good sign. On the left-hand bastion were represented a woman and a child; only their faces and hands were painted; their busts disappeared under a silver plaque representing clothes. A roof in yellow-metal filigree curved over this portrait, and various knick-knacks—a pearl necklace, other necklaces, a miniature leg in gold—were hanging from it. All this was visible only through a hedge of lighted candles, which made the brasses sparkle, the silvers shine and invested the gaze of the woman and child with a hypnotic dimension that the painter could not have foreseen. At least those two looked like a real woman and child, with a bulging forehead, cheeks in relief, shadows, modelling, a tender, mysterious expression, that bore no relation to the daubed, two-dimensional figures on the panels

217

forming the wall of images at the back of the platform. This wall, with its cupolas, crosses, curtain, red lamps hanging from their brass chains, was covered with faces lacking any physical reality, surrounded by swords, goblets, books, wings, mottoes, fantastic animals: they were no longer faces but ideograms. The whole, condensed into this reduced space, ready to burst like an atom of uranium, seemed nevertheless to conform to some rules that determined its necessary structure. It was an exalted place, isolated from the rest of the building by a protective barrier of candles. It was also a décor lit by footlights, representing something that it was not. And, like everything else here, pierced with eyes. A moment of hallucination: what if all those eyes started to wink in an irregular rhythm, like clocks chiming in a shop, or all together?

Then, nothing—nothing happened. Voices rose and fell. A new voice, well pitched and rounded, joined the pitiful choir, chanting with restraint the same continent melodies. Why did the others not keep quiet? Why did they not let her sing alone? Their God would undeniably have been the better off for it. And why did she not sing out? It would not have been difficult for her to drown these rivulets in her river. But her voice stood out only at certain moments; the rest of the time it melted into the kolkhoze. Another voice was reading aloud some sibylline text, pouring out the stereotyped phrases in the same fixed, monotonous rhythm. It was the height of absurdity: listening to a reading that one cannot understand. The choir, probably in a hurry to finish, intoned its amens before the reader's voice fell silent: not very polite. Human larvae crept along the walls, which they kissed with devotion. A different melody was heard and it was suddenly as if four humble voices of the choir had taken hold of the four corners of the building, lifting it up in the air like a sheet, and transported it elsewhere, far away, into a world of gentleness in peril, four angels, three of them extremely wobbly on their legs, carrying with the utmost care an ark—but what is an ark?—which was supposed to contain some irreplaceable treasure. The airvent: the melody came from there! Block up the airvent! Wall it up! No, it didn't really matter. A thin candle, melting in the heat, bent in the middle.

Above, it was completely dark: one could not even see that the roof was made of glass. How could one have known that one was in Paris, in that year? It was easier to believe oneself transported in some interstellar space-ship, outside the grid of the space-time coordinates of this world. A man appeared, preceded by a small boy.

The boy was wearing a yellow robe that fell straight from the shoulders to the ankles. It was a bit short for him: his shoes and his thick, red socks were visible. He had a very round head, very fair hair, very blue eyes, an attitude not self-important, but dignified. A good lad. 'I, a young pioneer of the Soviet Union, in front of my comrades . . .'—eyes fixed on the coveted scarf. But this boy kept his eyes fixed on the man he was attending, antici-pating his wishes, finding an evident satisfaction in carrying them out immediately: more than satisfaction, a sense of accomplishment.

The man had nothing about him of the greasy pope of tradi-tion: no long, oily hair, no severity of expression, no beard, no belly stuffed with capons extorted from the people. He must have been a pope all the same, judging by the costume, the breed hated above all others, keeping the masses under the anaesthetic of a fictitious hope, theophagous vermin of repulsive habits, to be crushed under foot, like sewer rats. He came forward, murmuring some chant, his body disappearing beneath a bronzed carapace that made him look like a beetle, a brocade hump weighing on him between the shoulders, black veils float-ing round his legs, as if they were not separated from one another, but formed out of a single block, like those celluloid manikins weighted with lead that are impossible to knock over—but no, one could, after all, see his short boots, tiny little boots encasing feet that were astonishingly delicate for a man; the whole man, indeed, seemed to have been produced in minia-ture: the small, deeply lined hand, the skinny neck, the slim bone-structure of the forehead caving in at the temples: every-thing suggested an insect's body swaying beneath the weight of a shell that was too heavy for it. At one moment, he held out his hand and the boy passed him an object made of chains at the end of which hung a small portable stove; at the same time, the boy

219

leant mechanically forward, and kissed the pope's hand, like those toy drinking birds that some counterweight forces to straighten up the moment they have touched the water. 'In the presence of my comrades I solemnly swear to be faithful . . .' With great dexterity, the pope started to wave the stove in all directions, in order to make smoke, catching it again on the end of its chain. The smoke escaped from an opening between the lid and the body of the stove, spreading that odour, which, thirty years earlier, had come out of the airvent. It should be noted that the pejorative and comic word 'pope' did not really suit this a-sexual, hardly physical, almost armorial, allegorical creature that became clearer as he moved forward with little ceremonious bows, without, apparently, executing separate steps: it was as if he ran on rollers and shock absorbers, a kind of mildly terrifying clockwork toy. It took some time to understand what he was doing, because he was doing two things at once; on the one hand, he was chanting in a low voice some consoling tune, irresistibly suggesting death, but a serene, acceptable, almost melodious death; on the other hand, he was moving around the building censing all the images in turn ('that's for you , that's for you') and all the congregation ('that's for you'). The worshippers stepped back as he passed, flattening themselves against the walls, as if pinned there like butterflies, merging so well with the images that one was then surprised to see them resume their places. The priest stopped, he set off again, he approached, swinging his censer in an almost menacing way—it reminded one of some 'disintegrator' out of science fiction and, in a more prosaic way, one could not help wondering what would happen if he let go of it—and his quiet chanting still rose from his lips, strangely resembling the smoke that rose from the burner, as if the chanting and the perfume were merely two different sensory aspects of the same phenomenon. He censed up at the pictures of an armed man, sword at his side, he censed down to the kneeling babushka, he censed sideways at the poor creature in the frock coat; he maintained them, so to speak, both within reach and at a distance from the censer; he picked them out individually, his regulars, his accomplices; he bowed before each person and

220

each image, though it was not clear whether he did so out of obsequiousness or because of the balancing movement imprinted on his body; it was as if he was labelling them, recruiting them: 'And you, too, St Ivan, and you, too, Ivan Ivanovich,' and they, making room for him, acknowledged him, recognized him, not in his psychological identity, but in his function or perhaps in something still more esoteric. They all belonged to the same crew. But there he suddenly was, quite near, making no distinction between the faithful and the unfaithful, simply picking him out in his row, between an ascetic saint and a bigotted old maggot; he stopped in front of the intruder as he was to do before all the others, putting him in the same fold. What impertinence! Did he not see that this was a wolf in the fold? He saw nothing. He levitated in his veils, in his odoriferous cloud, and he censed everything he encountered. Now he brought his arm back as if to strike, and his gaze transpired all of a sudden as it became aware of the strange presence, a gaze of prodigious penetration, which struck as lightning from that falcon's head inclined to one side, a total gaze in some sort, which seemed to encompass the hooked nose, the withdrawn mouth, the cheeks furrowed with vertical wrinkles, the protruding cornice of the asymmetrical eyebrows, as much as the eyes themselves, which had no reason to envy those of the images on the wall, being as fixed, as impenetrable, as stylized as they and, to cap it all, of different colours: the right blue-grey, at once milky and leaden like that of a dead bird; the left grey-green, of a disturbing marine transparency. An odd bird, that priest. It would be easy, if one believed in those things, to take him for a clairvoyant. With the hunch-backed effect imposed by the chasuble, with that lolling head, that drawn face with different-shaped eyebrows, and with that gaze seemingly projected by the whole being (as in karate it is the body as a whole that strikes and not only the three joints of the clenched right hand), he would have made an excellent intelligence officer. A pity that those energies were being wasted in the interests of the biggest practical joke of all time. No matter, he was the enemy, and it seemed intolerable to receive from him the homage of this censing, so manifestly symbolic, to be

pointed out by the movement of his little stove to a higher attention, to see oneself irremediably lodged by him in the pavilion of
the censed. Should one move back? The wall prevented it. Hide
one's face? One would look ridiculous. Heavens! Not the censer!
Not this smell of airvent in the nostrils, not this impalpable and
fatal seal.

To protect themselves against the devil the superstitious
make the sign of the cross; but what can an atheist do against a
fumigating chasuble? A glance at the child, standing there, in
the distance, alone, following, open-mouthed, the progress of
the pernicious levite. '. . . To be faithful to the precepts of
Lenin, to serve unshakeably the cause of our Communist Party,
to ensure the victory of Communism. I promise to live . . .'
How close the past was! The red scarf in the hands of the guide
and, in the heart, that knot of strength, that unequalled density
of the childish will. By what right was that little boy, fair-haired
and blue-eyed, that honest little Russian boy of the twentieth
century, forced to breathe the drugged miasmas that reigned
here, to kiss hands, to wear skirts, to venerate baubles? Help,
little boy! Commit some saving incongruity, kick that candlestick over or at least pick your nose with your little finger! But
the wondering child remained impassive, like Isaac under the
knife; no hypnosis could turn him away from the sacred butcher
who held him spellbound; his full, pink cheeks shone like
apples; he was happy with his absolute alienation. '. . . To live
and to study in such a way as to become a citizen . . .' The holy
formula! One swotted away at it of an evening, the blanket
pulled over one's head, one's eyes open in the darkness, one's
mouth forming tirelessly and noiselessly the sacramental words.
How afraid one was of forgetting them the day one had to say
them, in front of one's comrades! How convinced one was that if
one forgot the slightest part of it, it would be a sign that the sacrifice had been rejected, that one would be condemned without
right of appeal! 'If I hesitate over a single word, I will throw
myself under the 6.53 train. No, not if I hesitate: if I forget. But
yes, even if I hesitate. What would be the point of living if I were
rejected?' The red scarf, the badge with the sharp pin (if one
pricks oneself and bleeds, it brings good luck, but one mustn't

222

do it on purpose), the oath that rasps the throat, caresses the tongue, files through the teeth, flies off gloriously from the parted lips and there, it's done, the gift is accepted, it was easy: '. . . to become a citizen worthy of my Soviet fatherland'. The scarf, the plump hand of the guide. How tall one suddenly feels, how invincible! The guide's voice (it's a bit rough in the upper register, but one refuses to notice it: he has the most beautiful voice because he is saying the most beautiful words): 'To struggle for the cause of Lenin and Stalin . . . be ready!' A tremor ran through the audience. One shut one's eyes to make the moment more intense; one opened the mouth wide, for greater force: 'Ever ready!' Ever, forever, world without end, to my dying day and also at every moment of each day and night, even when it feels so good to skate on the Kliazma, even when it feels so good to curl up in bed, ready. Ready to set forth and ready to drop dead, ready to have one's fingernails pulled out by the White Guards, ready to be buried alive by the Fascists, to spit in the face of bourgeois torturers. Ready to give all: life and the toy soldiers and the stamp collection and the beloved old teddy-bear that Babushka mended and which one hides under one's pillow out of respect for one's pals. What decent-decadent Westerner would ever understand the absolute generosity of this childish gift? Their Dostoievsky was right: there's nothing more noble than a little Russian boy. We mowed him down, Dostoievsky, and quite right! The priest's hand opens lightly and the censer flies up. One bows like the others, so as to escape notice. It doesn't matter. The censer exhales its poison. The magus passes; the smell of thirty years ago rises in coils that one imagines to be illuminated with acanthus leaves and foliated scrolls; its waves majestically invest defenceless nostrils; they reach one after another the cells of the mucous membranes, depositing in each their pollen.

Block up the airvent!

Now an invisible man was reading meaningless words. Occasionally a single word stood out, and then one realized that there was nothing to understand, that even decoded, it was still gibberish. How could modern, so-called enlightened men pretend to believe that virgins give birth, that carcases resuscitate, that elements are transmuted? It's their class-interest, that's all, either because they find in these beliefs a means of exploiting others, or because they look to them to compensate for their own unhappiness. The martyrs were mad businessmen who believed they had found a wonderful opportunity to invest . . . They must have pulled a face when they saw that there was no payer on the other side. Only they no longer possessed a face, so they saw nothing at all. The candles guttered on the candlesticks: the specialized gleaner must be deep in prayer or having a snooze. There was reading and singing: there was no reason for it to end. The space-ship was suspended outside time, and these people liked that. So that's what the others had been doing in their cellar? The whole building, with its oblong and trapezoid shape, was reminiscent of a coffin, but an intimate, padded, almost warm coffin, in which one might forget life in relative comfort. What shame, to be thus tamed for death! What is that child doing here, in this obscene place? What children need are hard, clear things; symbols, yes, but clear symbols, like the triangular scarf signifying unity of the three generations of Communists, but above all not mystic symbols, even Hegelian ones, thank you. The candles went out one by one; they were not replaced; the space-ship sank into the void; one could hardly see a thing any more. The singers sang more quietly; they had no more breath, no more voice left, they were chanting mere ideas of chants, on a single, transparent note. But the words they were saying were becoming gradually clearer: 'Glory to God in the highest, and on earth (or the world) peace to men of good will'. Gibberish! The old sacred language seemed to grow a bit clearer as the light fell, but only to reveal how fussy and, in the final analysis, insignificant it was. 'Glory to God in the highest', perhaps there is an idea there all the same: God spreads his glory in the highest and those on high spread it on their subordinates, unless it's the other way round: the subordinates harvest the glory that they hand over to their superiors, who pass it on to God. Or it is to be understood as, 'the glory of those in the highest is for God.' None of that seemed to disturb the little boy, who should have been in bed some time ago. Instead of remaining on his knees, his bust erect, as he should, he sat

224

back on his heels and looked around him. No discipline! It was quite different when we put one knee to the ground to kiss the golden fringe of the heavy red standard embroidered with the portrait of Ilich.

We got up early, washed carefully, put on clean, perhaps even new clothes; may be we had gone without dessert the night before out of reverence; later, for hours on end, we were to respect our own fingers and lips; we were to avoid swearing, for fear of soiling our mouths, which had been sanctified by this kiss. Poor little Russian boy! Your stateless parents have uprooted you from your earth, deprived you of the milk of truth; they will turn you into a failed Westerner, or into a fanatic of deceit. Yet you might have served . . . Pity! For every one lost, it is true, there are ten to take his place. Russia has never had a problem with numbers. Ten thousand little boys like you are born in Russia everyday. One could have a kid like you tomorrow. But one would need a woman, and women, once one has mowed them down . . .

Would it never stop? Soon there would be no candles at all, or congregation. One could see the night again, through the glass roof, because the night was clearer than the inside of the building. Now only a single voice rose from the right-hand bastion, an old, cracked voice, like a sad chime, hurrying through some chant or other. The rest of the choir must have gone home: they'd had enough. Understandable. The pope, too, was nowhere to be seen. Odd phrases surfaced, all the same, like bubbles: give us our daily bread! Forgive us our debts! What could be more materialistic than these idealists? And suddenly, from one knew not where, from the depths of the sky or the centre of the earth, as if he was already dead or risen from the dead, came the voice of the omnipresent priest:

'For thine is the kingdom, the power and the glory, Father, Son and Holy Spirit.'

The cracked voice added, breathlessly, 'Amen', and continued faster than ever.

The kingdom, the power and the glory. Those people are not entirely out of their minds: they know what is good. But how do they dare to name those magnificent things in this old garage

225

with its concrete floor covered with a worn out carpet, with no more than a dozen of these woodlice to drill? The weak should not be allowed to use the sublime vocabulary of the strong.

On the platform, one of the wall images swung noiselessly. A black ghost, carrying a candle and a book, glided to the middle of the platform, where he stopped and, facing the wall of images, turned towards the absent congregation a smooth back, clad in a long, black, elegantly waisted tunic. There was no hump any more, but he was recognizable by the way the head lolled on one side. So he had been hiding? He had taken off his chasuble-armour: he must be in a hurry to get back to the wife. He stood motionless, but not frozen, a tree, not a post, concentrating inwardly, dense, radiating shade: it was almost as if he were growing. One could no longer see the candle he held before him, but the image at the foot of which he was standing reflected, from its varnished reds and blues, the light, trembling flame. The whole wall began to gleam with its burnished golds and when the priest bowed, a cavalcade of shadows ran through the building. At last the voice of the old reader stopped, as if a spring had snapped. One felt almost sorry: one had got used to it. The priest turned towards the hall, which must have gaped with darkness in front of him; he could not even see whether a single worshipper remained; he blessed them in their absence; he, too, disappeared. It was time to be off, but one really didn't want to; one would happily remain a few more minutes contemplating the death throes of the last candles, obscurely repeated by the metal and the polished wood.

Then, emerging from behind the counter placed next to the large entrance doors, appeared a character who had not yet been seen, a stunted gnome, moving with little steps, almost without lifting his feet, his legs wide apart as if he suffered severely from piles, his arms swinging loose like those of a big monkey, the shell-like eyelids closed, as if he were asleep on his feet. He dragged himself from one chandelier to the next, put out the last candles, threw them into boxes, emptied the boxes noisily into a larger box and unceremoniously blew out the lamps at the centre of the chandeliers, climbed up on to the platform and, by means of pulleys, lowered the red lamps to within reach. It was like a fairy story, those stars descending, once the people had left. They were put out and left there, swinging in the night. It was pleasurable to spy upon him in this way, as he performed his little chores. Now the hall seemed to be lit only by the glass roof, which had reverted to blue. Above, there was moonlight. Here below, nothing shone, but a few pale forms—banners, lecterns—retained some luminosity. The gnome came back to his counter where, under a cowl, shone—one could hardly see it—a strip-light. This gave one a glimpse of his bulbous head covered with short, white down. His eyes opened, globular and thoughtful, like horses' eyes. He suddenly realized that he was not alone, tottered over to the back, made half-a-dozen hasty signs of the cross, murmured the popular exorcism, 'Our place is holy', then suddenly came back to earth.

'What are you doing there, good soul?'

Silence.

'Perhaps you want to see Father Vladimir?'

The intruder did not answer.

The gnome spoke more slowly and more loudly, as he thought he should when speaking to particularly stupid persons, foreigners, for example: 'He is gone. Gone away. To the house, gone.'

He added in what he believed to be French: 'Priest house. Understand?'

Then the intruder asked in Russian, in a voice 'that was not his': 'Well? Is everything finished here, then?'

The gnome nodded emphatically: 'Finished, finished. Quite finished. It is go you must.'

The other man did not move. In the moonlight one could see his white irises. He looked liked a madman, a killer, a mad killer. He went on: 'When does it begin again?'

'What?'

'I don't know. This mass you had here.'

The gnome could not believe his ears.

'What do you mean? What mass, good soul? Masses are on Sunday. Or on feastdays . . .'

He went on in French, more sure of conveying his meaning that way: 'Tomorrow, mass. Tomorrow, tomorrow.'

227

The stranger asked drily in Russian: 'What time?'

'Eleven o'clock, eleven.'

Curiosity gaining over fear, the gnome questioned in turn: 'You cannot be from here, eh, Monsieur? Where do you come from, then?'

He would not have been surprised if the intruder had replied: 'From the other world.' But the intruder did not reply. He swung round on his heels and walked towards the side door. Suddenly, he yelled out: 'And today, what day was it today?'

'Today? The vigils . . .'

'And here, what is it?'

'Here? Well, a church . . .'

'Which church, I mean?'

'The Dormition of the Most Pure.'

'Dormition? . . .'

The name rang a bell, even if one did not know exactly what it meant. Popov stepped out briskly, crossed the courtyard, walked along the corridor, past the postern, made a mental note of the address, jumped into a taxi and was driven to the Rue de Grenelle. He went into his office, flooded it with dazzling light, took out from the filing cabinet the yellow folder marked 'Zmeïka', unfolded it on the table and, in the space reserved on the pink form for places and hours of contact, added: 'Church of the Dormition. Vigils. Masses.'

21

Bourjols and I had taken refuge in the *bistrot* opposite the corner occupied by the church. From there we were able to observe both the main gateway that gave on to one street and the postern that gave on to the other. From a broom cupboard smelling of floor cloths, I telephoned Rat.

'Well, my boy, you certainly are making us look good! Have you any idea of his motives?'

I had no idea. I heard a few clicks of his false teeth, then, with a decisiveness that surprised me, he gave me orders that were not pleasant to follow, but which were undeniably well founded. The black Peugeot 203 arrived twenty minutes later and I showed the chauffeur where to park so as to preserve our tactical advantage. With great satisfaction, he moved into a place where parking was forbidden and our vigil began. Every now and then, Bourjols grumbled: 'What the hell could they be doing?'

Once he said: 'You don't think they're getting married, do you?'

The idea of Marina in sable coat and Popov in a lumber jacket moving around a lectern, followed, step by step, by altar boys holding gilt crowns above their heads did not even make me laugh. I was stupefied with astonishment. How could my morning mood have betrayed me so much? I had been so sure of my luck! In fact, it was not my luck that had deserted me, but Marina. Why?

I had expected to see Popov emerge like a devil from a holy-water stoup, but no; he seemed to be enjoying the service. Or—my head was now filled with the craziest ideas—had

229

Marina had him kidnapped by some émigré group, White Guards or Black Hundreds, using some passage unknown to me? I was tempted to go back into the church to see what was happening, but I had felt so ill at ease under Marina's insistent gaze that I couldn't face it again. What a situation! I in the doorway; Popov, seen from behind, standing a yard away from me, and Marina, who had just kissed an icon, turning round to us, smiling, not like Gioconda, but like the angel of Rheims, whispering to us both, sarcastically associated in a single look: 'Welcome!'

Popov must have taken the snub on his own shoulders, but I had no doubt that it was also addressed to me. So it was in God's house that she spent her weekends!

Two or three people came out, then some others: a young woman accompanied by a little girl, some old women, one or two old men.

'The end of the mass?' asked the chauffeur, a young man with a fair moustache, very much the colonel's chauffeur, familiar rather than impertinent. 'Not much of a crowd, sir!'

'It's the vigils, Marty. And I don't think it's the end yet. The Russians leave when they've had enough.'

'The vigils? What's that?'

'On Saturday, pious Orthodox have a special service to prepare for the next day's mass.'

'You mean that for them it doesn't count as a mass?'

I shook my head. He whistled.

'Well, blimey! They make 'em work, them orthopaedists! Glad I'm a Catholic, not that I practise. Not much of a believer, either. Still, I suppose they don't have a collection on Saturdays?'

'Two, I believe,'

'The only ritual common to all religions, eh?'

We giggled in the little rain-beaten car. Bourjols jibbed: he did not approve of our freethinking: 'Everyone believes what he likes. Come on, open the window a bit, young man: can't you see we're steamed up?'

The well maintained engine purred patiently.

'There she is!' Bourjols said at last.

Marina had come out between two other women. Was she being careful? It might make our job more difficult. No sign of Popov. Either he was still inside, or, more likely, we'd missed him. It didn't matter: it was not him we were concerned with. Everyone was standing about saying goodbye. The two women, one fat, one thin, walked towards us. Marina went off in the opposite direction—alone.

'There's a sight for sore eyes!' remarked the chauffeur, releasing the hand-brake.

'I can do without your comments, Marty.'

I got out. It was the first time in my life I had been in charge of an operation of this kind, or even taken part in one; but I knew the drill and I was in no doubt that I would pull it off. Marina was walking some twenty yards ahead of me on the right-hand pavement. Fifty yards ahead there was an intersection and no car was parked at the corner: in a way, the luck that had been with me most of the day had not abandoned me. I felt no shame. The hunting instinct prevailed.

I overtook the sable coat on her right, five or six yards before the empty parking space.

'Marina?'

She turned round without stopping.

'Ah! You're still there. Did you like the service?' she asked in Russian.

It was beyond my strength to answer her in the same language. She used it only as a gesture of insolence, for the contrast between its soft, raucous sounds and the impudent expression on her face. I forced myself to walk on the inside.

'Marina,' I went on, pretending to be quite annoyed. 'I don't understand. Where is he? You should at least keep me informed.'

She was still walking. We reached the corner. The Peugeot came to a halt. I grabbed Marina by the right fore-arm.

'Marina . . .'

Stupidly, I didn't know what to say. When she saw me hesitate, she tried to snatch her arm away. Bourjols had just opened the rear door of the car. Marina looked to the left and drew back towards me. Bourjols grabbed her by the wrist and

231

pulled her off balance with a sharp tug. I took hold of her by the shoulder and bundled her into the car. Though I say it myself, it wasn't bad for a beginner. As I slammed the rear door, Marty opened the front door for me and let me in. The car moved off.

'Smashing, sir!'

I turned towards Marina. Bourjols was still holding her firmly and said to her: 'Don't make a fuss, little lady, or we'll have to use handcuffs.'

'I'm having much too good a time to make a fuss,' she said coldly. 'Are you having a good time, too, Cyril?'

And, by way of insult, she translated into Russian: 'Are you finding it amusing, too, Kiril Lavrovich?'

'We're going to blindfold you,' I said. 'Don't resist.'

'*Rocambole*, episode thirteen,' she remarked.

Bourjols blindfolded her with a scarf, taking care not to pinch the skin or tie it too tight. A lamb to the slaughter, she settled comfortably on her seat, as if embarking on a long journey. She was breathing rather more quickly than usual, but her muscles were relaxed.

Intimidation is the first lever. Sometimes it works on its own, but more often because the victim imagines—with a little help—that this is only the beginning. Being temporarily blinded, not knowing where one is and what happens next usually produce excellent results, especially with people of a certain intellectual level. It's different with more simple souls: they demand proof of violence before starting to quail. I hoped with all my heart that Marina would frighten herself: we did not have the means and I certainly did not have the inclination to resort to any real violence. It was surprising enough that, in his fear of Silbert, Rat had gone so far as to risk an action as illegal as a kidnapping. For the moment, Marina didn't seem to want to play it our way—she maintained a proud, attentive silence. I suppose she was observing her feelings in order to reproduce their internal symptoms when she would have to play the part of a prisoner. The Stanislavsky method is above all a storing away of sensations. Bourjols, distant and vigilant, obviously did not approve of our adventure; he had been taken on as a leg-man, not as a 'heavy', and probably was sorry he had ever agreed to take part

232

in this new phase of the operation. Marty, on the other hand, was not at all sorry to miss his Saturday night out: it wasn't every day a colonel's chauffeur kidnapped Mata-Hari.

The gates of the Invalides were open for us. The guard, a career NCO, cast a curious glance into the car. On orders, he had removed all his conscripts from view. Apparently, the Shopkeeper did not think Marty was the type to write to his Member of Parliament (we must have had some sort of hold on him). I helped Marina out of the car.

'If you need a hand, sir,' said Marty, 'don't hesitate to ask.'

I refrained from answering: that suggestive tone might have a good effect on Marina. Bourjols touched his cap with three fingers and moved off into the rain; he was not pleased with us and showed it. He was convinced that no one would lay a finger on Marina, but the fact that she might think that we would already seemed to him incompatible with the honour of a retired gendarme. Or perhaps he had seen Olga Orloff on television? Or perhaps she reminded him of some niece, or granddaughter?

I held Marina's arm under mine and guided her to my familiar quarters. Marina's heels tapped gaily on the old, worn steps and pink linoleum, but suddenly I became aware of how sinister the situation might seem and I felt a deep sense of compassion, for perhaps the first time in my life. It was not with a view to intimidating her—or, if it was, only to an insignificant degree—that I whispered in the chubby ear that I found so close to my mouth: 'Tell everything and nothing will happen to you.'

My good deed was not well received: 'I'll tell everything if I want to,' Marina snapped. At the time, I did not understand the tone of her voice: it suggested menace rather than restriction.

I had just knocked on the colonel's door when another door, further up the corridor, opened and Tolstoy, wearing a close-fitting sweater—it was Saturday—approached.

'Congratulations!' he said, subjecting the prisoner to an admiring scrutiny. 'If I were you, I'd take her home with me.'

He gave his slanted smile. His eyes insolently riveted to mine, he added: 'Love is blind?'

He passed behind us at the very moment Rat called out: 'Come in.' I pushed Marina forward with some impatience,

233

shut the door behind us and hastened to say—I think I stammered a little: 'You can take that off now.'

She took off the blindfold without haste and dropped it at her feet, like a stripper dropping her last layer. Then, with the deliberate gesture of an actress coming on stage and taking her bearings, she took in the place I had brought her to. The huge, neon-lit office, the filthy, untidy table under the window with its lowered blinds and the old man with the lantern-shaped head, wearing a moth-eaten pullover, none of this seemed to intimidate her. 'Where are the rack and thumbscrews?' she murmured (she had played Estelle in Sartre's *Huis Clos*), looked around for a chair, found none (the Shopkeeper must have removed them as a psychological tactic) and, after moving down-stage, as it were, to the footlights, stopped in the middle of the stage in a simple, but decorative pose: Joan of Arc before her judges. I cannot believe that deep down she did not feel some anxiety: after all, she had just succeeded in making a fool of the secret services of the French Republic and there she was in their hands; but she was so wrapped up in her role of heroine that she had no attention left to devote to her true emotions. To look at her, one would have thought that she was enjoying what was happening to her.

Personally, I was feeling far from happy. I knew that I was responsible for an operation that had failed superbly; Rat would throw all the blame on me, whatever his share of responsibility; if the business of the day-book was discovered I could end up in a court martial. My mouth was dry and my hands moist, but I think I managed, as much out of respect for myself as from calculation, to conceal the fact: if I was to wriggle out of it, it would not be by giving in to despair.

The most frightened of the three of us was Rat. He had, as they say, aged ten years. His jaundiced complexion had turned positively green; his slack lips moved with difficulty; the sounds that came out of them were almost hollow. He did not manage to hide the foetid fear he felt; he simply tried to pass it off as anger. I could tell that he had Silbert's mask floating in front of his eyes, and then his home in the suburbs, his bank account empty, his shrew-wife unchained, his central heating down to 60°.

'Well,' he yapped weakly, after a long silence intended to disconcert the prisoner, 'perhaps you'll explain to me what all this means?'

And he couldn't stop himself continuing, out of senile impatience rather than to rush her:

'What's this supposed to prove, what you have just done to us?'

Marina took a deep breath, threw back her chin, formed her carefully made up lips into a curve and said: 'It proves, sir, Whom I serve.'

A melodramatic style (which is nearly always the case when an actor writes his own lines), but impeccable diction, with explosive consonants and vowels powerfully sustained by breath.

Religious considerations were so alien to Rat that he misunderstood. He replied, with a distrustful look at me: 'I thought you had settled everything with Volsky.'

'I did settle everything with Volsky.'

'Or he's been stringing me along.'

'He has told you the truth.'

She sent the ball back to him forehanded, just skimming the net, hardly leaving him time to finish the attack before riposting.

'You agreed to . . .?'

'Yes.'

'Then what's come over you?'

This time, as one has to with a long speech, she gave herself time to breathe, then, on a more serious note, more slowly, she said:

'Do you really imagine that, in order to ensure M. Volsky's advancement and perhaps yours, I was going . . .? *You* perhaps may be excused, because you do not know who I am. But *he* . . .' Her voice swelled. 'Given his origins, he must have known that between them and us there can be only war.'

I intervened: 'It was an act of war I was asking you to perform.'

'There are limits to what you can ask an actress to do,' she said, without looking at me.

'What is all this belated virtue?' I asked, succumbing involuntarily to her tennis rhythm.

235

She turned on me violently: 'Don't you understand a thing? Yes, I agreed to make war with the weapons that God gave me—and I put my health on the line, as you know. Don't push me too far, Volsky. I might really tell all.'

Rat, a hunted look in his jaundiced eye, asked wearily: 'What's she insinuating now?'

I couldn't guess.

'I've nothing to hide from you, sir.'

'Well. We'll see. Don't be afraid of him, young woman. Out with it.'

'I'm not afraid of him nor of you. Aren't you capable of understanding that there's a difference between seducing an enemy and making him fall in love with you?'

'Ah! So you don't think you're capable of taking enough hold on him. Yet I'd have thought . . .'

The old man had just taken stock of this woman's charms. She smiled contemptuously and closed her eyes, as if calling on her reserve of patience.

'Of course I do. That's just it. Love . . . Love is sacred.'

The Shopkeeper scowled at me and snapped: 'Who have you brought me here, Volsky?'

Then, turning back to her, he brought his fist down on the table. Papers flew in all directions, but nobody picked them up.

'And the cash I give you, I suppose that's not sacred, young woman? What about the 30,000 francs you pick up each week?'

She smiled at him with a different kind of smile, broad, luminous, revealing all her small, moist, gleaming teeth in battle array. I had never seen her smile like this before. She took three steps towards the desk, opened her bag composedly, took out a signed cheque, the payee's name left blank, turned it politely round towards the colonel and put it in front of him, on the yellow blotting-paper, between the chewed pencils and the cigarette ash.

'I'll keep my Fragance fees,' she said. 'I've earned them. Here are your thirty pieces of silver.'

Rat did not bat an eyelid at the unwarranted allusion. His mind, so ingenious in sordid matters, was scouring the countryside. What could this girl want of him? She could have sold us to

Popov, but, in that case, the practices of the secret services are very strict: the sums of money received by the double agent from employer A go wholly into the account of employer B. So what trap was concealed beneath this appetising cheque? Of course, there was no question of accepting it. Giving it back to the Division would be an admission of his incompetence; putting his own name on it, however tempting that might be, would be to fall into the trap. So that was it? The KGB wanted to compromise the Shopkeeper with his own money? Tied up with red ribbon. He flicked the bit of paper away from him.

'What is paid is paid,' he said magnanimously.

Marina stood in front of him, quivering like an arrow in its target. How she must have looked forward to that simple, yet telling gesture of placing the cheque on the table! What pleasure she must have known, piling up her treasure from week to week, only to hand it back in one magnificent gesture! Rat leaned back in his chair. His cunning was gradually returning to him.

'What has there been between Volsky and you?' he asked point-blank.

She did not answer at once. Again, he could not wait.

'If his presence embarrasses you, I'll have him leave.'

I wondered if he was thinking of appropriating the cheque without a witness. Marina gave me an amused, but not over-expressive look.

'He doesn't embarrass me. There was never anything between him and me.'

But that's not what he was talking about. He could not have cared less about our personal relations.

'Come, come, young woman, I'm not deaf. It's quite clear you have something on him. You threatened to tell *all*.'

He extended his long, yellow fingers towards the cheque, picked it up—like the teeth of a crane closing on a load—then, moving the left-hand back and the right-hand forward, he folded it diagonally, as if about to tear it. He thought he held us by that cheque: 'Tell *all*, young woman,' he said, shooting a surreptitious glance at me.

There was a long silence during which Marina slowly reverted to being the Slav Gioconda, the Sphinx of the Urals.

She smiled as if only to herself, and goldfish flitted across her eyes. She seemed to feel a mysterious, intimate voluptuousness. Finally, once, almost imperceptibly, from left to right and then from right to left, she moved her head. She was denying something to a person more powerful than she and derived a certain delicious satisfaction from the fact. To be weak and to reign: what could be finer? The David complex. Gathering pinches of imaginary dust on his desk, Rat said:

'Young woman, I can see you're a bit dotty, but I think you've got enough upstairs to understand that this is a serious business that could have very pleasant or very unpleasant consequences for you. Espionage in peacetime is hardly punished by the law, I know, but that is because very few spies get as far as the law courts: most of them disappear en route. Put that in your little head and think about it. France offered you hospitality, but . . .'

'I'm a French citizen.'

'Quite right. You're a French citizen who is still alive, still very pretty, one to whom I should have great pleasure in presenting something close on half a million francs.' He waved the cheque like a flag. Lowering his voice he added: 'If Lieutenant Volsky has been cooking up something else on the side, it's in your interest to tell me at once what you know about it. You'll feel much better afterwards, I promise you.'

I gave a rather naive start. Rat had spent his life betraying people: it was natural that he should suspect me. Was it not I, who, by recruiting Marina, had aborted Culverin, which I had thought up myself in rather unlikely circumstances? But what did he hope to get by questioning my accomplice in front of me? After a few clicks of the false teeth, he went on, without looking at me:

'There may still be time for him to redeem himself . . . and we might, the three of us, set up some scheme that might pass muster. Crr rr . . .' He pretended to tear up the cheque. 'What do you think, you two youngsters? Shall we put Popov in the batter and fry him?'

I looked at the incorrigible old rascal and, since I was innocent and had consequently nothing to barter against my security, I began to be afraid in earnest. Local rivalries would no doubt prevent me from being handed over to the specialized teams of SDECE and, as a soldier, I could not be brought before the National Security department, but, Military Security did not exactly have a reputation for being tender-hearted either. Although I had gone into combat with a good grace the very idea of an interrogation literally took my breath away. I would admit whatever horror they wanted me to. I remembered my pathological and literary temptations where betrayal was concerned. I was no longer sure that I had not succumbed to them.

'Right!' said the Shopkeeper, getting up with a new influx of energy, 'I'll leave you two youngsters to chew it over alone, I'll be back in ten minutes.'

He shuffled off. I went straight for Marina.

'And what precisely have you got against me? I've been absolutely open with you. It is you who've cheated.'

'Cheated? Yes, perhaps. I am a cheat, didn't you know?'

She added in Russian, as if the word had an even better taste in her mother tongue: 'A rather successful cheat.'

That was all I needed.

'Ah! No, don't. Please don't speak Russian here. He'll think we're hiding things from him.'

'You mean he's listening?'

'Do you think he's a fool? Well? Why have you done it? Why have you done this to me?'

'Don't you see, Cyril, that I've seen right through it all?'

I walked up and down, explaining to her that she was betraying France, our service, me, her own word. But it was no use: I got nowhere. Rat couldn't absent himself indefinitely. Convinced either of my innocence or of my inadequacy, he came back, looking even older, the flesh hanging off the bones and the skin hanging off the flesh. He didn't even pretend that he had not been listening to our discussion. He dragged himself over to his desk, on which he had left the cheque. He noticed, with some disappointment, that it was still there. He dropped into his chair, stuck his forefinger into his mouth, felt for a spot that he must have had on his gum, croaked rather than sighed and, taking the cheque between two fingers, said, with some difficulty: 'Mademoiselle, take back your property. I don't want to see you again.'

She did not move. The cheque fluttered to the floor.

I made a move to pick it up: 'Sir . . .'

He had the eyes of an exhausted dog.

'I don't want to see you again, either. Disappear.'

There was no alternative but to leave with Marina. We were no longer playing at blind man's buff. The bluff hadn't lasted long. Culverin was dead and buried. What did it matter if Marina recognized the Invalides? My 2CV was waiting for me at the foot of the steps; a military driver must have retrieved it for me. I wouldn't be driving it for much longer. I opened the right-hand door. Marina got in. I drove through rain to the Avenue de Suffren; we said nothing; we didn't even exchange a glance. When I stopped in front of her door, I decided to make a last attempt.

'And you won't explain to me . . .'

She gave in at once.

'If you insist.'

'I don't know what you mean.'

'I was salvaging your self-respect, Cyril. Was I wrong?'

She was sitting next to me. It was dark. Cars with double haloes hissed by over the wet surface. We had been, among other things, friends.

'You can't really be unaware . . .' she began wearily. 'You've never forgiven me . . . When the opportunity presented itself to humiliate me, as you thought you had been humiliated, you jumped at it . . . You knew Popov's unusual tastes . . . He was your double: you entrusted him with your honour as a male, and gave him the job of avenging you . . . You really wanted me to tell that to your colonel or whatever he is? . . . Between Popov and you there's not as much difference as you think: you both serve the prince of this world . . . I'm interested in another kingdom.'

I was no longer listening to her. I turned towards her, stupefied. Emancipated women sometimes have the oddest ideas.

'You believe in all that psychoanalytic mish-mash?' I shouted.

She looked straight ahead in that concentrated way one associates with broody hens and mathematicians.

'In any case,' she murmured at last, 'that's how it ought to be played.'

22

On Sunday morning Major Igor Maximovich Popov took the métro and, after a few changes intended to shake off any shadows, got off at Convention. He liked precautions to be laid layer upon layer, like *bliny*. If he had not managed to shake off any unknown comrades entrusted perhaps with the task of spying on him, it did not really matter: no one, but no one, could be less suspected of religious feelings than he: had he not proved as much? He was going to the church of the Dormition to contact an agent, the file was there to prove it; now, Russian churches, where everyone goes in when he likes and leaves when he likes, where it is quite usual to change one's place or talk during the service, are well known places for making contact. Major Popov had worked out the following argument:

'The comedy-ambush that she has taken so much trouble to set up, surely without her case officer knowing, shows that she is caught. She thought that she was being sarcastic when she asked me to come back; in fact, she was expressing her own desire to see me again. It is clear that the French are being tricked in all this. I still don't know what advantage it will be possible to extract from the situation, but in any case the contact must be exploited to the maximum, if only in the interests of personal hygiene.'

When he thought of Marina, he never gave her a first name. He saw a compact, harmonious body, well-endowed bosom, a face so perfect that it invited a desire to damage it, but he referred to her simply as 'she' and 'her'. She was one more 'she'. She had led him on, only to disappear, but he was not angry with her: he should have been mad with rage right up to the moment he would get his revenge, but no, he took it quite calmly, as if she had not gone beyond her rights. This passivity would have disturbed him if he had had any tendency to introspection, but that was not how he lived. Action alone mattered to him and, in so far as a cool head was good for action, he congratulated himself that he had kept a cool head.

Having got off at a station he did not know, he managed to reach the Dormition without getting lost, along a street in which he had never set foot: the one that led into the church through the main gate. He looked up and made out a half-effaced inscription in Slavonic: 'Temple of the Dormition of the Most Holy Mother of God'. Below that, under the porch roof, crowned with a three-branched transversal cross, an icon represented a recumbent human form surrounded by standing human forms. Below, a red lamp glowed. Popov pushed open one of the doors, stepped over the porch threshold and entered an irregularly shaped courtyard, planted with a few trees. Sparrows were flitting about in their bare tops. The snow had completely melted; here and there, blades of grass stuck up out of the ground. To the right stretched the thickset, ungainly mass of the former garage. Above the main door was another icon, this one enclosed in a small glass house. It depicted the same subject: a woman lying down, surrounded by various figures with their arms raised up, the whole crudely executed without perspective, without depth. But surely it couldn't be an old icon? A typically Christian retrograde attitude—to produce an ugly imitation of the ignorance of the past.

Popov raised his head and looked around him. The courtyard was surrounded by buildings inhabited no doubt by émigrés, Russia's spittle, vomited by her in her salutary epileptic fit at the beginning of the century. It amused him to find that he felt no animosity towards them: they were dead and he had no time to hate the dead. Under the garage icon was another lamp, also lit. So they weren't as dead as all that? There still remained a vestige of the old Russia the new Russia had not succeeded in crushing under her foot? Bah! In another generation or two it would all be finished: the map of atheistic progress left no doubt on the matter. An old woman, bent in two, appeared from he knew not where, crossing herself over and over again, and slipped into the garage like an earwig. Popov followed her in, this time, through the main door.

At first, he had an unpleasant surprise. As soon as he was inside, he found himself at the top of four steps leading down: the level of the courtyard was raised in relation to the building. It gave the appearance of a catacomb and it uselessly reminded him of the cellar he had never entered, but whose airvent exhaled that smell of damnation. Besides, it was paradoxical to go down into a church, to slip into it as a rabbit slips into its warren. Popov even tried to stop on the topmost step, but it was too narrow for his big feet. So he went down. On the left, he recognized the gnome's counter, on the right the side door through which he had come the day before.

The atmosphere that morning was different. The red lamps had resumed their places, but the light that fell through the glass roof effaced them: one could not tell whether or not they were lit. There were almost no candles on the chandeliers and they spread no visible light. The topography was no longer enigmatic: Popov recognized without difficulty that of the churches, now turned into museums, that he had visited in his own country. The screen of images that rose on the platform and did not even reach the ceiling—which gave it an unfinished look—was pierced by three doors. The middle one was double, but so low that a mauve curtain had been added to block the opening and hide what took place behind, in the pope's lair. In front of the screen, on the platform, was a red carpet stained with circles of wax where the candles had dripped down. On either side, half-screens serving as bastions hid the two ends of the platform. The various lecterns had been covered with white, starched embroideries. The smell was no longer only that of the airvent: he could also make out the smell of furniture polish, another polish used on brass, then an almost indefinible mixture of wax, wool, ironing, spices, smoke, vinegar, something rancid that reminded him of the Near East. A voice rose from the right-hand bastion, a flat, sexless, unintelligible, but inoffensive voice, reading something or other in an expressionless tone, without changes of rhythm, on an unvarying melody, inter-

244

rupted only occasionally by a short silence to take in breath or to turn a thick, dry page. The church seemed to be empty and there was something welcoming in that particular emptiness: it was as if the images had retreated into the walls; they did not impose; it wouldn't be a bad place to have a nap.

The Pioneers' Hall had also smelt of polish, but of honest polish, without any superstitious ingredients, and the total silence had not been emphasised by the presence of a thin thread of a voice. Only the floor, an old *ancien régime* parquet floor, which squeaked underfoot, might betray his doubtless unauthorized presence. Igor had never dared to ask if it was permissible to go inside for a moment's recollection, unsupervised. On the days when he decided to go there, escaping from home or from class, he would make bets with himself: 'When I touch the handle, the door will open—it won't open . . .' If he concentrated enough, he was never wrong, and the latch-bolt receded or remained blocked depending on whether or not he had felt in advance the double-ended handle turn in his empty hand. But even when he knew he would not be able to go in, he did not hesitate to run off, enter the old park, slip up to the first floor and put his hand on the brass egg. It was as if he had been given an order, and his own presentiments did not permit him to disobey. If the door resisted, he went down the staircase again, hiding behind the bannister, rail by rail, forcing back his tears: he had not been judged worthy. If the heavy door with the carved panels opened, with an impressive creaking as he pushed it, he held his breath, well aware of the holy sacrilege he was about to commit: he, who had not yet been admitted to the Pioneers, was going to drink at their source, recharge at their battery, contemplate their treasures, steal their fire . . . Often, to make the adventure even more dangerous and the initiation even more stunning, he would move forward with his eyes shut and open them only when he had reached the middle of the hall; in this way, if someone else were already there, he would have had no escape.

The hall was vast, white and green, high-ceilinged, with cornices, carved panelling, internal shutters on the two twinned windows, whose deep and highly decorated embrasures looked out on to the foliage of the park. The marquetry floor glistened—it was treacherous beneath one's clod-hoppers. On a mahogany pedestal table, supported by four sphinxes, stood the model of the future Pioneers' Palace. In the glass case, not only the buildings were displayed, but even the apple-green trees dotted around the paths, and people walking about, men, women and young Pioneers. The right-hand wall was covered by a gigantic map of the USSR, dotted with multicoloured drawing-pins representing the links, detachments and companies. Above, in red, block capitals was inscribed: 'In our country, there are 13,856,299 young Pioneers of Lenin.' This number was kept more or less up-to-date by the chief guide, but Igor liked to think that it was strictly accurate by some miracle of Soviet science, that as soon as one more little Ivan, somewhere in the depths of Kamchatka, pronounced the oath, one more unit was automatically added to this number. That's how it would be when he too was admitted into the organization: he would enter that very hall, head high, and find the sacred number increased by one unit, like those station clocks whose big hand marks the minutes not by reptation but by small jumps.

On the rear wall were four portraits. The topmost one did not interest Igor very much: it represented a fat, bearded gentleman with dreamy eyes; it more or less fitted Babushka's description of her old God, who didn't exist, and all the ill one was supposed to think of God somehow rubbed off on to the gentleman who had so loved the people.

He so loved the people that he had written many books: this was not, for little Igor, a very convincing proof of love. A bit like the other one who had so loved the people that he had sent them his only son. 'Don't you think it would have been better, Babushka, if he had come down himself?' he once asked. Below, there were two other portraits hung at the same height. The one on the right was in colour, which made it more attractive, but there was something overbearing about the face. His thick, gleaming moustache reminded Igor of the disappointing formula with which Babushka ended the bed-time stories she used to tell him:

> I was there at the feast,
> And the honey I tasted:
> None entered my mouth,
> On my moustache 'twas wasted.

It always seemed to him that the moustache in question was that one. However much of a genius the statesman, warrior, writer, scientist, philosopher, might have been, his moustache always seemed to be stuck down with hydromel, and Igor already had no sympathy for the downtrodden and slow-witted. This impression was not helped by the foreign-sounding accent of the universal genius on the radio. In the dialectical triad he represented the negative moment of the antithesis. 'And I', thought little Igor, holding his breath, 'I shall be the synthesis.'

The left-hand portrait was quite a different matter. It was impossible to look up without crying out inside one: 'It's him!' Just one look at that mug convinced one that the source of truth had at last been found. Though no less exotic than the other mug—it was obviously Tartar in its bone structure—and almost embarrassing in its suggestion of an intellectual, it was indisputably true, true like a right note, or a square root. It was the only one to be depicted in profile and facing, of course, to the left (that is to say, for people who read from left to right, towards the future), this head was not a head, but rather a moving fist, a prodigious concentration of strength ready to explode, a thunderbolt contained in a ball (an atom of uranium, as Igor was later to say). The swelling of the forehead, the twist of the eyebrows, the swollen eyelids, the projecting cheekbones, the pouting lower lip, the vertiginous line of the nose-moustache-goatee, everything was thrust outwards, swollen from inside by the thermal pressure of thought. The expression of the eyes and mouth was neither kindly nor particularly creative, but so superbly cunning, so vibrant with strength! One felt that here was a fellow who would never let you go, or rather that one would never let him go, for he could very well dispense with you if necessary. He was a man as completely removed from his past, from his background, from all other men, as a painted portrait that had left the canvas and his two-dimensional similars to become embodied in the third dimension.

Under the two grown-ups was the child Pavlik Morozov, the pioneer of Pioneers, their hero, their fourteen-year-old martyr: his forehead, doubling the height of his little, stunted, proletarian face, his cap . . .

The child crossed the church. He had changed his socks, but he was wearing the same golden robe; in the daylight one could see the wear under the arms and round the collar. The hem was new: the bottom had been taken in where it was fraying. The child was carefully carrying a tray on which were arranged several small loaves on squares of paper with inscriptions printed on them, some in black, others in red. He disappeared into the den at the back. Two or three babushkas had come in without Popov noticing and were wandering around, stopping in front of this or that image, prostrating themselves, kissing various objects, lighting candles, asking one another, in a loud whisper, the poor, deaf old things, for news of their varicose veins and chilblains, feeling more at home in the house of God than in their own homes. Popov was surprised by this familiarity. He had only been to Catholic masses, which he had attended out of a diplomat's curiosity, and which he preferred for their well-drilled discipline; but, he had to agree, if one set about imagining a Christian paradise, one would see it more easily in terms of this amiable Russian confusion, in which everyone went and said his own prayer in his own corner, than in the smooth order of the Roman ceremonies.

Having advanced two more paces, little Igor fell on his knees before the principal object of his secret visit, the standard of the giant condor with folded wings that stood in a corner of the hall retained by a ring encircling its staff, and which filled the whole hall with its red reflections. It was as if it did it on purpose, as if it was sitting on something warm under the heavy undulations of its feathers. Igor held out his hand, conscious of his audacity, expecting to feel a burn or an electric shock. His finger brushed along the heavy, stiff, golden fringe, grasped the corner of the material and, moving back, he closed his fist over it, and gently pulled. The folds opened out slowly, revealing pieces of embroidery whose gold thread formed as it were dried crusts on the surface of the glowing material. On one side a few letters of

248

the motto were visible, a few rays from the star, a few tongues of fire; on the other, one or two numbers and, if one dared to pull back the folds that far, one could make out the Face that dwelt in the depths, always the same Face, irreplaceable, aggressive, vibrating with internal combustion and so geometrical that it would have been easy to scribble it to infinity in the margins of exercise books had there not been too grave a risk of blasphemy in doing so. Igor never unfolded the material entirely: horrible things would have happened if his temerity had crossed that final barrier; the Thoughts of the Standard circling like harpies with razor-sharp claws, would have sprung out at him, horrified, from the last folds; beating their still-short wings, bleeding, their flesh still poorly covered with feathers, they would have hurled themselves at the ceiling, at the windows, at the walls, at the furniture and at last struck the rash one who had violated their gestation.

The linear voice continued its reading. Since the evening before, a change had taken place in Popov's receptive circuits; his childish memory must have undergone a shock; it was as if his ears had been unblocked: he recognized and understood more words. The text that the voice was reading at that moment was one Babushka had repeated to him every night at bed-time; he had learnt it by heart in spite of himself; it was the one that spoke of bread being given and debts forgiven. The reader had hardly finished when the astonishing effect of the night before was repeated: a disembodied voice, falling, it seemed, from the glass roof, but in reality hidden behind the mauve curtain, proclaimed: 'For Thine is the kingdom, the power and the glory, Father, Son and Holy Spirit.'

The whole thing was becoming absurd: what power could be felt in this caravanserai? Was not all the power of the world concentrated into the fist-shaped face, so asymmetrical that one would have thought it was two halves of different masks stuck together by mistake, much more asymmetrical than that of this shrimp of a pope?

Whenever the rear door opened a draught lashed one's ankles; new characters, old, young, men, women, children made their entrances, as in those modern productions, where the actors come on to the stage one by one, with the curtain up, as the audience are settling into their seats, so that one never knows at what precise moment the play begins. It was the same here. Distant greetings, noisy conversations, scowls, smiles passed back and forth, the eyes of the devout raised to heaven, a whole intimate commotion and, above it all, those eternal signs of the cross, quite without order, imaginary forests swept by unpredictable winds. Babushka blessed herself more seriously, with gentle pressure, a slight swing of the thumb, fore and middle finger conjoined, skewering in turn the forehead, the stomach, the right shoulder, the left shoulder. The Greeks then place their hands on their hearts; the Old Believers crook the middle finger; the Catholics crook all of them; the Protestants don't cross themselves at all. Boloney!

In the middle of the church stood a lectern covered with a pale pink cloth; an image with a brass frame was placed upon it, surrounded by a few flowers. The more bigoted prostrated themselves before the lectern; the lazier were content to touch the ground with their fingers; most of them kissed the image, the obsequious in the lower right-hand corner, the bolder ones smack in the middle. Parents lifted their children and swung them over the lectern: smacking kisses resounded. A young woman, wearing a white crêpe-de-Chine bodice and a black skirt, had just stooped down in turn; without interrupting the smoothness of her movement she placed her forehead on the wax-stained carpet. It was as if she had, throughout her whole body, from top to toe, only a single muscle, capable of executing any movement with limpid phrasing, so different from the breaks, gasps and jerks of the others. She remained for a long time in this pitiful, this ridiculous posture, her nose in the dust, her rump in the air, but Popov found it neither ridiculous nor pitiful: in the shape so freely adopted by a body so perfectly 'in good shape', there was an ease, a pride that he appreciated. The young woman rose up at last, with the same melodious sinuousness, made a broad sign of the cross over herself, bowed over the lectern as over a cradle and kissed the icon as if it were a sleeping infant. Then she crossed herself again and, with the air of having accomplished some significant task, she went over

250

towards the right-hand bastion, which enabled Popov to see her in diminishing profile. When he recognized her, he felt neither anger nor desire, but rather a curious impression of satisfaction, of confirmation: everything was in order, everything was taking its course. 'She' was there.

The comparison between this woman's prostration before that thing and his own childish kneeling—he had spent long minutes on the floor of the Pioneers' Hall, bruising his bare knees, his head buried in the folds of the Standard as in those of his mother's skirts, his lips pressed against the silk—emerged entirely to Popov's advantage: his abasement had been simply the compression of a spring; she, deep down within herself, would never straighten up. Another man, as infatuated as he was, would have said to himself: 'I shall cure her of it, I shall really teach her to live.' But that was not his way. He did not believe in improvement below a certain level of quality. He was really modern in that respect, and he knew it: the liberals might hope to change men, the existentialists might deliver them from moral condemnation, the orthodox Marxists might judge them in terms of a whole battery of ideas. Popov was a Leninist, and he had understood that Communism owes its victories not to a superseded body of doctrine, but to the men it attracts and the means it employs, which has everything to do with opportunism. You pick up a tool, you examine it; if it is sound, you use it; if you suspect it of the slightest flaw, you toss it out! There was no Leninist salvation for 'her', but it was good that she was there in her place and good, too, that she should disappear into her bastion, present but invisible, so present that she had no need to be seen.

Yes, the compression of a spring. Life is not walking but running left, right, left, right, never both feet on the ground at the same time. Was it not the Christians themselves who said that if one stopped and looked back one would be turned into a statue of salt. Why salt? Fairy tales! Nevertheless, among those busy human beings and those flat images, each of them preoccupied with the same ineptitudes, one was easily induced to rummage among one's most secret luggage. If only they hadn't started cooking up that smell of purple and death again, which, a quarter of a century earlier, four thousand kilometres away, had come up through the airvent! If souls decay, they must stink of incense. The pope with his smoking saucepan was wandering around again, picking out the images one by one, the spectators one by one, handing out to them equal swings of the censer, like an irrefutable *coup de grâce*. He had to give a similar one to 'her' and now he was going to give one to Popov, though Popov did his best to hide behind a portly woman wearing a flowered hat. No use. The hunchback's professional, parti-coloured eyes photographed him with a curious expression of undifferentiated attention, the censer flew in his face, and he just stood there, as if picked out for identification, then thrown back into the bed of the recognized. What was it all about? Overtaking. Initiation, overtaking, initiation, overtaking: a staircase. Popov recognized in it the form of his own destiny. Others are initiated and satisfied, or initiated and disappointed; for him, everything was a step upwards. He did not even know what disappointment or weariness were. As soon as he had assimilated anything, he worked on it. His whole life had been one increasing tension, from the day he joined the Pioneers to his membership of the Komsomol. Then the radical transmutation took place: the ticket. Westerners say 'the card', a replete, satiated term, suggesting the sleep of a boa-constrictor. But one is a member of the Party, not of a club! 'Card' is infected with the bourgeois (bogus) security of cardboard; 'ticket' rustles with the proletarian insecurity of paper. 'Card' is the past: veterans' card, large-family card; 'ticket' is the future: a cinema ticket, a railway ticket. One is given a card; one takes a ticket (sometimes one hands it back, like their Dostoievsky, to one's God). A card is held on to, like a privilege; a ticket is torn up almost at once. 'Proletarians of all countries unite to have visiting cards engraved!' A card was menschevik. One would never do anything with those card-carrying, cardboard Communists.

Yes, Popov had bought a ticket—it was the right word—for every successive supercession. It would be childish to take into account a certain lassitude, a certain impatience, that had over-taken him of late. As a child, he had dreamt of conquering the world for Lenin; well, now, he had boarded the train (he was *en train*, as the excellent French expression put it)—and the rails were laying themselves beneath the wheels of his locomotive.

A concert of voices rose behind the right-hand bastion, thin voices, almost all of them inadequate, or broken, or breathless, but nevertheless harmonious, producing not exactly music, but witnessing all the same to music. Popov recognized the one unflawed voice: juicy, deep, a good mezzo, lacking in refinement, perhaps, but broad and deep. He imagined it was 'her' voice. What a pity she allowed herself to be crushed between the walls of those ritual chants! She would have sounded so good in, 'Only he who knows' or in some Great-Russian cantilena, *Luchinushka* . . . The church was now a quarter full and it went on filling: a constant stream of people were entering, crossing themselves, buying candles, sticking them in the chandeliers, kissing the walls, prostrating themselves, exchanging news, curiously at ease in this world, which was nevertheless, so obviously, an enclave, a pocket, of the beyond. But this was because those people felt at ease in the beyond. They had friends among the saints, and knew each one's particular character and speciality; the etiquette of the place was familiar to some, others invented their own, convinced that whatever they did would please God. Vexingly easygoing. If ever these poor people learnt that anti-Christ was standing among them. . . What a stampede there'd be! Popov could not help smiling at the thought, though without malice and, to hide his smile, he bowed his head and, out of a professional concern for disguise—he didn't believe, did he? One couldn't be taken in by one's own cover—he joined his thumb and first two fingers of his right hand as if to take a pinch of salt, crooked the other two against his palm, and touched his forehead, breast and shoulders. He felt a certain irritation at doing so, but only because he had rediscovered so naturally a gesture that he had not made for thirty years, did not even have to hesitate as to whether one moved from right to left or the opposite. He remembered that he had had some difficulty distinguishing his left from his right and Babushka had often repeated to him: 'But it's so simple: which hand do you cross yourself with?' As a Pioneer, when he had to move off left foot first, he still, to his shame, used his grandmother's method: the foot he set off with was on the opposite side to the hand that made the sign of the cross. How insidious were these reflexes acquired in childhood! How right one was to extirpate the opium of religion in the earliest years! The last time he had asked himself what hand he made the sign of the cross with was when he was taking his driving examination: priority on the right. . .

Suddenly the choir intoned, to some almost martial tune, a propaganda piece that was almost entirely understandable.

'Blessed are the demoralized, for theirs is the kingdom of heaven.'

Unlikely. Isn't morale the main strength of armies?

'Blessed are the cry-babies, for they shall be consoled.' But one should neither console oneself, which is cowardly, nor console others, which is reactionary. On the contrary, the wounds should be whipped to make them bleed more. As for the mourners, they are parasites to be eliminated.

'Blessed are the submissive, for they shall inherit the earth.'

On the contrary, cursed be the submissive for they get only what they deserve—like Chekhov's Old Firs and Uncle Tom. As for inheriting the earth, they'll soon see: they shall be mown down.

'Blessed are those who hunger and thirst for *pravda*, for they shall be satisfied.'

But *pravda* is to be found in a newspaper. *Pravda* is changed every day with one's socks. Those who are satisfied with it are useful fools. One has to keep one's distance from it, fatten others up with it, go through it like a train goes through a station.

As these slogans filed past, Popov listened to them with more and more attention, because it gave him all the more pleasure to think how obviously wrong they were and how patently out of place a wolf like him was in each of those successive sheep-folds—unless he intended to dine there.

'Blessed are those who have pity, for they shall be shown it.' But Popov would have felt just as dishonoured if he had felt pity as if he had inspired it! Anyway, was it not some bourgeois thinker—or aristocrat, if there was any difference between them—who remarked that pity was not necessary in a well-made soul? Pity was such a slimy thing . . . A bullet in the neck was better. And did God think that he could buy him with that?

'Blessed are the clean of heart, for they shall see God.' Ah! cleanliness, the ideal of the idle rich! Whiteness! The Whites, so well named, white cuffs, white flags, white liver, lily-livered as Shakespeare put it. . . The pallor of defeat, cowardice, capitulation, sterility. They should be left in their whiteness! Nothing horrified Popov more than those who kept their hands clean, the scrupulous, those eaten up with remorse, the innocent, the quitters, the cowardly. Have a clean heart and see God! He thought of the rich little black girls, mincing about in their First Communion dresses, that he had seen at Brazzaville. Thank you! Anything rather than that ignominy: to be clean in a world of slime and blood! Could they invent anything more abject? He listened with a vigilance bordering on voraciousness. He hoped that the Slavonic would not become more difficult, that he would miss none of its absurdities!

'Blessed are the peacemakers, for they shall be called the children of God.' Yes, they will be called all kinds of names, but in fact the peacemakers, those liberals, those cowards, those poxy-brained dreamers are merely sub-bourgeois struck by a characteristic curse: reality crumbles at their touch and they destroy the peace they preach as they preach it, for there is no peace without order, and they do not like order.

Popov did not catch the last, long beatitude. It was probably worth all the rest. No, there was nothing useful for him in that *kasha*. He was surprised to find himself almost relieved. The curious thing was that, however pitiful those slogans might be, they emerged between those walls with such assurance, bobbing like sailing ships on their musical, sinewy waves, that they suggested by the fullness of their form the very thing the message they bore claimed to destroy: strength, grandeur, harmony and—yes—order. Yes, all that mish-mash was not without its own order, and there was no order without potential energy, without gravitation. Gravitation—yes, that was the word. In the circular evolutions of the hunchbacked, gilded idol, accompanied by the little satellized boy, in the spirals described by that lesser satellite, the censer, in the disposition of the images, flowers, lecterns, doors, walls, banners, sputtering candelabra, one could divine a pre-established astral order, a coded grid placed over the world, a stencil, a system of spatial coordinates, relations, the mercator projection of a higher order. This place, as different from ordinary space as, for example, a weightless chamber, was, Popov suddenly realized, like a sportsfield, with strictly defined areas, constricting, arbitrary, but universally recognized. The lines that divided up a rugby field, its touchlines, or a soccer field with its penalty areas, or the numbers corresponding to the various holes in café pin-tables were so many conventions that were not essentially different from those to be found here. Popov noticed for example that one did not cross the bisectrix of the wall of images without paying duty in the form of a sign of the cross, and also it was impossible (except for a few fools who were obviously out of it) to cross it between the central lectern and the curtained double doorway. This curtain, sometimes drawn, sometimes open, also obeyed strict rules and, Popov had been really naive earlier not to understand that this screen had as much *raison d'être* in the system as, for example, a traffic light in the street: red, green, off, on, one only needed to know the code, which was different on land, on sea, and in this carefully beaconed place. The side doors pierced in the screen of images—an iconostasis, that was what it was called—opened and closed, the initiates bumped into the landmarks or moved round them, the choir intoned or fell silent, the monotonous voice of the priest executed his fiorituras, or not, as the case may be, all according to a particular plan. This idea of a plan—not a five-year plan, but an eternal one—impressed Igor Popov. From the time of Peter, Ivan, Vladimir, the same bowings and scrapings had been performed. A net had been thrown over the world and its meshes remained caught at the same places. For a man who thought of little more than the future, there was something particularly provocative in a spectacle that had not changed for fifteen hundred years and claimed to remain unchanged for as many times more as was necessary. How many masses had been said since the first one? And if it had taken four or five centuries for a certain stabilization to take place, there was no doubt that if a fifth-century Byzantine came back to life in this ridiculous garage he would have been perfectly at home, because the penalties and corners had not changed: bows, swings of the censer, kisses, alternate doors, irruptions of the choir borne on centuries-old melodies as on archangels' backs, everything would be as he knew it. Even the same eternal little boy, chubby-cheeked and thoughtful, who, with his tray covered with small loaves, had just bumped into Popov's hip and passed by, preoccupied, superior, without a word of apology.

Who was he? Where did he live? Did he speak Russian? Yes, no doubt, as well as Igor, and he was there, after fifty years of exile, a scandalous symbol of the perpetuity to which this *pravda* laid claim. The last beatitude caught up with Popov several minutes late. Had there really been a 'blessed are the exiled' in all that? Impossible! The exiled have put themselves outside the law. They are not plugged in. They live an ersatz life. How could *they* be blessed, these fish out of water? It was a patent lie. How different it was from the legitimate desire to win the middle of the current, to go straight ahead, steadily, to suck the honey of history straight from history itself, to add to the collective hope one's individual effort—the reasonable drunkenness that Popov had known so well! He suddenly remembered the breath of fresh air on waking, that clear, good air, vaguely reminiscent of bran and iron oxide, that light without source, since the sun had not yet risen, that aspiration of his whole being to the plenitude to come—the morning was only a suction cup applied to the belly of the day! Ah! How Russian and how Red he had felt that morning, a fine Russian red, like an Easter egg, trusting, pure, resolute. How the sacrifice of the evening had gloriously, joyfully, come to him! It was not a deal made with destinies. It was not an 'If I say my formula without mumbling I promise to . . .' No, it was an 'I shall say my formula without mumbling and I. . .' The little yellow teddy-bear with its crumpled ears, the black pearl and brown pearl that served it as eyes, its bit of a nose that was half coming away and its plush chest half pierced by the slit of an internal whistle that no longer worked, the little teddy-bear Mishka was still asleep on the pillow, the edge of the sheet covering the lower half of its body,

257

indifferent to the events that were to mark that unique day. Draw with full hands the cold water from the tank and apply it in great quantities over a shivering body that must be cleansed of all impurity; don't use too much soap; wipe the floor; put on clean, fresh-smelling clothes, carefully ironed by a mother of no importance whatsoever; wet his hair, smoothe it down, take a final look in the mirror ('That's the boy who today. . .'), run at last out from the detested, petty-bourgeois house where so many superstitions still lingered, and run on, in the red light of dawn, jumping from sleeper to sleeper along the railway track with its glittering rails that led to the holy city where the dead god resided.

There was a relatively organized commotion, with more signs of the cross and genuflections, the choir fell silent and, as if sucked in by the void thus produced, there stood in the left door of the iconostasis, which seemed to open of itself, a monster. Above a legless body covered in gold leaf, swayed a disproportioned cranium formed by a book bound in gold, dotted with precious stones. It advanced slowly, emitting, from the depths of its visible pages, murmured invocations.

It was not until the figure was in profile that one could see that it was quite simply Father Vladimir bearing the Gospel, holding it with both hands against his face as if it were a child being shown to the people. Popov could not suppress a tic of irritation: what tricks was he up to now?

The chemical factories were smoking in the morning light. The five now only partially gilded onions of the cathedral still captured some gleams from the sun. The Kliazma was driving a holiday sky. The birds were singing fine, red, Russian songs to the glory of the Bolsheviks.

A plump fellow, disguised as a pope, had just moved to the middle, an ordinary book in his hand, and began to growl out something, gradually raising his voice and raising himself on tiptoe as he did so. His neck was getting redder and redder, as the voice rose in pitch and intensity. An incomprehensible text. The double doors were open and one could see the priest sitting in the depths of his lair, while the public remained standing, except for a few old dodderers slumped on benches along the walls.

Mother had skipped the ceremony. When he risked a look into the crowd, he had recognized his father, a sad, bespectacled figure, present not because he approved, but because he did not have the firmness to object to anything; indeed, he was worried at the thought that his wife or mother might find out that he had gone to see the child swear his oath to the devil. After the beginning he had slipped into the third row where his tall figure made him more conspicuous than he would have liked; before the end, he merged into the mass and no doubt he did not even have the sense to impress his bosses with the gesture of loyalty that he had made. Meanwhile, at home, mother, her bust always arched backwards to support the weight of her figure, had probably lit a candle under the secret icon, and Babushka was salaaming in front of it enough to give her bumps on the forehead. 'I, a young Pioneer . . .'

It was like when he had stood before the horizontal bar and watched the queue of young comrades melt alphabetically from B to V and from I to K, then found himself all alone at the foot of the high thing on which he would have to hoist himself and throw himself over head first, the trunk carried by the centrifugal legs, or like at the swimming-baths, when there were only three, then two, then one single candidate at the end of the diving board and he had to take a deep breath and invoke his faith in order not to flinch: 'A Communist fears nothing. Lenin, don't let me shame myself!' Suddenly there was the great, sand-covered square, the Standard waving in the middle, like a red tree in the wind, like a benevolent and voracious dragon. . . Set off with your left foot, take twelve paces, come to attention, put one knee to the ground.

'I, a young Pioneer, in front of my comrades . . .'

The heavy folds, familiar from his secret visits, but now very different, no longer smelling of the moth-balls of secrecy, but of the pollen of the open air, and more curiously, of curdled milk, beat down on his now close-cropped head, covering and devouring little Igor as he kissed the material, not with the passion he had expected, but with a rigour that was the same passion carried to a higher degree, conscious already that this culmination was a new departure, that he had simply changed trains as

259

one would to go from Riazan to Moscow, that this kiss, real in anticipation, would become symbolic in memory.

'I promise . . .'

The red scarf around his neck: that harness, that tourniquet, that wreath; to work, to suffer, to rule. The guide smiled as he tied it. He was a good, well-fed fellow with generous biceps, a bit of a rutting boar who was shortly to be expelled from the Komsomol over some piece of skirt. Did this scarf mean so little to him that, as he was tying it, he could make eyes at Nastia, the singer of *chastushki*? In any case, he made nothing of the tears that filmed over the neophyte's gleaming eyes. He had hurt him when he stuck the badge into his shirt and then, with a great curved paw he gave him a friendly tap on the back of the neck.

'All set, kiddo!'

This great likeable brute had a high-pitched voice and a lisp. After a pitiless crescendo, the singer had finally strangled himself on a soprano's note and he had gone off muttering something between his teeth. The priest was once more standing on the platform and he raised his hand to curse the assembly. Christians, no doubt, imagine that they are receiving a blessing, but whoever blessed anyone by forming in the air an instrument of torture? It was not the first time Popov had been cursed since the service began, but this time it was particularly disagreeable, because it seemed to him that the parti-coloured eyes had sought him out in the crowd, that the priest had thrown his sign at his head like a club, that, having got him in his sights, as they say, he would go on belabouring him with great blows of the cross. The boy was pulling a lectern that was bigger than himself into the opening of the double doors. The metal-bound book that had served as a head for the monster was placed on it as on a tray and the priest began to read, still in that baroque language that sounded like Russian but was just sufficiently different to prevent one making it out. It was evil and ridiculous, like the language of the law to an illiterate defendant. Yes, Mother had not come to the oath-taking ceremony; her full, modestly corsetted figure was missing among the group of mothers. These were of all kinds, ancients, teenagers, ex-bourgeois, paupers, sluts, soaks, meritorious workers, all so different, but all having a single virtue: the fact of being there. Only the tender, frightened face of his great pole of a father (he looked like a bespectacled giraffe) had accompanied Igor in his march to the Standard. Not that it mattered: Mother had ironed his uniform impeccably, that was enough.

It was a quarter of a century since he had thought of his mother, not out of remorse, but because it was useless to dwell on it. Mother had come from a petty-bourgeois world that was superior to the petty-bourgeois world from which Father came; Mother, with her austere gentleness, her uncompromising pride; Mother who had breast-fed him for so long—was it two years or three? He thought he could still remember it—Mother, that most secure of assurances . . . He remembered clearly the grey eyes and the rigid principles, that insistence, always heavily stressed, on perfection. How it suited her, her capital M: ample, open, majestic and, even in its very flowering, affected. Babushka was the opposite: bustling, grumbling, scolding, her drooping lower lip always in movement, her short-sighted eyes almost misted over, but even more obstinate in her uselessness. The day when Igor had coldly declared: 'I don't believe in your God; I want to be a Pioneer,' Mother had understood. The tears had welled up in her beautiful grey eyes, but she had not insisted; she had stopped praying in his presence (probably to spare him opportunities for blasphemy) and she had ironed in silence his little Anti-Christ's shorts. Babushka had taken to crossing herself more than ever and invoking specialized saints. Individual differences, but the same race: irredeemable. As for Father, he had never been anything but a wet rag.

The priest finished reading and, having closed his book, he put one more cross on his audience. Under so many weekly crosses, was it surprising that men had taken so many hundreds of years to raise their heads? The dialogue began again between the priest and the choir, always the same words, but in a different tone, more hurried, humbler. Suddenly a curious call resounded:

'Let the dumbfounded depart! Let the dumbfounded depart!' No one moved; on the contrary, everyone became quite still as if the serious matters were at last going to begin.

261

This was followed by a silence, to mark the break. The airvent smell intensified; the crowd knelt down; the choirmaster gave the tone on three notes. Everyone waited. A new melody, like none of the preceding ones, rose *pianissimo*. Popov knew enough about music to realize that if the voices had been fresh, this chant would have been pleasing and moving. He liked this romantic sweetness. However badly performed it was, one could feel that the heavy caravel of the liturgy had managed at last to cast off its moorings and reach, clumsily but surely, the open sea. The cabin-boy had once again crossed the deck. Did he still sleep with his teddy-bear?

The days when Popov had entered the KGB, or had been given his ticket, or had been admitted, at fourteen, to the Komsomol, which he had experienced as successive initiations, he had not found a satisfying sacrifice to make. The Komsomol and the KGB had been marked by nothing; in honour of the Party he had given up without too much difficulty a not very deeply ingrained habit of smoking (which, in fact, he had recently resumed, without knowing why, with contemptuous self-indulgence): from the age of fourteen, he knew that sacrifice in itself did not matter and several times, when already grown up, he had regretted subjecting himself to the heartbreak that had marked his entry into the Pioneers: it was all right for Christians to count on 'God will reward me'; a Bolshevik keeps or discards: he does not sacrifice. But at the moment, he no longer regretted anything: it would be good, he thought, for this serious, chubby-cheeked boy to go without whatever it was he liked most in the world, to cut himself, quite deliberately in the side with a grafting knife. He clearly remembered his return from the city, after a picnic in a wasteland that had since become the Park of the Sixteen Republics. The basement flat in which the Popovs lived was empty. Father would be home later. Mother and Babushka must have gone to peel potatoes in the communal kitchen, on the ground floor: it was their time for the kitchen. All the better: he hardly expected a family celebration, after all. He slipped into his room. The teddy-bear was sitting on the chest-of-drawers where mother had put him after making the bed. She liked Mishka's sentimental functions—familial and familiar—bourgeois functions, in other words. It was she who had bought him second-hand and given him to little Igor for his name-day on June 5. The dishonoured bear (bears are naturally ferocious beasts, those who allow themselves to be transformed into monkeys deserve nothing but contempt) sat there, legs apart, his right arm raised vertically as if in salute. Mother liked to play with Mishka; she always left him in a different position on the chest-of-drawers (on all fours, or kneeling, or with his head to one side). Was the salute ironic? Or had mother reconciled herself to the idea that her son's teddy-bear should congratulate him for dedicating himself to the miscreants? Did it conceal some peaceful intention? No matter. Mother did not count. Igor grabbed the teddy-bear.

He had loved this object, loved that accepting, easy tenderness that neither demands nor imposes anything, loved that glassy, rather facetious look and that dusty smell of worn cloth. How many nights had they spent together in each other's arms? Two thousand? More? The bear had consoled him when he could not sleep, reassured him when he woke from nightmares. He had played every role that Igor had been pleased to entrust to him on their nightly journey to the land of nod: he had been a sailor in the bark, a passenger in the taxi, a little brother on the sledge, more often a fellow-soldier in the tank. There had been a time, soon repudiated, when little Igor, taught by Mother, had even knitted a scarf and rompers for Mishka. The shame of it! Now the naked bear no longer recalled that period of ignominy, but nevertheless Igor still had to hide the bear's compromising existence from his friends: it would not only be sublime, therefore, but particularly fitting to get rid of him. Yes, even then, Popov thought back with satisfaction, he had known how to grasp an opportunity. He left the house, carrying the little thing pressed for the last time against his breast, head downwards, one leg stuck up its back. While continuing to run, he had quickly given the bear a more natural posture—he still felt a little sorry for his weakness. He was no longer hiding it, but carrying it aloft in his left hand, his thumb pressed into the whistle, his fingers coiled round the little familiar body, his eyes dimmed by sorrow or rage, he did not know which. He had to cross some sloping ground, then climb up the embankment covered with nettles to reach the railway line. Igor ran quickly, too quickly, he began to get out of breath, several times he nearly tripped up, the iron on his left heel grazed his right leg. He arrived at last at the top of the embankment and stopped. But he could not breathe deeply: his throat was tight. The blood from his shin was running down on to his sock. Filthy, filthy bear! He threw it on the yellow and grey gravel, which looked pink in the twilight. The bear fell on its back and stayed there, indifferent, docile, becoming once again the bag of bran that it really was.

Igor knelt down, picked it up, examined once again the muzzle on which he had placed so many kisses. How stupid to kiss a lifeless thing like that! However it depended on him to preserve in that thing what served for life: its shape. He could keep for himself the secret passenger of his nocturnal journeys, or give it to some neighbour's little girl who didn't have a teddy-bear to sleep with, or throw it on the rubbish dump, where someone would pick it up, cajole it, kiss it in his place. He remembered all sorts of games: in the restaurant with Mikhail Ivanovich, visiting with Mikhail Ivanovich, at the mausoleum with Mikhail Ivanovich . . . He placed the bear across the rail, belly up, the four limbs slightly apart. Then he got up, his knees pricked with gravel, which he brushed off. That was that.

No it wasn't: the engine wheel might push the condemned object aside and everything would have to begin again. There was no question of abandoning him to his fate, purposely leaving him a chance to escape. That would have been a typical case of Slav negligence, superstitious, incompetent, a hangover from the old order. Igor took a piece of string out of his pocket, knelt down again and secured Mishka to the rail, firmly, angrily, breaking a nail as he tied the knot. Filthy Mishka! Every now and then he cocked an ear: the 6.53 was sometimes early. He felt a vibration in the rail. This was followed by the panting of the engine. He got up and stepped back three paces. Coils of smoke, as in a child's drawing, rose above the trees into a golden yellow sky. The priest appeared on the threshold of the central door, took in the congregation with a sweeping, semi-circular glance, appeared to rest his gaze on Popov, crossed his forearms over his breast and bowed, saying in a distinct voice: 'Forgive me, my brothers and sisters.'

Forgive him what? The humbug! Too easy! The engine, seen head on, appeared: a gigantic black, gleaming buckler mounted on wheels that one imagined cutting like razors, heavy as millstones. There was still time to save Mishka, and the idea of running the risk tempted Igor for a moment. He had spent his childhood beside the railway tracks and trains had loomed large in his childish imagination: Lenin's sealed train, Trotsky's armoured train, Tolstoy's train-executioner, Dostoievsky's trial by train. He liked the idea that his sacrifice was being offered up to a train. He also liked the idea of snatching from that god the victim he had promised him. 'You want him? Well, you shan't have him!' That would be really Bolshevik. But how would he know later if he had not given into feelings of pity for Mishka— or for himself? He turned on his heels and fled, sobbing.

Halfway, his curiosity returned. He climbed back up the slope and returned to the same place as before. The train was coming: chuff! chuff! chuff! chuff! Mishka seemed quite tiny on the rail. Now it was too late. The innumerable wheels mowed him down one after another, tearing the material, splintering the wood, scattering the bran, tearing off the limbs. Igor did not wait for the results: perhaps out of weakness, or contempt for easy emotion, or both. When, next morning, Mother bent her large body over him and asked him where Mishka was, he looked her straight in the eyes and said: 'I tied him to the rails.'

She jumped back, stung by a pain infinitely more acute, it seemed to him, than when he had denied her God. He could still see her, half turned away, as in a low angle shot, filling the screen of his memory, infinitely gentle, yet as hard as a rock. The silent lips formed a word that sounded like a long hiss: *chudovishche* . . . His only reply was a stupid giggle, the kind of giggle that gets a slap in families given to that kind of thing: the Popovs were not given to slapping. Suddenly the image of Antonina came into his mind. Why? No doubt because they were two quite unimportant women, he said to himself. He was drawn from his daydreaming by the music, which was swelling in volume.

The half dozen Sunday singers, obviously imagining that they were the combined choirs of the Red Army, attempted a crescendo, majestic in conception, but pathetic in its effect. The old, cracked voices—there were to be more of them as time passed—and the beautiful mellow voice combined to form a sort of magnificent hydra whose sinuous necks entwined round one another, whose heads were raised, whose eyes grew bigger and bigger: it was becoming unbearable, it would explode . . . Popov picked out the phrase:

'Raising to the Tsar . . .'

What! Hadn't this dyspeptic White Guard scum forgotten the Tsar yet? He guessed all the same that the words might refer to some other Tsar. What power lay in the intention! What a cacophony in the execution! Why, then, do these dead-beats persist in singing the praises of force? At that moment, the left-hand door of the iconostasis opened and, as the choir, having reached a climax, remained suspended in a silence of incredible tension, the phantasmagoria began again in a cloud of incense. The creature who appeared this time was two-headed—an eagle?—and each of his two unequal heads was covered by an impenetrable red veil. The few spectators who were still standing fell to their knees and a powerful thrust from behind threw Popov into the same position, weighing on him first at the level of the shoulder blades, then, as he resisted, descending to the small of the back. His forehead hit the carpet, which smelt of vacuum cleaner and candle grease, and a wave of furious hate passed through him. He felt the breath knocked out of him, as when he had fallen on his back while roller-skating.

When he raised his head, everything was smoking around him: the candles, the incense, the red lamps under the iridescent icons, the impalpable mass of prayers. Lit by a sunbeam that fell diagonally through the glass roof and that was a-whirl with dusty galaxies, the priest stood in front of the central door, brandishing two receptacles, one broader, the other taller, covered with little individual cloths, and intoned a monody that also rose like smoke. At his feet, the child slowly swung the censer-airvent.

From that moment on, Popov, sometimes standing, sometimes prostrated, borne on by a commando of ghosts, could no longer detach his pulsating attention either from the past or the present; the images that filed past within him were super-imposed on the encirclement that was closing in on him, the whole sustained by that newborn hatred that astonished even himself. To hate had always seemed to him to be a particularly idle form of amateurishness; but this time it was quite unmistakable: without knowing exactly what he hated so strongly, the hatred hissed in him like a blowlamp, devouring everything around it, like a phial of acid exploding in his guts, throwing over everything around him a tinge of burnt yellow, a smell of sulphur. It was both unbearable torture and a strange liberation.

'The doors, the doors!' the priest called out, but it was not clear which doors he was referring to, nor whether he wanted them opened or closed. Suddenly the entire church, under the direction of the choirmaster, a little old gentleman who had sprung up from his bastion like a jack-in-the-box and was beating time with his hand, broke out into a list of incredible idiocies, each chopped off from the next as if by a cleaver: 'Visible and invisible . . . begotten of the Father . . . descended from heaven . . . incarnate by the Holy Ghost and the Virgin Mary . . . buried and rose again . . . ascended into heaven . . . seated . . . will come to judge the quick and the dead . . .' Talk of the ultimate confidence trick!

The crushed teddy-bear, the airvent (four rusty bars sealed with cement into the brickwork) and suddenly the back of the old man's neck, a smooth-shaven surface of skin, exploding under the impact of a heavy bullet, and the surprise of feeling nothing at all at the idea of having killed his first man. The KGB was not a melodramatic institution: no one forced you to pull out the eyes of a living cat to toughen you up (as was said about certain SS units, it seems); only reliable candidates were recruited, ones who had no time for such childish pranks. Popov might well have made a career for himself without ever killing with his own hands, but the opportunity had presented itself and he was sent to take advantage of it, like a new recruit sent to the cat-house. He had despatched the old man with less curiosity than he had possessed his first woman (on the upper floor of an aristocratic pre-Revolutionary building, a fat redhead whose first name he couldn't remember, who had then burst into tears and wiped her nose with the back of her hand). In doing so, he grazed the middle joint of his forefinger on the trigger guard, not expecting the recoil. A funny fellow, the old Rittmeister! Killing Reds on every front during the Civil War, just escaping from Budienny, Dzerzhinsky, Ezhov, emigrating to France, joining the Foreign Legion in Morocco, re-enlisting in Hitler's army, staying behind the Soviet lines after the retreat, finally betrayed and captured, resisting the Cheka for years, subjected to cold and hunger, months in the cooler, constantly beaten up, recovering as quickly as a dog, never brought to justice because the hope of finally breaking him and making an example of him persisted, never missing his evening prayers or his morning exercises, becoming something of a character at the Lubianka, a terrifying buffoon, famous throughout the prison for the insults he hurled at one's colleagues. 'Do you really imagine that there was more justice in your Tsarist Russia?' one of his interrogators asked sarcastically. 'Certainly', replied the prisoner from his bed of torture, 'because then you were looking after pigs.' 'What are these daily gymnastics in aid of?' he was asked by a general bursting with fat. 'Tomorrow I'm going to have you rubbed out.' 'It's to see you roast in hell all the more slowly.' 'So that's where you're off to—it's you who said it!' chortled the general, slapping his thigh. 'No, my boy, but it's where I'll go on leave.' In the end, room had to be made and it was decided to eliminate this useless mouth. Just as he was about to descend the stairs that led down to the cell, as he did every day, the Rittmeister turned to young Popov, whom he had never seen before and whose weapon was not visible. After looking him up and down, he suddenly pointed to his own rachidian bulb: 'Here, you good for nothing oaf! And try not to miss it, or God help your mother!' There was no satisfaction in any of that.

'Mercy of the world'—or was it 'mercy of peace'?—sang the choir, in a different tone, as if a new refraction had taken place in the luminous path of the liturgy, a new transformation of quantity into quality, as Engels would have said. The priest on the platform raised not a hand, but a veritable instrument of torture reproduced in miniature, and with it delivered a discharge on to the heads of the consenting congregation:

'The grace of our Lord Jesus Christ and the love of God and of the Father and the fellowship of the Holy spirit be with you all.'

'Not with me! Not with me!' Popov protested to himself.

No, Popov was certainly not a killer. He had derived much more pleasure from the American physicist, a Harvard-educated Bostonian, with his grey, striped flannel suits, his thick, square glasses, that way he had of dragging his feet when he walked, to show that he feared no one. Time and again they had tried to compromise the virtuous intellectual who attended all the international conferences. He smiled, his mouth full of white gold: 'This is the H-bomb era and the Soviets are still playing at cops and robbers . . .' We had arranged for him to marry a dangerously innocent, plump little redhead and he had fallen head over heels in love with her with all the ardour of which his puritan heart was capable. Once in Moscow, nothing was easier than to have her seduced by a specially appointed gypsy, nothing more satisfying than to lay out in front of him a set of photographs like a conjuror with a pack of cards. And the proud Anglo-Saxon melted into tears, his love and his vanity deflated at one go! In the end he realized that he could still save his career. What a delicious duty it was, explaining to him what the price would be.

The instrument of torture was pointed to the heavens, followed by the austere gaze of the parti-coloured eyes.

'Let us lift up our hearts to the mountains.' Popov understood him to say, then, 'Let us give thanks to the Lord.'

'And what should these old rejects thank him for?'

He felt himself raised on the point of a pin like a periwinkle about to be devoured.

Yes, the Harvard-man in the flannel suit had given in even more quickly than the other drip, Evdokimov, the first man Popov had

269

managed to turn into a Zombie . . . Thanks to this solemn, silent old pipe-smoking professor, regarded by his students as a model of intellectual integrity, we discovered in time the madly audacious plot hatched by a group of young atomic scientists who hoped to liberalize the regime by threatening to explode a stock of bombs. At first he had refused to cooperate. One night in a cell was enough: picked up at midnight, taken back home at four in the morning without anyone so much as laying a finger on him, he had signed everything we wanted. And how noisily he had lapped up his hot chocolate! How quickly he had put on his waistcoat! His wife looked at him with a mixture of tenderness and repulsion (she had guessed), while warming his chocolate on the primus stove. The great man was no more than a glove-puppet: to put him on like a glove had been sheer delight.

Whether it was because the words of this part of the liturgy were simpler, or because he was getting used to the old language, it seemed to Popov that, apart from one or two mistakes, he could now understand what was being said. Above the glass roof, which sent the voices of the choir bouncing back, the sky shone royal blue with all the crude insolence of spring. In the hate that consumed him, Popov could no longer hear the choir as it really was, but as it ought to have been, reconstituting in his ear the formidable music being massacred here.

'It is worthy, it is just, to worship the Father, the Son, the Holy Spirit, consubstantial and indivisible Trinity.'

Worthy? Unworthy? Just? Unjust? What blasphemies Popov would have invented to defy the trinitarian tyranny if he had been more religious! But he lacked a sacrilegious imagination. His very guts were in revolt, a bubble of saliva oozed from the corner of his lips; he would have liked to explode on the spot, to soil this place with far-flung entrails, splattering the assembly with his flesh.

With Pavlusha, pleasure had had a different taste. To get him to accept at last the idea of bathing together—he had never bathed with the other kids—it had been necessary to become his friend, which was difficult for him and all the more delightful, for he was very shy

270

and distrustful. One day, the two boys had slipped into the reeds on the edge of the Kliazma and taken off their clothes. Pavlusha turned away slightly, as if out of modesty, which seemed out of place in a boy, and dived in first, though he claimed to be afraid of water. But, splashing around in the stream, he had forgotten his reticence and, when they were back on the bank, he no longer thought of hiding the brass cross that hung on a chain around his neck. 'Do you always wear it?' 'I never take it off. It would be sacrilege, you know.' And then, scrupulously, Pavlusha had added: 'Except for the medical examination and even then I'm afraid . . .' A month later—it had needed that delay to avoid any suspicion—four little toughs leapt on Pavlusha in the middle of class, pulled off his sweater and shirt, and pointed to the shivering pink chest, marked with a cross. His comrades howled their disapproval. 'Obscurantist ignoramus! Opium peddler!' yelled the poor schoolmaster, spluttering with indignation (he had himself 'crossed over' and was out to prove himself). Pavlusha cried, protecting his cross with his hands, while the boys tried to twist his arms behind his back, to display his infamy to all. Popov had not taken part in the action. He had carried his finesse to the point of secretly remaining Pavlusha's friend, with no particular intention, simply out of a taste for concealing the seams. The secret of his maestria lay in the smoothness he had acquired in handling men, in the care he always took in the finish of a job.

'Song of victory exclaimed, proclaimed, announced, pronounced,' chanted the priest.

In an ineluctable crescendo, the choir—no longer a few old men and a fine, but unpolished mezzo, but angels and saints in unison—took up a triumphant theme and filled not only the old replastered garage, but the primeval universe in which the stars revolved.

'Holy, Holy, Holy, Lord God of Hosts. Heaven and earth are full of Thy glory. Hosanna in the highest . . .' Hosanna, hosanna, the dark valleys resounded, hosanna, hosanna, the snowy summits echoed, awaiting the universal Conqueror.

'Maestria' was not too strong a word.

271

Take Crocodile. Moscow was getting worried by a certain fall-off in his inflow of information. But to get this epicurean eunuch back to work—he saw himself as a pasha of the intelligence service—all he had to do was to show him meticulous and circumstantial contempt: 'You think you're a Marxist, but what you've been giving us for the last six months is crap. Don't imagine that your scribbling will protect you: a pig is always a pig. As for the French . . . Do you think I'd give myself the trouble to have you kidnapped? You fly too low. I'll go and see the French myself. And they'll give you a dip, old chap, a real dunking—preferably in a swimming-pool, given your dimensions.' How overcome Crocodile was! What protestations of loyalty! He had even burst into tears (and not Crocodile tears) . . . What conditioned reflexes! All in all, it's easy to play the great human mechanism! One only has to press the button marked FEAR or APPETITE and one is on the way to becoming the master of the world. No mistake, no failure. Accidents, but no failures. Unless Antonina . . . But that wasn't in the line of duty, it didn't count. Anyway, why did he go and marry that Chekhovian heroine, when the daughter of the procurator general, a fine, strapping young woman—not so generously endowed, perhaps, but she was crazy about him—would have accelerated his career even more?

If he had married Decabrina, he would now have his own directorate. Instead of that, he had allowed himself to sink into the quicksands of Antonina's grey eyes. Was it love? He knew he was incapable of a low passion of that kind. Caprice, rather: he needed those eyes, that throat, that cracked voice, that walking wound, that pain, which he was making his own. He remembered how, one evening, he had even tried to treat the wound and calm the fear. But the rest of the time he felt only a raging desire before so much integrity, a need to ravage and bring down this incorruptible sanctity. He had, after all, chosen this virgin simply to be sure of violating her innocence, to be sure of soiling her. How he had worked on her to possess her! Despite all the efforts she had made to let herself be ravaged, she had always eluded him. She had carried her good will so far as to receive him one day in black stockings and suspender-belt, she, the vestal virgin of atheism, the reconverted nun, as if she had hoped to exhaust that appetite he nourished for her fall. 'I'll mow you down!' he cried, throwing himself on her.

Turned inside out like a garment, bleeding, sobbing from the desire to appease this insatiable voraciousness, she had remained in fact out of reach, to the day she died. Good riddance!

Now it was like a military review in which, from the lowest of the rookies to the most be-ribboned of the generals, the same terrifying hope, in a graded, collective irrigation of hearts, spread through the hierarchical, descending channel, as the generalissimo approached.

'Blessed be he who comes in the name of the Lord.' This was God's own version of, 'Fall in!'

Another peal of hosannas, another rumble of ecstatic apprehension left hanging in the air, and the Triumphant One would appear. A few deafening explosions would crown the previous outburst! What blinding glory would extinguish in its light the previous lightning-flashes! Everyone was already prostrated: all that remained was to burrow into the earth. The king of kings was about to step ashore . . .

In that void cleansed to welcome the greatest plenitude, the rasping voice of the priest, alone, inadequate, naked, offered a derisory gift: 'Take, eat, this is my body.'

Then, even more inadequate, if that were possible, he passed from the solid offering to the liquid: 'Drink all of this, this is my blood.'

What an insupportable paradox to fling in the face of reason! A new threshold crossed, one was now plunged into the hyper-continuum where nothing rational existed any longer. It was like being in the middle of a pulverised sun surrounded by revolving pieces of débris. The iconostasis opened and shut. The curtain was pulled back and drawn again. The choir chanted and fell silent. The priest appeared and disappeared. One was swimming in a different order where there was no longer any possible progression. Words heard earlier resurfaced like bubbles, then vanished in a slow maelstrom . . . Mother of God, cherubim, seraphim, Pavlusha, Evdokimov, spiritual perfumes, let us offer up our bellies to the Christ God, and again the bread and the debts, again those intolerable blessings, like boiling oil, like molten lead; it was stifling, nerve-racking . . .

The child (Pavlusha?) was still circulating in the opposite direction with his small, round loaves; the prostrated worshippers rose like infantry after a dive-bombing attack, the babushkas began to dance around the candelabra, men bowed and passed, carrying plates in which people threw money (Popov put in a small coin), the gnome, with generous thrusts of shoulders and elbows, cleared a way for himself to the front, to that proscenium where one felt that quite fantastic things would soon be taking place. The proceedings stopped and started, noise alternating with silence. It was all a gigantic puzzle in which church bits and KGB bits mingled together pell-mell, in a state of weightlessness. At last, after an embarrassing pause, the curtain opened with a jangling of rings on the rail, the double doors also opened, there was a commotion in the auditorium, some dozen spectators, with their forearms crossed on their breasts, were carried to the front. Popov allowed himself to be propelled along with them. The gilded hunchback rose up to meet them, a fierce expression swelling his features. At arm's length, in both hands, he brandished a golden thing covered by a square of red cloth. He took so many precautions, he moved forward so cautiously, he held his breath so reverently, one might have thought that the thing was a primed bomb, capable, if dropped, of blowing up the entire world.

23

I slept late that Sunday morning; whenever I woke, I turned on to my other side and forced myself to go back to sleep, knowing that an unpleasant situation awaited my return to consciousness. The telephone pulled me from the last, superfluous slumber, the one that makes your mouth dry and gives you a headache. I pretended not to hear it, but without much conviction. I was tempted to get up without answering it—if it was Rat, he could wait till tomorrow—but curiosity won. It was Marina.

'Hello, Kiril?' She spoke in Russian, with a touch of agitation in her voice. 'He was there.'

'Who? When? What? Where? What time is it? Who do you want?'

She laughed, her soft, throaty laugh.

'One day you'll miss the kingdom of heaven, oversleeping. It's a quarter to one, Sunday, and Igor Maximovich was at mass this morning.'

I leapt blithely into the train of reconciliation.

'For your beautiful eyes, one would go anywhere, Marinochka.'

'It wasn't for my beautiful eyes, which he didn't even look at. He . . .'

She continued gravely: 'He wanted to take communion.'

I put my feet down on the prayer mat I bought in Beni-Izguen and used as a bedside rug, and uttered various sounds of surprise. My mind was a blank.

She laughed again: 'That's stunned you!'

My intellectual cogs were gradually engaging. I said in

275

French: 'Tell me all about it.'

Marina, singing 'The body of Christ receive, taste at the immortal spring,' had seen Popov join the queue of communicants, his forearms crossed, looking crazed, his white eyes fixed on the chalice. He was last but one in the queue. The smaller children went first, followed by two old ladies, then an ex-officer, then a young woman decked out and perfumed as if for a ball, then a mujik who was wider than he was tall, then a long-haired student, then it was Popov's turn. Marina was still singing the same ritual words and could hardly believe her eyes.

No one remained between Popov and the priest. Father Vladimir, the sacred spoon plunged into the chalice, looked at the unknown man from under his black eyebrows. The stranger stood motionless, his mouth open.

'What do you want?' the priest asked at last, quietly but severely, almost menacingly.

Popov did not answer immediately. After a moment, he shut his mouth, painfully swallowed, pointed to the chalice with his forefinger without removing his forearms from his breast, and said: 'Some of that.'

It was as if, Marina said, the priest had swollen up, his feathers ruffled, as if he had grown armour to protect the holy Gifts. His nostrils quivered and the rasping sibillant voice asked:

'Who, may I ask, sir, heard your confession?'

'Why? Is it obligatory?'

The priest's chest swelled up under the chasuble-carapace. He took a deep breath before answering: 'To partake of the most pure Gifts, it is indispensable that you first be purified.'

He added, either out of indignation or, on the contrary, out of politeness, out of human respect: 'Even if you were a saint.'

For a moment, everything hung in the balance. This proscribed pope, this God reduced to a mere pittance, were defying Major Igor Maximovich, officer of the KGB, counsellor at the embassy. How implausible! He must have thought of snatching the chalice from the priest's hand and draining the contents, for his gaze wandered to the two men flanking Father Vladimir, the verger, a sort of Quasimodo, on the left and, on the right, a thin, fair-haired young man, with intense eyes, wearing a short cassock pulled in at the waist. There was little chance that Popov would manage to take communion by force, there was a very good chance that he would profane the communion. Marina was the only one still singing: the choir and the entire congregation, guessing that something unheard of was taking place before them, were waiting, consumed with terror and curiosity. After a moment's reflection—which seemed interminable to Marina—Popov said at last, in a voice—how could one describe it?—in a thunderstruck voice:

'Well, I . . . Why not? . . . When does that take place?'

The parti-coloured eyes looked attentive, almost respectful.

'If it's urgent, the moment you like. Usually, on Saturdays after the vigils.'

The priest added, understandingly: 'About half-past eight. Here.'

Popov nodded two or three times, turned round, walked off the platform and, with hastening steps, through the church. People moved to one side to let him pass as if he were a prince or a plague-victim. Suddenly, he swung round to the left, towards the side door that led to the postern.

'Then,' Marina concluded, 'then, Kiril, something extraordinary happened. You know that intense gaze that the icons have. Well, it was as if all the saints and the Saviour himself turned on him alone: they followed him with their eyes, I saw them. He left, banging the door behind him. I don't think he did it on purpose.'

I have already remarked that Marina's literary tastes were not irreproachable: for my part, I would have done without that collective gaze raking Popov's back. The facts were crazy enough without bringing in the supernatural. It did not occur to me that by bringing in the supernatural—not necessarily at Marina's intellectual level—they might seem less crazy. I was careful to hide my scepticism, but Marina must have guessed it, for she went on, excitedly: 'Perhaps I shouldn't have told you all that. I thought it . . . I don't know . . . would console you.'

All things considered, her decision to telephone me did

perhaps require an explanation. We had left each other on fairly bad terms. Did she want to show me that her intervention had not been so catastrophic? Or to share her stupefaction with me? Or, good girl that she was, to 'console' me, as she put it? I asked her something else:

'How do you explain that he came back this morning? Did he want to see you again? To amuse himself, taking you at your word? He is surely too atheistic to amuse himself by blaspheming. Anyway, he seems to have behaved correctly, doesn't he?'

After some hesitation, she replied, in a very serious tone, but in French (either out of a sense of decency, or to distance herself from her own hypothesis, or because she could not find an appropriate Russian word): 'Personally, I think he has been touched by grace.'

The idea struck me as absurd, but one of my talents is that I do not turn my back on the absurd. I simply exclaimed: 'Popov?!'

'Why not?'

'A major in the KGB?'

'We have to believe that God loves majors, too.'

I had no opinion on the matter. However, I seemed to remember that he loved centurions well enough. I was still convinced that there were other motives for Popov's inexplicable behaviour, but, to discover what they were, one would first have to examine the obvious explanation, however unacceptable it may be.

'Did he say that he would go to confession?'

'He indicated that he was not against it.'

'Did he notice you at any time? Did you catch his eye?'

'No.'

'What was the reaction of the congregation? Did they have any idea who Popov was?'

'There was something of a commotion, as you can imagine. Some old biddies went to tell the priest off: "How can one refuse communion to anyone who asks for it?" Some thought he had escaped from over there: he seemed so unfamiliar with the practices. The verger thought he had seen us together last night—I denied it.'

Various possibilities came into my mind. First, we had to find out which side Marina was fighting on now. How could I ask her?

'Has Popov tried to get in touch with you again?'

'Not yet.'

'If he does, will you warn me?'

This meant abandoning any semblance of pressure. I was throwing myself on her mercy: this couldn't have escaped her attention.

'It depends,' she said after some hesitation, and I had to content myself with this answer.

In fact, I did not remotely believe in Igor Popov's sudden conversion, but I began to think that he might be playing the convert in order to get his hands on Marina again. If this were the case, he was really nailed for good; there would be no reason not to ressuscitate Culverin. I thanked Marina again effusively and, after weighing up the psychological implications, I called Rat. 'Of course he's here: where do you expect him to be?' replied Mme Rat with her usual charm, and I heard her grumble under her breath: our conversation would stop her listening to her radio play. Rat did not seem too pleased to hear from me either. I reported the facts as briefly as I could.

'What cock and bull story is this you're giving me?'

He had resigned himself to the idea of giving up the operation. It upset him to have to go back to it: he was old. But I had no doubt that with a little time his hopes would revive.

'Marina wouldn't lie to me, sir, not when I could check what she says with an entire congregation. It's simply a question of interpreting what happened: either he's undergone a conversion or he's pretending that he has.'

'Conversion?' the Shopkeeper chortled. 'Talk of a turn-around!'

'Why not? Millions of men , from St Paul onwards, have been converted. In many cases, it is precisely the sworn enemies of religion who suddenly change sides.'

'There was a chap called Polyeucte,' Rat muttered.

'Polyeucte and St Vladimir and Paul Claudel behind his pillar, and many others. There may not have been a KGB major yet: all the more reason, statistically, that there should be one some day.'

'And we've found him?'

'Someone had to find him, of course. It so happens that we did. We have to exploit the situation, sir.'

'Exploit' is also a key word in the military vocabulary: I mean it opens doors. I used it on purpose.

'Converted? What a joke all the same,' Rat giggled. 'And sudden, too.'

'It's almost always sudden. An ox of a man, committed in one direction, suddenly leaves his furrow and sets off in the opposite direction. The harder he pulled one way, the harder he'll now pull in the other. The boomerang effect—it's well known.'

'Can you see me reporting a conversion to Silbert? Now *that* would make me look good!'

'As you yourself have observed, sir, conversion is a turning at its most typical. However, in this case there is another possibility: Popov is a sham, but he's been seriously hooked by our girl, either for professional reasons—through her he hopes to get to us—or for the kind of personal reasons we've been counting on from the beginning. She refuses him on religious grounds and in order to get what he wants, he takes up religion.'

'Well . . . One way or another, he certainly wants to hoodwink someone . . . A KGB officer at mass! You have to be joking. Perhaps he wants to hoodwink God? Look, old chap, I don't mind asking General Poirier what he thinks.'

It was a partial victory: Silbert, apparently, still did not know how bad our situation was. Everything still seemed possible. I took Frisquette to Ermenonville. Next morning, I thought it was wiser not to go to the office, in case Silbert happened to call me in. I telephoned Mme Krebs and told her I had a hangover; apparently, the Shopkeeper was also suffering. What a coincidence! I spent a studious day at the Mazarine library. That evening, Rat called: lunch tomorrow at the usual restaurant. Poirier was interested in Culverin again.

He was looking distinctly wan: the marbling of his skin seemed bluer, the arterioles more evident, the mouth smaller, almost childlike in the great hunk of meat, soaked in Calvados, that made up his face. But he was once more heart and soul for our scheme. We discussed Popov as we savoured our *tripes à la mode de Caen*.

'Well, spout,' said Rat.

I took out my files and spouted, alternating, I'm afraid between pedantry and buffoonery.

'As the colonel must have told you, sir, I think the fact that Popov went to church might be explained in various ways, but since he asked to communicate, only one hypothesis remains: conversion, whether true or false. I see the argument against it, especially against the hypothesis of a false conversion—it's improbable. Truth doesn't need as much probability as dissimulation. But, on the one hand, a young woman's criteria of probability, especially one who is herself religious, are not necessarily the same as yours or mine; and she's the one who has to be convinced. On the other hand, having thought about the question a little further, I've come to the conclusion that in fact it isn't entirely improbable that Popov should have undergone a genuine conversion nor, consequently, that he should have decided to play the convert for us. It is true that we don't often have an opportunity of witnessing conversions, but that's because we live in a society in which Christianity is either taken for granted or regarded as *passé*. In fact, conversion, from *convertere*, 'to turn, to change oneself', is the very essence of Christianity. The first thing John the Baptist asked of those who heard him (*Mark*, chapter I, verse 4), is, in the French translation, to repent, but in Greek, to μετανοεῖν: *to change feeling*. "The time is come," he tells them, "the Kingdom of Heaven is at hand, so change feeling" (*Mark*, I, 15). In the desert of Judaea he went about proclaiming: "Change feeling, for the Kingdom of Heaven is at hand" (*Matthew*, III, 2), and when Jesus began to preach, he used the same words: "Change feeling, for the Kingdom of Heaven is at hand" (*Matthew*, IV, 17). The verb ἐπιστρέφω: "to change, to turn," is used—the numbers are probably not accidental—seven times in the Gospels and twelve times in the

281

Acts. Seven and twelve, sir, are mystical numbers, and this fact emphasises the primordial importance given to the idea of turning. As the colonel remarked the day before yesterday, conversion is turning *par excellence*.

'Our whole Western civilization is the fruit of millions of conversions. Some are particularly important. Constantine sees a cross appear before him, accompanied by the words *Hoc signo vinces*, "By this sign thou shalt conquer", gives Maxentius a hiding, and heaves the Roman Empire, that is, the civilized world, into Christianity. Vladimir, seeing a painting of the Last Judgement and realizing that the lot of the damned will be as unenviable as that of the saved will be sweet, has a river and a whole people baptized at one and the same time. Clovis, converted after Tolbiac by St Remigius, hears the saint tell him: "Rise, proud Sicambrian, worship what you have burnt, burn what you have worshipped"—which is a veritable compendium of turning—and the dove of the Holy Spirit brings him the Holy Ampulla in its beak. It may be a legend, but it's telling: all the history of the kings of France is encapsulated in it. In our own day, there's no shortage of conversions: the philosopher Gabriel Marcel, the philosopher Simone Weil . . .

'From the Christian point of view, specialists recognize several sorts of conversion: some have intellectual motives, like the quest for truth, others rest on a desire for moral perfection, others again are triggered off by an emotion, often a collective one. A question that theologians believe to be important has been debated throughout the centuries: is it man in his freedom who seeks and finds conversion, or is it a grace that God sends him? The Council of Trent made up its mind on this subject: "Whoever expresses the opinion that without inspiration and the previous help of the Holy Spirit a man might believe, hope and love or repent as he must to receive the grace of justification, let him be anathema." St Thomas Aquinas clearly shows that it is God who takes the initiative in converting man, who merely has the duty to cooperate with God. In other words, transitive conversion is the cause of intransitive conversion. Orthodox theologians, who are more attached to freedom, think differently. Bulgakov . . .'

'Let's stay with the Catholics, shall we? That's quite enough gas as it is,' said Poirier. 'Waiter, we're dying of thirst here. No, no, the wine's all right . . . Calvas—that's the boy. Right! Carry on, Volsky.'

'Often conversion takes place gradually, especially in the case of intellectual conversion, but when it's an emotional phenomenon, a matter of illumination, then usually it's sudden. In Scripture, this was the case with Zacchaeus, Matthew, Lydia, Timothy. Jawcett wrote: "On the first Christians, the influence of Christianity was almost always immediate." Savonarola also admitted that "a single word had sufficed", and you'll remember the suddenness of the turning of Claudel and Frossard, who were both converted in churches. Here, if you'll bear with me, sir, we have the question of what is called internal grace and external grace: external grace is the occasion offered by God, for example George Herbert's poem "Love" in the case of Simone Weil; internal grace is the evolution of one's mind towards the acceptance of the truth. The archetypal conversion, of course, is that of the Apostle of the Gentiles, Paul of Tarsus.'

'The road to Damascus . . .?' murmured Poirier, anxious to display his knowledge, yet fearful at the same time of making a gaffe.

'Precisely, sir. The conversion of St Paul has become a great feast of the Church, celebrated in the West on January 25th; it has inspired innumerable paintings, including ones by Murillo, Caravaggio, Carraci, Giordano, etc., etc.; for us non-Jews, it represents the starting-point of our evangelization. Allow me to remind you of the facts. Paul is a convinced reactionary, a pure, extreme Pharisee, a Christian-eater; he took part in the stoning of Stephen, the first martyr; he went to Damascus with a view to carrying out systematic repression. On the way, a light struck him like a laser beam. He fell. A voice, which his companions also heard, said: "Saul, Saul, why are you persecuting me?" '

'Why Saul?' asked Poirier, who wished to grasp the situation completely.

'Because he only assumed the name of Paul when he became a Christian, "another man". He asked politely: "Sir, who are you?" Remember he had seen nothing except this light which, in the strict sense of the word, blinded him. The voice replied: "I am Jesus whom you are persecuting." He then asked: "Sir, what do you want me to do?" Jesus ordered him to get up, go into Damascus and await further orders. Saul got up. He could no longer see. He blinked, he rubbed his eyelids, perhaps he washed them: nothing! In the meantime, Jesus appeared to the Christian Ananias and commended Saul to him. "I've heard about this Chekist," Ananias replied; "he's not to be trusted." The reply is unanswerable: "But he is my chosen vessel." Ananias was not convinced, but nevertheless he went and saluted Saul as a brother. The scales fell from Paul's eyes, he had a bite to eat and right away he became the greatest apostle of Christendom. It was he—and he spoke from experience—who produced the theory of conversion. Whoever leaves a dead religion for a living faith is no more a renegade then a widower who remarries is an adulterer. There is progress from error to truth and when one has "known God", it becomes meaningless to subject oneself to the rudiments of knowledge by which one has run one's life. "What matters is not being circumcised or uncircumcised, but being a *new* creature." "Be transformed by the *renewal* of your spirit." *New* Testament, *new* wine-skins, *new* man. I have the references if you like. In the Orthodox Church we sing at Easter: "Let us drink the *new* draught."

'You may think all this is a lot of religious nonsense. Christ may not have gone to Damascus, but Saul of Tarsus did. From our point of view, it amounts to the same thing. Modern psychologists are quite right: the most atheistic of them study conversion as a well established psychological phenomenon. William James regarded it as a natural event, in which an ego, conscious of being in error, inferiority and unhappiness, achieves unity and awareness of its own rectitude, superiority and happiness. Owen Brandon considers that conversion is the response provided by the individual to a stimulus "concerning a particular orientation, whatever it may be, of the mental attitude and/or behaviour". Freud . . .' The other two cocked their ears: they knew the name and expected some juicy morsels to follow. 'Freud saw it as the child's sense of vulnerability and his nostalgia for the father. Leuba, Starbuck, Coe regard conversion as a manifestation of the unconscious without any divine intervention. Jung notes that all religious activity belongs to the specifically human activities of man, and Schaff-Herzog maintains—this is of particular concern to us—that there are two types of conversion: one is an act of will by which one tries to become different, to turn over a new leaf; the other, on the contrary, is an abrogation of the will, corresponding to an "invasion from a subliminal region, through which, after a more or less prolonged incubation period, one freely identifies oneself with God. Experiences, too, are partially due to high sensitivity with a tendency to automatism and suggestibility of a passive type."

' "Automatism! Suggestibility of a passive type!" Exactly what one expects of the Communist ideal, which finds it quite normal to change truth every morning. All you need is for someone other than Lenin to take over secretly and the natural Communist will be shown up as a shock Fascist like Mussolini, or a democrat like Koestler, or a believer like so many of those who have perished behind the curtain.'

'Well preached, padre,' said Poirier, with approval. 'I find it difficult to accept your revolutionary idea of Catholicism: for me it's more a matter of pennies in the plate, sheets over the window, sugared-almonds at baptisms, and first communion dresses, but you're quite right: for those born outside it, it must be quite an adventure. Believing in the crucified Christ, that's quite something, I tell you. But Popov, now, of all people . . .'

'Precisely.'

'A hardened lecher . . .'

'Vladimir had eight hundred concubines: and he evangelized Russia!'

Poirier gave his fleeting smile.

'How old was he when he died? Right. O.K. It's possible. What are we to expect from all this?'

'Nothing good,' said Rat. 'It's too bent, even for me.'

It was amusing to see the two old cynics disarmed not before religious illusion, but before the illusion of illusion: in fact, increasingly convinced that a conversion was not improbable, they were still thinking—as I was—in terms of a fictitious conversion, simulated with a precise objective. Since this objective could hardly be anything other than Marina, I suggested having her observed electronically: I liked the idea of an inanimate witness concealed in the privacy of her home, transforming her secret life into electro-magnetic signals, thus giving me an almost supernatural advantage over her. Judge me as you will—I judge myself—but not by some bourgeois yardstick. I was a 'novelist'. If Stendhal had been able to hear what Mathilde said when he was not there, can anyone suppose that he would not have put his ear to the keyhole? Perhaps I already had an idea of the use I was to make of Marina, that second possession by which I finally took possession of her. In any case, when we'd had our Calvados, I insisted on getting my microphone.

There could be no question, of course, of getting the assistance of our rivals.

'We might try Sergeant Lavallière,' Poirier suggested.

He had kept up an episodic relationship with this specialist, now retired, who continued to do odd detective jobs, putting his expertise and equipment 'borrowed' from his former employers at the service of jealous husbands, greedy wives and suspicious bosses.

Poirier got up, staggering slightly; his trousers sagged behind him. In his day this old wreck had been regarded as a dandy! He disappeared in the direction of the telephones.

'You and I are on the tightrope,' said Rat, observing the general's swaying posterior, 'while the old joker's having his fun at no risk at all.'

The old joker returned. A meeting had been arranged for me, for of course it was always I who had to serve as lightning-conductor. All that remained was to decide where the receiver was to be installed. Lavallière's emitters had a restricted radius. Rat remembered he had a friend whose office formed a corner with the Avenue de Lowendal. He would agree, given a slap-up meal, to house the Ecole Militaire's receiver and tape-recorder. (We had several in stock that could be taken out without Tolstoy's permission.)

'And why shouldn't we put Tolstoy in the picture?' asked Rat.

'You must be joking,' said Poirier irritably. 'Tolstoy has his 144, that should be enough for him. Compartmentalization, that's the name of the game.'

I interpreted this jovial, but brutal way of interposing, with a fluttering of his thick, but thinly distributed, colourless eyelashes, as a 'You're not going to play with my toys', which suggested a certain incipient senility. But Poirier was of course undeniably right: protection and information must be segregated as distinctly as possible. That is a dogma of the business. The mere fact that Rat so much as dreamt of transgressing it should have put me on my guard.

I met Lavallière in an anonymous café, at the time when wine goblets begin to replace the beer tankards. He was tall, dark, hollow-chested, with a triangular head and pointed ears. He was wearing a red shirt under a very worn suede jacket. The sergeant was not a great talker. It seemed to me that I had never heard him utter more than two words, always the same. I explained what I wanted him to do.

'No problem,' he said.

Through the traffic jams, he drove me to the Avenue de Suffren in a car that was too short for his long legs: to get into it, he had to fold himself up like an accordion.

Marina's building was flanked by two alleyways perpendicular to the avenue. There was one window per apartment: if you were in the right alleyway, all you had to do was count. It was raining. By not getting out of the car, Lavallière gave me to understand that I was to do the reconnaissance: the expert would bestir himself only when this had been done.

I stepped out into a puddle, raised the collar of my mackintosh and took the left-hand alleyway, on the even side. I paddled my way to the eighth window. A light shone reflected behind the shutters. Marina must be in her bathroom, with the door open: it was seven o'clock, she was getting ready to go out. I returned to the car. Lavallière lowered the window an inch. I told him we would have to wait.

'No problem.'

I got in to the back and sat on the street side, my eyes fixed on the front door of the building. The tricolour lights reflected in zigzags on the roadway, the blinding headlamps, the sprays of water from the cars, the glittering puddles prevented me from seeing as distinctly as I would have liked. Marina might leave without my noticing.

I repeated my reconnaissance two or three times. On the last occasion, I found the light out and as I ran back along the alley-way, I almost bumped into Marina who, wearing high heels and carrying an umbrella, was trotting over to a black Mercedes, double-parked, with the door open. 'The boor!' I was jealous and soaked, while that lout sat in red plush comfort behind his steering wheel! Marina did not seem to have noticed me. I crossed the roadway behind the Mercedes: 'Let's go.'

Lavallière unfolded himself. He was wearing, I remember, one of those transparent raincoats with metallic highlights reminiscent of a spacesuit. We entered the long corridor with its bright blue walls and its lugubrious ceiling lights, which would not look out of place in a science-fiction crypt or morgue. The isolation was complete: one's feet sank into the carpet and all one could hear was some jazz tune, faint and muffled. We stopped in front of number 8. I tried the door and commented stupidly: 'It's shut.'

'No problem,' said Lavallière.

He was carrying a big brown bag of imitation leather, suggesting a doctor or an abortionist, rather than an electronics engineer. I expected to see him take out a burglar's precise, gleaming tools. But the expert was content to slip a rectangle of celluloid into the jamb-lining of the door and calmly slide it back and forth. The latch-bolt retracted, the door opened, we went in. Lavallière calmly switched on the light.

The mobiles, the pictures, the nicknacks, the rugs, the icon in the corner were all familiar to me. A sheepskin, thrown over an armchair, hung to the floor. The rough, nigger-brown sofa, all right angles, opened up, I knew, into a soft, white bed, like a coconut. A disturbing memory. I walked a few steps around the room. This violation of privacy was, all the same, a sort of pos-session, the only kind permitted to the 'novelist' over the heroine. I glanced at the bookcase with its red and green bindings: *La Vouivre, Spartacus, Sparkenbroke* . . . On another shelf, the *New Testament* in Russian. I pulled out a book the spine of which carried no title: Antonin Artaud. I went and looked into the kitchenette: there was nothing to see. I emboldened myself to open a drawer: lingerie. I shut it hastily: I still had some moral scruples. The wardrobe was filled to overflowing with coats, dresses, skirts, trousers, furs and, below, innumerable pairs of shoes. Mitsuko reigned, what a heart-ache! I turned round to Lavallière. His bag lay gaping wide on the floor, he had put on pale green rubber gloves and, armed with a screwdriver, he was performing a caesarian on the telephone. However, instead of taking out, he was putting in. A magnetized parallelepiped, the size of half a matchbox, was stuck to a metal surface. I watched, all the more fascinated in that I found it incomprehensible that this mass, once primed, would transmit not only the heroine's telephone conversations, but also all the noises in her room, suspending its activity when silence was re-established and resuming its emissions as soon as it was interrupted. Lavallière screwed back the base, put the telephone back in place, looked at me defiantly, as if I had ever doubted his abilities.

'No problem!' he declared with a shrug of his shoulders.

He turned out the lights. We were already in the corridor when I remembered that I had not closed the door of Ali Baba's cave—I mean the wardrobe. I had no wish to look ridiculous by admitting it. In any case it was quite unimportant, either one way or the other. Marina would think that she had left it open herself. I don't know why I am relating this incident. I still dream of that door open in the dark before that store of accessories from which filtered that odour of sorcery—in vain, since no nostril was there to pick it up.

We still had to go into a café to ring Marina's number in order to prime the emitter. It was strange ringing that number, knowing that it would remain for the moment, silent, but that it would never be deaf again: the ringing that I was causing in the Avenue de Suffren was already being recorded in the Avenue de Lowendal.

24

On Monday morning, Major Igor Popov opened the yellow file marked 'Zmeïka', tilted back his plastic and chrome chair and, staring at the map representing the progress of atheism, pressed the bell push with his foot. Lieutenant Arbuzov entered. He was a thick-set fellow: he had a big, chubby, pale face, with thick, almost negroid lips. I never met him, but I have been through the documents: a run-of-the-mill KGB man of little talent. He was to be recalled shortly afterwards for having given himself leave to transgress, like his boss, the puritanical code of the service.

'Comrade Major?'

He trembled like a cocker-spaniel at the idea of not pleasing his master.

Popov pulled towards him another file, while leaving the first open in front of him, and declared: 'The Gospels.'

'The Gospels? . . . How do you mean? . . . The Gospels?' Arbuzov stammered, not knowing whether he would displease more by his stupidity or by asking a question. 'What kind of Gospels?'

'The Russian. Pocket-sized edition. Published abroad, of course,' said Popov absently, without looking up from the file.

'You require a copy of the Gospels, Comrade Major?'

A fist thumped the desk.

'How many times do I have to tell you, you idiot? Are you going to fetch it or do I have to get it myself?'

An hour later, Arbuzov reappeared, trying to conceal the nervous trembling of his hands by pressing them hard against his trouser seams. Unlike his peers, Major Popov did not like people to be afraid of him.

'I'm terribly sorry, Comrade Major. There is not one copy of the Go . . . Gospels in the whole of the embassy. Except perhaps in the ambassador's own quarters . . . I did not dare to ask him without orders.'

'Cretin!' said Popov.

Then, three seconds later, he added: 'Buy one.'

He returned to his dossier.

It took Lieutenant Arbuzov two hours to learn the existence of the religious book-shop in the Rue du Val-de-Grâce, to understand that what he called the Gospels was referred to there as the *New Testament*, to verify that there was such a thing as a pocket-sized edition in Russian and to buy one. Arbuzov remained prudent and cunning when there was no need to be; he imagined that the shop might contain concealed cameras planted there by the Americans, and that if the Americans got hold of a photograph of him buying a copy of the Gospels he would never escape their blackmail; it also occurred to him that his boss might have invented a particularly mean method of getting rid of a subaltern who irritated him. That is why, instead of going himself to get his purchase, he sent in a taxi-driver, who took his time. In the end, holding the little brown book with the finger-tips of both hands, Arbuzov laid it on the major's desk.

'See this door, idiot? Shut it—from the outside.'

When Popov was alone, he looked at the book for some time, as if he expected some absurd miracle to take place, of the kind to be found in the *Old Testament*: an explosion, perhaps, a peal of bells or a cloud of smoke issuing from its pages? A flight of black birds with sharp talons? A cluster of bats rising to hang upside down from the ceiling? Then he pulled towards him the yellow folder, pulled out the yellow form and under the heading 'Written Communications—Codes', wrote, in his carefully linked handwriting: 'Code book: Gospels.'

He picked up the little volume, opened it without fear and copied out the exact reference of the edition. Then he rang. Arbuzov appeared.

'Did you note the item of expenditure?'

291

'I simply wrote "book", Comrade Major,' Arbuzov replied with a crafty look.

'Nitwit!' said Popov. 'What are you trying to do, have me suspected of buying that for pleasure? Scram.'

25

Silbert had asked to see us and we appeared before him on the Wednesday, Rat quaking as he did before any superior, I, hardened, cold, knowing that I was playing for high stakes, resigned to losing, yet ready to be agreeably surprised if I won, devoid of any illusions and not suspecting the fatal fork in the road that lay just ahead. Estienne, the red-haired warrant officer, kept us waiting before announcing us and then, Silbert himself, after we had been announced, kept us waiting almost as long as he had kept me on the last occasion: Steel Wool liked to show his subordinates that, seen from the top, the differences that separated us were negligible. Mathematically, he should have emerged enhanced from the operation, but no one was taken in: on the contrary, our opinion of him fell still further. He was still wearing his blue-tinted spectacles and the currycomb that served him as hair seemed stiffer and sharper than ever. Nevertheless, he asked us to sit down: a good sign.

Once we were seated at a respectful distance from him, and a less respectful but still considerable distance from one another, we awaited what was to follow, I with military fatalism, Rat sweating and wriggling beneath the invisible gaze that served to enhance his discomfort still further. In the end, Silbert, in his trenchant, sibilant voice, with its incisive consonants, declared: 'Costly business, eh, costly business!'

And, developing his idea, he went on: 'Costly business, this Culverin, and it's not paying off!'

His hand gripped his paper-knife and he examined his nails as if he had been to a manicurist for the first time in his life.

'I'm a patient man, eh, but all the same . . .'

'Sir,' Rat began. Out of humility he had renounced the protection of his yellow-tinted spectacles (as a defeated dog presents his jugular vein to his rival). 'Sir, as I have had the honour to report to you, we are on the point . . .'

I was congratulating myself on my low rank when Silbert interrupted: 'Who's in charge of the operation?'

'Volsky, sir.'

'Then let him speak, if you don't mind.'

The blue-tinted glasses pivoted towards me with an impatient upwards movement of the head. I thought I could detect in the tone, beneath the obvious sharpness, a hidden docility. After all, if I succeeded, Silbert would reap his share of the laurels: a share commensurate with his rank. I replied with calculated dryness.

'We are approaching the phase of exploitation. From the beginning, we had guessed that Major Popov was a relatively weak link in the chain. We attributed this to a certain excess of sensuality. It appears that things are not quite so simple. Two possibilities present themselves: either Popov is in the grip, as expected, of an uncontrollable passion for our informant, whom we planted on him, and, in order to win her over, he is pretending to entertain religious feelings: in which case, we will exploit the situation as planned, either by turning or by compromising him; or the unpredictable has happened, and Popov really believes that he has undergone a conversion. The Slav soul is a matter of race, not of regime. In the second case we are in just as good a position as in the first. Either the new man will disown the old; in which case, if he refuses to work for his bosses, he will sooner or later be induced to work for us and, at the very least, we can expect a complete unloading of all the information in his hands; nor is it out of the question that, as a neophyte with ambitions to martyrdom, he might agree quite simply to change sides, in which case we have at our disposal an admirably placed agent, resolved to undergo every sacrifice: what more could we want? Or, if the new man decides to make his peace with the old, he's bound to compromise himself before long. He will then be in our hands and we can force him to work for us in whatever way we see fit.'

As a supreme token of benevolence, Silbert took off his glasses. He had cold eyes but perhaps not as hard as he would have wished. He pursed his little purple lips. We spooks like to bet on the odds and evens together, but in the regular army, from which he came, that was not how things were done. Each situation answered to one single strategy.

'When will you know which way he has jumped?' he asked, almost politely.

At least he had not dismissed out of hand the idea of a conversion, whether sincere or pretended. He accepted the facts. If Popov was going to church, he must have a reason.

'Next Saturday, sir, I presume.'

I had to explain the Orthodox system to him; no confession, no communion. He liked that. He asked if one had to show a confessional ticket and was disappointed to learn that the practice had almost entirely died out.

'Then it's just a technical matter: all we have to do is . . .' he said, with the tone of a leader who is well ahead of his foot-slogging subordinates (though without the slightest criticism intended: the leader is *necessarily* more intelligent).

Suddenly I guessed what he was going to say. Once stated, his suggestion entered my disarray belatedly, confirming the bruise, but not causing it, since I had already received the shock from the inside.

Ten years have passed since then. I, who, at the time, was an amiable agnostic, have been restored to myself, and thence to the bosom of the Church. I say this without irony, and if I am playing a little on words, it is out of a simple sense of strait-laced *pudeur* that I have not succeeded in shaking off. At various moments, we all have a nostalgic desire to return to the womb, but it is given only to Christians to satisfy it in a specific way; by not being of a physical kind, the sense of protection, of enclosure, is perhaps even more complete: one rediscovers one's (earthly) mother in the bosom of the common Mother. I have known the sense of peace that results from cutting oneself off from one's pride and crying 'Mother!' I am forgiven, washed, pardoned, whitened, amnestied, *amnesia-ed* . . . God himself has forgotten and, according to our beliefs, it would be a major impiety to accuse myself of a sin that he has given himself the trouble of extirpating in the past. But—is this a paradoxical sign of my incurable frivolity, of that twisted scale of values of which I was once so proud, and which I now deplore, but of which I can probably never cure myself?—I cannot forgive myself for the offence to which I am now coming, the recital of which costs me infinitely more than that of all the crimes and acts of cowardice that I may have committed, more even than that of my humiliation with Marina. Shall I admit it? I've long sought a means of relating this story while suppressing the incident or attributing it to someone else: it seemed to me—it still does—that to retell it is to commit the same offence again. All the same, in the end, I've opted for the truth. Why? I have no respect for what is called realism, I am convinced that fiction is quite capable of surpassing life in interest and in imagination, I derive no pleasure from vilifying myself, public confession holds no attraction for me, yet there is a grain of reality that I have been unable to toss out from the sieve. It is as if, in certain cases, life were still the best poet and that it is a lack of taste to seek other solutions than its own. In short, Silbert said: 'One simply has to bug the confessional.'

Immediately I poured out a flood of bad arguments to counter a decision that I know I was unable to prevent, a decision in which I could already see myself participating in spite of myself. To begin with, sir, there are no confessionals in the Orthodox churches, and anyway, sir, there is no way in which we could set up a listening post near enough, and in any case, sir, we don't know whether the confession will really take place. What is more, sir, supposing Popov detected our attempt, what a loss of face that would be for us!

'No confessional?'

I explained that the priest and the penitent usually stood side by side in front of a lectern on which a copy of the Gospels had been placed. This was certainly not a piece of secret information, but in briefing Silbert on our rites I felt as if I were betraying secrets. The lectern, I added, was placed outside the view of the faithful, behind one of the semi-partitions. Silbert, who was interested in topography, wanted to know what these semi-partitions were. I had to scribble a plan of a Russian church on his memo-pad (I moved my hand towards the larger pad, but he pushed the smaller one towards me), with the sanctuary hidden behind the iconostasis, the ambo in front, with the nave and the narthex further on. Betrayal had piqued my curiosity; now it nauseated me.

'Curious, curious,' repeated Silbert.

I showed how the two ends of the ambo were masked by two semi-partitions parallel to the iconostasis. At the church of the Dormition, the choir was placed behind the right-hand one; behind the left-hand one confessions were heard.

'Put the lectern on your sketch.'

I sketched in the lectern.

'Is it well lit in that part?'

'In the evening, it's very dark.'

'What does this lectern look like?'

I described the high desk covered with a cloth hanging to the floor.

'Would there be room underneath for a tape-recorder?'

The suggestion struck the Shopkeeper and myself as scandalously simple. We were not, after all, amateurs. We liked two-way mirrors, cameras concealed in photometric cells, microphones in telephones . . . A tape-recorder under a lectern was plain daft. Rat himself broke his silence to remark that the equipment would have to be put into position before the service, that Russian services were devilishly long and that the tape would have run out before the confession began. I went further. The vigils lasted at least two-and-a-half hours and there were certain to be other confessions beside Popov's. The argument was quite invalid—and we knew it. Silbert, always a step ahead, explained to us that there were delayed-starting systems that the Deuxième Bureau was quite capable of attaching to any tape-recorder. He was right.

This discussion in which I intervened so clumsily did not really affect me. Deep down, I had, as we say in Russian, gnawing dogs. It seemed to me that some terrible catastrophe was building up, as they build up in nightmares, and that I could do nothing to avoid it: I was caught up in it, I was standing on an escalator descending into hell. The colour drained from the world around me. I had a clear impression—even now, I hesitate to write the word as if in itself it represented a risk—of damning myself. And yet why? The secrecy of the confessional is a matter for the priest. No one has ever thought to propound a dogma forbidding secret eavesdropping, electronic or otherwise. I would commit no listed sacrilege; I would simply be doing my job. Anyway, did I even believe in God? Scarcely, and surely not in the pomps and works, ecclesiastical or otherwise. For me, the Church was above all memories of childhood, of boredom and tenderness mixed in more or less equal parts. I had been very happy, I remembered, on Sundays when, dressed in a sailor suit and little white shorts, I went to take communion without going first to confession, not having yet attained the age of so called reason, and when adults, both family and friends, treated me until the evening with a deferent solicitude that I found very much to my taste. I had been less happy when, later, I had had to perform interminable stations standing at the sabbatical vigils, arriving at mass on time, not moving before the end of the sermon: 'Brothers and sisters, the Gospel for today teaches us that . . .' But yes, I had understood, I was not deaf. I remembered in particular the irritation that came over me on days when the parable of the sower had been read, the meaning of which was so clear and which Jesus himself had spelled out to his disciples, but which the worthy cleric felt the need to spell out further—perhaps because, for once, he ran no risk of committing an error of interpretation. I had been even less happy when, mature enough at last for confession, I had to confront the insoluble dilemma of admitting the inadmissible or of keeping silent on precisely what ought to be said. As soon as I was my own master, I had dispensed with these tortures; in view of this, I no longer took communion and hardly put in an appearance in church except in pleasant circumstances as, for example, to show some Parisian tourist the exoticism of the Easter service (everyone kissed each other afterwards—it was obligatory), or the majestic pathos of the office of the dead celebrated in honour of the martyred Tsar. And I now had to return and commit that act for which there was not even a name, not even a punishment, as was the case for parricide in some Greek city or other? Profoundly repressed mystical inclinations began to uncoil within me. But I already knew, of course, that I would not refuse to obey for the good reason that I did not yet have any serious reason to disobey.

Silbert seemed unaware that something was troubling me, when I suggested that someone other than myself, the chauffeur Marty, for example, should set up the device. It would be better, I respectfully remarked, to avoid the risk of being recognized in that church, having attended bits of services there once or twice a year. But Silbert patiently pointed out that, in view of what I had myself just said, my visit would surprise no one, whereas Marty, or anyone else who would have, quite uselessly, to be brought into the secret, was bound to attract attention by not knowing the correct way to behave. Of course, he was quite right.

'Can you see Marty performing exercises in front of the icons?'

I left the office toying half-heartedly with the idea of resigning. Rat seemed not to have a care in the world.

'Well, we've got rid of that one. The chief's on our side. And if by some chance it works . . .'

Clearly, the lieutenant-colonel already saw a full tally of gold stripes on his epaulettes. Then he came back to me and, squeezing my arm, he examined me with those yellow eyes of his in which cunning and a knowledge of men stood in for intelligence and imagination. At the same time, he was making terrifying grimaces with his big, loose lips; I guessed that he was trying to put his false teeth back in place. 'Well, well, my boy,' he said, with a mixture of fellow-feeling and contempt, 'so it's back to our first communion?'

I kept my temper sufficiently to reply: 'First communion is exclusively a Roman rite.'

He smiled. I realized that he had seen right through me and was amused by what he saw.

26

Twice a day I went to collect the information that was being recorded at the Ecole Militaire. An old lieutenant of the noble service of the Chancellery pointed, without a word, to the receiver-recorder lying on the floor in a corner. I removed the tape and put in a new one. I put the first tape on to a second tape-recorder; I put on the head-phones and sat in a chair, facing the wall, and listened. Visits and calls followed one another: invitations, gossip, flirtations, business conversations. All this had no interest whatever, but the fact that it was possible was interesting. It was incredibly exciting for me, an intelligence officer, to unveil this woman, a woman who meant something to me as a man. I suffered each time the mercurial voice answered with one of her hellos, so charged with expectation and promise. I let myself be deliciously rocked by it when she expatiated endlessly as to the relative advantages of moisturizer prepared from a yogurt base and masks consisting of marine algae. I never pressed the PLAY button without wondering if, this time, I would not hear too much, and what I would do if this particular recording violated Marina's intimacy even more than the previous ones. Jealousy, a kind of unhealthy curiosity, remnants of scruples, the passion of the 'novelist', all this was mixed together and put me into a cold sweat . . . I was at once happy and unhappy that it was I who had conceived of this eavesdropping, which I hated, yet could not refrain from. I do not remember being all that much concerned about the professional advantages that I was supposed to derive from it.

At last, one evening—I think it was Thursday—I heard:

'Well, Marinette, what have we been up to? Have we got a

moment for our favourite Popolisson?'

Trembling with anticipation, I expected passion, perhaps sensuality, not vulgarity. I got exactly what I deserved.

Marina gave me some hope by trying to discourage Popol: she had a headache, a part to learn, but she spoke to him familiarly—and a few moments later, because the tape-recorder skipped the silences, I heard the old lecher start up again: 'I'm bringing a bottle. You've got ice?'

Instead of throwing the boor out, she laughed softly with her cooing laugh and he cracked silly jokes as he emptied her refrigerator: 'You want some chicken?' Crack, crack. 'It's the leg I go for. I like chicks' legs.' Why did it hurt me so much? Marina, after all, was nothing to me, was she? When, by certain clues, I had identified the Popol in question as a journalist who was beginning to make a name for himself in the theatrical press, I was, to some extent, relieved: Marina did not love him, she was sacrificing herself to her career. But, apart from that, there was no room for doubt: she had been, she would still be, his mistress. I almost pressed the STOP button. But professional conscience required that I listen to the end. Would I, in any case, have been able to stop myself? I examined the Louis XVI parquet floor at my feet and, behind his desk, the chancellor, who seemed to date from the same period. I imagined the nigger-brown sofa-bed opening like a fruit. The world was nothing but bitterness and filth; life, a crude joke.

'Now, now, Marinette, what's bugging you this evening?'

'This evening, Paul, the answer is no.'

Hope returned to the world. But no, Marina would give in. She was only trying to titillate him with calculated refusals. There was almost a row in the tape-recorder. Ah! How I would have liked to transport myself to the Avenue de Suffren the evening before! How the instincts of *homo habilis* soon rise in the muscles! I made no claim to Marina myself, but I could have kicked the bastard in the nose and in the crotch. Did he really imagine that a woman could not do without his certainly over-rated favours? What suspense! Popol alternated propaganda ('You'll see, it will be fabulous'), interrogation ('Are you ill or what?'), blackmail ('Your little friend Doris has been making eyes at me'), offers of help ('I'm getting an interview on Radio Luxembourg') and attempts at rape. The amplifier was excellent: it was like being in the room itself. I had never felt so much a 'novelist': all knowledge and no power . . . Suddenly there was an 'ouch!' which poured balm on my wounded heart.

'You've shattered my shin,' Popol whimpered

'I don't think so,' Marina's reasonable, almost maternal, voice replied. 'You see, Paul, no one likes to say yes more than I do. But when I say no, I mean it.'

'But why? Why?'

'Have you never felt the wish to stay chaste just for one evening?'

She asked the question with such gravity that the lechery froze on the wretch's lips. He went off, giving himself the double satisfaction of bad behaviour and ill humour. Good for Marina! By what right did the granddaughter of General Kraievsky play games with such riff-raff? I was delighted. I did not think to ask myself why, that evening, Marina had opted for chastity.

The next evening, extraordinarily, she did not go out. She had systematically refused all invitations. I heard her busying herself in her kitchenette, then rehearsing a part. For a 'novelist', there is no more winning woman than an actress, and I did not tire of hearing her repeat 'Yes? Yes! Yes . . .!? Yes . . .? Yes? . . .' in every possible tone of voice. Sometimes she would mumble to herself, going through the script in her mechanical memory without concerning herself with the meaning; sometimes on the contrary she would reinvent it, adding interjections, onomatopoeas, sometimes bits of sentences of her own, to commit it to her unconscious. The telephone rang once again. First she let it ring and went on working at her script: 'But, darling, I told you . . . But, darling I told you . . . But, darling, my love, my honeypot, my custard-tart, I . . . with my mouth, my tongue, my eyes . . . But, you fool, it's your wife after all . . .' The telephone was still ringing. She couldn't stand it any longer: 'Hello?'

How many times had I heard that 'hello?' repeated over and

over again, with accelerated cadence, leaping over the hours of silence! But I did not tire of their fluid rotundity; I'd always wanted to answer: 'Hello, Marina, it's me. I love you. Let's be happy together.' This time, at the other end, there was nothing but a suddenly interrupted breathing. Marina repeated 'hello?' with a less gilded limpidity. Still nothing. She hung up. It's always strange, always rather disturbing, a silent call coming from one knows not where: from a café at the street corner or from the other world.

Later I had occasion to check with the appropriate Intelligence service. The call came from 79 Rue de Grenelle. Did Popov perhaps want to know whether Marina was asleep or not, or simply to derive solace from hearing her voice? No one will ever know. Anyway, he must have been having her watched since, that same evening, obviously knowing that there would be no other visitors, he rang at her door.

It must have been about ten. I did not see Marina then, but I can see her now. Curled up on the angular sofa-bed, reading her part to herself, awakening the vigilance of the microphone only by sudden exclamations, which came over on the tape as a strange hotchpotch: '. . . er . . . sfool! . . . why? . . . but what is truth I ask you . . . sinnocent, go on!' The doorbell rang. I can see Marina raising her head, tilting it to one side, and I can hear her, as I then heard her, in a voice that betrayed a touch of night-time anxiety: 'Who is it?' Then, since there was no answer, I could see her putting on her slippers and, with a sigh, go and put her eye to the spyhole.

Suddenly, she said in Russian: 'Igor Maximovich, it's you!'

I could not really see her at the time, of course, but now I can see her, in my mind's eye, unlocking the door, a meditative expression on her serene face, her hands still, a long house gown encasing her luscious body like a pod; her body she withdrew for the moment into the background, in a way we often treat our bodies, indispensable as they are and, in the final analysis, so underestimated.

Popov was wearing thick shoes, his plus-fours, a rough, shaggy sweater, an unbuttoned mackintosh. He looked younger than usual, his big ears pointing innocently upwards like those of a little boy, his eyes shining and flat like silver coins.

'You live here,' he remarked after a while.

Popov examined through the gloom everything that caught the light from the dim lamp: the mobiles, a theatrical poster, the sheepskin, the book bindings, the icon. He looked, Marina thought, like a pilot guiding his plane between cliffs (!), as the dignitaries of dictatorships let loose in free countries often do. She had moved back, looking at him from a distance. He walked, turning slowly, this way and that, before dropping at last into an armchair.

'Give me your mackintosh.'

He did not hear her. He was still looking. In the end he asked: 'Do you have other rooms?'

She was standing in front of him: 'Look!'

She opened the doors of the kitchenette and the bathroom. She even opened the door of her wardrobe with an expression of vulnerable, amused delight.

'That's it.'

'Too little,' he said. Then added: 'You're an actress.'

She showed him her photograph album and press cuttings. He turned the pages absent-mindedly.

'What would you like to drink?' she asked.

'Give me some whisky. Don't bother with water and ice.'

She jokingly poured him a full glass of dark-coloured Scotch, which perfumed the whole room and which he drank in mouthfuls, like wine. I, the invisible partaker in this scene, a voiceless member of this assembly, could not understand his silence. If he had something to say, why didn't he say it? If not, why had he come? It only occurred to me later that he did not know whether his own security service had bugged the flat. What he had to say would have to be understood differently by her, by them, by us, and perhaps also by another witness. It was hardly surprising that everything he said sounded so stiff, or even that he was deliberately muffling its resonance, as one silences the reverberation of a glass with one's finger. In the end, he said (how different from the inspiration of his earlier conversations!): 'I was married, you know. She . . .'

He smiled for the first time: 'She did not look like you.'

Marina was still standing, looking him up and down. 'Kiril, you've never seen such a smile in all your life.' I tried to get her to describe it. She could find no other adjective than 'nice'.

Popov went on, labouring over every word: 'She's dead. It was a mistake.' It was not clear whether he meant her death or the marriage. 'And you . . .' He looked up. 'Have you always been . . .' He stumbled over the word . . . 'a believer?'

'Always', said Marina.

She asked, quite naturally: 'Was she?'

He shook his head, his eyes downcast.

'She did believe, but in something different. In the Revolution.'

He smiled again, this time more 'charming' than 'nice'.

'A failed nun.'

He delivered himself of these scraps of phrases with such effort, such anguish that one would have been forgiven for thinking that he was drunk. She listened to him, trying to anticipate his wishes, his needs. She was sure that he had come to her for help. He creased the skin of his forehead from top to bottom into great furrows. He was sitting very low, his legs wide apart, his knees pointed, his shoulders high. He held his glass with both hands between his thighs.

'You expressed a desire to work with us,' he began, on an easier note. 'To begin with, you might provide us with background information on intellectual and artistic circles. Opinion-formers are very important these days. Secondly, you might keep an eye on the group of sympathisers to which you belong. Thirdly, you claim to be in contact with an espionage centre. We have checked on this, and what you say is quite true. So you might . . .'

She was lost. She had meant, by taking him to the church, to show him clearly enough that her offers of service had been no more than a bait and a sham. Seeing him come back to church and then ask for communion, she had thought that some trans-formation had taken place in him. But there he was obtusely returning to the old propositions, as if nothing had taken place in the meantime. She tried to interrupt him: 'Igor Maximovich . . .'

He cut her short and went on: 'You don't have to provide any information for the time being. We'll settle the details later. Even if you're hesitant, trust us. We'll find a way of meeting you on every point.'

'But don't you understand that everything I told you . . .'

She had tricked the Red unscrupulously, but she could not bring herself to disappoint the man. In one of her flowing movements, she slipped to her knees and put her chubby hands around the two bony hands clutching the glass.

'Igor Maximovich, I lied to you. I have never . . . Don't you understand that to the very marrow of my bones I'm . . .'

She was going to say 'a White'. He cut her short again.

'I know; in fact, I didn't believe you. It's of no importance. Let's drop all that. You aren't refusing to communicate with *me*, are you?'

He stressed the word 'me'.

She shut her eyes.

'No,' she said, 'I'm not refusing to communicate with you. You may be a Red, but you aren't like the other Reds. So you'll go and take communion next Sunday?'

Two souls were trying to tell each other the truth. There are no birth pangs more painful, nor more sublime.

He put the glass down on the carpet and, gently, giving her plenty of time to stop his gesture, he raised his two hands towards her and placed them on her cheeks, framing her heart-shaped face with his huge, flat paws. They stayed like that, without moving, for a long time. Igor's hands were dry. A little blue was reflected in his white eyes. She moved closer to him, on her knees, nestling up between his knees, inscribing herself in him, he open, she given, forming together an ideogram that I have still not wholly deciphered. At last the intensity, but not the sweetness of the moment, abated and Marina said: 'But I'm still the same, you know.'

She meant that their new understanding—she noted it—did not dissipate their older differences: even if she were to become his lover, she would remain his enemy. He gave a brief smile, again lowering the tension of their common emotion (just as trapeze-artists let go of the trapeze cautiously, careful of their own safety and that of their partner): 'Yes. Yes. I expected as much.'

This was his masterpiece of ambiguity. He dropped his hands, resting them on his knees and picked up his glass. She swung to one side, curling up on the rug, more kittenish than perhaps the occasion demanded, but unintentionally, simply becoming once again herself, outside the common transfiguration.

'I've brought you the book we'll use as a code on days when you'll have to send me information in writing,' he went on, in a didactic tone of voice.

'But Igor, don't you understand . . .'

She looked at him incredulously. It was the incredulity one always feels so violently at the beginning: so it's him? so it's her?

'The French call it the Rémy code,' he went on 'For us, it's the code of the chosen book. You will have to get the same edition, from a bookshop in the Rue du Val-de-Grâce. In view of your prejudices, it's an ideal choice. Our code pages will be 3, 18, 40, 77. Repeat the numbers.'

She had an actress's memory. She repeated them. He began to explain the code. I can hear him now: clear and pedantic. One chose one of the four pages at random. The message began with a group of four figures; divisible by 4, this group indicated that the fourth page had been chosen; by 3, the third; by 2, the second; by 5, the first. Then one looked on the page for the first letter of the message to transmit and one noted the number of the line on the page, followed by the number of the letter in the line. For example, if the first letter of the message was B and B was the eighteenth letter of the ninth line, one noted the group 0918 and one passed on to the next letter. Since there were several Bs on the page and one never used the same one twice, this very simple code was indecipherable for anyone who did not have the book. If the desired letter was not to be found on the key page, one chose another page, which one indicated by noting the group 00 followed by two other figures, chosen at random. The four pages had been chosen because they contained within themselves the entire alphabet. 'You understand? Repeat.'

Strangely enough, the little brown book that Popov held that evening in his left hand, moistening the forefinger of his right hand to turn the pages, now lies in front of me, on this old wooden desk, which seems so out of place in this New World, and on which are piled the 179 pages (with the exotic format of 11 inches by 8½ inches) of my manuscript. I have often questioned myself, sentimentally enough, about the memory of things. If dried flowers, little lace handkerchiefs, the clothes adapted to our shapes, the furniture deformed by our weight remember us, how much less this little book, whose pages 3, 18, 40 and 77 still have their corners turned down, can have forgotten Igor Popov. How vulgar of him to turn down the corners! Yes, Popov did lack refinement. But we should not be surprised by an act that seems, at first sight, so unprofessional. The major had never intended using his code. Having explained it, he picked up his book and went off, having fooled all his listeners except for One.

27

PRIEST: *O God our Saviour, who by Thy Prophet Nathan didst grant unto repentant David pardon of his transgressions, and didst accept Manasseh's prayer of repentance: Do Thou, with Thy wonted love towards mankind, accept also Thy servant, who repents of the sins which he has committed; overlooking all that he has done, pardoning his offences, and passing by his iniquities. For Thou hast said, O Lord: With desire have I desired not the death of a sinner, but rather that he should turn from his wickedness and live; and that even unto seventy times seven, sins ought to be forgiven. For Thy Majesty is incomparable, and Thy mercy is illimitable; and if Thou shouldest regard iniquity, who should stand?*

For Thou art the God of the penitent, and unto Thee do we ascribe glory, to the Father, and to the Son, and to the Holy Spirit, now and ever and unto ages of ages.

Let us pray. O Lord Jesus Christ, Son of the living God, both Shepherd and Lamb, who takest away the sins of the world; who didst remit the loan unto the two debtors, and didst vouchsafe to the woman who was a sinner the remission of her sins: Do Thou, the same Lord, loose, remit, forgive the sins, transgressions and iniquities, whether voluntary or involuntary, whether of wilfulness or of ignorance, which have been committed unto guilt and disobedience by these Thy servants. And if they, bearing flesh and dwelling in the world, in that they are men, have in any way been beguiled by the devil; if in word or deed, whether wittingly or unwittingly, they have sinned, either contemning the word of a priest, or falling under his anathema, or have broken their oath: Do Thou, the same Master, in that Thou art good and cherishest not ill-will, graciously grant unto them these Thy servants the word of absolution, remitting unto them their anathema and curse, according to Thy great mercy. Yea, O Lord and Master, who lovest mankind, hear Thou us who make our petitions unto Thy goodness on behalf of these Thy servants, and disregard Thou all their errors, inasmuch as Thou art exceedingly merciful; and loose them from punishment eternal. For Thou hast said, O Master: Whatsoever ye shall bind on earth shall be bound in heaven, and whatsoever ye shall loose shall be loosed in heaven.

For Thou alone art without sin, and unto Thee do we ascribe glory, to the Father, and to the Son, and to the Holy Spirit, now and ever and unto ages of ages. Amen.

Behold, my child, Christ standeth here invisibly, and receiveth your confession: wherefore, be not ashamed, neither be afraid, and conceal nothing from me: but tell me, doubting not, all things which you have done; and so shall you have pardon from our Lord Jesus Christ. Lo, His Holy Image is before us: and I am but a witness, bearing testimony before Him of all things which you say to me. But if you shall conceal anything from me, you shall have the greater sin. Take heed, therefore, lest, having come to the physician, you depart unhealed.

IGOR: Is it me now?

P—Yes, go on.

I—Tell me first what I'm supposed to call you. Otherwise, it's a bit awkward.

P—Whatever you like. It really doesn't matter. As I told you, I am only a witness.

I—How d'you mean?

P—It is to Him you are speaking. You may call me father. It's usual, but not essential. If it bothers you, don't do so. Your only true Father will hear you in any case.

I—You see, for me, it isn't easy. I've never made a confession before. Do you find that surprising? Or laughable?

P—Put that idea aside. It doesn't seem laughable to me. Have you been baptised?

I—I'm almost embarrassed to admit it . . . You see, yes. My grandmother . . . Anyway, there's no need to blame her for it

310

here. My parents were in favour. We always say it was grandmother's fault, because she's old, or dead, and anyway, who cares about *her*.

P—Have you ever taken communion?

I—As a child, you're made to do things ... One isn't responsible. To tell you the truth, I don't know. To begin with, there was no church in operation. Later, they were afraid of me. Even before I told them that I did not believe. Still, it could well be that when I was six months or so ... How should I remember a thing like that? Does it matter? I don't know your rules.

P—You mustn't attach too much importance to the letter.

I—Don't apologize. Everything counts. I'm quite willing to do everything according to the rules. The trouble is. . . I don't know what they are.

P—Were you never given any religious instruction?

I—No. I was given a lot of anti-religious instruction. Once I even gave a course in atheism. Everything I know about religion I owe to atheism.

P—We're in the same position with regard to heresies . . . You were saying that you used to be an atheist?

I—Of course. When one doesn't believe, it's so obvious that God does not exist! After all, what have you got to go on—there's not a sign, not a clue, not a sound or smell. As for the proofs . . . To think that there are numbskulls who insist on believing—it makes one spit! One wants to split them open and stuff their brains with a bit of sense.

P—Yes. And when one does believe, it's so obvious that He does exist. One may feel angry when one thinks of the numbskulls who insist on disbelieving. But one has to find other ways to bring them to their senses than by splitting their heads open. Always.

I—You're a man one can talk to. Look, all this must remain confidential for the moment. I've checked you out: you don't appear to be working for us.

P—How do you mean, for you?

I—It would be known. You aren't employed by the Fifth Section. As for the army . . . it would be outside their competence.

P—We have plenty of time. Explain yourself clearly—I am bound by the secret of the confessional.

I—You must allow me to doubt . . .

P—Not at all. There may be priests who have transgressed it. More often in operas than in life, however. For most priests, whether Orthodox or Roman, confession is sacrosanct. Even if we wanted to divulge its secrets, we could not. Besides, we forget a great deal . . .

I—I don't think you'll forget so quickly what I have to tell you.

P—Human pride is always laughable, especially in evil.

I—Well, I think you'll jump out of your skin when you know who is standing next to you.

P—It's quite possible, but you mustn't worry about that. I hasten to tell you that I am unworthy of the function I fulfil.

I—You admit that yourself?

P—But He who stands between us will not be afraid. He's seen it all.

I—It seems to me you're getting a bit worked up. Excuse me if I shock you, that's not my intention. I've never spoken to a priest before. I don't know how it's done.

P—Forget, if you like, that I'm a priest, and speak to me simply as a man who is a little more versed than you are in these matters.

I—I don't know you.

P—And I don't know you. That doesn't stop me from regarding you as a brother. Brothers don't need to know one another.

I—Possibly. I never had one. Never wanted one. You know, you've really arranged things in your church to set one dreaming about one's past! I've spent a lot of time here remembering myself in short trousers.

P—It's an excellent habit to begin at the beginning.

I—With you, I'd rather begin at the end.

P—As you wish.

I—I wanted to ask you. The other day . . . Why did you chase me out?

P—The rule is strict and for your own good. If you are not ready to receive the Sacred Gifts, we believe you would do yourself irreparable harm in consuming them. It's a devouring fire that

312

consumes all evil. If, through contrition, you have separated yourself from the guilt that is in you, that alone is incinerated. But if the evil still clings to the walls of your soul, those very walls themselves, those delicate mucous membranes, will be damaged.

I—Am I to understand that metaphorically?

P—Listen. No one can gain access to faith without grace from above, and I don't expect you to believe what I am saying. But you have it in you to understand. For the time being, I would ask you only to understand.

I—I find no difficulty in believing. I simply want to be informed.

P—You mean that, although you are a great sinner, you have faith?

I—Is that impossible?

P—Sin is like a cataract: it is difficult to see the truth through that veil. Even while abstaining as much as possible from sin, one gains entry into pure faith only, so to speak, from time to time. At certain moments, the heavens open, one sees cherubim and seraphim ascending and descending, one sees the reflection of the glory of the Father . . . The rest of the time one is blinded by the false light of the world. Nevertheless it is true that there are cases when the true light explodes within us like a bomb. It breaks the veil from within. A time-bomb placed by an angel in the corner of your soul, a long, long time ago . . . But don't flatter yourself. What is uncommon in religion is not as desirable as you might think.

I—Why not?

P—Much is expected of those to whom much is given—the risks are in proportion. It is better to be satisfied with a humble salvation: to take the lower place. If the master of the house takes you by the hand to offer you a better place, all well and good. It is better to take a back seat.

I—I'm not sure I understand you. Don't forget that there is a religious rhetoric, as there is also a rhetoric in Marxism, for example. One speaks through quotations, allusions, there is a common system of reference. If I taught you Marxism-Leninism, I'd have to explain to you the rudiments at each stage. In religion, I know nothing. You may not like it, but that's how it is.

P—No, I don't dislike it, and thank you for correcting me. It is up to the patient to guide the physician's hand. I haven't had much experience of cases like yours. I see scarcely anything but the stale loaves, or the working of the leaven in the very young . . . But they are so frivolous and the world is so tempting . . . I concern myself with theological articles. I hardly ever take risks, I mean . . . with the souls of others. I'll do whatever I can for you, but don't hesitate to correct me as you have just done. We are so ignorant of anything outside our routine.

I—That's true of every job. I hardly know what to ask a pope. Sorry—a priest. I've read the Gospel: nothing there about priests. I don't even know exactly what use you are.

P—We are the gleaners.

I—Rhetoric again?

P—Actually, there is a priest in the Gospel: the high priest.

I—You mean Caiaphas?

P—I mean the Lord Himself, the High Priest according to the order of Melchisedec. But you'll accuse me again, quite rightly, of using a system of reference that is alien to you. Yet it is quite true, the Son is the High Priest of the Father, and our role consists in imitating Him as far as possible. There are certainly bad priests: those who imitate Him badly.

I—Explain to me what I must believe. No details. Just a summary.

P—'I believe in one God, the Father Almighty, Creator of Heaven and . . .'

I—Without formulas, if you can. Explain to me what you are, what all this is about, this whole business that we have not yet managed to liquidate: yet we've tried hard enough, at one time anyway. In the end, we tolerated you: why? It wasn't only because of the war. We were already resigned to leaving a little room for you, not to smoke you out of your little mousehole. We mowed you down and you stood up again. Why? Anyway, when I say 'you', I really don't know who I have in mind. I believe, but I don't know what's to be believed. Teach me. That's your speciality.

314

P—You believe you believe?

I—Yes, yes. There'll be no difficulty there.

P—(Lord, my God . . . to fail . . . one would have to . . .) Excuse me. I'm not used to this sort of thing. I'll tell you quite frankly: I'm afraid. Usually, I see people who know quite a bit about religion, but who complain of a lack of faith: one has to allay their doubts, their scruples, plaster over their cracks . . . For the rest, they're just ordinary good people. With you, everything is upside down.

I—Don't apologize. It's good that you should expose your inadequacies. I've no time for know-alls. And don't be embarrassed to speak to Him in front of me. I shall speak to Him, too, when I know how.

P—What exactly do you mean when you say you *believe*?

I—That I know that it's all true.

P—All what?

I—That, I don't know.

P—Good. Let's try . . . Where shall we begin? . . . No, we mustn't prepare ourselves. Love created the world. You understand well enough that the world could not have created itself by itself?

I—Don't give me your agit-prop. Expound. I believe in advance.

P—Love created the world because Love is creative, it is His property to create. The Bible affirms that the Creation took place in six days. That, of course, is symbolic. One mustn't allow oneself to be scandalized by excessively naive fundamentalist interpretations.

I—Don't worry.

P—Love created man. He created him immortal and free. In order to experience his freedom, man turned away from Love. He became mortal. That's what we call the Fall. Then, instead of forcing man to obey Him, Love decided to humiliate Himself before man, to put Himself at man's mercy, totally, in order to give him back his lost dignity: that is what we call the Cross.

I—Clear enough. Go on.

P—All the rest is secondary, providing one has Love.

I—I don't.

315

P—You don't know what you're saying. Why would you be here otherwise?

I—Because I know that you Christians are right. By the way, this story of the apple and the serpent . . . How is it to be understood? Excuse the expression—I don't know whether it's decent to use it in your presence: is it a . . . sexual story, or what?

P—It's a very mysterious, very venerable myth that teaches us the first use that man made of his freedom: he wounded himself with it.

I—What about Jonah? Do we have to believe in him?

P—It is by no means indispensable. His story is a poem that foretells the Lord's stay in hell.

I—And the Bread and Wine? Do we really . . . ?

P—Yes. Love offers Himself to us in the humblest form. That's what one wants to do, when one loves someone: feed him, give him to drink, become his food, his drink. It is not within man's power to do it, but it is within God's. And also, to some extent, woman's. They know how to produce milk for their children. That is why they are holier than we.

I—So God is Love?

P—And Love is God.

I—But what is Love?

P—This is what it is: to diminish oneself so that the other may grow, what we call the *kenosis* and which we symbolize by our poor rite of the washing of the feet. It's what the Lord lived through on the cross, on the cross of love.

I—So Love is not to possess?

P—It is not to possess.

I—Is it to be possessed?

P—It's not quite that either. Love is to prefer the other to oneself. Not to sacrifice oneself, but to prefer.

I—That's what I thought. I don't care for Love.

P—How can you dare to say such things?

I—It doesn't matter. I knew there'd be something of this kind. Don't worry, I'll make myself like it. I'm used to succeeding when I set my mind to a thing.

P—If I have all knowledge and all faith, but have not Love, I am

316

nothing. If I give away all I have, and if I deliver my body to be burnt, but have not Love, I gain nothing.

I—A quotation again?

P—I'll try to do without them. It will be difficult. They are our weapons. It's not so much that we reason with arguments based on authority, for we know very well that a quotation means nothing out of context, but they form so many furrows in our minds, circuits that our thought is used to running over. However, since you don't have the same . . . I must try to pretend that I am a missionary of the early Church speaking to a pagan struck by grace. As for Love, you must allow me not to believe you entirely. You may not have enough Love—who has?—but you cannot be as devoid of it as you say. Your mother: is she still alive?

I—My mother? She's croaked.

P—And your father?

I—Dead.

P—No children? No wife?

I—No children. My wife is dead.

P—Don't you miss all these dead?

I—Not in the least.

P—So you are quite alone. It's hard.

I—I don't think so. My work is enough for me. Anyway, one is always alone. Whatever one does.

P—One is never alone.

I—Yes, I've come to realize that. The Eye is always there. It never leaves you, or, if it does . . .

P—What is your name?

I—Why do you have to know?

P—I only want to know your Christian name.

I—Then you'll want to know my father's?

P—Yours will be enough.

I—Igor.

P—Lord Jesus Christ, have pity on Thy servant Igor. Most Holy Mother of God, pray God for God's servant Igor. Holy Father Igor, pray God for us. I think we can now begin your actual confession. Would you prefer to speak to me or would you like me to ask questions?

I—Why would you trust me? Anyway, I don't know what to say. To tell you the truth, I won't be surprised if you seize up when you know who I am.

P—I keep telling you, I am of no importance. I must trust you, but you do not have to trust me. I am only an ear. I have no mouth to repeat what I will hear. I have no brain to judge you. It is He you must trust. Do you understand the purpose of confession?

I—It's to be able to take communion.

P—It also has a practical purpose; we'll come back to that. Why do you want to take communion?

I—I want to do the right thing. He said we were to do it, didn't He? So I want to do it. I want to do whatever He commanded us to do.

P—And you don't love Him!

I—You don't have to love to obey. Just as well!

P—It also has another purpose: to put everything that is bad inside you into a heap and burn it, to renounce, to destroy in yourself, the old perverted man, so that you can become a new, pure man, the man God loves, the man he saw in you when you were a little, innocent child, the man you have chosen to pervert and persecute, and whom, with the help of God, you will become once again.

I—I suppose there's the investigation as well.

P—Investigation?

I—Before you're accepted in the Party, your past is taken apart bit by bit, everything is put on the table, everything is brought to the surface. Confession must serve the same purpose.

P—Why do they do that in the Party?

I—To know what kind of a man you are.

P—With us, all that matters is what kind of a man you will become. For that, you have to renounce the man that you have been. To renounce him, you have to take him apart and examine him, piece by piece. Only you can do that.

I—I want to do everything as it's laid down. You must tell me what to do.

P—I'd like you to understand . . . Love is light; evil is opacity. That's all. First, you have to scrape off inside yourself the

318

biggest patches. Then, little by little, you will become sensitive to the smaller flakings. In the end, the slightest scratch on the window of your conscience will bother you, and you will not rest until you have confessed, so that the light may flood into you unhindered. For the moment, first things first. Let's move the sandbags that you must have piled up in front of your windows throughout your life.

I—Try not to speak in images. I'd like to be sure I understand you.

P—Let's take everything in the right order. What is the memory that weighs most upon you?

I—I don't know . . . Everything's always gone well for me . . . Perhaps some blow a sergeant gave me, and which I couldn't give back because of my career. In fact, it wasn't really a blow, more of a slap. I've never told anyone about it. You're the first. As for Dmitriev, he's probably still slogging away in his copper mine, unless the son-of-a-bitch has already had his chips . . . Excuse me.

P—But it wasn't your fault . . . ?

I—He lost his memory when he was drunk. It wasn't difficult to get him to confess that he had said something he hadn't said. Article 57.

P—You denounced him?

I—If you want to call it that.

P—And it still troubles you?

I—You surely don't imagine I feel any remorse? Oh, yes, for you, there has to be, doesn't there. No, no. It's simply that, when I think about it, my cheek burns. My left one.

P—I expressed myself badly. I meant to ask you what is the greatest sin you have committed.

I—Sin, sin . . . I was always in order. Are you thinking of murders, for example?

P—Were there murders?

I—And what about your lot, then!

P—The Church is not immaculate.

I—Ah! So you practise self-criticism, too?

P—You were going to tell me about murders.

I—Not for the pleasure of it. Anyway, they hardly gave me any

319

pleasure. None at all, in fact. There was one in self-defence. Another on orders: a buffoon! a monarchist! There were some others, not by my own hand—I simply signed recommendations. I couldn't tell you how many. Does it matter?

P—Excuse me. I wouldn't like you to think that I lacked Love. It's a long time since I heard the confession of a murderer. It's always rather overwhelming, a poor soul who has swollen up so much at the expense of another. I had a lot after the war, but then war's not quite the same thing: I'd have done the same myself, if I'd had the opportunity. I'll tell you something: I did envy them at times. My greatest temptation—I'm telling you this so that you will realize that I, too, am a sinner—occurred at that time: I wanted, may the Lord forgive me, to rip my cassock to shreds and apply for a rifle.

I—Why?

P—Who knows? Perhaps there are such things as atavism, after all. If there had been no revolution, I would have been a hussar. You see how things turn out, without our opinion being asked . . . Now I'm Christ's hussar. But in your case, it wasn't during the war was it . . . ?

I—A Bolshevik is always at war.

P—Have you ever suffered from the fact?

I—No.

P—But from the moment you thought you *believed*.

I—No. Do I have to?

P—Anyway, what do you call *believing*?

I—Like one believes one's eyes, one's nose, one's fingers.

P— . . . Apart from those men who died under your responsibility, have you caused any serious wrongs to anyone? Have you placed temptation in the way of anyone?

I—What's that?

P—Have you led other men to commit what they believed to be evil?

I—Who do you think you are talking to? That's my job; do you want examples? There was the white-haired American married to a nymphomaniac. There was the pipe-smoking professor who clung desperately to his petty comforts. There have been . . . dozens . . .

320

P—What is this horrible profession?

I—I hold the rank of major in the Committee of State Security.

P—Did you choose freely to do these things?

I—Enthusiastically. Gratefully.

P—Why?

I—It suited me.

P—In what way?

I—For one thing, I had the necessary qualities. For another, I found it quite impossible to waste my time in any other profession. I wanted to be at the point of maximum intensity, where I might serve the best.

P—So your ambition was to live for others?

I—I make no distinction: I, others ... I chose the greatest acceleration. I suppose that's what you'd call a sin? When I was 'a little innocent child', I had a friend who wore a cross and prayed to God; I denounced him; he got into a lot of trouble and I was rewarded for it. I took pleasure in mowing him down.

P—In what spirit do you tell me that? You don't seem to be ashamed of it.

I—Should I be ashamed?

P—Have you never had pity on anyone?

I—I was taught that pity was a hypocritical, bourgeois sentiment. One chops wood, the chips fly. Pity? I felt pity for my teddy-bear, which I threw under a train, the day I took my oath as a Pioneer. That little pile of scattered bran made me weep many a night ...

P—You see.

I—But you can't base a whole system, even yours, on childish sentimentality. You asked me if I ever felt shame: yes, I was ashamed of those tears.

P—But now, you see ...

I—Now I want to serve a new master and I'm ready to change my method. What was good for others is bad for him. I know how these things happen. You do understand, don't you? I'm not just anyone. I'm a counsellor at the embassy and I'm in line for promotion to lieutenant-colonel. At my age! Between you and me, no one would be surprised to see me at the head of the Committee in twenty years' time. And from there . . . Believe me, I'm not boasting. You must understand that I don't come empty-handed.

P—Those are not gifts that the Lord would appreciate. You must come to Him with your heart and pride smashed into pieces. Indeed your hands must be empty if you are to reach out to Him. It doesn't matter if they are bloody, but they must be empty.

I—I don't trust your rhetorical flourishes. It must be more agreeable to God to reclaim some big chief than some mere peon.

P—Only if the big chief is also a big sinner, as appears to be the case. Let us leave your career to one side for the moment, since you still seem to take pride in it. The day will come, I hope, when you will regret not having been, in the service of evil, a mere peon. There is another domain in which we run the risk of becoming particularly opaque, because nothing is more different from the truth than what sometimes bears the same name.

I—Are you referring to the newspaper?

P—The newspaper? The church does not have political feelings. I am referring to the seventh commandment.

I—I don't know the numbers.

P—Many of our contemporaries do not understand why the Church, which is firmly based on the New Testament, puts so much stress on a sin that appears to do nobody any harm. But, from what I understand, your own rules are rather strict on this matter and there may be a fortunate coincidence for you there. The saying 'no fornicator will enter the kingdom' weighs heavily on many consciences. But we must understand what it means. It is not so much sensuality in itself that is bad—though there is in it a downward deflection of energies that might be better employed—as the fact of treating another human being as a means, as Kant would have said.

I—You've read Kant?

P—Every human being must be treated as an end. The human body is the temple of the Holy Spirit: to treat it like a toy . . .

I—You know, perhaps we had better not talk of these things. At least not in your church. If I told you aloud what kind of a man I am from that point of view your chandeliers would sway and your icons come clattering down off the walls. For me, it has never seemed important. There are gourmets and there are gluttons. Personally, I was a glutton, and I like to see blood.

P—And you aren't married?

I—I was. She died of it. I already told you so.

P—From your ill treatment?

I—If you want to call it that.

P—But what depths . . ! Excuse me. Son, brother, excuse me. But what is your heart made of then?

I—I've always liked to think my heart is like a fist. But you must understand: I am quite willing to unclench it. I think I feel it opening a bit already. I thought a fist was the strongest thing in the world. The other day, I realized that it wasn't. There was something better.

P—When did you realize that?

I—When you said that absurd thing . . . I understood that what one eats and drinks is stronger than the person who eats and drinks it. If we did not eat and drink, we would be nothing. The meat that we think we are eating forms us; the water that we think we are drinking . . .

P—Wait a moment. I must get this quite clear. You have believed in God for a long time, and last Sunday you realized that . . .

I—Last Sunday, for the first time in my life, I realized that God exists. Then I had an opportunity of checking it out.

P—Had you noticed in yourself, previously, any movement, any dissatisfaction, a feeling of anxiety perhaps, which might have led you . . .?

I—No. No. I was master of my own fate.

P—You know, no one is less inclined to believe in miracles than a modern priest. Perhaps we now go too far in that direction, because in the past we went too far in the direction of credulity, if not deception. God spits out those who are neither hot nor cold, and the history of Christianity is full of persecutors who are suddenly converted and become apostles and martyrs. They were usually crude, single-minded men.

When Love was given them, they gave themselves to it with all the richness of their virgin nature. Your case seems to be different. You were already in possession of an idea, and it consumed you. How could it finish burning inside you without completely burning you out? Or, while being, I presume, a Communist, were you not the enemy of Christ? If that was the case, you must have been a very bad Communist.

I—I was an excellent Communist, I'm telling you. I was not a specialist in the anti-religious struggle, but I knew how vital it was. It was just that I believed the battle practically won. I didn't want to waste time mopping up the remaining pockets of resistance when the thing was to forge ahead. The struggle for scientific supremacy—especially in the field of nuclear physics—struck me as another priority.

P—Have your political feelings changed since . . .?

I—You mean my opinions about the ownership of the means of production, the class struggle, the dialectic? I haven't had time yet to settle that question. For men like me it is of secondary importance. Ideas are tools—they get worn out. One of Marx's main ideas was that capitalism had to be allowed to rot on its feet. Lenin succeeded in doing precisely the opposite. So what? What do I care? I don't believe in dogmas. Trotsky, with his internationalism, was probably a more orthodox Marxist than Lenin: that's why he deserved to be eliminated. Sclerosis is the only true enemy of Bolshevism.

P—What is Bolshevism?

I—Maximum growth. When you design an aircraft, you try to create the one that will go the fastest, the farthest. You get a prototype; it's satisfactory; you adopt it. Then technology progresses. You build another, more quickly, with an even more extensive radius of operation, and you sell the other one to the under-developed countries. It's the same with ideas. I realized that one could go further with God than without Him.

P—For you, God is a form of Bolshevism?

I—It's an advance.

P—You mean that the cross traced on the world is the + sign?

I—Now that's an interesting coincidence.

P—I think I'm beginning to understand you. You've had a

brilliant career, dedicated to progress. You arrive at an age when, like many successful men, brilliance is no longer enough for you. An age when adventures can only be vertical. You've felt that things would always be the same in the world. That the scope for progress was limited. You've begun to dash yourself on the bars of your cage. You're still only a major, but you've foreseen that even as a general . . .

I—Why only a general?

P—Well, minister, if you like, president, dictator . . . You would still be at more or less the same point. You've seen that the pleasures of power are almost as monotonous as those of the flesh. So you've looked for a way out . . . and you've found one: you are like the point that was getting bored on the straight line and discovered the plane!

I—I don't know whether there's any use in your understanding me, but I must tell you you're mistaken. My life has unfolded from stage to stage, from initiation to initiation. I had every reason to expect that it would continue to be ever more satisfying. You speak of the monotony of power, that's because you haven't experienced the pleasure of imposing your will on others. Quite recently I had the greatest spy of the century grovelling at my feet. Under my predecessors, he had begun to go his own way. There's a certain intoxication in it . . . You wouldn't understand it. I was, if you want to put it like that, happy. I could see no obstacle at the end of my straight line. The fact that God exists disturbs me. But I'm not going to be so childish as to stick to a hypothesis that I know to be false. If God exists, one must draw the consequences. I am drawing them. I have come to you. What more do you want?

P—How can you be sure that He exists?

I—What's this: sabotage or what?

P—*I* know He exists because I love Him. One can't love what doesn't exist, unless one is under some illusion. The touchstone is love of one's neighbour. I love my neighbour; so I know that I am under no illusion when I say that I love God. But you . . .

I—If what you are trying to do is to persuade me that my

certainty is bogus because it hasn't gone through the hierarchical channels . . .

P—What is it based on, then?

I—So that's what's bothering you? Well, that's quite intelligent of you. Usually we are so pleased to see others believing what we believe that we forget to ask them their reasons. It's like the Marxist loyalism of that man; my predecessor accepted it without checking: how can one not be a Marxist? I had my doubts; you have yours. Very well. God imposed Himself upon me with all the force of evidence. If you think that a Leninist is ill-equipped to recognize such evidence, you're mistaken: we are pragmatic, we grab hold of any evidence within reach. We pounce on it, we build on it. Indeed the dialectic . . . we know better than anyone that the Far East is the same as the Far West, and by turning up the heat one can achieve unpredictable transformations. The fact that power raised to the divine scale liquefies in God's blood is no more surprising than to see the fourth state of matter.

P—I thought there were only three.

I—And what do you do with plasma?

P—But what kind of evidence? You mean intellectual evidence? Mathematical evidence?

I—Evident evidence. Politzer made fun of Berkeley: he wouldn't deny the existence of matter if he was knocked down by a bus. God has knocked me down.

P—Do you think—excuse me, I've no wish to hurt your feelings—do you think you've had a vision? If that's the case, I must very seriously put you on your guard . . .

I—No, no. There was no vision. It was much more like a punch between the shoulder blades. It was like somebody jumping on my back. I'd been thinking of my childhood, then bang, that was it. He'd won and I knew it. It explained a lot—in particular, that we've failed to crush you. Anyway, regard it as a fact. It must be easier for you than for me.

P—You talked of verification?

I—It isn't a sin is it? So there's no reason why I should discuss it with you, is there?

P—Perhaps not. You must forgive me for being rather taken

aback by your confession. I'm a man, a sinner; like everybody else, my intelligence is disturbed by the unusual. That in no way affects the powers I possess or the compassion I feel. Let us agree on this therefore. Last Sunday, you had a revelation of the existence of God. Do you believe that He is present in the Church I represent?

I—Yes, yes. God, the Church, it's all one. I learnt that when I was a kid.

P—Were you a religious child?

I—I was an atheist at five. Much younger than Lenin. And I went further than him or I wouldn't be here now.

P—You are now going to begin a Christian life. Do you know what it begins with?

I—You have to give money for the popes?

P—One has to look back on one's past life and contemplate it in all its horror. Till one shudders, till one weeps. Then one has to burn it and set out in another direction.

I—What does that consist of, in practical terms?

P—Do you regret the evil that you have done to Love, to men and to yourself? Do you sincerely regret it, with all your heart?

I—That's a funny question. I changed sides, all right. But you know very well that I have been against you and I have done all I could to crush you. Yes, I have done what you call evil, but for me, at the time, it was good. I can't regret having done good. The more evil I've done, the bigger your catch. Regrets would be pointless.

P—But the damage you've done yourself . . .

I—That's probably what brought me here.

P—When you have walked for a long time in the wrong direction and suddenly you realize it and set off in the right direction, don't you regret each of the steps you took?

I—I'm not aware of having changed direction. Your music rose, rose, it was the power and the glory . . . And then: drink and eat. Did you change direction? I've always walked towards greater light. The greatest was not the one I thought it was, so what? I've kept on walking.

P—Conversion is a revolution. The soul, which was inside out,

327

is turned back the right way, like a garment. One must turn one's back on the world before raising one's eyes to Love.

I—Why do you always say Love? Isn't it rather sentimental?

P—How shall I call you? Servant of God Igor? Servant of God Igor, you profoundly disturb me. As I told you, I ought to be no more than the ear of the Lord, but we've long since abandoned the confessional routine together. This talk we are now having is also a meeting, a promise, a rather poor catechism class . . . Try to understand: I'm responsible for the Body of Christ and I'm responsible for your soul. I can do nothing lightly, just to please you. Answer me. This child, this comrade you handed over to your leaders, could you then look him in the eyes?

I—Look him in the eyes? It's just a phrase. I became his best friend.

P—That woman, your wife, and those other women, for, if I understand you correctly, there were several others . . .

I—Don't ask me how many. I couldn't possibly tell you.

P—Was there not a single one for whom you felt some feeling of friendship?

I—Friendship? But that's not what I . . .

P—Precisely. That's why I . . .

I—Friendship . . . I don't think so. I had a better time with some than with others, it was more amusing. There's one I liked to give presents to.

P—Because that gave her pleasure?

I—Yes, and also because it humiliated her. There was one who tried to resist me . . .

P—What happened?

I—You embarrass me, you know. I enjoyed that even more.

P—Did you feel that it was wrong? Or at least do you feel that now?

I—I know it didn't conform with your code. But what does that matter? I wasn't on your side at the time.

P—I was about to say to you just now: one should distrust the flesh; it sends us back a faithful image of ourselves. The first man you killed . . .

I—An old officer of the Tsar. I don't know: perhaps you're a

Tsarist. As far as I was concerned it was as if I had crushed a slug.

P—It isn't customary, but having gone so far already . . . I'll tell you a story. I was seventeen and was fighting against your side. One day I was ordered to shoot some prisoners: we didn't have enough to feed ourselves. The squad consisted of a disabled old veteran, an apprentice cobbler and the officer on duty: me, as it happened. We were trying to save ammunition. I was given charge of a sailor—I had to sign for him. They were the toughest, most convinced men. I took him out into the garden. I had him tied to a tree. My hands were trembling. I couldn't tie the knot myself. The old veteran did it, crossing himself with each turn of the string: 'This isn't good work we're doing,' he muttered, 'but it has to be done. Lord Jesus, have pity on us, most pure Mother of God have pity on us. And on him too,' he added, squinting at the sailor, a big, tall, serious man with hairy arms, who said nothing. The apprentice cobbler giggled: 'The devils will gnaw at your tootsies.' The sailor was a good head taller than us. He could have knocked us out and run off. He didn't move. It seemed particularly horrifying to kill a man so much taller than us. He rejected the blindfold with a gesture, without a word. At last we took twelve steps back. 'Take aim!' But I couldn't. How could I send metal flying into that flesh? As a child, I'd gone hunting. I'd shot woodcock and chamois. But this man, this big unarmed, resigned, haughty fellow . . . And yet orders were orders, and I knew it was my life against his . . . I ordered the squad to ground arms and went and untied him. With my own hands, so as to have full responsibility for it. He still said nothing, not a word of gratitude, but suddenly he opened his shirt, and we saw on his tanned chest an enormous allegorical tattoo. There were two crossed flags, the tricolour and that of St Andrew, the portrait of the sovereign, a ship in full sail, a cannon, a bayonet, a scroll bearing the words 'God save the Tsar' and, below, another scroll, probably of more recent date: 'Death to the bourgeois'. I looked at this huge exposed chest, which was almost hairless, unlike the arms, and all those signs crossed by a scar or two, like creases on a map . . .

The whole thing rose and fell in an accelerating rhythm, filling itself with the air that it had been so close to losing. The man's face was expressionless, but it was hallucinating to see below it that allegory panting like another face . . . The old veteran came up. 'What's this, then?' he asked. "God save the Tsar", and "Death to the bourgeois"? Whose side are you on?' The sailor spat on the ground. 'It was the bourgeois who destroyed the Tsar,' he replied, and it's true, you know. This dinosaur then became one of our most faithful combatants, so much so that I wasn't even punished for sparing him. I should like to know whether, in your life, as in mine, there was ever a moment of weakness . . .

I—Not as far as I know. Anyway, it's quite true that it's the intermediate classes that . . .

P—Listen. You did have a mother.

I—I did without her very early on and very easily. Don't start blackmailing me with mummy.

P—What was she like?

I—A fine, big woman, very strict and religious. She walked with great dignity. Like this, you know: arched backwards, as if she was afraid of upsetting a tray. When she bent over my little bed, she occupied the whole horizon. I couldn't even see the lamp.

P—Did you weep when she died?

I—I didn't know she had died at first. Anyway, I didn't care.

P—Have you a friend you prefer to anyone else?

I—A friend in *my* job?

P—Have you ever had an animal to which you were particularly attached?

I—I'm not a hunter. I don't ride.

P—Are you really a man without a flaw? Or are you perhaps only pretending to be? . . .

I—What do you mean?

P—I don't know how to take you.

I—But you already hold me. What exactly do you want of me?

P—Are you sure that you aren't playing—I don't mean for my benefit, but for your own—the rather improbable role of a man without a flaw? You'd be quite capable of glorying in the fact. But how will God enter you if there is no hole?

I—He has entered.

P—Has He? You claim to be sure that He exists, very well. But not all those who cry 'Lord' . . . One must do His will.

I—I intend to.

P—And, yet, you're engaged in the service of the devil.

I—I've thought of all that. I intend to change my job. I haven't been idle during the past week. I'll study whatever is necessary and I'll become a bishop. I want to be one of those in the highest in whom God's glory is to be found.

P—In the highest?

I—It's something you sing: 'Hosanna in the highest' . . .

P—That means: 'Hosanna in the highest heavens.'

I—Too bad. But it makes no odds, does it? I want to serve the master.

P—Don't you know you must serve Him with humility?

I—I'll cut off whatever is necessary.

P—You'll give up sensuality?

I—I'll get married. And this time it will be different. I won't destroy this woman.

P—How come?

I—Because it will be a Christian marriage. You have rules of continence; I'll contain myself.

P—In the Orthodox Church, a married priest cannot become a bishop.

I—No married bishops?

P—Only in the Anglican Church.

I—Yes, but since our Church is the true one . . .

P—Do you already know the woman you want to marry?

I—Does that concern you too?

P—I simply meant: do you love her?

I—If anyone so much as thought of doing to her . . . Don't let's talk of that.

P—You have discovered the holiness of love. So everything is not opaque in you. You are, after all, a man like other men. That's a weight off my mind. I'm sure that even before this meeting . . . You may have been hiding your light under a bushel, but it was there.

331

I—Can you only talk in images?

P—It befits Christianity. Perhaps because man himself is only an image. Let's see now, cast your mind back. When you became a Communist, didn't you burn with a desire to save mankind?

I—I don't think so. I've never been sentimental.

P—What? Just the will to power, no more?

I—Another big word. I've read your bourgeois pseudo-revolutionaries, too. No, it wasn't the will to power, it was Bolshevism. The desire for a higher state of being, if you like. And if, to be more, one has to accept being less, I still reply: I'm ready.

P—Let's leave that now and go back to your plans for the future. You are going to leave your . . . job?

I—Of course.

P—Do you think they'll let you go?

I—Of course not. I shall ask for political asylum in France.

P—Will the French give it you?

I—They'll be only too happy to! I could have done a better deal with the Americans, but they never know when to stop squeezing. Besides, these moves are always a delicate matter. Here I have a contact. She will arrange everything, under my direction.

P—The French may want to question you about . . .

I—I've already microfilmed my files.

P—Won't you feel you're betraying . . .

I—One doesn't betray the devil. I was taught at school that when Prince Vladimir became a Christian, he dragged the idols through the mire. The pagans wept, the soldiers laughed. Is that true?

P—So they say.

I—That's how idols should be treated. I shall drag the Party through the mire. I won't be a bishop, but I'll become a saint. And don't tell me there are no married saints.

P—Aren't you shocked at changing sides like this?

I—I don't find it shocking to put one foot in front of another to move forward: first the left foot, then the right. You don't know the dialectic, that's your trouble.

P—So it's because of that woman that . . .

332

I—It's because God exists, and because He exists one cannot live as if He didn't.

P—You spoke of becoming a priest. One should not speak of these things lightly. All Christians, even some of the best, are not called to the priesthood. So where did this idea come from? Or this desire, let us say?

I—If one recognizes a master, one has to tool up for him. It's logical.

P—Ah! My dear, dear friend! How I would like to help you! (Lord, help me!) I have no doubt, I do not wish to doubt that your vocation is a noble one. As for your logic, how shameful it is for us Christians to practise it so little! But have you any notion what the priesthood is? Do you realize what level of self-denial one has to reach even to think of it? Yes, your ambition to serve is a noble one, I repeat, but do you feel ready to be no more than a pane of glass, as transparent as possible? To suppress in yourself all the opaque density of your own self? To become a conducting wire, with no resistance whatever? We are recommended not to talk about ourselves, but who do we know better? These memories are coming back to me today because you are the first to come to me from over there . . . It seems to me that if I can teach you something, prevent you from making some irreparable error, my methods will be forgiven. Listen. When you drove us to the furthest point of the peninsula, to the last thread that still bound us to our homeland, when we had boarded our overloaded ships—and I was one of the last to stop shooting, with my feet already in the water, literally, it was curious, the bullets ricocheting on the surface—then when we found ourselves in a foreign land, I understood, I was one of the first to do so, I think, that we possessed, that I possessed *nothing*. God had given me the extraordinary grace of depriving me of *everything*. No family, no future, no country, no hope, no money, nothing. I was as naked as one can be under the eye of God. Around me, people were clinging to their rags, to bits of flotsam, to hopes . . . Someone had salvaged a diamond, another an icon, another a woman's letters, another the determination to continue the struggle . . . What terrible

333

poverty! These people had saved their lives. Your people would no longer crucify them, would no longer carve initials in the skin of their shoulders or cockades on their foreheads; they were, by comparison, lucky survivors. But what awaited them? Factory work, eleven hours a day, standing; the spray-gun, and two litres of mílk a day as an antidote; eyes worn out embroidering; hands ruined with washing; most of the men without wives; the few surviving couples broken up because a woman had married a Guards officer and now found herself married to a miner; hunger—yes, old men hanged themselves because they were dying of hunger—and drink, of course, sometimes double-dealing, prostitution . . . There have no doubt been similar disasters in history, but there has never been one on such a scale, that lasted so long and was more tragically sordid . . . I felt then that this misfortune had been given to me and that I could give myself to it. I would never be a hussar in the Imperial Army, but I might be able to go to those people and help them to make the best of their misfortune. That's how I became a priest.

I—Didn't you feel any disgust? It's so squalid, misfortune!

P—You have to learn to wash its feet. We succeeded, up to a point. To wash them and even to make them clean. Through all its absurdities, it's pettinesses, its schisms, its hatreds, its betrayals, our diaspora was on the whole to be exemplary. In our fidelity to our language, to our Church, to our culture, to our truth—and not only to our pirozhki-vodkas—we are second to none, except perhaps the Jews. The day will come when you will be proud of us: us, your emigration. I don't deny that Russia is above all over there; but she is also scattered, fragmented throughout the world. That's her Christic side: she is torn to shreds and yet she nourishes.

I—Russia, I *do* love.

P—Thank you for telling me that. So you do know what Love is.

I—Are you married?

P—I'm separated from my wife . . . It's a great scandal for the faithful. There's nothing I could do about it. My marriage was a mistake. I had a vocation for complete poverty. Now I write articles. That, too, is a mistake. One never totally succeeds in one's poverty. But we shouldn't be talking about me. Do you think you will be able to bear exile?

I—It may not be for long. I shall return there as a conqueror.

P—Perhaps it may be your turn now to labour under illusions?

I—Russia is seething with unsatisfied Christianity. That's obvious to anyone who has fought her. She's the only country where a Christian revolution is imaginable.

P—So Dostoievsky may have been right?

I—And Lenin.

P—You're still fond of Lenin, aren't you?

I—I have gone further than him. Anyway, tell me—don't we have to go through some formality now . . . I mean so that I can . . . communicate.

P—There's the absolution. But how can I absolve you?

I—You haven't got more tricks up your sleeve?

P—First you must condemn yourself.

I—I do condemn myself.

P—But with all your will, all your intelligence . . .

I—I condemn myself.

P—With all your heart.

I—I condemn myself.

P—You must do so sincerely.

I—I am sincere.

P—You must sunder yourself from yourself, renounce yourself, put yourself in God's hands.

I—I renounce myself.

P—You must prefer His will to your own.

I—I prefer it.

P—You must accept to be whatever He makes of you.

I—I accept it.

P—'God, save me by the ways of Thy choice!'

I—So be it.

P—You understand that only the sins you have confessed will be forgiven.

I—And the others?

P—If you deliberately conceal them, their weight on your soul will redouble.

I—Absolve me.

P—And the communion that you take will turn against you.

I—Absolve me.

P—Let us pray together.

I—Well, let us pray.

P and I—Our Father who art in heaven (P—He who is not here)
hallowed be Thy name, (P—at the expense of mine)

Thy kingdom come, (P—whatever it costs me)

Thy will be done, (P—and not mine)

give us this day our daily bread, (P—however bitter it may be)
and forgive us our debts, (P—since we will never be able to
acquit ourselves of them)

as we forgive our debtors, (P—or rather better than we forgive
them)

and lead us not into temptation, (P—our own already surpass
our strength)

but deliver us from the evil one, (P—which is inside us)

for Thine is the kingdom, the power and the glory, in the
name of the Father and of the Son and of the Holy Spirit.
Amen.

P—You repeat those words with too much pleasure. You enjoy
their earthy savour. I fear the old man is still here with us.
That you haven't sufficiently taken leave of yourself . . .

I—As much as I can.

P—Do you feel ready to receive the sacrament of absolution?

I—I will answer as a Pioneer: always ready!

P—But that's not it, that's not it at all . . . My God, forgive me if
I am making a mistake, and may it be rather by an excess of
mercy than of sternness. Kneel down. *May our Lord and our
God Jesus Christ, through the grace and bounties of His love
towards mankind, forgive thee, my child, Igor, all thy
transgressions. And I, his unworthy Priest, through the power
given unto me by Him, do forgive and absolve thee from all thy
sins, in the Name of the Father, and of the Son, and of the Holy
Spirit. Amen.*

I—Is that all?

P—That is all.

I—No, it isn't all. I haven't told you everything.

P—Have you forgotten something?

I—It's not something one forgets.

P—It's never too late.

I—That verification . . .

P—Doubt may be a sign of humility. Thomas verified.

I—Listen. When I learnt that God existed, I bought His book, I began to read it. From the beginning. Soon I understood that one shouldn't read it like that. That particular story didn't interest me. I remembered what my parents . . . my mother . . . used to do. She'd open the book at random and put her finger on a paragraph.

P—A verse. Dostoievsky did that too. There's no harm in that. All the verses are good.

I—I opened the book and read: 'I have conquered the world.' Then I understood that I had not made a mistake, that this God really was the God of victory, that He was a God for me. But I didn't know if He wanted me.

So I opened it a second time and read: 'When you were under the fig tree, I saw you.' Then I understood that I had been recruited. I had spent all my life under God's eye. He saw me when I took my oath as a Pioneer, when I secretly visited our standard, when I discovered Israel's nuclear plans, when I was with those women, when I exterminated the old buffoon, always. Under the fig tree. But I had to verify that too. God might only have been pretending.

I opened it a third time and read: 'And the children will rise up against their parents and put them to death.' Then I knew, I knew that He had really been watching me. And He was still watching me as I read His book. It was settled. I had been penetrated: all that remained was to let myself be turned. But, you see, I'm a professional. I've tricked too many people to let myself be tricked, even by God. Information of such importance has to be cross-checked before being acted upon. I decided to allow myself one final verification.

I opened the book a fourth time and to be even surer, I chose another of the four authors. When I opened my eyes and lifted my finger I read: 'And the children will rise up against their parents and put them to death.'

337

P—Yes, Mark and Matthew, two of the synoptics. But what meaning . . .?

I—Didn't it ever occur to you, with all your knowledge of souls, that I'd had an astonishing career for someone of my age, and that there must be a reason for it? Some token of my loyalty?

P—You frighten me.

I—I told you you'd be afraid. I was thirteen. People talked to us about nothing but Pavlik Morozov. His portrait hung on the wall, with those of the great leaders. A real little Bolshevik's head, hard eyes under his cap. I wondered what I could do to spit further than him. I came from a Christian home, but I wasn't forced to do anything. I had thrown away my cross. My father hid his, but he sympathized with the women—Babushka and Mother—whom I'd seen praying in front of the empty corner where an icon had once been, long ago. Kneeling, prostrated, standing, kneeling, talk of a pack-drill! Hasty little signs of the cross from Babushka; slow, broad signs of the cross from Mother over her broad bosom. Their eyes somewhere else. Where? I was beginning to worry at this time. How were little girls made? It was the year I learnt what parents do together when children are supposed to be asleep. We only had the one room for the four of us, you see. In the evening, I shut my eyes, but not entirely, and I watched my mother doing her gymnastics, her lips moving, her eyes raised to heaven, her body bending and straightening up . . . All those displacements of air. From my bed, that mass pointing into the air looked like a gun carriage . . . My father was waiting for her, already in bed. He, too, must have said his prayers, but with his head under the blanket. You understand nothing if you think I didn't love my mother. She breast-fed me until I was . . . I think I can even remember sucking her nipple, I don't know whether that's possible. Poor woman: it wasn't only out of tenderness—she did it to save money. I wanted to get her to leave her God; I repeated to her the propaganda I'd learnt at school: 'Mother, how is it God doesn't fall out of the sky? What does He hold on to? . . . Mother, if God is all powerful, could He make a stone so big that He couldn't lift it up?' She didn't reply, she didn't punish

338

me, she made the sign of the cross over me as if I'd mortally wounded her, she retreated into herself, she prayed twice as hard . . . You see, at the time, the official religion was already tolerated. There was even a church open. Anyone who wanted to could go to it. It was guaranteed by the constitution. But Babushka and Mother didn't trust the fat, greasy, excuse me, archdeacon who officiated there; the real priest was just a pale ghost, thin as a rake, who barely put his feet on the ground when he walked; but the archdeacon was a Cheka agent. He had a deep bass voice, as if he'd swallowed an organ! And a card index! Everyone knew. There was also a secret church, which was illegal. It was called 'the church of the catacombs'. The name always scared me. My father went there so as not to be seen; Babushka and Mother, so as not to have to pray for Stalin. The premises changed all the time: one never knew in advance where the services would take place. The priest led a double life. He worked like everybody else, he'd shaven off his beard, no one knew who he was. The militia were looking for him, but the community was so united it was impossible to penetrate it. We talked about it at the Pioneers. Oh! If only we could carve up the dragon of superstition! My conscience gnawed at me, like a dog gnaws a bone. I, a young Pioneer, having taken my oath, allowed this dragon to survive, to drag its slimy rings into my house, into the room in which I slept. I claimed to be worthy of Lenin, yet I lived under the same roof as the hydra? But if I did my duty, who would iron my shorts, who would put clean handkerchiefs in my pocket? In the morning, when I was with my schoolfriends, I wondered if they would detect the smell of pterodactyl on me. I had slept in premises poisoned by the influence of men in black whose insignia was an instrument of torture and who told a lot of tedious stories. It was a terrible time for me. That struggle of duty against weakness, sentimentality, comfort, animal instincts . . . I sawed through my own umbilical cord with a penknife. One night, I made up my mind. I had taken the precaution of asking Babushka to teach me how to iron, and it wasn't as difficult as all that. In the morning, my pillow was drenched with tears, but I had become a man. I knew that the

Saturday night and Sunday morning services were usually said in the same place. On the Saturday I followed the women. My father came from another direction, out of prudence. It was in a district of old brick warehouses, by the river, beyond the railway. No one lived there, but the old, rusted tramlines were still embedded in the roadway. Tufts of grass had sprung up between the cobblestones ... It was the first time I shadowed anyone. Of course, I lost them: I'd been too frightened of being noticed. I ran like a madman, really like a madman, through that wasteland, past old rickety railings, under trees covered with red dust, over bumpy pavements, in front of wide iron gates which slid on ball-bearings. I didn't find them. That was it! They'd escaped. I'd never have the strength to start again. And I sobbed, and I stamped my foot, and I bit my knuckles, and I asked myself whether, after all, God might exist, and I set off again ... I found them through the smell. At a street corner, I suddenly caught a whiff of it. I recognized it at once. When very young, my mother had taken me to the church, and I'd never forgotten that smell. You know how strong the olfactory memory is. I advanced step by step, like a hunting dog, sniffing, sniffing. It was a sweet, pungent, stifling smoke, God's own special smell ... It seemed to be coming from the pavement ... So it must be coming out of some grill ... I knelt down, still sniffing, filling my lungs with that damnation. The smell of purple, the smell of the terrifying word ANATHEMA. I can still see the yellow bricks forming the basement below the red bricks of the wall, the rusty bars, the dust piled up in a corner, the weed with jagged leaves that had managed to grow there, some kind of wild carrot, the dark rectangular hole and, when at last I dared to lean over, the glittering in some deep cellar, of twenty or thirty candles. There rose up towards me that stifled music, curling upwards with the smoke ... I wrote down the address. I ran to see the Pioneers' guide. The good fellow was all embarrassed. He lisped. 'I don't understand ... You mean, your parents will be there ... Do you really want to? ... Think about it.' I was only a kid, but I said: 'If you don't help me to denounce them, I'll denounce you.' The

340

mousetrap was laid for the following day, Sunday. I saw Mother leave for the mass. Just as she was going, she nearly kissed me, which she didn't do any more. Then she gave a deep sigh, with all her chest, you know, and she turned away. I never saw her again.

P—My brother, forgive me. My brother, let me kneel before you. The more sick you are the more I must . . . How you must suffer! I prostrate myself before your evil. Why didn't you say anything about it before? Were you ashamed?

I—Why are you kissing my hands? No, I was afraid. You wouldn't have let me go to communion.

P—But you're telling me everything now?

I—When you put that strip of material on my head, it was as if you were pumping me out.

P—Simply admit that you horrify yourself. That's all I ask. You will be able to go to communion.

I—I would like to lie to you . . . I feel no horror. Not yet. But I shall lead a different life. I shall no longer kill. I shall marry. I shall be a priest. I shall serve. I swear. Can I communicate now?

P—Jesus . . . Through Thy name, through Thy name as Thou hast promised . . . From now on, it is I who . . . Kneel down . . . Such a desire . . .

   'By the power of our Lord, Jesus Christ, Son of the Living God, I, his unworthy priest, truly unworthy, a parricide, I absolve thee, child.'

28

I pressed the STOP button. Poirier with his pipe and Rat with his gaspers had smoked up my room. They'd also polished off my bottle of whisky, the one complaining that it wasn't Calvados, the other that it wasn't his brand of plonk. The hundred and eighteen minutes of Russian—I provided them with a French résumé during the gaps—had exhausted them. The alternation of the two voices, the smooth and the rough, of the two tones, the flat and the thoughtful, moving together towards the final hysteria through all the narrations, speeches, whisperings, stifled cries, set all our teeth on edge, but especially so for the other two, who could not, like me, imagine the empty church, the smell of cold incense, the crippled verger in his corner, impatiently awaiting the departure of this loquacious penitent so that he could lock up (in the end he had given up and gone off to eat, banging the door loudly—Father Vladimir could lock up himself) and, facing the lectern on which were placed a book and a crucifix, these two men, seeking each other and avoiding each other by turns in the half light, the two parti-coloured eyes and the two white eyes sometimes fastened on one another, sometimes repulsing each other, like ships standing by to grapple, while the icons and chandeliers glittered feebly in the moonlight falling through the glass roof and while, under the lectern, the scrupulous machine reeled in yards and yards of secrets, like a Chinese conjurer swallowing ribbons.

'What wind-bags they are, those Russkies,' said Rat.

'Coming from a schismatic, this absolution isn't even valid,' observed Poirier, who believed scarcely in God, but one hundred per cent in the Pope.

His ill-temper was assumed, simulated partly out of decency, partly out of superstition. When you're a spook and about to carry off the coup of the century, you don't put out the flags, you pretend to sulk. Popov was virtually in the bag; all that remained was to wrap him up and tie a knot . . .

'The SDECE lot won't be too pleased!' Poirier chuckled.

'They won't look too good,' added Rat.

I knew he was seeing himself in dress uniform of a full colonel, perhaps a swagger-stick under his arm—seven hands, thirteen knots—reviewing an imaginary guard of honour. And the bank account would get fatter . . . I turned to Poirier. Beneath his pretended and predictable irritation, I did not perceive the internal jubilation the occasion merited. He was drumming his fingers sombrely on the table, depicting to himself the mortification of his ex-rivals ('And the Security Police, too!'—'Yes, and the Security Police, too, sir!') as if something were still missing, if not from his victory at least from his peace of mind. What bothered him, I think, was that he could not count on any reward; I accused him of envy, of baseness, of childishness: a true spook ought to be proud to return to the shadows . . . How I despised men at that time! Yes, in fact, it was I who deserved the contempt. (I still deserve it about as much, but I'm aware of the fact, and no longer avenge myself on others for my own pettiness.)

'He did mention microfilms, didn't he, Volsky?' asked Rat.

'Yes, sir.'

'And a contact? A woman?'

'Yes, sir.'

'So that would be your filly.'

'It's in the bag,' said Poirier, rising to his feet.

'He doesn't say exactly when he expects to come over?'

'No, sir. It won't be before his communion, I suppose.'

'And that will be . . .?'

'Tomorrow morning.'

'Providing nothing happens to him between now and then.'

'Nothing will happen to him,' said Poirier.

I thought I could detect a certain peevishness in his voice.

'A Soviet agent who has turned round, someone of such calibre . . . Never seen anything like it,' purred the Shopkeeper. 'There've been fellows who've chosen freedom, true, but without being manipulated: there's no art in that. Even Penkovsky came and threw himself at the Yanks. There's no particular merit in catching such a prostitute of Intelligence, eh, sir?'

Poirier gave his fleeting smile, but somewhat absent-mindedly. His hands in his trouser pockets, his burgundy-coloured sweater pulled up at the back, he was looking out of the window. It was gone eleven.

'Right, it's in the bag. I'll be on my way.'

'You've pulled off your finest coup during your retirement, sir,' Rat pursued. 'I must say, it doesn't surprise me, coming from an old rogue like you.'

'My coup, my coup,' Poirier grumbled. 'You've had the decency to consult me along the way. I've done nothing. Nothing at all.'

He whistled between his teeth. Rat's little flattery had been rejected. I was too tired to ask myself seriously why. I expressed hypocritical regret at not having another bottle to prolong our celebrations. Poirier hooked off. The Shopkeeper stayed a few minutes longer to luxuriate in our success, under the pretext of settling the details: where to hide Popov? How to protect him? What did he eat? Which vodka did he prefer? Then he looked for flaws in our success and found none. Was there nothing to fear from Marina? Why had she not given us an account of Popov's enigmatic visit? If, on her side, she had fallen for him, wouldn't she deter him from his praiseworthy intentions? On the contrary, she would be delighted for him to betray for her. Anyway, he would certainly insist that she act as intermediary. So we had everything to hope for.

We were doubtless not to count on keeping Popov in the KGB as an agent in place. Even Rat understood that. The metaphysical reasons eluded him, but he knew from experience that when a professional decided to get out of it, the worst thing to do was to try to dissuade him. For the time being, we had every confidence in Popov; we thought that his confession was sincere and that he really had decided to 'drag his idols through the mire'. But we only had to rub him up the wrong way to make him feel homesick for his old office, and if we did that we'd have to look out for disinformation! We'd strike not oil but a reeking jet of home-made hokum. Only a drop, thanks! Yes, we had been counting on receiving intelligence in the form of regular dividends, but we wouldn't turn up our noses at a tidy capital sum instead. And some capital! To begin with, Popov's career and those of all his friends and acquaintances. Secondly, the battle order of the KGB brought up to date. Thirdly, the list of Soviet agents and informants in France, including the redoubtable Crocodile. And fourthly . . . once we had all this information we would be able to trade it with all the friendly services, the French ones in the first instance, and the Allies later. There the Shopkeeper would be in his element. If only Silbert showed enough authority to keep Popov in the Division—and there were excellent reasons for that: after all, we were in the Defence department, we owed nothing to the Special Services— we would see the whole of France beating a path to our door: beginning with SDECE and the *Surveillance du Territoire*, followed closely by General Intelligence, Military Security, Naval Security and, of course, the President's own security services, who poked their nose into everything. When that was all done, the Yanks would demand their share (they would even demand it earlier, but the Head of State could be relied on to keep them hanging about as long as possible). They'd be given some, but half a minute!—they wouldn't get it for nothing! A manna of information was about to fall into the lap of the Deuxième Bureau. Each of the experts admitted to interview the defector would be invited to drop his penny in the plate on entering—and on leaving, too, if I knew Rat. Such details as the order and duration of visits would probably not be settled higher up, unless Silbert managed to corner all the exploitable advantages—and he had neither the guile nor the tact necessary. The head of GEST would collect a variety of small perks such as foreign decorations, membership of various clubs, letters of recommendation, Stock Exchange tips, ways of blackmailing a croupier at Deauville, or of getting round a customs officer at

345

Annemasse, reductions on a Chevrolet or a Wollensack, the addresses of clinics in Geneva, massage-parlours in New York, opium dens in Chinatown, a Dutch banknote torn in two, which would be recognized by some receiver in Amsterdam, or a German banknote recognized by some madame in Hamburg, everything, of course, exchangeable for other more enviable, or more appropriate advantages (somehow I couldn't see the lieutenant-colonel making the trip to Hamburg) . . . He was about to leave me when he suddenly slapped his thighs:

'And I was forgetting,' he exclaimed, 'Israel! Popov worked on Israel when he was in the Lebanon. That, my dear Volsky, is bullion. The Jews are businessmen. Even our orderlies will be feathering their nests.'

Lacking his experience, I did not know how much all this was worth in terms of extensions to the suburban house, or char-woman's hours, or glasses of banyuls, or games of *belote* judiciously lost so as to provide opportunities of winning others, but I could see these various advantages reflected in his yellow eyes. In a surge of affection, the Shopkeeper gently massaged my back-bone.

'We could never have hoped for this, Volsky! In a sense, it's so much better than anything we could have expected. A complete turn-around. Like a glove. Like a rabbit-skin. A conversion. Yes. These defectors always hide some little secret, out of prudence, self-respect, or shame, or whatever. But with God on our side, that one won't be satisfied till he's scoured out every corner of his soul. Once you've acquired a taste for confession, there's no stopping you. And if he does marry the filly, who is French after all, he really will become a new man and spill the beans. Mind you, we did foresee that he would really fall for her head over heels.'

'Yes, sir, I foresaw it.'

He tapped the pocket into which he had slipped the tape.

'Sold his father and mother, eh? Little rascal! We'll bleed him like a pig, Volsky. We'll suck the marrow till there's nothing left. You'll transcribe all that into Russian and translate it for me. In two columns. Word for word. Don't skip a thing. It will all be useful. Even the bit when he was a snotty-nosed kid. It's full of juice, Volsky, I'm telling you. Culverin may not have been entirely above board, but, after all, you have to know how to shoulder your responsibilities when you're the boss. And you've backed me up well. Are you in line for promotion? Captain, maybe? At any rate a decoration—perhaps a little stud? Or even a palm! I'd say you'd certainly rate a palm.'

I had to push him out—well, almost. He was still prattling on over his shoulder as he descended the stairs. If I got a palm, he was sure to get the Legion of Honour—a full colonel without the Legion of Honour . . .

I opened the window. The cold, damp air flooded eagerly into the room, making the smell of smoke seem even staler. I poured myself out three last drops of whisky. I, too, should have been happy, but that didn't come without effort. The confession we had heard, as we smoked and drank, sickened me. Not the smoking and drinking—the confession itself. At least that's what I thought. I pictured myself again, the night before, arriving at the church before anyone else, carrying the case, entering through the main door, almost tripping up and falling flat on the steps leading down, going up the length of the nave, mechanically crossing myself before the crushed-strawberry curtain over the royal doorway, stepping up into the ambo, finding myself stuck in the little left-hand *klyros*, between the iconostasis and the back of a tall icon of the Mother of God, a corner shared by the candle-snuff, rags used to polish the candlesticks, a tin containing candle ends, and the lectern. It all looked like a small lumber-room, and the failing afternoon light did not predispose me to mysticism. Nevertheless I avoided catching the eye of the various icons leaning towards me: I remembered too clearly my childish terrors in a similar place. Apart from Christ Himself, always so accusing in His torment when He is on the cross, apart from His mother, the very sight of whom began to make me uneasy because I had started lying to my own mother, and John the Baptist, who survived on nothing but ants whereas I liked *crème caramel*, there had been all kinds of other saints, St Seraphim of Sarov, who conversed with the Holy Ghost, and St Helena, who used torture to find the True Cross, and St Nicholas, the miracle worker, and St Pantelemon,

347

whose relic was concealed in a secret place in the church, and St Mary of Egypt, who had been an abominable sinner, which gave me a sneaking sympathy for her, though I vaguely suspected that she must have done something more iniquitous than stuff herself with *crème caramel*, but whose exemplary repentance struck me as inimitable. They were all against me: 'He knows, they all know, but they want me to tell them these horrible things . . .' What terrifying minutes I had spent there waiting for the priest to decide to open for me the eternal register in which I was to write one more bad confession, not so much out of malice as out of respect for these sacred places that I had a horror of soiling with the confession of my vices . . . And Popov, a mature man, whom no one could force to pass under these Caudine Forks, who, on the contrary, risked a great deal in venturing there, was he going to subject himself to all that for nothing, for the sheer pleasure of it? I *literally* shuddered, shuddered at the idea of ever going back myself to confession. I hastily slipped the tape-recorder under the lectern and started the postponement mechanism. The holy green brocade fell back in place and I left with a feeling of having committed, in spite of myself, one of the most significant acts of my life. Since the office was usually shut on Saturday, the cursed tape-recorder had had to keep me company in my apartment since Friday evening; it mocked me from the dark corner where I'd put it and several times I was tempted to sabotage it, by damaging either the motor or the postponement mechanism (which would have been even funnier: we would have recorded two hours of vigils), but I abstained for a number of inadequate and complementary reasons, the first being that I knew nothing about electronics. Now this tape-recorder, having ingurgitated not only the confession that interested us, but also the innocent admissions of a little girl and the confused bleatings of an old woman, which I tried, by means of the Fast-wind switch, to hear as little as possible of, so as to limit my sacrilege to what was indispensable, this tape-recorder, still sitting in state on my table, struck me as the king of this décor which—I then realized—I had always hated: the furniture with its stupidly hexagonal motifs, those square, unyielding cushions, those cut-off corners, those

348

flattened ornaments, which reminded me only too well of the period of my defeat, consummated some years before my birth and attached like a millstone round my neck.

'The Fall,' I suddenly thought . . . 'For me, the Fall is the Russian Revolution.'

I had a headache. Before my own whisky, I had drunk some bad brandy on top of some adulterated Alsatian wine in a café opposite the Dormition, while those interminable vigils were taking place. Several times, contemptuous of the ordinary security procedures I went back to listen at the door: there was singing, chanting, reading, reciting, muttering; Popov was in there, simmering in that pot . . . Would he really make his confession? What would he tell Father Vladimir? I went back to the café and ordered another drink, my eyes riveted on the corner of the wall, waiting for the exodus. From time to time, one of them lost patience and decided to go home, but the service still went on. I was getting furious. Popov had gone in through the postern gate through which Marina had taken him the first time: he would probably come out the same way. Had I not missed him if he'd gone out through the main gate into the other street? The vigils finally drew to a close, the black beetles had hobbled off, even Marina had gone and Popov had still not emerged. Had he slipped off earlier without going to confession? Had I, then, committed a sacrilege for nothing? It was too stupid. I slipped into the church through the main gate. The crippled verger was pottering about in the narthex.

'You there, what do you want?' he called out in a rough voice.

The church was deserted. The icons with their staring eyes seemed to be holding their breath under the spell of the moonlight. All the candles were out. The big red lamps hanging from their chains were dimmed. I thought at first that there was no light and no sound. Then I made out a murmuring and a glow coming from behind the icon of the Mother of God. There, feebly lit by a dying candle, two men must be standing, two Russians, one bearded, the other beardless, the theologian and the anti-Christ, the priest and the master spy, the future saviour and the future saved, with, concealed at their feet, the

349

man-eating machine, digesting, at so many millimetres a second, the mystery of salvation.

I beat a retreat. I walked around in the courtyard. Through a window in the garage I could see the blue palpitations of a dying candle. It finally went out. A red glow lingered for a time, then nothing. Still the two men did not come out. The Soviet must be taking his conversion seriously. Or it was a very subtle game he was up to. A new idea occurred to me: 'What if, in fact, Father Vladimir was one of Popov's informants and this confession was a contact?' I particularly liked this possibility, for that would mean no sacrament and, therefore, no sacrilege. From the lighted windows of the buildings that overlooked the courtyard there came a few snatches of a Russian song. At last a door slammed. I just had time to see Popov, a fist stuck into his left pocket, as usual, goose-stepping his way through the corridor leading to the postern. I went back into the church. There was now a light behind the iconostasis, a flat electric light, with nothing of the anthropomorphism of the candle. The priest was in the sanctuary: he must be putting something away, or perhaps praying. I walked the length of the church without making a noise, I stepped on to the ambo, slipped into the *klyros*, bent down to pick up the tape-recorder from under the lectern and bumped into something.

'Who's there?' asked the unsteady voice of Father Vladimir.

I said nothing.

'Is it you, Agathon Petrovich?'

The tape-recorder vibrated from all its batteries like a living being. I pulled it towards me. I had some difficulty lifting it up, it was so heavy. I walked back down the church. On the doorstep, I turned round towards the darkened iconostasis, with, behind it, that vast feeble light and that mysterious bustle; I moved the tape-recorder from one hand to the other: I was staggering a bit—and, with a short bow, I risked a hasty, ill-executed sign of the cross.

'For what it's worth, coming from me, take it,' I muttered.

Then I went out into the cold, ignorant of what message I carried in the depths of that buzzing case, with its multi-coloured intestines. Now I knew it all: Popov was turned,

Culverin a success, Lester hood-winked, my career assured, Frisquette satisfied, the prince of this world and the King of the other perfectly served.

I was in the habit of taking a shower every night, but tonight—it was already almost one o'clock—I was content to undress, put on my pyjamas and slip between the sheets without even my sacrosanct, vesperal footbath, finding some strange satisfaction in thus wallowing in my own filth (all things being relative, of course—I had a good scrub that morning). The last picture, half dream, half imagination, that I carried with me into unconsciousness, was that of the priest unrolling his stole over the head of a kneeling Igor. A radiance seemed to come from the priest, as if a light had been placed behind him: twice I had observed the same effect that evening (when the candle had shone behind the icon of the Mother of God and when the electric lights had been switched on in the sanctuary). Igor, on the contrary, remained in the dark—a darkness of supernatural density—and it was terrifying to make out that semi-human form, the head disappearing under the band of stiff material placed over it, as if the sight of what was there might have petrified the world. I dreamed that I woke up with a start, tried to chase away this nightmare, went back to sleep and fell back into it. This happened three times: each time, surrounded with its halo, the attentive, serious, terrifyingly serious face of the priest; each time the same teratological tadpole at his feet. I wanted to cry out, but I could only open my mouth like a fish washed up on the sand, and I saw that fish gasping for breath, and I understood that it was that tadpole that had become this fish. I was awoken by a bell ringing.

I opened my eyes. An icy wind was blowing in through the open window, but it had still not managed to dissipate either the tobacco smoke in my room or the alcohol in my head. A red mist covered Paris. My limbs, encrusted in a thin skin of dust and sweat, did not quite belong to me. The bell—it was the doorbell—rang again. Frisquette? I looked at the luminous dial of my watch. Five past one. No, it wasn't Frisquette. A friend would have telephoned first. Then it occurred to me that it might be Popov. Yes, it was he, and if I opened the door, I would see him on the threshold, with the light behind him, decapitated, politely presenting to me his own head on a platter . . . I fell asleep again. Again the bell rang.

This time someone had put his finger on the bell-push and kept it there. The neighbours would complain. I threw back the sheet and, not finding my slippers, ran bare-foot over the cold floor. Through the spy-hole I could see nothing: the hall lights, on a time-switch, had gone out; the bell was still ringing. I did not know who was standing a foot away, behind the door.

'Who is it?'

By way of an answer, the ringing stopped, the lights came on and, deformed by the lense, a huge head on a tiny body that seemed to end in a fish tail, a sober, dark tie in the opening of the military-style, white, double-breasted, belted mackintosh, I recognized my friend Captain Tolstoy.

My hands had some difficulty finding the chain and bolt.

29

His fresh, innocent, fair cheeks glowed. He kept his hands stuck in the slanted pockets of his mackintosh. I stood before him in my crumpled green pyjamas. His nostrils twitched as he looked at me. He didn't like the smell that still lingered in the apartment. He ran his eye over my furniture, which now became twice as tawdry, twice as hideous.

'Come on scribbler,' he said at last. 'Get dressed.' And, as if I had some deformity to hide from him, he added: 'I won't look. Promise!'

I went into the bathroom and banged the door in his face. I ran the shower. I swallowed two aspirins. I splashed myself from head to toe. I kept my linen in the bathroom, my clothes in the bedroom wardrobe. I came back in my underpants, my back still damp. Tolstoy had sat down in an armchair—he had chosen the one with the worst prolapse—and crossed his legs. I had to crouch down in front of the chest-of-drawers, a few inches from one of his black, pointed, none too new, meticulously polished shoes. What was he after? Had Popov decided to defect even before taking communion? But what had that to do with Tolstoy? Perhaps some other GEST matter demanded my attention. I was not going to give Tolstoy the satisfaction of refusing me an answer. An officer is on duty twenty-four hours a day. I went back to the bathroom without asking anything and decided to shave. Over the hum of my Remington, I heard: 'No need to doll yourself up, Volsky. We're not going to a literary cocktail.'

I cut short my shave, reproaching myself for doing so. I reappeared, ready for anything. Tolstoy had shut the window.

'I'd take an overcoat, if I were you,' he said.

'I was going to.'

He watched me put it on, as if I had just told some childish lie.

We walked down the stairs, his shoes sliding noiselessly beneath him; he turned round once or twice, irritated by the noise mine made. His car was double parked, headlights dimmed. It was a black Ford; it almost completely blocked the street.

'You go for a shapely American chassis, hey?'

He looked at me with amusement. We had between us our common Russian blood, to which we never referred: we were both French officers.

'I need it to pull the caravan,' he said. 'When I'm on leave, we Tolstoys go camping. It's the only way when there are seven of you.'

I thought I'd caught him showing off; he put me in my place, explaining that, on the contrary, he was pretty broke. He, his wife (a Breton aristocrat) and the five little Tolstoys out shrimping, coming back in the evening for soup in the caravan: each had his little bunk and his own little locker, but no more than two toys each—somehow I couldn't find the picture as ridiculous as I'd have liked. And Tolstoy himself, in Bermuda shorts blowing on the camp fire, must have looked a fine figure. The mastodon moved off sweetly; there was no gear change.

'Do you like automatics, sir? Don't you find them a trifle unresponsive?'

'It all depends on the size of the engine.'

We were doing nearly forty on the wet roadway: it felt like fifteen.

'How did you expect to use him?' Tolstoy asked. 'In fairgrounds, as a two-headed calf?'

I didn't answer at once. Who was he talking about? Popov? But how would Tolstoy have found out?

'You'd probably do better getting your answer from the Shopkeeper,' I said at last.

'The Shopkeeper is a lightweight. This one's too big for him. He'll choke on it. Who does he think he is? This sort of thing is decided at a national level. He still thinks we're in the Second

World War, when there was room for individual initiative. It's always dangerous to employ lightweights, even in supporting roles. What's planned for the debriefing?'

I might perfectly well have remained silent; perhaps I was flattered that Tolstoy should side with me in running down the colonel, but I heard myself saying:

'As far as I know, nothing very precise has been decided yet. There's nothing to be gained from alerting our competitors.'

The vocabulary of a grocer, Tolstoy no doubt thought to himself: all part of the democratization of the cadres brought about by the Resistance.

'Only you four know about it?'

Natural authority is a strange property. I had to steel myself to reply: 'I don't think you are in a position to question me on that point, sir.'

What could be more pleasant than to tell Tolstoy to get lost? But it didn't come easily and I couldn't help myself adding, as if to soften with a touch of irony the hardness of my refusal (already mitigated by that 'sir' and that 'on that point'): 'Anyway, with you there are already five.'

Why the devil had Rat let him into it?

The streets were deserted. We were driving fast. I thought for a moment that we were heading for the Dormition. But from the 15th arrondissement we passed into the 14th. Tolstoy stopped, double parked, thirty yards from a street corner.

'Come with me.'

He took the ignition key with him. We turned the corner. A splatter of rain stung us in the face. Tolstoy stopped in front of a building of semi-bourgeois appearance.

'If the concierge stops us, ask for Dr Béral. He's an obstetrician.'

The concierge did not stop us. There was no lift. We climbed up to the fifth floor. I tried to make as little noise as Tolstoy. There were three doors. He pointed to the one on the right: 'Ring the bell.'

I shrugged my shoulders and rang discreetly. An indefinably plebeian smell invaded our nostrils. After a minute, I rang again. I still had a headache. Behind the door, there was some rustling, then nothing. Tolstoy pressed his finger on the button and, using the same method as before, kept it there. We could hear the ringing echo insolently through the apartment. Someone shuffled to the door, then an ill-tempered woman's voice called out: 'All right, all right, we can hear you. Don't wake up the whole building. What do you want?'

Tolstoy was standing in front of the spyhole. He didn't bother to answer and just winked at me. At last the door opened a crack, with the safety-chain on. In the gap appeared a large woman's mask with dishevelled hair. I thought I could detect some resemblance to Colonel Rat: her flesh seemed to be peeling off the bone in great, worn strips: the eyelids, the lips, the bags under the cheekbones would not last much longer. But she had no doubt been a beauty, fifty years before, and hatred of the entire world had kept her alive ever since.

'Well?' she barked at us, scrutinizing us with her beady eyes.

The captain's pretty, moist lips, curved over the consonants of his own name: 'Tolstoy,' he said in a low voice, his eyes twinkling with mischief, as if he had just made some deliciously improper confession.

The witch of Vesuvius emitted a groan and disappeared.

'With a little luck,' said Tolstoy, 'the old bitch won't go back to sleep until morning.'

She came back and dropped the chain. We entered the narrow hall. Tolstoy—I can never find light switches—stretched out his hand and turned on the light. A twenty-year-old, brown and yellow wallpaper rose above imitation panelling painted a glossy brown, with broad strokes of the brush, leaving hairs in the paint. A smell of reheated coffee floated in the air. In the half opened door stood the stooping figure of the lieutenant-colonel, a brown dressing gown opening to reveal none too clean, beige and white striped pyjamas. Without spectacles or false teeth, ill supported by his backbone, groggy with sleep, he looked like an inmate in an old people's home. His poor yellow eyes blinked in the light of what could not have been more than a 40-watt bulb.

'Well, Tolstoy, what is it?' he spluttered.

Mme Rat, her arms folded over a thick strawberry-coloured

356

dressing-gown, examined him in a way that boded no good. All she needed was a rolling-pin under her arm. We might have been drinking companions who had come to debauch the colonel under his own roof.

'The general wants to see you,' said Tolstoy. 'He wants to hear the tape.'

'What general?' Mme Rat broke in. Tolstoy turned to look at her, but said nothing.

'I don't know, Silbert, I suppose. It must be Silbert,' said Rat, coughing. And his wife snapped back, mechanically: 'Don't you see enough of him at the office?'

Rat gave a deep sigh. If there were to be a scene, it would be for the thousandth time. I thought I could see a tear roll down from under one of his loosely hanging eyelids. He half raised his arms in a gesture of impotence, turned his back on us, and was about to disappear, when, thinking better of it, he came back, turned on the light in the sitting-room (60 watts, perhaps) and, with a sweeping, almost noble gesture, invited us into the room.

'Sit down, gentlemen. I'm afraid I've nothing to offer you. I won't be long.'

The little sitting-room was stuffed with Charles X furniture, upholstered in red and gold stripes. The window was blocked by a heavy crocheted curtain; on a dejected-looking upright piano, in a metal frame, stood the photograph of a beautiful young woman in a wedding dress. Tolstoy sat down in an armchair that squeaked under his weight. Mme Rat looked daggers at him. A trace of contempt for the fragility of her furniture crossed his face. I remained standing. So did Mme Rat. I looked at her big feet, her ankles protruding over the red pom-pomed slippers. An invisible clock ticked in another room, probably on the dining-room mantelpiece. Rat came back, the knot of his tie askew. A pathetic white down covered his great loose cheeks. Perhaps he was somebody's grandfather.

'Go back to bed,' he commanded his wife. 'One never knows how long these emergencies take. Well, gentlemen, I'm ready.'

'For all the good it would do me!' she sneered. 'Do you think I'd get back to sleep?'

357

Tolstoy winked contentedly. I was the only one to say goodbye to Mme Rat. She didn't return the compliment.

We walked down the stairs, trying not to wake anyone. Outside, the biting wind set Rat's old carcase shivering under his trenchcoat. My head felt as if it had been split open. We walked to the car. I opened the rear door for the colonel. But he got in front and gestured to me to sit next to him.

'A luxurious beast you have here, Tolstoy,' observed Rat, surveying the rows of dials, levers and switches.

'Second-hand,' Tolstoy replied.

The second-hand car took off effortlessly. The thick wipers scraped across the windscreen forcefully and efficiently. When, after having our cards duly checked by a shivering sentry, we entered the Division courtyard, it was 2.25 on the Ford's black dial.

The long, broad corridor that led to General Silbert's office, filled in the daytime with a bustle of officers, an undulation of secretaries, was now deserted, airy, dark. Night lights divided up its length. At the end, on the right, a half-opened door threw a wedge of light into the rectangle of shadow. It was one of those doors with coded and interchangeable numbers. It led into a bare, oblong room, furnished only with a long wooden table and chairs. General Silbert presided, his hands in front of him on the table, looking unhappy without his usual accessories. He was wearing a navy blue track-suit: the only correct dress, he must have thought, for such an incongruous hour.

We were hardly inside the room when something incredible happened: without so much as a word of salute to the general, Tolstoy said: 'Anyone called?'

And Steel Wool hastened to reply: 'No'.

I noticed a telephone placed on the floor at the end of the room.

'Sit down, gentlemen.'

Rat sat down on Silbert's right; I on Rat's right. Tolstoy walked around the table, took off his mackintosh and sat down on the third chair on Silbert's left, isolated from everybody else. Rat and I looked at the general, the general looked at Tolstoy.

'Well,' he said at last, 'perhaps you will explain to us what this is all about.'

'I took the liberty of giving the Greek Fire alert and asking you to meet here while we wait for a call from Up There. Meanwhile, we can clarify a few things. Colonel Rat, you are in charge of Culverin.'

'Well,' said Rat, beginning to open his umbrella, 'Culverin is under my authority but it's Volsky . . .'

'Right, so it's Volsky. I presume, nevertheless, that you know quite a lot about the affair. And the tape,' he added, in a significant tone of voice.

Rat plunged his hand into his pocket and pulled out the tape. He handed it to Silbert, who did not seem inclined to take it. Rat, surprised, was left holding it. Silbert grabbed hold of it and slid it quickly across the polished table to Tolstoy, who stopped it by cupping the palm of his hand over it.

'Who, apart from Volsky and yourself, sir, knows about it?' asked Tolstoy.

Rat kept his eyes lowered. He shot me a glance that was intended to be accusing, but which only succeeded in being pitiable: he must imagine that it was I who had tipped off Tolstoy. Did he take me for a fool? For the first time in his life perhaps, his contempt for men betrayed him.

'There's no one else,' he declared. He immediately corrected himself: 'And, of course, General Poirier, who ordered the operation.'

Tolstoy looked amused, a cat playing with a mouse (what is pity?): 'Didn't you employ any personnel? Take out any equipment?'

'Who d'you think you are, Tolstoy!' Rat exploded. 'I don't have to account to you.'

'It's the general who is talking to you through me. Well? Personnel? Equipment?'

I observed with muted surprise. The Special Services are always a bit like waxworks: nothing is what it seems to be. I still remember my astonishment, that first evening, when I discovered an NCO passing himself off as a colonel with the permission of his commanding officer, who was wearing sergeant's stripes on his sleeve. All the same, I couldn't get over the obsequious way Silbert looked at Tolstoy.

'Two shadows,' Rat admitted. 'A chauffeur. Recording equipment.'

'And also, if I'm not mistaken,' said Tolstoy, 'a lady informant on the payroll and a contact agent, who already belonged to another operation.'

'I don't know the details. I left Volsky free to handle it as he saw fit. After all, it was his idea.'

Tolstoy smiled contemptuously and turned to me: 'Well, Volsky?'

Rat's baseness had exasperated me. My headache had gone. I replied curtly: 'With respect, sir, I don't think you are in a position to question me about a project ordered by the high command.'

We stared at one another. I stared him out. He sat back in his chair, indulgent.

'Very well, scribbler, we'll make something of you. You deserve some sort of explanation.' He turned to the general. 'Don't you think so, sir?' The general did not demur. 'It's some time now since your little plot with the colonel attracted my attention. I've questioned Marty, Planacassagne, Bourjols and other chaps in the Shop. The postponement mechanism attached to the tape-recorder seemed to me significant. I took the trouble to have you followed. Today, I was waiting for General Poirier as he left your apartment. He was surprised to see me, but he talked.'

'Poirier?'

'He seemed rather relieved to make a clean breast of it.'

If Poirier had mentioned the subterfuge of the day-book, it was a court martial for me. Tolstoy watched me struggling between truth and lies. I was not sure what proportion to use.

'Scribbler,' Tolstoy continued, in an almost kindly tone, 'when General Poirier ordered Operation Culverin, he forgot one little detail. Perhaps it was due to age? Or his forthcoming retirement? The prima donna's last, definitely final appearance? There are plenty of possible explanations if one wants to find them. Personally, I don't think he really believed

Culverin could succeed and thought that there would be no harm in toying with it. All the same, it takes a greenhorn like you to think you can turn a KGB major—and to bring it off. But, what General Poirier forgot when he ordered the operation . . .'

He didn't take his sea-dog's eyes off me. Tolstoy, stressing his words, was trying to get something across to me: was it that he would not look at the business too closely? That it wasn't important if I had cheated a bit since an unhoped for success had resulted?

'What he forgot, Volsky, was quite simply that he had no right to order such an operation. You were not to know, but he knew, that Popov's zone overlapped the zone of Greek Fire, which has an absolute priority.'

So the whole thing was simply a demarcation dispute? Tolstoy, who handled Greek Fire, was worried at seeing me get too close to his preserve? I wouldn't have thought him so petty. Silbert turned on Rat with intemperate violence: 'As for you, you've certainly served us well!'

Tolstoy contradicted him flatly:

'Officially, the colonel does not even know who Greek Fire is. It's an oversight of General Poirier's that has got us in this mess. These things happen. He's retired. We'll just have to get ourselves out of it as best we can.'

He looked at me as he spoke. What was he trying to tell me?

Rat's old eyes wandered from one side to another. He finally summoned up enough courage to speak.

'We may have trespassed on your domain, Tolstoy. If so, I'm sorry. But if you'd heard the tape . . . Popov is about to come over to us lock, stock and barrel. Not to the Yanks, to us. He's microfilmed all his files. It will take us ten years to use all that. A turn-around like that, sir,' he added to the general, 'happens only once in a century. The SDECE will be furious to think that it was your Division . . .'

Tolstoy cut him short with a calculated vulgarity that took my breath away: 'Stop sucking up, sir. Can't you see it's not getting you anywhere?'

He turned back to me: 'For a reservist, you didn't do a bad job

361

with your little scheme. To succeed against all odds—well, that's neat. Do you accept that General Silbert has a right to question you? Well, he has transferred his powers to me. Right, sir?'

'As far as Greek Fire is concerned, certainly,' said Silbert, decidedly ill at ease.

'Make up your mind, Volsky: I shall have to give some kind of explanation,' said Tolstoy persuasively, shooting a glance in the direction of the telephone.

'Spout, Volsky. That's an order,' Silbert declared.

I didn't understand what it was about, but I was beginning to enjoy this carnival. Anyway a number of peaks were emerging from the mists. By virtue of the fact that he handled Greek Fire, Tolstoy possessed, in the balance of powers, a weight that I hitherto had not suspected. Now, suspecting (or even knowing, depending on Poirier's discretion) the initial irregularities of Culverin, he was giving me a chance to drown them in oblivion, on condition that I agreed to playing his game. The telephone on the floor and the suggestive way in which Tolstoy had alluded to 'Up There' were not without their effect on me. Rat oscillated miserably between two attitudes: sometimes he took himself for the organizer of an exceptional operation, sometimes he passed off on to me the responsibility for a flop. Nothing could be expected from him: he was heading for the dustbin. Each time he opened his mouth, a bad smell came out.

'The only person to know of the operation, sir,' I began, turning to Silbert, 'apart from yourself, General Poirier, Colonel Rat, myself, and now Captain Tolstoy, is, as far as I know, the actress Olga Orloff, whose real name is Marina Kraievsky. Various auxiliaries took part in various phases of the operation, in particular the mole who enabled Mlle Kraievsky to make contact with Popov. Of course, he did not know what he was doing.'

'Who's that?' Silbert asked, to demonstrate that he still took himself seriously.

'A certain Roger Moutins, an army ex-NCO, ex-OAS killer, at present director of a para-Communist youth centre. He does a lot of undercover work for us.'

'And you mentioned Popov to nobody else?' Tolstoy continued. 'Your memory ought to be your best friend, Volsky,' he added, with surprising gentleness.

It was strange to take the operation apart in this way, to expose to the light of day the labyrinth of an ant's nest, constructed with such a care for secrecy. Without looking at Rat, I named Malmaison, Algy, Lisichkin, Lester. For Tolstoy, these were mere names; for me, they were living people; but as I mentioned them and as they obeyed my summons, one with his pastel yellow waistcoats, another with his imaginary theatres, yet another with his excessive glances at the legs of passing females, they became something else: characters, who, in turn, were gradually transforming me into their 'novelist'.

Tolstoy listened to me, took notes, interrupted me occasionally with a question. Silbert glanced nervously at the telephone, which awaited its hour. When I'd finished, Tolstoy said: 'Good. We'll have to put a stop to it.'

This time I looked at Rat. He had no resistance left. Were we to stop Culverin? So near the goal? Anyway, how could we stop it? The turn-around was now consummated. Or did Tolstoy mean that Popov was to stay in place, as we had sometimes hoped? He had only to listen to the tape to understand that this was out of the question.

'Put a stop to it?' I repeated, incredulously.

Tolstoy looked at me gravely and said nothing.

The silence continued. Silbert was playing with a gold-plated fountain-pen. We were waiting for the telephone to pass its opinion. It seemed incredible that the fate of an operation that had lasted months, occupied so many people, cost so much money, hung in the balance on that ill-shaped object lying in the corner. We had only to cut the wire, after all. But no one would cut the wire. Besides, I was still expecting a favourable oracle. Major Popov was the resident officer of Bureau T in Paris, Crocodile's case officer: the secret services would really have to be perverse to let such a man slip through their fingers. It was unthinkable. Were we just going to hand him over on a plate to our dear Allies? But perhaps—the thought came back to me—Tolstoy had not understood that Popov's decision to come over was, for religious reasons, irreversible? He could not become a priest while remaining an officer of the KGB. Did anyone have the temerity to explain to him that he would serve God better as an agent of the French secret service? I was about to open my mouth to declare that such an idea was grotesque when the telephone rang.

There was a moment of hesitation: who would answer? Being the youngest, I made to get up, but suddenly Silbert forestalled me. He looked almost elegant in his track-suit, but since the wire was too short for him to answer the telephone standing at attention, he had to double himself up, which made him look oddly servile.

'General Silbert reporting,' he declared, in a tone appropriate both to a great leader and a valet, with a kind of thin smile that was enough to set your teeth on edge.

Then, visibly disappointed, he said: 'It's for you.' He handed the receiver to Tolstoy, who took it without haste and crouching down next to the telephone, one knee almost on the ground, the other raised, in an attitude both relaxed and ready to leap.

'Captain Tolstoy . . . Yes, *sir*.'

A long silence ensued.

'Yes, *sir*.' The tone was quite different. He was now talking to a different general. Suddenly, Silbert, Rat and I were all little boys in the same class. With all the simplicity of comradeship, we exchanged glances in which an almost sacred terror and amusement at our terror were mixed.

'Certainly, *sir* . . . I'll pass you over to General Silbert, *sir*.'

Silbert rushed over and opened his mouth. The Other was already speaking. Silbert, bent double, his elbows apart, his backside in the air, his mouth open, looked like a caricature. We strained our ears to recognize the tricks of the familiar Voice, but before Silbert could present his compliments there was a click. We saw our general hesitate, then he presented them all the same, knowing perfectly well that he was talking to a dead microphone, but wishing nevertheless to observe the strictest discipline, indeed ready to forget the detail of the event and to write in his memoirs: 'During our talks on the subject, the Head of State and I . . .' He was not quite at that point yet. He looked rather lost. He waved the receiver in the air, in the hope that someone would take it from him. As no one decided to do so, he clumsily bent down to put it back himself and, returning to his place, declared to nobody in particular, in the tone of a spoilt child who is not getting his own way: 'He said: "Leave it to Tolstoy." '

He sat down and, with a majesty behind which one recognized another majesty, he said: 'Well, Tolstoy, what are you going to do?'

Captain Tolstoy was standing, his hands gripping the back of his chair, looking down. He knew—and we knew that he knew, though he pretended to hide it—that he had reached a decisive moment in his career, if not in his life. When he spoke, his voice seemed for the first time unsure of itself: 'What is at stake?' In a firmer voice he continued: 'What's at stake is to protect Greek Fire at all costs.'

The indispensable Silbert interrupted him: 'In front of Volsky, captain?'

'Volsky made the gruel, sir. Now let him taste it.'

It was an allusion to a Russian proverb that the general could not possibly know. It was, therefore, a hint to me.

'Anyway, short of bringing in a whole lot of new elements which I don't think would be desirable, we will need everybody and, preferably, the chaps who are already involved. Volsky did not do so badly in setting up his meccano: he'll manage somehow or other. Anyway, it's in his interest to do so.'

Yes, if Culverin was to be dismantled (which I could not yet believe), it was undoubtedly in my interest to make sure that the operation was carried out without hitch. Without appearing to touch it, Tolstoy had already put his forefinger in the hollow of my neck and was pressing. But why the devil had Poirier tipped him off?

'But requirements of compartmentalization . . .' objected Silbert, punctilious as a neophyte.

'If there'd been a little less compartmentalization, sir, we wouldn't be in the regrettable position we now are. If Volsky had known that Crocodile's case officer was out of bounds, he would have gone on quietly running his errands and writing his masterpieces. The country is going to be put in an impossible situation through an excess of compartmentalization. We can't ask Volsky to do what has to be done without giving him a reason.'

'But you don't understand, sir,' I managed to get out at last, addressing Tolstoy. 'Popov has been turned for good. He's not simply compromised, he's been converted. He wants to serve. He'll be taking communion tomorrow morning.'

'I know,' said Tolstoy. 'Our only hope is that he doesn't start anything beforehand. I suppose he has to contact you through Culverin? Culverin's home is under electronic surveillance, I suppose?'

I explained the system of the tapes, which I listened to periodically.

'That's not enough. If Popov calls her, will she report back to you immediately?'

'I don't know.'

'Don't you have her under control any more?'

I had to make the most difficult confession for a case officer: 'I'm afraid not.'

He expressed no criticism.

'We must have a man there the whole time, sir,' he said, turning to Silbert.

'Certainly. Rat, where have you got your gadget set up?'

Rat named his friend in the chancellery. He would have to go to his home to borrow the key to his office. An officer from the Division would have to be posted to listen to the tapes twenty-four hours a day. Silbert was in his element here: telephoning in all directions, rousing his underlings, getting them moving. His metallic voice resounded in the room. I was beginning to realize what was happening to me. The serpent's egg that I had been hatching for months was being snatched from me and would be thrown away. Someone else would listen to Marina's intimate conversations. A wave of revolt rose up inside me: 'Assuming I still am in charge of the operation. . .'

Tolstoy looked at me without sarcasm. Did he understand what I was feeling? He walked round the table, pulled out the chair on my right and sat down astride it. This stressed the privacy of our conversation.

'You will understand,' he said patiently.

And, with no more emphasis than if he were reading the weather forecast, he went on:

'Greek Fire is our main source of scientific, in particular nuclear, information not only on the USSR, but also on the USA. When I say our, I'm thinking not of the Division, I'm thinking not even of the army, I'm thinking of the country. The Americans have their reconnaissance planes and other non-traditional means of obtaining information; we can afford only traditional information, obtained through informants. Greek Fire is irreplaceable. He is important to us not only for military purposes. Our Scientific Research Centre, Nuclear Research, even industry, everything works twice as fast because of what he brings in—from one side and the other.'

'Greek Fire informs us about America?'

'You're about to understand. Just bear in mind that in a few seconds you will know the one secret of all French secrets which is the most highly secret.'

He said that with the smile of a poet that I did not recognize in him.

'I'm classified COSMIC. Is that sufficient?'

'It makes no odds. Either I throw you out or I explain. It is in both our interests that I shouldn't throw you out. You've heard of Crocodile, the star of Soviet informants.'

'Yes, but . . .'

I was being obtuse.

'You've heard of Popeye, the star of American informants? In fact, they have other pseudonyms. It doesn't matter: those are the names under which we know them. Well, Crocodile, Popeye and Greek Fire are the same guy.'

His eyes seemed drunk with repressed excitement. His face was so close to mine that I felt his fresh breath on my cheek.

'To handle such a bird, one needs, as you will readily imagine, not just a case officer, but a whole factory, for what is involved is not only the exploitation of what he brings in to us from the USSR and the USA, but also the manufacture of misinformation to feed to the Soviets. To disguise this factory we created

GEST, and we put in the window a few incompetents to show that it was an ordinary, run-of-the-mill organization, like so many others. The mere sight of your boss is reassuring, don't you think? In fact, *without any of its members knowing*, the service is working ninety per cent of the time for Greek Fire. There are a few cover activities, like your own, but the only real *raison d'être* for GEST is to feed and exploit the tidy little operation I'm going to describe to you . . .'

'You mean the Shopkeeper is the figure-head of the ghost ship?'

'I'd say rather that he was a complacent cuckold, paid to keep his eyes shut. Listen, the Americans employ Popeye against the Soviet Union. Our little secrets don't interest them. They know that Popeye is also a Soviet informant and they think they have turned him. They provide him regularly with questionnaires, plus a carefully dosed pittance of information-misinformation to prime the Soviet pump. On top of that, Popeye, who has contacts, gathers items of information from them that they are not aware of communicating to him.

'The Soviets use Crocodile against the USA and against France. They know that Crocodile is also an American informant and they, too, think they have turned him. They know that Crocodile is employed by France. But they do not know that he is working for us as, among other things, an agent. They provide him regularly with questionnaires about France and the USA, plus two beakfuls of information-misinformation, one directed at the USA, the other at France. On top of that, Crocodile, who has contacts, gets information from the Soviets that they are not aware of communicating to him.

'Of course, neither the Soviets nor the Americans are entirely taken in by this. They know that the information provided by a double agent is largely rubbish, but rubbish that always contains a few nuggets of the real stuff, which slips in without anyone knowing. Modern methods of cross-checking make it possible to separate the gold from the dross. Moreover, when one has established on what points the adversary can allow himself to tell the truth and those on which he has recourse to misinformation, one can deduce, in negative as it were, a second

368

batch of information, which is often of considerable interest. In other words, misinformation is a form of information that may not be of very high quality, but which the great powers certainly take care not to ignore.

'Our position is different. We only deceive the Soviet Union incidentally: in fact, we even pass on a certain quantity of valuable information, but look what we get in exchange:

'—Washington's misinformation intended for Moscow, from which we draw conclusions about the state of scientific advance in both places;

'—Moscow's misinformation intended for Washington, from which we draw parallel conclusions;

'—the Washington questionnaires;

'—the Moscow questionnaires; (and I wouldn't insult you by telling you that a well framed questionnaire is already, in an expert's hands, a mine of information;)

'—information secretly collected in the USA;

'—information secretly collected in the USSR;

'—plus information concerning Langley's methods, organization and personnel;

'—ditto for Lubianka.

'In other words, thanks to Greek Fire, we practically help ourselves to Soviet information and, above all, to American information, which, as you know, is of considerably greater scientific value. All that is injected into research, industry and the General Staff. Now do you understand why we need the whole of GEST to keep Greek Fire working at full stretch?'

He was trying hard to control his creative emotion, but I could sense the 'novelist' at work. The captain describing to me how Greek Fire operated was Balzac contemplating the Human Comedy laid out at his feet. I looked at him with more understanding than sympathy. It would be pleasant to spoil his satisfaction.

'Is it not rather naïve, sir, to imagine that a triple agent who so obviously deceives two of the three sides is being a faithful servant to the third? How can you be sure that Popov—or, for that matter, the American case officer—doesn't think exactly as you do? Your schema strikes me as something of a merry-go-round. Perhaps if we could question Popov . . .'

'Good reflexes, Volsky,' said Tolstoy coldly. 'Distrust, always distrust, eh? So you've picked something up in your training. But, don't you see, over and above money, there still remains . . . human nature.' It was odd to hear him use such an abstract term: the 'novelist' was suddenly revealed. 'The Americans pay their Popeye well and calculate that they get good value for their dollars. The Soviets imagine that they have persuaded their Crocodile of the eternal truth of Marxism-Leninism; they pay him little; what he's repaying them for, they think, are their ideas rather than their kopeks. Money and political beliefs are perfectly valid motives to risk one's skin, when there are no better ones. We, however, do not pay Greek Fire; and we even pocket his kopeks and dollars.'

'We don't pay him at all?'

'Not a franc, not a centime. What could we give him, anyway? France is so poor, compared with the others! Greek Fire works for us out of love.'

'Love of France?'

Tolstoy thought for a moment. Was he about to yield up his final secret? He could see that I was incredulous; he wanted to convince me.

'No, Volsky, not exactly. Love of a man.'

We looked at each other for a long time. In the end I took my eyes off his to shoot a glance towards the telephone. I read a certain acquiescence in Tolstoy's expression. I sighed deeply. I now knew who Popeye-Crocodile-Greek Fire was, and I knew, by the most certain of all sciences, which is faith, that Popeye and Crocodile might betray their employers, but that Greek Fire would remain forever an unshakable pivot of fidelity.

Fidelity is no doubt the least explained human phenomenon, but it would be falsely cynical to deny it and stupid to refuse to build anything upon it. It hardly mattered whether or not the man who benefited from this passionate and unshakable love deserved it. For the moment, he was able to benefit the country with the, perhaps grotesque, devotion he inspired—and we were on the country's payroll. I had myself enough loyalty not to seek further.

It took me a few seconds to take in the news, to enlarge the image I had of a person whom I believed, up till then, was deserving of my contempt, and to persuade myself that by a miracle of duplicity—or rather an ingenious and systematic triplicity—a hermaphrodite, tender-hearted foreigner was, in a sense, bearing France on his shoulders.

'I don't see why all that prevents us from . . .'

Tolstoy squinted at me, sarcastic once more: 'Really, Volsky, you don't see?'

Well, yes, I saw all right! I saw the evidence sparkle in the sea-dog's eyes. Greek Fire could work for us only so long as the Soviets did not know that we knew that he was working for them. If Crocodile's case officer defected to our side, Operation Crocodile was finished, and so, too, would be Greek Fire. Now, this set-up was worth more to us than all the files, all the codes, all the methods, all the plans we might get, because it provided us, not so much with Soviet gossip, as with American scientific secrets. Once Popov had gone over to the French, the Soviets would have to eliminate Crocodile before the French thought of getting a half-nelson on him in order to question him really thoroughly. It was clear, clear as crystal. Answer: Kill off Culverin before it throttled me.

I swallowed. Silbert, having made his telephone calls, had resumed his place at the head of the table, a prima donna out of work. Tolstoy turned to him, with the air of a surgeon who has just grafted a kidney:

'Our young colleague has the picture, sir.'

He got up slowly, walked round the table, sat down in his place, took up his notes and resumed the interview at the point he had left off.

'So you didn't talk to anyone about Culverin?'

'No.'

'And you, sir?' he asked the colonel.

He had to repeat his question. Rat shook his head.

'General Poirier also told me that he has said nothing to anyone about it. Do we know at what moment Popov intends to cross over?'

Rat, humiliated, said nothing. I answered: 'No.'

'I haven't time to listen to the tape. There's no doubt about his intentions? I'm relying on you.'

'He's undergone a conversion.'

'He might just be pretending.'

'I did think of that. I don't believe he is.'

'There's no way of keeping him in place? Through the holy *starets*, for example?' Tolstoy pronounced the *r* of *starets* in the French way, which gave it a perhaps unintentional effect of sarcasm. 'If we had some hold on the holy *starets* . . .'

'He's not concerned with the *starets*, sir. He's concerned with God. If you had a hold on God . . .'

Tolstoy looked at me as if I was a fractious infant.

'Through the beautiful Marina, then?'

Rat came back to life: 'There you have something. The filly gains nothing from his turning his coat. She might persuade him to carry on making a bit on the side. We could promise them, for the future . . .'

His experience as a wheeler-dealer was bound to make him totally misjudge a monolith like Popov. I couldn't repress a snigger—I now regret it, because at that moment the Shop-keeper deserved nothing but pity: 'For the future, a nice little corner newsagent's business? Don't you understand that Popov's never been one to "make a bit on the side"?'

Silbert was pushing back his cuticles with the clip of his pen. Tolstoy went on.

'In short, the fish is a bit oversize, but if there is no smaller one, it's a fact we'll have to accept.

He looked at me encouragingly: unlike the two old fogeys, he and I had already grasped what the inevitable solution was, and we were to continue as if they, too, understood. I went along with it.

'All we know is that he will go to the church. We could do it as he leaves his apartment.'

'Not easy. The building communicates—and for very good reasons—with the Boulevard des Invalides. Which exit will he take? Anyway, he may have slept at the Rue de Grenelle, in order to sort out his papers. Which church is it?'

'The Dormition of the Most Pure.'

Rat was beginning to understand.

'Coming out from mass? Unthinkable,' he said, to show that he was still in the discussion.

I contradicted him: 'There are two doors. The main gate and a postern door that gives on to another street. He prefers the postern . . . Very few people use it . . .'

'It might work,' said Tolstoy. 'As he arrives or as he leaves, then? That would give us two chances.'

Silbert chewed his lip.

'You're not seriously thinking of . . .?'

No-one answered.

'And . . . and . . . and what about diplomatic immunity?' he stammered.

Tolstoy shrugged his shoulders and smiled. What a time to be thinking about such trifles!

'You must be mad, my boy,' cried Steel Wool. 'You've been reading too many spy stories! I suppose you've heard of the Court of State Security?'

Tolstoy got up, went to the telephone, crouched down gracefully and began to dial a number.

'What are you doing?'

'I'm going to wake him up, sir, you'll get your orders.'

'Very well, very well,' said Silbert, 'sit down.'

Tolstoy dialled one more digit.

'All right, I tell you! We'll knock him off, your Russky.'

Tolstoy came back to his seat visibly irritated by so much amateurism.

Unlike the secret police, the secret services are not staffed with men of blood. On the contrary, the professionals of 'information' tend to regard violence with as much disgust as a chess player feels for a stalemate. On the rare occasions when there has to be recourse to a cleaning-up operation, it is almost always because someone has made a blunder—it generally costs him his career. Anyway, even if it can be done, it must not be mentioned, hence the euphemisms 'elimination' (French), 'maximum prejudice' (American), 'wet business' (Soviet). Post-Christian, democratic sentimentality, which tends to regard human life as sacred, acts in a similar way: bloodshed is avoided

373

for reasons of style and one is delighted not to shock the honest folk who form public opinion. Besides, the decline of virility or, if you like, the progress of humanitarianism has seriously reduced the number of competent killers, at least in the West. The Secret Army Organization failed for lack of killers, and the regime triumphed only by recruiting them from its own prisons. All these are facets of the same picture, and it should be realized that the price we were going to pay to keep Greek Fire going seemed exorbitant even to us. It had needed a decision from Up There (not that Up There was very respectful of French life, but a counsellor at a foreign embassy, especially a Communist one, can't be liquidated without a good deal of thought, as, for example, could several thousand moustachioed mountain folk, who have been stupid enough to believe in the word of France). In short, Tolstoy and I did not find it easy to call in the Cleansing Department, and we found that the less one talked about it, the more professional decency would be respected. And here was our amateur superior officer talking of knocking off the Russky!

'Question One,' said Tolstoy; 'who'll carry the can?'

'The Chinks,' suggested Rat.

'Good idea! Any Chinks up your sleeve?'

Rat shook his head.

Tolstoy turned to Silbert: 'Any Chinks, sir?'

'No Chinks. What about an extreme right-wing commando unit?'

'It wouldn't look serious.'

'Neo-Nazis, then.'

The Neo-Nazis have a broad back, but it was already five past three. You can't produce a Neo-Nazi movement in a few hours if you don't have the police on your side. We all racked our brains. One would imagine that the whole world detests the Soviets, but try to find someone to kill one off!

'What about a crime of passion?' suggested Silbert with inexhaustible inventiveness.

Proof would be needed, and it was six minutes past three.

'To deal with a Russian, you need a Russian,' said the Shopkeeper.

He was getting there slowly.

'For example that old Tsarist who has been living for two months overlooking the embassy. Lisi . . . Lisis . . . kin.'

'No one would believe in a Tsarist,' said Tolstoy. 'But we could make him a Solidarist.'

'Providing we didn't tell him,' I agreed.

'He'll need an alibi.'

'Easy: it's the time for Sunday mass.'

'Has he any family?'

'None.'

'It will cost less to send him to Chile.'

'Why Chile?'

'Good climate. Temperate. Besides, I've got passports.'

Lisichkin's fate had been settled between Tolstoy and me.

'Question Two,' said Tolstoy.

There was no need to state it. We were asking ourselves the same question. He merely said: 'I'm in intelligence, not action. I don't have anyone. Any ideas, sir?' he asked, turning to Rat.

'No! I used to have a lot of little fellows, but at the moment . . . They must all be working for the secret police. I knew a gypsy: he went up with El Biar's villa. There was a Catalan, too, but I don't know where to get hold of him now he's no longer inside.'

'What exactly do you need?' Silbert asked. 'A . . .'

We were not going to let him utter another indecent word.

'What we need,' said Tolstoy, with some haste, 'is a crack shot with a pistol, or simply a good marksman with a sten-gun.'

He took the trouble to explain: 'Shouldering a rifle in the back of a car tends to be noticed.'

'Well, there's no problem, then,' said Silbert. 'Take a chap like old Rabah—I brought him back with me from Kabylia: if I told him to cut the Pope's throat he'd do it before breakfast.'

'Lend him to me, sir.'

'Rabah? But everyone knows he belongs to my outfit. The commanding officer of the Intelligence Division can't be compromised in such an affair. You're not thinking what you're saying, Tolstoy.'

And, feeling himself threatened, Silbert added, threateningly:

375

'Anyway . . . A man you can depend on, a good shot . . . If that's not in your line . . .'

Tolstoy turned towards him, his chin thrust forward: 'No more than in yours, sir.'

Silbert sighed. For a moment their eyes were fixed on one another, like two lobsters grasping claws. Then both looked away. We had all killed, but none of us was an assassin: even Silbert could understand that.

'Gentlemen,' Tolstoy went on, 'we have been given the mission, from the highest authority, to rectify the mistakes made in this service. What are we doing to carry out that mission?'

'I remember transferring a Corsican lieutenant who broke his commanding officer's jaw,' said Silbert. 'He was playing poker. He might need money.'

'Has he any experience of this kind of operation?'

'I can't guarantee it.'

The four of us seemed to be racking our memories for a killer. No doubt Up There could have provided us with one, but we were grateful that we were being left to do our own house-cleaning. All the same, France was not going to be deprived of the benefit of Operation Greek Fire because we were incapable of finding a competent and discreet killer! The colonel was collecting invisible pinches of dust on the table, the general had put his pen down in front of him so as not to touch it . . . That legionary would have done the job, but he ended up strangled with a guitar string, that policeman downgraded for brutality had become an alcoholic, that Colonial NCO was now married with six children.

'If only we had more time,' said Silbert. 'After all, we don't know when the bugger's likely to approach us . . .'

But we couldn't run the risk of waiting.

I let them stew for a bit, then announced modestly: 'I have someone.'

Tolstoy, who until then had managed to hide his anxiety, now betrayed it by allowing an expression of hope to spread across his face. For me, it was important to appear as the saviour of the situation; but a deeper worry already troubled me. There was something satisfying for the 'novelist' in seeing the various plots that I had kept going simultaneously help to resolve one another, their elements being used to the maximum, all the squares being filled and all the files exhausted, all the characters of the ballet appearing for the last time on the stage, grouped in a new combination, more harmonious than the earlier ones and clearly definitive. (Beyond this aesthetic satisfaction, a superstitious fear gripped my heart, whatever effort I made to behave as a civilized Westener. If the chord really was being resolved as expected, would not the signature—or rather the mark—of this piece of dovetailing be rather too easily recognizable? When everything begins to take off with such unexpected elegance, with such excessive smoothness in the transitions, with too delicate a phrasing in the events, how can one not see it as the work of the prince? I am referring, of course, to the prince of this world.)

I described Moutins' qualities. Not only had he himself asked to play the role for which we had found no actor, but, by acceding to his wishes, we would lead him to give us an absolute guarantee of his fidelity, which I was now beginning to doubt: he would not go over to the Soviets after liquidating a major of the KGB. Besides, by using Moutins, we would not go outside the circle of the semi-initiated and Moutins knew Popov, an advantage that it would be unforgivable to ignore. I saw all three pairs of eyes turn towards me, filled with approval. I was once again at the head of Culverin. They were delighted to throw the head of Culverin at me. It was half-past three. Rat yawned, spreading around him the smell of his gastric juices.

'How much do you think he'll want?' Silbert asked. 'I presume *I* shall have to pay him.'

'He'll do it for the pleasure of it, sir. However, we'll have a better hold on him with a cheque. Let's say a hundred thousand francs.'

'Old francs?'

'Certainly, sir.'

'No problem. I'll give you that by hand, you'll just sign a receipt.'

One of the reasons why killers are difficult to find is because the profession is not rewarded in proportion to the risks incurred.

I realized that Silbert, with his receipt, wanted to hold me, as I wanted to hold Moutins with my cheque.

Silbert looked worried again. 'The weapon . . . The weapon. It mustn't be identifiable if he gets nabbed.'

'Moutins has weapons of his own, which he knows. Brought back from the Algerian war. They can't be traced. But it would be better to buy one off him and get him to throw it into the Seine afterwards. Allow 50,000 more.'

'50,000 francs for an old sub-machine-gun?'

'He's attached to it. It has its price.'

'All right. And the vehicle? Should we pinch one? It would be safer. We'd only need some fool to make a note of the number . . .'

Now we were organizing an operation, the general was once more in his element. He went himself into his office to fetch a sheet of paper on which he ruled the columns and squares that he regarded as necessary to the planning of the operation. He filled up every available space, square by square, with pleasure and efficiency. Once our plan had become OPS, it no longer shocked him. He made a few good suggestions, telephoned Air France to book a flight for Lisichkin, drew a diagram of the area of operation, and was the first to ask the crucial question of the driver. He did better: he gave us the impression that he was completely behind us—nothing is more indispensable to those who go 'into the cold' than to know that there is someone in the 'warm' who cares about them. It was twenty-five to five when, having rediscovered his usual aplomb, he declared with a blue flash of his glasses: 'Thank you, gentlemen.'

30

It had stopped raining. The night was at its darkest. One felt that it would end. One day.

Silbert had stayed inside, on the grounds that his dignity prevented his emerging with us.

'Will you drop me off at home?' Rat asked.

'There's a taxi rank at the corner,' Tolstoy answered.

Tolstoy and I went back to the big, comfortable car, while Rat walked off, stooping, counting his change in his pocket. Tolstoy put the lever on D and we moved off. In the Rue de Bellechasse, he double parked.

'I'll wait for you.'

I climbed the stairs, opened the door with my key, the chain stretched. An unhealthy-sounding snoring reached my ears.

'Lev Mikhailovich!' I whispered.

Springs. Pattering of bare feet. Light. A nose.

'Oh! Lieutenant! I thought it was the *tovarishchi*!'

He dropped the chain. He was wearing nothing but a shirt. He was trembling slightly, with cold and embarrassment.

'Not quite in uniform, lieutenant, not quite properly dressed,' he remarked with a poor smile.

I pushed forward a soap box and sat down on it, leaving the naked old man standing in front of me. I didn't find it easy, but this was not the moment to forfeit an advantage.

'Lev Mikhailovich, Chile is a beautiful country. They like Russian émigrés there.'

'Chile? Kiril Lavrovich?'

'Chile, Lev Mikhailovich.'

'It's true what you say, Kiril Lavrovich. I remember my

379

major has a chocolate factory at Mendoza. He asked me to go and work for him there.'

'When was that?'

'Well, once in 1929. And again, after the war. Then again, more recently, ten years ago . . . I never had enough to pay for a ticket.'

'Your ticket is ready. Booked in your name and paid for. You'll leave tomorrow night. If your chocolate maker doesn't want you, you will go to a certain Señor Hernandez at Santiago, who will find you work and lodgings. Have you got a passport photograph?'

He ran over to one of the bundles of papers lying on the floor. Bent double, he held down his shirt with one hand.

'Showing one's behind to an officer, tut tut! It really isn't done, it really isn't done at all!'

In the end he found an old crumpled photograph, which he handed to me. One could just recognize his fox's profile, the wrinkled lower eyelids, that expression combining naïvety and cunning. I pulled out of my pocket the Chilean passport in which Tolstoy had written the name Leon Lisichkin, the number of which would indicate to the Chilean police that it was a passport of convenience, delivered under government orders.

'You stick this photograph here. When you get there they'll stamp it. Allow me to congratulate you. From now on you're a Chilean subject.'

After thirty years of fidelity to a Russia that no longer existed, the good fellow had spent twenty trying in vain to become a naturalized Frenchman—it is so exhausting, in the end, to belong to nobody—and there he was, as in a fairy story, without the slightest effort, the proud possessor of a passport (not a resident's permit, or a tourist visa, a real national passport).

'A Chilean subject, Kiril Lavrovich? But, I mean, how is such a thing possible? I don't know a word of Spanish.'

'You'll learn, Lev Mikhailovich. Spanish is an easy language. Are you going to church in the morning?'

'Certainly, I'll even have a special service said to bless my journey.'

'Excellent idea. Which church will you go to?'

'Perhaps to the Dormition of the Most Pure. It's not too far from here and they have the right ideas there.'

'Out of the question. Strictly forbidden. Any other church.'

'The one in the Rue Daru?'

'Perfect. One more thing. Have you, by any chance, any NTS literature among all your papers?'

'Certainly, lieutenant. One gets all kinds. It's not my fault. You know me, I'm Faith, Tsar, Fatherland. All those Solidarists are redder than the Reds. I'd . . .'

'Well, don't take that literature with you. Don't destroy it. Leave this room in the morning before mass and don't come back. Understood?'

'It's not very . . . very clean, lieutenant. I'd prefer to clean it up a bit . . . and I really would like to get rid of that Solidarist filth . . .'

'I'm not interested in your preferences. If you see any friends, tell them the chocolate manufacturer has paid for your ticket. Be at the Invalides air terminal at nineteen hundred hours. Your ticket will be waiting for you at the desk.'

'Paid in advance?'

'Paid in advance.'

'When do I get to Chile?'

'The day after tomorrow, about eleven in the morning.'

'Lieutenant?'

'Yes, Lev Mikhailovich?'

'You know, I've also got a friend in Canada who's asked me to join him several times. Perhaps it would be more convenient, because of the language? He's a trapper, it seems. And they speak French there. Because I don't speak a word of Spanish . . .'

'Señor Lisichkin, or rather Don Leon,' I said severely, 'you are a Chilean subject and you are leaving for Chile. I hope you are not going to be lacking in patriotism? That would surprise me in a man like you.'

'No, no, I, what, why, not all, Chile it is, Chile it is . . .'

'That's better. Lev Mikhailovich, thank you for all your services.'

He attempted a salute, his legs still bare, and came out with the old motto of the Tsar's army: 'Delighted to strive, sir.'

I got up. He stopped me, putting his hand on my arm.

'And him, down there, the son of a bitch . . . What about him?' He winked in the direction of the garden.

'That son of a bitch,' I said, 'is none of your business. Don't forget to go and pray in the morning and make sure you're seen by all your friends. And above all, don't miss the plane. For the rest, don't worry. Good-bye.'

I left the building. It was five to five.

31

Tolstoy looked at me enquiringly.

'Everything's fine. He asked no questions.'

'He'll have time enough for that in Santiago. What's the address?'

I gave him the second address with some reluctance. First, I didn't at all like putting at his mercy a private informant that I had once defended against his 144 organization; secondly, however much I envied his hardness, I had to confess that, hardened as I had myself become, it did shock me. He had not read the pages of Kant, or if he had read them, he had used them for his wife's hair-curlers: men for him were decidedly only means to an end and, if he had no use for them, he threw them away like non-returnable bottles. At any rate, this access of purity was not to last long and soon I was again flattered by my association with this 'novelist' so manifestly destined to succeed: young, strong, clever, unscrupulous, we were together going to clean up the mess our elders had left us with. It felt good driving fast through a deserted Paris. As we plunged through the night that belonged to us—we were, in more than one sense, the forces of the night—I wondered what Poirier had said about me to Tolstoy. I tried to reconstruct the sequence of cause and effect: Poirier had agreed to play at Culverin out of sheer boredom; seeing that it was about to succeed, his conscience pricked him; Tolstoy, waiting for him outside my apartment, seemed to him like a heaven-sent confessor. Result: he spilled everything he knew, either out of remorse or, on the contrary, out of decency, accusing himself and protecting his subordinates. Possibly.

Tolstoy stopped in the Boulevard de la Gare: 'Go, my young comrade, for the love of literature, go!'

He sat back on his black cushioning, his feet under the heater. I jumped out. Moutins had no telephone, but he was not supposed to sleep out without reporting to me: so there was a good chance of finding him at home.

I did not know the district; it is sinister, like most of those crossed by the overhead métro. Under the evil-smelling piers that bear it, one can make out a swarming mass of human vermin, and if one has any imagination, one walks with all one's senses alert, ready to throw up, or to riposte. The Rue du Chevaleret, which ends there, winds its narrow length between high walls leading into sundry depots and warehouses. From time to time, an apartment building rises up in the midst of this windy desert. Dawn was still far off, but the temperature was falling. I had warmed myself in the car. I now jogged along, shivering.

A shoddy modern building. No concierge. Numbered letter boxes with the names of tenants. I found 'Moutins Roger 2nd right C' easily enough. There was a lift (descent forbidden), and out of lassitude, I shut myself up in the tiny box to ascend two floors. It was a mistake: surrounded by obscene graffiti scratched in the red and green paint, a sensation of claustrophobia overcame me and I heard someone say in my ear: 'I'm suffocating. You must change something . . .'

No doubt I was talking aloud to myself. I shook my head violently to bring me down to earth again.

Second on the right. The magic eye in the plywood door. A visiting car: 'Monsieur Roger Moutins, industrial designer.'

I was torn between two principal emotions. It is always pleasant to wake people up in the small hours: it gives one an extraordinary sense of power. There they are, batting their eyelids, naked or in crumpled night clothes, ridiculous, smelly, unarmed, unmasked, caught in their meanest truth, and one dominates them with all one's daytime armour. No need to shake them: the pleasure is gratuitous. To have these advantages over Roger Moutins did give me pleasure. But, on the other hand, the power one exercises is never really absolute—one can

384

imagine only God totally devoid of human respect, and not the Christian God, at that. It is embarrassing, therefore, to come and disturb people at an unsuitable hour, like some boor; one may have very good reasons, but it is wrong all the same and one knows it. That night, for the first time, a third intuition was already raising its head inside me: Lisichkin's excuses for his involuntary exhibitionism had provided me with a limit in a certain direction: I couldn't get Kant's quotation out of my mind; the remnant of feeling I had was beginning to melt on the surface. I rang brutally, insistently, *à la* Tolstoy. All the more brutally in that I was a little afraid of M. Moutins.

He let me ring for a long time; when finally the door opened, it was suddenly, noiselessly, and to a darkness hardly penetrated by a pale light filtering through opaque curtains. The polyhedron of electric light from the landing caught only the light-coloured wall of the tiny hall and, beyond the door, the blade of a dagger. How many such hungry warriors are there throughout the world who still play, at night, at running risks! As it happened, that blade was welcome: it showed me that Moutins was still very much on his toes. I entered the darkness. The door shut behind me, in the best oiled silence.

'Monsieur Moutins . . .'

A whispering in my ear, the breath swallowing itself up unpleasantly and blurring consonants: 'I'm not alone. No point in you being seen. Wait for me at the corner of the boulevard.'

The door opened behind me, masking once again the master of the house whom I had still not seen. Melodramatic, perhaps, but one had to admit that Sergeant-major Moutins took effective precautions.

As I retreated, I whispered: 'Leave your Sunday free. For action.'

Having laid my bait, I went down to warn Tolstoy, who moved off. Moutins was already coming, stooping forward, his hands thrust into the diagonal pockets of his wind-cheater, his delicate spectacles on his nose, his cheeks so pink and clean-shaven that one wondered if the hair ever grew on them. He held out his hand first.

'I was with a lady of the night,' he said, a trifle pretentiously.

The icy wind whirled about us, whisking up discarded Gauloise packets under the viaduct—for once the emblem of the winged helmet found real occasion to fly.

'Moutins . . .' I deliberately cut out the 'Monsieur' in order to galvanize the ex-sergeant. 'I haven't come to tell you of your transfer, but I'm giving you a chance to prove yourself. It's not an order, mind you. I've chosen you and I've pulled a few strings, but . . . it's up to you to refuse if you want to. There's a long queue.'

Apparently phlegmatic, he gave me a look that I don't know how to describe. His emotion was something like that of a lover in the grip of a desire at once of the most pitiless and pitiful kind. Despite the belief that killers are also insatiable sensualists it struck me, on the contrary as wellnigh impossible that the same man could find equally intense pleasure in such dissimilar activities: Moutins, I said to myself, must be the very opposite of Popov, and the prostitute, if she had been there since the previous evening, must have done well for herself: a night spent with one, not too demanding, man. I needed a killer; I had found one: a use could be found for his appetites . . . I had to congratulate myself, but I felt ill at ease under that greedy gaze.

'The decision has at last been taken in the highest quarters. Major Popov of the KGB will be eliminated. Are you willing to do the job?'

'Yes, yes,' he replied absently.

'Everything will be done to throw the police, the press and the Party on a false trail, but if you're caught, you'll have to fend for yourself.'

'Yes.'

He was dreaming.

'We'll do our best to get you out, of course, but only if you don't spill the beans.'

'O.K.'

'If, for example, you mention my name, I'm sure I shall be reminded of the Delta Networks.'

'Yes, yes.'

We walked back up the boulevard. I set about explaining the plan.

'Are you listening, Moutins?'

He hadn't heard a word. I think he was contemplating the murder that was growing and blossoming inside him.

'When's it for?' he asked.

'Tomorrow morning. This morning.'

'What technology is envisaged?'

For a fraction of a second, I didn't understand what he meant. He went on: 'I'm using a blade?'

He was beginning to frighten me, not for myself, but for him. How could God save a thug of this type? Father Vladimir had asked himself the same question about Popov and we were going to resolve it for him: Popov, assassinated in a state of grace, would pass through the broad gate of the martyrs.

I explained that firearms were necessary and suggested buying one of his off him. He didn't seem too disappointed.

'Have you got ammunition?'

'Yes, yes.'

Then I talked about the vehicle. He agreed. He always agreed. Deep inside himself, he was following some great musical dream that was quite beyond my comprehension.

'Pity you didn't warn me in advance,' he said. 'I'd have had more time to get ready.'

What he meant was: to savour it. I talked about money: 'A hundred thousand for yourself. Fifty for your weapon. Twenty-five for the driver, if you provide him.'

We were still walking against the wind, up hill. On our right was the viaduct; on our left, a row of buildings, each with its complement of sixty sleeping petty-bourgeois, plus one or two who had got up and switched the lights on: early risers or insomniacs. Suddenly there was a rumbling: a refuse lorry was coming down towards us.

Moutins was beginning to emerge from his daydream: 'Haven't you got anyone?'

'Yes, of course, but compartmentalization . . .'

I knew I would have to do it myself if Moutins didn't have a pal he could depend on. Tolstoy had refrained from the slightest threat to me, but I thought it less and less likely that Poirier had not told him about the day-book.

387

'I'd rather be responsible for everything myself, anyway,' said Moutins. 'You feel safer with people you know. And financially I get more out of it .'

'Have you someone in mind?'

'Her.'

He jerked his thumb back at his apartment behind us.

'Her?'

'A Spanish woman from North Africa. She thinks our Charlie's a Communist agent. I'll tell her that Popov is his case officer. She'll do it for nothing. O.K?'

'She won't talk? It'll hit the headlines, you know. She might be tempted.'

He chuckled.

'In the ten years I've known her, I've never heard her say ten words. She works in silence and recollection, d'you get the picture?'

Everything was working out so smoothly . . . The viaduct was shaken by a vibration, and a chaplet of yellow squares crossed the night above us: the first empty métro. Suddenly Moutins stood in front of me in that thunderstruck attitude we curiously call 'at attention', his body leaning forward as if he were about to fall over, his chin raised as if he were about to take flight; a cloud of vapour escaped from his mouth.

'Thank you, sir. I shall never forget.'

32

I have always loved the sunrise, that masterly clean sweep that
chases away the shadows, clears first the larger surfaces, then
pokes into the corners, scrapes out the cracks, polishes the
facets, and finally crushes the last shreds of night left hanging
here and there. I've always felt that each morning is the first
morning, as if the Father were giving Adam one more chance,
while each evening is the last evening, as if the angels were
putting their trumpets to their lips in the sunset to announce
the arrival of the Son. It may be because my mother taught me
my religion in a book for rich children, sumptuously produced
in Russia under the Ancien Régime, with a kind of Father
Christmas floating on clouds over the first page, but I have
never been able to adopt the general attitude, which consists
in seeing the Father as the vengeful Jehovah of the *Old Testament*, while the Son appears only as the gentle Lamb of the
New. Personally, I find the Son frightening: I imagine him with
the terrible gesture attributed to him by Michelangelo in the
Sistine Chapel, the Father remaining the kind daddy with the
floating beard that I knew so well in my childhood. So the
morning belongs to the Father. That morning, in particular
(say what you like, Sundays are not, from a cosmic point of
view, days like any others), the sky of Paris was traversed
by a cavalcade of grey clouds, a froth of creamy clouds, a
splash of unfinished glory, which not only heralded the spring,
but also aroused quite unnatural longings for virtue, or rather
innocence. The morning was approaching so quickly: at
a gallop. I feared that it would overtake me: I still had so
many (hardly innocent) things to do to abort Culverin at the

foetal stage. But I anticipate.

While Moutins went back home to sort things out with his driver and to collect a few necessities, I had rejoined Tolstoy, curled up in his car like a pearl in his oyster, his complexion as healthy as ever, his eyes still bright.

'Well?'

'We're all set.'

Nothing betrayed his relief.

'And the driver?'

'He's got one.'

Nothing betrayed mine. I did not specify the driver's sex, suspecting Tolstoy of misogynous prejudices.

'And the weapon?'

'He's got one. Vehicle?'

He handed me a key.

'Right, Volsky, play this one like a big boy and we'll wipe the slate clean.'

He might easily have given me a friendly tap on the shoulder as I left. The insolent look in his eye told me: 'My attitude horrifies you. I know. It's good for morale.' Culverin no longer belonged to me. I walked off. The sky had already changed from that indigo characteristic of Parisian nights; it was no longer black, as just before dawn, but it was streaked with tangled swirls, black and white; one sensed that the clouds were low, the wind strong, the weathercocks turning in all directions. It was half-past five.

I met up with Moutins at the crossroads. He was wearing a balaclava helmet, muffled up with a scarf, crammed in an anorak. His face was masked in goggles and he was astride a motorbike. I mounted pillion, in my velvet-collared overcoat. We took off. I clung to his shoulders in an almost feminine gesture that was hardly compatible with the dignity of command.

At five-past six, when we stopped in a forest track near Bièvres, I was stiff with cold; my arms and legs felt as if they were made of wood. I walked up and down for about ten minutes clapping my arms about my chest, as coach-drivers once did, it seems. The sky was turning a lighter blue-grey, with, here and there, unimaginably delicate patches of a velvety, dove grey. The earth smelt of mushrooms and rotten wood.

Moutins came back. He was carrying a packet of newspapers to which a few bits of red, clayey soil were still adhering. He laid the packet in my arms, as if it were a child. Then we were on our way back to Paris. I no longer had to cling on to him: I had found my 'seat'; I gripped with my knees as if the riding master had placed coins under them. We reached the outer boulevards and turned off left. At five to seven, Moutins stopped a hundred yards from the Porte Brancion. I gave him the key. It belonged to a van Tolstoy had rented some months earlier from a service station. He had made a copy of the key 'just in case'. He must have his pockets full of those 'just in case' s—as he did of Chilean passports. Moutins walked off. I stayed there, next to the motorbike standing on its rest, holding in my arms some twenty pounds of weapon parts and ammunition clips. The sky was brightening every second. A window slammed. Two cars passed. No more: it was, after all, Sunday morning.

An almond-green van, with rounded corners, a sort of bubble on wheels, rusted here and there, turned the corner and stopped next to me. I wanted to jump into the back. The door was stiff. I'm clumsy with objects. Moutins came round to help me: 'Why don't you get in the front?'

I beckoned him in after me and, when we were both inside the metal box, I gave him his parcel back.

'Put it together. Let's check that it works.'

'My weapons always work.'

'Do as I say.'

None too pleased, he undid the newspaper. A little light came through the two round windows giving on to the driver's compartment. Moutins opened a transparent bag, with yellowing sides, inside which globules of oil rolled around. He took out several substantial parts and four ammunition clips, all gleaming with oil. He had not greased them for fear of getting the springs stuck. He took out a rag from his pocket and carefully wiped each part. He cleaned the barrel, pulling through a cloth on a string which was all prepared in the bag, by way of viaticum. Then with efficient clicks, the inert parts came together, their function bringing them to themselves. A block of steel became a breech; a piece of wood became a butt. It was like the resurrection of the dead in *Ezekiel*; the bones were covered with flesh, arms and legs came together, the spirit breathed once again into the bodies, which became men once more; similarly, the barrel and the butt fitted together, the clip clicked home, these various things gave each other life— since function is what gives life to things—and, by a series of efficient sharp movements, a Thompson sub-machine-gun was reconstituted.

Crouching there, I watched with fascination the cartridges garnishing the clips. Eleven forty-three, it's only a number, but when one sees a snub-nosed bullet nearly half an inch in diameter and one imagines getting that in one's flesh, one tends to grit one's teeth. An instructor once told me that if one of these projectiles hit your little finger it would throw you to the ground by the sheer force of the impact; I don't know whether that's true, but the mere sight of those copper cylinders with their lead, hemispherical ends, combined with the idea that I knew which chest, which belly, which skull they were going to tear open, impeded my breathing. Moutins showed me the completed assembly with the air of a head waiter presenting the lobster that will be boiled for you. He worked the trigger and then moved the heavy breech, holding it back with a gesture that I could only describe as erotic. The moving part slid with marvellous smoothness. I showed I was satisfied. He wrapped up the weapon again in the newspaper. It was, I remember, *L'Echo d'Alger*.

Moutins got out of the back of the van and returned to his motorbike, while I got into the driver's seat. It was a veritable cortège: I followed Moutins and I was followed by a big Ford with double headlights. I got used to the position of the gears fairly quickly. The idea that I was driving a stolen car did not particularly disturb me. The service station was shut on Sundays, so the owner could not notice the van's disappearance until the next day. Besides, I had the French army behind me. About half-past seven, I reached the Place d'Italie, where I parked the van. I hid the key under the mat as agreed and set off, on foot, in the direction I had come. Tolstoy caught up with me.

'Come and have a coffee.'

I had black coffee, with croissants. Tolstoy observed me, trying to detect some sign of weakness. But my appetite did not betray me. We hardly spoke. Tolstoy simply said: 'You'll have to take your fine overcoat to the cleaners. Put it down to expenses.'

I looked down and saw that in fact there was grease on the left tail.

When we left the café, it was light: no more need for headlights. At a quarter-past eight, Tolstoy dropped me off at my apartment. This time, I got no encouragement, either ironical or seriously intended.

The apartment still smelt of stale tobacco. I opened the window and dashed into the shower. I found it odd to be washing my smooth skin, when, in two or three hours, another skin, no doubt as smooth as mine, would be opened up in several places and lie hanging off in strips. I looked at my chest and belly and wondered what holes the bullets of the 11.43 would make on entering or emerging. I imagined a continuous jet of singeing, heavy bullets drilling themselves into me in a light pattern, as into a target; one here, one there, one on the left nipple, another comically placed slap in the middle of the navel.

I shaved and dressed carefully, as one should when one is going to mass. Indeed, curiously enough, it struck me that I owed it to Popov: a last courtesy. . . A stiff white shirt, cufflinks made of five-rouble pieces (rather on the large side, but patriotism may sometimes get the edge on good taste), a waisted, navy-blue suit, a tie of the same colour, starched breast-pocket handkerchief. And I tried to take off the grease with a detergent. I didn't succeed; however, the stain did not show too much.

The telephone rang. Tolstoy was calling me from a public call-box. The listening device revealed that Marina had spent the night at home, alone. An American actor, some gaga academician, that playboy Popol and a few other panders of less substance had telephoned her. She had politely got rid of all of them. From Popov, nothing.

I took the métro, so as not to be noticed by any driver or policeman, and so as not to have to park my 2CV near the church. If they had listened to me I would not have shown my face at the Dormition that day, but Silbert and Tolstoy wanted one of us to be there. In so far as I was not to take part in the action, I tended to think that they were right. I got off at a relatively distant station, for fear of being remembered by an idle ticket inspector, it being Sunday morning, and I walked the rest of the way. The sky looked as if a broom were busily at work: clouds were being swept across it at an ever increasing, almost comic speed. On the ground, bakers' shops were opening one by one, and little ladies in coats pulled over crumpled pink pyjamas were nipping out to buy their croissants.

I had given Moutins a plan of the quarter. I reached the intersection where the church stood, and walked about fifty yards in each of the four directions, but no green van was to be seen. It was five to ten. I went back to the Dormition, made a sign of the cross at the gateway and entered the courtyard. The lamp was lit under the icon: so the verger had arrived. I pushed open the church door. At first I thought there was no one there, then I made out a few old biddies stuck to the walls. A silence reigned there that was not simply an absence of noise, but an element in itself. A solitary candle was lit on a chandelier. A serene muttering came from behind the iconostasis. I went out again. I was going to have a man killed. It was not the first. Whether it took place entering or leaving a church did not concern me unduly: I might be superstitious, but I was no hypocrite.

The day had turned out fine, bright, windy. Coloured rubbish floating in the gutters caught the light, the puddles levelling off the hollows of the pavement gleamed. The green van appeared, coming towards me. Why wasn't it already parked? I followed it at a leisurely pace. It stopped alongside a line of parked cars fifty yards farther on. I stooped down to the right-hand window, which was lowered as I did so.

'Well, Moutins?'

With his goggles and balaclava he was unrecognizable. There was no weapon to be seen. The driver—a young woman with black hair—had turned away, exposing a bronzed neck.

394

'There's nowhere to park, sir.'

It was true. Bumper to bumper, the consumer society had taken over both sides of the street.

'Keep moving.'

I turned round and saw Popov arriving.

He was wearing a ribbed white sweater, plus-fours, a tweed jacket. His legs thrown forward, the dome of the forehead broadly exposed to the elements, he was approaching at a quick pace, his left fist stuck in his pocket, his right gripping the handle of a huge yellow pigskin briefcase, with visible stitching. One could sense that it was heavy and that he was carrying it lightly. He dashed in through the postern gate. I had no doubt been noticed in the *bistrot* on the intersection the night before, so I found another, small and sinister, a bit further on. I rang the office.

'Culverin here, yes?'

Tolstoy's voice. I felt a pang of regret at the thought that he had at last succeeded in taking over my operation, signing my 'novel'.

I gave him the telephone number of the *bistrot*. I waited five minutes. Would he ring me back as arranged from a public call-box or did he have a safe telephone at his disposal?

He rang back: 'Report.'

'We missed the arrival. No room to park.'

It took him a second to take in the news. We had had two chances; now we had only one.

'Alert?'

'No.'

The second chance was intact.

'Keep me posted.'

I recognized that brief, serious tone: it was how orders were given, by radio, during battle. Tolstoy was no doubt going to report to Silbert; would Silbert panic? There was nothing I could do. I felt supremely calm. I went back to the church: all this coming and going was quite normal among the Russians and would disturb no one.

I had never come to mass so early. I had always cut it short a bit at the start and finish. The liturgy-proper had probably not yet begun. I didn't know. Someone was reading something somewhere. Ghosts were beginning to congregate in the corners. Popov stood to the right, in front of the crucifix, stiff-backed to make up for the shortness of his legs.

I went out again. In the courtyard people were chatting. An old gentleman caught sight of me:

'Ah! Kiril Lavrovich! Come and tell us what they think of the political situation in the high government circles in which you move.'

I kissed the hand of a decrepit princess who sported false eyelashes, false teeth, false hair and a false title. That I should fulfil my Sunday duties in the courtyard and not in the church caused no surprise. By doing so, I would simply be categorized as belonging to that species my grandfather ironically called 'courtiers'. The weather being fine, there was no lack of courtiers. I went back into the street. The van was still circulating. It would be noticed.

I stopped Moutins: 'Move off. Come back about eleven. Someone may have gone off to the country by then.'

I went back into the church. Things had got going: there was singing, incense was smoking, old women were cackling quietly away to themselves, the priest was chanting my childhood —which did not interest me. Popov, half hidden by the crowd, had not moved. What was going on in his head, in his heart? What did it feel like to be a convert?. . . If only I'd . . . If I'd been he, I'd have been dead.

I went back to the *bistrot* and had a glass of white wine. There were enough Russians around who expected to benefit from the main part of the mass, but who considered it rather excessively pious to arrive on time, for the *patron* to think me one of them, providing I didn't use the telephone. I wondered if Lisichkin was consolidating his alibi at the church in the Rue Daru. I really did wish no harm to the old blighter.

I returned to the courtyard. The bearded beggar had taken up his station at the entrance. His bluish, iridescent nose would have sickened puritanical philanthropists, but not me; I put my hand into my trouser pockets, pulled out all the change I had and gave it him, without counting. Then, remembering, it is

396

true, that my wallet was almost empty, and with a glance round to make sure that no one was watching me, I opened it, pulled out all the notes, still without counting, and gave them to him. Why on earth did I do that? It was not very professional behaviour. The man broke out in blessings. I went into the church to escape him.

It was now full of people and I found to my surprise that I could no longer regard that praying throng with my usual contempt. I remembered what Father Vladimir had said about his emigration: when all was said and done, it had been nobly borne. Beyond their squalor, their absurdity these men deserved—no, does one ever deserve?—they consumed, they absorbed, the love he bore them. Throughout the centuries there had scarcely been people more destitute. Surrounded by coils of incense, the false princess was weeping away her cheap mascara before an icon of the Virgin and, by a kind of mirror effect, I also found something of the icon on her poor creased, over-painted face.

I looked around me and had the feeling that, apart from the liturgy, something essential—something crucial, I was going to say, if I may be excused the pun—was taking place here. Someone was doing something. What? Who? I did not know. Between two heads, I caught a glimpse of the carefully shaven back of Popov's neck and his so undistinguished profile, with its domed forehead and nutcracker chin. I remembered that he had been to confession the day before, that he had been absolved of all his sins and that, consequently, in the eyes of the Church, he was as innocent as a new-born lamb. Popov innocent? Don't make me laugh! I suddenly remembered the old Russian riddle: 'What do you call a cannibal who has eaten his father and mother?' Answer: 'An orphan.'

I looked at my watch every few seconds and invariably I forgot what I had just read on the dial. All around me were snatches of tunes torn from my past, tremulous tears in old eyes reflecting the candles, kneelings, prostrations, illuminations, kisses. The icons were kissed, the books, the ornaments, the altar, and everybody bowed to everybody, the faithful to the priest, the priest to the faithful, and the priest and the faithful together to the icon, and the icons, up on their walls, seemed to bow to us.

I had no idea how the liturgy unfolded. Phrases, that I interpreted wrongly but that I recognized, struck me, coming sometimes from the sanctuary, sometimes from the right-hand *klyros*, which held the choir, among whom I recognized the beautiful, slightly coarse voice of Marina. I was struck by a particular expression that recurred again and again:

'A Christian end to our life, without suffering, without shame, in peace, and a good defence before the fearful judgement of Christ, that is our request.'

And Popov? The end of his life might be a Christian one, but it would be neither blest with peace, nor free of suffering. His death would be violent and his eyes would stop, like those of all the assassinated, on a vision of unspeakable horror. Hadn't I seen enough of those eyes turned to glass by the final terror?

The priest invoked, begged, threatened, blessed, and I, out of politeness, performed the gestures recommended to the faithful with more care and punctiliousness than the regulars around me. I took ridiculous pride in doing so, not considering that the emotion that many of them felt was far superior to the outward show that I was observing so scrupulously. Suddenly, the priest appeared before us. Less hieratical, less musical, this side, so to speak, of the liturgical transfiguration and, gathering up his brocaded robes in a gesture at once broad and humble, he also gathered us together in a deep bow addressed to us and said in a clear voice: 'Forgive me, my brothers and sisters.'

What had I to forgive him for? Knowing that one does not leave the church as long as the royal door remains open, I waited for the latch to fall and the curtain to be pulled, then left. My head was spinning. I had lost the habit of this Orthodox liturgy that intoxicates the soul and, sometimes, transports it to Mount Tabor. Closing my eyes, I caught sight once more, through a gap in the congregation, of Popov's head, half turned away, his hair very blonde under the sunshine streaming in through the glass roof. I had told Silbert and Tolstoy that I was familiar with the mass, but I now realized that I didn't know it at all: every now and then I felt sure that it was about to finish, but it went on, serene, as if it were never to end. It was equally capable of

398

suddenly stopping before my equipment was in place. The beggar gave me a deep bow, fool that I was. I went back into the street. There had been another rain shower and the sun was reflected in the puddles. The van was double parked in front of the main gate—the gate that Popov would certainly not use! I dashed to the van door, anger giving me all the authority I had been afraid of losing at certain moments.

'Sergeant Moutins, are you mad? Are you mad? What are you playing at? I'll have you shot!'

His goggles protected his eyes. All the same, he looked very sorry for himself, that much was obvious. The driver turned a pretty, somewhat irregular face to him: 'I told you, Roger: it's the little one.'

I went on berating him, sincerely enough, but thoroughly enjoying the effect I was producing: 'If you can't read a plan, I'll bust you, Moutins. Got that? I'll bust you.'

I don't know precisely what I meant by the term, or what he understood by it. He no longer had a career in the army to be destroyed, and, physically, I was ill-equipped to frighten him. But he stammered, his lips pale: 'I'll get him, sir. I'll get him. Promise.'

Had anyone seen us? In a sense, I didn't care any more: I wanted only one thing, the death of the bull. I went into the church and saw everything.

Father Vladimir was standing on the ambo, holding the chalice in his left hand and the spoon in the right. The stem of the chalice was wrapped in a red material that the priest held with two fingers. A step below, on his right, a slim, fair-haired young man, wearing a short cassock, pulled in tight at the waist, seemed ready to assist him. On the left, the misshapen, twisted, red-faced, tottering verger was raising a corner of the same material with his bear's paw. The parti-coloured eyes of the priest, the beady eyes of the young monk, the old, washed-out eyes of the verger, all seemed caught up in the greatest concentration. They were fixed on a point somewhere between the chalice and the long cranium of the approaching communicant. Instead of having his forearms crossed over his breast, as was the custom, Popov moved forward this time with his arms hanging at his sides, the right one weighted. Suddenly the red material stretched to form an inclined triangle, the apex of which was formed by the stem of the chalice, and the two lower angles by the hands of Quasimodo and the angel of the Annunciation. Popov threw his head forward, while, at the same time, raising his face, and I saw, by the bulge of his jaw muscles that he had opened his mouth. At that moment, his head was enclosed in an imaginary polygonal box formed by the three faces—one seen full face, two in profile. And what profiles! The base was provided by the red material; the lid was missing. All around people were bustling to and fro, candles were being extinguished, prayers and greetings whispered; one was aware of the familiar presence of the ineffable; the choir was chanting on a single, endlessly drawn out note: 'The body of Christ receive, taste at the immortal spring.'

How many years was it—ten, fifteen?—since I had communicated? I thought, without knowing quite what it meant, that it would be right and proper to communicate today. Right? Proper? What was happening over there? The fair-haired angel was whispering with what I took to be fury:

'Kiss the chalice. Kiss the chalice, I tell you!'

Other communicants filed past, following the servant of God Igor, who came down the steps, still gripping his pig-skin briefcase. The angel reminded him:

'And the warmed wine?'

Poor Popov did not know what he was supposed to do, but he was keen to do the correct thing. An old lady pointed out to him the boy who was standing, wearing a sky-blue robe, behind a table on which had been placed a jug of warm wine, a sort of wine-taster, and a basket containing a few pieces of bread. This was no longer the communion; it was already, so subtle is the progress of transfiguration with the Orthodox, so lively our faith in the hierarchy of mediations, a means of reminding oneself of it. The old lady kindly showed him what he had to do. Popov helped himself, under the serious, disdainful eye of the boy.

I went out by the side door, crossed the corner of the courtyard, went down the steps, along the corridor, and, after a moment of panic at the idea that the postern might be locked, pushed it open and found myself on the pavement. The almond-green van was double-parked with the engine idling, fifteen yards to my left, at the exact spot Silbert had marked on his plan with a hard, newly sharpened pencil. If Popov turned to the left, he'd be caught full-face; if he turned away, he'd be followed and get it in the back. I crossed the street in the direction of the *bistrot*. I still had plenty of time for another pick-me-up before the end of the mass.

I was about to push open the door when an engine revved up behind me. I was wondering whether authenticity would be better served by my turning round or not, when the Thompson went into action. I did turn then, but I could see nothing, because the van came between the target and me. Echoing between the stone walls, the volley sounded like thunder. The explosions, the vibrations, the echoes, pursued one another in an apocalyptic series of thunderclaps. When would it end? I felt it would go on forever, till the end of the world. More and more palpitating detonations, more and more whining richochets. A single burst would have been enough, but it was a long time since Moutins had fired on a man: two or three shots would not have satisfied him, he needed the orgy of the whole clip. I distinctly heard the last percussion click empty, in the void. 'So long as the idiot doesn't reload!' No: the roaring engine was at last freed and the van, skidding over the wet roadway, the wheels at an angle, the tyres flattened and screeching, plunged into the left-hand turning, contrary to the plan—no doubt Moutins was taking precautions to protect himself against us. Fair enough!

Popov was mincemeat smoking on the pavement. The right hand was still clutching the thick handle of the briefcase, but the arm was missing. Standing with her back to the wall, her legs bare, her arms crossed over her breasts, was Marina. I ran up to her. She was dripping with blood. Small pieces of minced flesh stuck in her hair.

'Are you hurt?'

She wasn't. Moutins had done a neat job. For some moments what seemed like an absolute silence reigned. The stink that was

401

spreading through the air made me feel sick. I made a conscious effort to overcome it. Suddenly, a few seconds later, a window shattered up on a fourth-floor. This dull tinkling seemed to free all the other sounds: the noise of Paris once more reached our ears; passers-by, slightly grazed by the ricochets, started to shout and scream in order to draw attention to themselves.

Marina could not take her eyes off the bloody mess at her feet, while I could not take mine off the briefcase, which lay intact and which might contain the entire network of Bureau T in France, including Crocodile's file.

Two policemen came running up. They wanted to free the briefcase. I put my foot on it and showed them my card.

'This man is a foreign diplomat. Don't touch anything. You, go and telephone the Soviet Embassy. You, stay with me: you will be a witness that the briefcase has not been opened.'

Other representatives of the law, medicine, the fire service, the press turned up. But I stayed where I was, my foot on the inestimable briefcase. I kept intruders at bay and, holding a handkerchief to my nose, I awaited my only allies, the Reds.

To what extent I had really become their ally, I understood only years later, when I finally had an intimation of Whom it was that I had arranged to shoot that morning coming out of church.

33

It is not that I am of timorous nature or am troubled by a delicate conscience, feeling some invincible repulsion for violence as such. No, I am convinced that violence, judiciously used and calibrated, constitutes in politics an effective, economical and, therefore, moral homeopathy. I often speculate what the history of the twentieth century would have been if, instead of the inoffensive Rasputin, who demanded peace and whom no one heeded, despite the legend, our three aristocratic assassins had had the happy notion of emptying their phials of poison and their revolvers in the carcase of a certain Vladimir Ulianov. Among other happy effects, these benefactors of mankind might have been able to save the throne of Germany and, consequently, erased the history of Nazism, not to mention Leninism, Stalinism, etc., etc. with a trickle of cyanide or a puff of smoke. The development of my religious feelings has in no way changed my opinions on that question.

It is not that I consider that justice has been violated. Igor Maximovich Popov was a monster and the death penalty, even for lesser criminals, does not in itself shock me. It is not that the Christian that I have become is revolted in the name either of the old commandments or of the new. I sincerely believe that God and Caesar reign over different kingdoms and that neither should be deprived of the proper means of executing his particular mission.

Nor is it, I think, the paradox of the situation that has disturbed me so much. No doubt there is something irritating, both in terms of my own feelings and of professional aesthetics, in telling oneself that Popov was coming over to our side, had decided to work for us, with us, and that we had welcomed him with 11.43s in the chest, belly and face, but these accidents are all part of the masked ball of the special services, and I am in no way—let Tolstoy have no doubts on the matter—among those who have been sickened by secrecy (editorial offices swarm with them at the moment). I can still not conceive of politics without espionage and counter-espionage, and I am still convinced that such games cannot be played without fouls. My loyalty is intact; I condemn none of the organizers of the execution, not even myself.

If it really must be expressed in so many words, I would go so far as to say that our action was *just*: it may not have been good, but at least it was necessary. When finally the Soviets arrived, in the shape of two particularly ugly customers, and I yielded up to them the briefcase and the hand, which they did not manage to detach, I felt I had carried off one of the great coups of modern undercover warfare. Silbert, still off target, pointed out to me that the briefcase probably contained proof of Popov's treason and that I would have done better to have destroyed any such evidence, but Tolstoy came to my defence: if the Soviets found proof of defection in the briefcase, they would never believe that we had voluntarily given up such a prize. Events proved me right: during the few years that remained to him, Greek Fire continued to pull the chestnuts out of the Soviet fire—and the American barbecue—on our behalf.

Nor was it, on reflection, that Operation Culverin failed to prove 'cost-effective'. On the national scale, we had, it is true, succeeded only in putting the country into an embarrassing situation from which no practical advantage would be extracted by way of compensation. But on the personal plane things were quite different: I had bet on turning Popov and turned him I had; his elimination had become desirable and I had eliminated him. Artistically, it was impeccable. 'Apply for a regular commission,' Silbert advised me. 'I'll back your application. We need pragmatic officers like you.' Tolstoy still laughed with his iceberg-blue eyes when he saw me, but I felt the effects of his protection, where the expenses and other more marginal profits were concerned. In all probability, I had been mentioned Up

There; the red-haired warrant officer Estienne hardly ever kept me cooling my heels. I was given a decoration—it gave me no pleasure, but this was not for any of the reasons I have just listed.

A transformation had been set in motion in my internal abysses. I watched my universe crumble around me, bit by bit, the plaster flaking away in chunks, taking with it large pieces of myself. What would remain? I did not know.

I had paid Moutins his 175,000 francs: after abandoning the van near a métro station, he had gone home with his assistant. He said he had thrown the sub-machine-gun into the Seine; I pretended to believe him.

'How's the bun in the oven?' he asked me.

'In the oven?'

'Yes. My transfer.'

There was a languorous look in his eyes, as after a well-spent night. I told him he would have to wait. For the time being, he would continue to provide us with the same services as before. There was no danger now that he would change sides.

The press, of course, pounced on the affair, but the Minister of Information must have got his orders from Up There, for the campaign came to an early end. Lisichkin's name was thrown to the baying pack and the propaganda of the Narodny Trudovoy Soyuz duly discovered in the room overlooking the embassy gardens. For three days it was thought that the assassin had been identified; Chile felt it suitable to make a discreet protest against the use made of its passports. Then witnesses turned up: Lisichkin was attending a religious service at the other end of Paris at the time of the assassination. That settled it. A journalist threw out an idea: Popov had been on the point of going over to the West and had been assassinated on the orders of his own government. The pigskin briefcase received its share of commentary; fortunately, Olga Orloff escaped the attentions of the press; we were happy to see that her preferences coincided on this point with our own. The police, of course, made a show of concern, but we were hardly worried on that score: they must have been given their instructions and, in fact, were conscientiously marking time. The embassy in the Rue de Grenelle and the French Communist Party were another matter: the Soviets demanded that the truth be told about the assassination of their diplomat, and they inevitably set to work on a secret investigation into the major's murder. Popov's successor imparted its conclusions to Greek Fire: the Americans, anxious to resume control of Crocodile, had decided to eliminate an overly clever case officer.

Marina had telephoned me, asking to meet me at the *Pont Royal*. She was waiting for me, her fingers closed around the stem of a glass of vermouth. My whisky arrived, brought as usual by Big Ears, without my ordering it. I put my hand over the plump little hand that resembled a heart-shaped face. The Slav Gioconda was dressed in black from top to toe: black jersey, black skirt, black shoes and stockings, jade necklace. Quite spontaneously, I spoke to her in Russian.

'Yes, Marina, tell me.'

'Kiril,' she announced, 'now you are like a brother. We can weep over him together, can't we? Now that he's been killed by his own people?'

It was an unexpected aspect of the situation. I denied nothing.

'You know,' she went on, 'I could have fallen in love with him. I'm surrounded by buffoons: he was a real man.'

Her chin was trembling. If being a man required you sending your father and mother to their deaths, plus your grandmother as make-weight, then Popov was undeniably a man. I expressed no opinion.

'One evening,' she went on, 'he came to see me.' (I knew.) 'I don't remember very well what happened.' (I could have provided her with an exact transcription of their conversation.) 'I don't think he told me he loved me, but I think that's what he meant.'

I thought so too.

'He went to confession on Saturday evening and to communion on Sunday. I went to congratulate him. He wanted to leave at once, without waiting for the end. As he was leaving, he asked me if we could have lunch together. His forehead was uncreased—he seemed happy . . . He had some presents for me.'

'Presents, Marina?'

'Yes. Some Russian records, Tchaikovsky, I think. Not my kind of . . . but it was one of their orchestras, their technicians, paper made with their trees . . . There was also something else.'

'What, Marina?'

'I didn't quite understand. He said: "An idol." I laughed; I repeated: "An idol? An *idolishche paganoie*?" He looked very serious: "Yes, an idol. Do what you like with it." We were leaving when . . .'

She shut her eyes. I squeezed her hand, fraternally.

'Kiril, I wanted to tell you something else. They came to see me.'

'Who?'

'Them. One looked like the grey wolf, the other like a fox. They were very polite, and even their Russian wasn't as bad as I had expected.'

The permanent electronic surveillance had been suspended, but the microphone was still in place. That evening I would hear what had been said that afternoon, and in what Russian.

'What did they want?'

'They wanted to know if I was working for him.'

'What did you say?'

Once again the safety of Greek Fire was in question.

'It was difficult to know what to say. Me working for a Red? All the same, I thought I owed him that, Kiril. I owed it to his memory. A sacrifice . . . It was the only way I had of assuming my widowhood. I said yes.'

'And they asked you to carry on?'

'And I said no. I explained that it was a special relationship between him and me. They showed me a copy of the Gospels. They asked me what it was. "The Gospels," I said. "Yes, but who was it for? For you? For you and him?" I remembered what he had told me that night. I answered: "It was our code." One of them seemed satisfied. The other asked me how the code worked. I explained it to him. He too seemed satisfied. Then, after whispering between themselves, they asked me—the wolf, not the fox—if I would like to keep the book. I said I would. Here it is.'

'You want me to have it, Marina?'

'I'm not sentimental. Or perhaps I'm too sentimental. I don't want to dwell on it. . . After me, you deserve it more than anyone.'

It was her way of ridding herself of a rushed mourning. She would be left with a few beautiful memories, as they say, not to mention Fragance's fees and the amount of the cheque, which there was no way we could cash. We parted on a friendly note. When I got home, I felt more and more as if I were witnessing a change of scenery, an avalanche, some geological slips or folds . . . Was Marina right by any chance? Was I, too, mourning Popov?

One Tuesday—my thick brown diary swollen up by the humidity mentions another of my imaginary toothaches—I had a rendez-vous with Lester at the *Cuisse de Grenouille.*

'Well, boyo, how's tricks?'

'My respects, Major.'

'Your government's looking a bit nettled, isn't it? Was it your lot who scratched out the big tit fancier? I'll tell you a secret, fella. We once thought of turning him, taking him by his weak spot.'

He mimed the action of turning Popov around, holding him by his weak spot.

'No, seriously, don't you know who did it?'

'We have information on it, but it's F/6.'

'Shoot all the same.'

'The Israelis.'

I saw Lester make a mental note, while sliding a glance at the first of the miniskirts.

'And how's Popeye, Major?'

'Popeille? Popping. And Greek Fire?'

'Firing.'

Puzo invited me to a psychedelic evening. I didn't know what 'psychedelic' meant, and neither did he. But there was herring in cream, there was Madeira, there were young writers who fancied themselves, and sex objects wearing dresses slit up to here—and the master of the house did not forgo the pleasure of recalling some delicious dressing down with which he had been honoured twenty years earlier. Divo appeared to be enjoying himself, but I suddenly felt sick. I thought of Popov rotting

408

somewhere, and the living rot that surrounded me suddenly became unbearable. I slipped away and walked in the direction of the esplanade.

Spring was in the air, gay and impetuous. Frisquette was waiting for me. A publisher was not entirely sure that he would not publish my first novel. And I walked, wondering why I was my I, breathing in the intoxicating air of a Parisian April, and not that other I, the Popovian I, whose mouth was now filled with Russian soil, if he still had a mouth, the I whose carcase was already feeding the verdant splendour of a Muscovite or Vladimirian April. An answer came to me. The only reason why his I and my I were different was that another I, situated at the centre of the circle, was directing on us two equal, but distinct beams of light. I don't know what such an explanation is worth in philosophical terms; at the time, it struck me as a flash of lightning.

I then discovered that the 'Murder in the Cathedral' aspect of my latest exploit had been gnawing at me for a long time. When the remaining walls of the surrounding structure had collapsed, this remained: I had murdered a man who was coming, not only to me, but to Christ. I was Nero. The excessive ease with which everything had taken place, the impunity and various advantages I had derived from it, now appeared to me in a different light. I wondered whether the whole story was not that of my own turning, but in a different direction: in what tends to be called downwards.

'No, that is not what I want.'

I had reached the point when one has to do an about-turn and take to one's heels.

My contract would soon expire. To the surprise of my superiors, I did not renew it.

'You're crazy, my boy,' Rat said. 'Mine's up in three weeks. If only they'd let me re-enlist. . .'

He had used that old trooper's word to be funny, but his voice cracked and I saw him picturing himself choking on his last bowl of air, at the end of a huge bed monstrously obstructing some tiny bedroom, under the contemptuous hiccups of his witch of Vesuvius.

Having left the profession, I wanted to leave the country. I found a teaching post across the Atlantic. I proposed to Frisquette that she accompany me, as my wife. To my relief, she refused. Meanwhile the publisher had decided not to publish me after all: I saw this as a reassuring sign. My sacrifice had been accepted. The moment seemed to have come to make my peace with Him into whose presence Popov had preceded me.

Everything wears out, even Orestes' crime. Having become a renewed, if not quite renovated, man, I felt a desire to retrace my steps, to attempt, after so many others, the transmutation of my life as lived into life as life-enhancing. From face to mask. But I did not feel I had the right: the loyalties of the *metaxu* come first, as they should. One day, opening a French magazine quite by chance—usually I avoided them, because they had nothing to say about me—I learnt of the death of Quatre-Etoiles, 'the great master of contemporary eroticism'. A heart attack. . . I then saw him in my mind's eye, with the greatest intensity, 'our national Puzograph', as M. Alexandre used to call him, a poor, fat, stateless hermaphrodite raising a sententious finger and crying once more: 'My friends, that reminds me of the day when the General was good enough to. . .' How we had misjudged him, though we saw him every day and how, since I had known better and come to respect his professionalism and his courage, no less worthy than those of a Sorge or a Philby, I had still failed to do him real justice! Of all of us, Puzo was perhaps the only one who knew how to love. Deprived by his nature of the joys on which the most destitute may depend, he had taken the mixed instincts that swarmed within him and divided them in two: the crudest he had sublimated in literature; the finest, in a limitless devotion, which we had so often mocked, but which I now saw only as humility—and grandeur. Poor, dear Puzo, with your wandering hands, you whom I did not like to be too close to! My heart, little accustomed to these gratuitous motions, contracts at the thought of your destiny. I know nothing of your childhood in Transsylvania or Illyria, of the torments of your puberty, of your hopes for eternal life. I think painfully of your slavery under the cold Tolstoy, of the brutal way Popov 'brought you to heel'. But in secret you laughed, did you not, at their stringen-

410

cies, and you were to die knowing that you had well served the object of your love.

With Greek Fire gone, no one would take his place. So nothing now prevented me from writing, rediscovering, after several years of sterility, a vocation that had been temporarily set aside. Having completed the manuscript, with the names altered and certain details disguised, I sent it to Colonel Tolstoy, asking him if there would be any objection to Operation Culverin being made public in fictional guise. Moutins, to his great delight, had finally been put at the disposal of the action teams of the Big Shop and would no longer be at risk, but I remained, in spite of everything, faithful.

The answer came back. A telegram that the American operator laboriously spelled out to me:

AFIZZLEDSPOOKALWAYSTURNSINTOAHACK

THE DAY OF THE JACKAL BY FREDERICK FORSYTH

'As a political thriller it is virtually in a class by itself; subtle, fast moving, superbly written, unputdownable, easily beating Ian Fleming on his own ground. The entire French background is convincing, and beautifully atmospheric down to the last whiff of Gauloise.'

Sunday Times

'A compelling, utterly enthralling first novel ... some of the tensest thriller writing I can remember reading.'

Sunday Express

'The tension, excitement and pace are brilliantly maintained to the last page.'

Sunday Mirror

'THE DAY OF THE JACKAL works beautifully ... I was held spellbound ... riveted to this chilling, superbly researched story. A remarkable ring of authority ... a superb piece of mystery.'

Guardian

'Electrifyingly exciting ... within or without the pages of fiction there can rarely have been such a meticulously efficient, cold-blooded human killer. Mr Forsyth is clever, very clever and immensely entertaining.'

Daily Telegraph

ISBN 0 552 11497 9   £1.65

THE ODESSA FILE BY FREDERICK FORSYTH, author of THE DAY OF THE JACKAL

The life and death hunt for a notorious Nazi criminal unfolds against a background of international espionage and clandestine arms deals, involving rockets designed in Germany, built in Egypt, and equipped with warheads of nuclear waste and bubonic plague. Who is behind it all? Odessa. Who or what is Odessa? You'll find out in *The Odessa File* ...

'In the hands of Frederick Forsyth the documentary thriller achieves its most sophisticated form – Mr Forsyth has produced both a brilliant entertainment and a disquieting book.' –

The Guardian

0 552 11498 7   £1.50

THE DEVIL'S ALTERNATIVE BY FREDERICK FORSYTH

'Whichever option I choose, men are going to die'. This is the Devil's Alternative, the appalling choice facing the President of the USA and other statesmen throughout the world.

As the gripping story gathers momentum, the reader is transported from Moscow to London, from Rotterdam to Washington, from a country house in Ireland to the world's biggest oil tanker which threatens to pollute the whole of the North Sea. The climax is the most exciting that even this master story-teller has contrived, and the last-minute surprises in the concluding chapters take the breath away.

0 552 11495 2   £1.75

THE DOGS OF WAR BY FREDERICK FORSYTH

The discovery of the existence of a ten-billion-dollar mountain of platinum in the remote African republic of Zangaro, causes Sir James Manson – a smooth, ruthless City tycoon – to hire an army of trained mercenaries whose task it is to topple the government of Zangaro and replace its dictator with a puppet president.

But news of the discovery has leaked to Russia – and suddenly Manson finds he no longer makes the rules in a power game where the stakes have become terrifyingly high ...

0 552 11499 5   £1.75

THE KEY TO REBECCA BY KEN FOLLETT

'Our spy in Cairo is the greatest hero of them all' Field Marshal Erwin Rommel, September 1942

He is known to the Germans as 'Sphinx', to others as Alex Wolff, a European businessman. He arrives suddenly in Cairo from out of the desert, armed with a radio set, a lethal blade and a copy of Daphne du Maurier's REBECCA – a ruthless man with a burning, relentless conviction that he will win at all costs.

The stakes are high, for the survival of the British campaign in North Africa is in the balance. Only Major William Vandam, an intelligence officer, and the beautiful courtesan, Elene, can put an end to Wolff's brilliant clandestine reports of British troop movements and strategic plans ...

In this desperate race against time, as Tobruk falls to the Panzer divisions and the sky of Cairo is blackened with fragments of hastily burned security documents, Vandam and Wolff become locked in a deathly struggle which will determine who wins – and who loses – the greatest war the world has ever known ...

0 552 11810 9   £1.75

A SELECTED LIST OF CORGI TITLES

WHILE EVERY EFFORT IS MADE TO KEEP PRICES LOW, IT IS SOMETIMES NECESSARY TO INCREASE PRICES AT SHORT NOTICE. CORGI BOOKS RESERVE THE RIGHT TO SHOW AND CHARGE NEW RETAIL PRICES ON COVERS WHICH MAY DIFFER FROM THOSE ADVERTISED IN THE TEXT OR ELSEWHERE.

THE PRICES SHOWN BELOW WERE CORRECT AT THE TIME OF GOING TO PRESS (MARCH '82)

☐	11810 9	**The Key to Rebecca** (50)	*Ken Follet*	£1.75
☐	11495 2	**The Devil's Alternative** (50)	*Frederick Forsyth*	£1.75
☐	11240 2	**The Shepherd** (72)	*Frederick Forsyth*	85p
☐	11695 5	**The Dogs of War** (50)	*Frederick Forsyth*	£1.75
☐	11498 7	**The Odessa File** (50)	*Frederick Forsyth*	£1.50
☐	11497 9	**The Day of the Jackal** (50)	*Frederick Forsyth*	£1.65
☐	11715 3	**The Spymaster** (50)	*Donald Freed*	£1.75
☐	11533 9	**Genesis** (40)	*W. A. Harbinson*	£1.75
☐	11594 0	**Out of Control** (50)	*Gordon Kiddy*	£1.50
☐	11352 2	**Salt Mine** (50)	*David Lippincott*	£1.25
☐	11246 1	**Savage Ransom** (50)	*David Lippincott*	£1.25
☐	10936 3	**The Sandbaggers** (100)	*Ian MacKintosh*	80p

All these books are available at your bookshop or newsagent, or can be ordered direct from the publisher. Just tick the titles you want and fill in the form below.

CORGI BOOKS, Cash Sales Department, P.O. Box 11, Falmouth, Cornwall.

Please send cheque or postal order, no currency.

Please allow cost of book(s) plus the following for postage and packing:

U.K. CUSTOMERS. 40p for the first book, 18p for the second book and 13p for each additional book ordered, to a maximum charge of £1.49.

B.F.P.O. & EIRE. Please allow 40p for the first book, 18p for the second book plus 13p per copy for the next three books, thereafter 7p per book.

OVERSEAS CUSTOMERS. Please allow 60p for the first book plus 18p per copy for each additional book.

NAME (Block letters)...

ADDRESS ....

....